For Kat :-

EQUAL
Parts

Cheers

Also by Vicky Moon

The Official Middleburg Life Cookbook

The Middleburg Mystique

Best Dressed Southern Salads

A Sunday Horse

The Private Passion of Jackie Kennedy Onassis

Equestrian Style

Golf Style

The Stylish Life Equestrian

EQUAL Parts

A Novel

Vicky Moon

WLM

Waverly Lee Media, LLC

The events in this book are fictitious. Any similarity to actual events is coincidental and not intended by the author.

www.vickymoon.com

First Edition, Waverley Lee Media, LLC, August 2016

Waverly Lee Media, LLC

Cataloging-in-publication data is available from the Library of Congress.

Moon, Vicky

EQUAL Parts: a novel/Vicky Moon- 1st ed.

ISBN 978-0-9617683-5-5

Book design by Pam Owens, www.pamowensdesign.com
Design consultant Greer Chapman
Illustrations by Big Truck Graphics

Printed in the United States of America

DEDICATION

For Lenny

and

My fabulous friends in Middleburg

In memory of

Bobby Abbo

Mo Siegel

and

Duke Ziebert

Contents

Men are not monogamous by nature.

—Jenny Holzer

Chapter 1

Cannelloni & Chianti

It was a balmy evening in Washington, D.C., the Thursday after Labor Day.

He had chosen the Roma restaurant on upper Connecticut Avenue. The garden patio was still open and the grapes on the ancient arbor were positively, perfectly ripe.

Isabelle, after all this time, still couldn't figure him out. Was he aware of this splendid though decayed setting? Did he know the very thought of the place made her heart jump at the sheer anticipation of a night out with him? Or maybe he chose it because it was off the usual trendy list of Washington restaurants, a neighborhood kind of place where they were not likely to see anyone who knew them?

He called between meetings earlier that afternoon. "Hey," he said in that familiar baritone. "`How about eight- fifteenish at the Roma?"

He always added "-ish" on any time...sixish, sevenish, or whateverish. She was always on time. With the election approaching, he always ran late.

When she left work that afternoon, she hurried home to primp for her evening out. Her friends and coworkers at the Georgetown interior decorating shop knew she was "involved" with a married man. They usually met on Wednesdays. She talked about him constantly with her closest friend, Tracy Curtis, always careful never to mention his name.

It was not always easy.

The front room of the Roma restaurant was empty, except for the one man in the third booth eating alone, with the September 7 edition of The Washington Post spread out in front of him. The news of this day in 1978 included a report that President Carter was meeting with Egyptian President Anwar Sadat and Israeli Prime Minister Menachem Begin for a Middle East Peace summit at Camp David. They had assembled at the presidential retreat near the majestic Catoctin Mountain, part of the imposing Bull Run mountain range which provided the leaders a breathtaking landscape. They gathered on a flagstone patio at Aspen Lodge, part of the 134-acre compound. It was funny, Isabelle thought, how people dining alone invariably had to have something to read, as if that could possibly substitute for human contact. She was happy not to be one of them.

Slick red Naugahyde booths lined both sides of the long front room, with pink cloths on each table. On the walls were trophies of exotic animals: a lion, gazelle, water buffalo, zebra, moose, and baboon. A massive lion and polar bear completed the ambience of the place. Each head was placed strategically above a booth with a photo of the original owner posed, gun in hand, with his kill on various safaris and game expeditions around the world. Thirty years ago, when Robert Abbo, Sr. started the business, it was one of the hottest restaurants in town. Then, he became a victim himself, killed by a hit and run driver seventeen years ago. Now, his son, Bobby, Jr., ran the place. He often spent the day at the racetrack playing the ponies with an enthusiasm that bordered on addiction. He showed up each evening at precisely six and greeted the customers, leading them to various tables and pausing from time to time to sit and chat with the regulars. The food was so-so, but no one ever left hungry. If you hit it on the right night, with the right person sitting across the table, it could be a thoroughly satisfying meal.

Patrons filled just about all of the twenty-six tables in the back garden. There was one man on the piano and another, a moonlighting Marine Corps band member, strolling from table to table playing the violin.

He ordered the Cannelloni Fiorentina. She had the stuffed manicotti. From the first time they met their conversations were always lively, spirited. They talked about his day, her day, politics, art, music...it didn't matter. They shared a bottle of Chianti. She loved every minute. She wanted to freeze their moments and save them forever. But now, she also feared losing him after the election.

They had a mutual interest and trust in one another that for the most part went unspoken. She heard someone on a talk show not too long ago say, "We have no control over our emotions. You can't make yourself unlove someone. What you can control is what you do about that emotion." Isabelle long ago acknowledged that she could not control her emotions for Johnathan. She went on to conclude that she would savor that emotion as long as possible—forever, if it came to that. She was perfectly content to remain the other woman in Johnathan's life as long as he was interested.

She knew it was best not to ask him about his other life. It was understood that she was never to ask much about Betty, his wife of twenty-six years. He preferred it that way, and she knew it. But sometimes, Isabelle couldn't help herself and at the end of the evening, on the ride from their meeting place, she would casually inquire, "So, where did you tell her you were going tonight?'

"A meeting," would always be his answer.

Oh, well.

"You'll never in your whole life believe who came into the shop today?" she said now, half-asking a question, while barely taking a breath to answer it at the same time. "Claudia Jasper," she announced proudly between bites of antipasto.

Claudia was the wife of George Jasper, one of the *Post*'s top political columnists. She was always in the news...giving a party, working on a charity event. She was one of Betty's best friends. She and her husband recently managed to save their marriage. Now as part of their reconciliation, she was redoing their cottage in the country. By all appearances, they were going to live happily ever after.

"She picked out some of the most luxurious chintz I've ever seen," Isabelle said, continuing without another breath.

He loved watching her talk, *she was so...so...young, vibrant, passionate in everything she did*, he thought. So open, so refreshing, so different from all those vacuous women he dealt with at home and at the office.

"Brunchwig and Fil, it's a navy blue background with tulips in various stages of development...you know...some are open just a bit and the others are so full that the petals are almost falling from the stems. Well, the flowers are in a sort of pinky melon color, that's very chic right now, and she's having the lining done to match in a plain glazed cotton that's also very expensive, with swags and tassels—the whole bit. Just for the sun porch, as she called it, the bill will be at least $8,500 for the fabric and labor and she's just getting started. She wants us to come over and measure some other rooms and work on colors and window treatments. I can't wait to see the place," she added.

Isabelle Benton Stoker grew up in Raleigh, North Carolina. Her father owned a large and successful insurance agency. Her mother taught art at a prestigious private academy and took no salary during the years Isabelle was a student in order to pay the tuition. Her mother knew it was worth it when Isabelle graduated in the top 10 percent of her class. She went on to college to major in design.

Isabelle's luxuriously natural blond hair was thick and heavy and fell past her shoulders. She invariably wore a headband of some sort, pulling it back loosely off her face. She wore it this way since just before turning sixteen; a classic look she knew would never go out of style. If she was going to a fancy Georgetown party or the Kennedy Center, she upgraded her look without a headband and with a matching or coordinating hair accessory such as a tortoise shell clip. She wore the same oversized gold knot earrings her parents gave her for graduation from Queen's College in Charlotte. Occasionally she wore the small diamond studs she bought herself two months ago on her twenty-third birthday. She had bottomless blue eyes and made it a rule never ever to wear blue eye shadow. She learned this from a friendly cosmetic saleswoman one day while roaming around Woodies, the foremost department store formally known as Woodward and Lothrup. The woman informed Isabelle that it was a "no-no to wear eye shadow that matched your eyes." So naturally, Isabelle, like most young career women, got sucked into buying a bagful of new (and expensive) Estee Lauder makeup.

Isabelle primarily wore pale grey shadow. Up close the arresting blue color emerged in her eyes, turning them a blue-black hue. She never wore lipstick, instead, just a clear lip-gloss, which she forever applied with her little finger. She kept a small pot in her purse and pulled it out on any and all occasions. She never wore any liquid foundation and once in a while used a bright pink blush. Her favorite perfume in the winter and fall was Shalimar. In the summer, she wore L'Air du Temps. Her manner and her long, taut body could best be described as...alluring.

"She's such a very sweet person," Johnathan said, referring to Claudia Jasper. "And I know she has fabulous taste," he added, deleting the fact that he and Betty had seen them at a Capitol Hill party less than ten days ago, and that they socialized frequently out in the country.

Johnathan Douglas Dent was what some women called drop-dead gorgeous. At 6 foot 2, he had a large frame usually draped in perfectly fitted Brooks Brothers suits, purchased at $600 off the rack at their L Street store. His hair was jet black, with a touch of gray at his temples, a look both men and women could envy. He had green eyes, a shallow translucent green. At almost fifty-two, he was in good shape, and he worked at it, with a rowing machine in his bedroom he used for thirty-five minutes every morning. Still, he was just a touch overweight—maybe eight to twelve pounds—the result of all those high-calorie lunches with clients, not to mention his weekly night out of pasta and passion with Isabelle. She didn't seem to mind, though—she thought it made him so very loveable. When he undressed, Isabelle smiled at the sight of the UVA tattoo that adorned his left rear cheek. She longed to pinch and hug every part of him. Dressed, he was the image of privilege and power, the consummate Washington lawyer.

She also knew he couldn't go anywhere without women stealing furtive glances. They'd forget their names and where they were when Johnathan walked into a room. And yet, Isabelle wasn't in the least bit jealous or insecure. In many ways it amazed her when she sat down and thought about it...and she asked herself, *Why don't I get upset, knowing that all these women he works with are just dying to take him away?*

And then, she smiled to herself and knew the answer.

The world would be astounded, but Johnathan Douglas Dent, the widely respected Washington attorney, most likely soon to be the next senator from Virginia, was a most insecure man.

Even Johnathan's wife didn't recognize it. Of course she didn't—she was half the reason. But to know him as Isabelle did, with all his insecurity was to adore him.

He grew up in Richmond. His mother stayed at home, looking after Johnathan and his younger brother, Robert. In her spare time she took in sewing, making curtains and slipcovers for customers. She performed her duties as a mother in just that manner...as if they were duties. She packed lunch for the boys each day, always including a package of cheese crackers with peanut butter. She took them to school plays and Little League games, but Johnathan always felt as if something was missing. Oh, she'd kiss them and tuck them in at night, but he always wanted more. Once when she was leaning over to tuck him in one night, Johnathan reached up and hugged her as hard as he could. "I love you mommy," he said.

"That's nice, Johnathan," she responded, while unhooking his arms. "Now sleep tight," she said as she turned out the light.

Johnathan's father operated a vending machine business he'd started from nothing, building it into what he described as a "good strong operation." He started out with a few machines at bowling alleys, gas stations, and the city's small airport. Then he added the University of Richmond, a hospital complex, and every police and fire station in the city.

Johnathan was fifteen when the business expanded. His father put him to work after school and during the summer. It was the most important period in Johnathan's young life.

It was late spring when he met Trudy. She told Johnathan she was twenty-two, but he later found out she had been working as a practical nurse at the medical center for more than ten years and had at least two other lovers. He didn't care. He grew to believe that he could never love a woman. The day after Johnathan graduated from high school, his mother left them and was never heard from until three years later, when someone sent a copy of her death notice from a newspaper in New Jersey. It was a mystery Johnathan never solved. It didn't matter now; he had stopped thinking about the woman who brought him into the world and subsequently abandoned him and his brother without any explanation.

What did matter was that Trudy taught Johnathan the simple joys of the flesh. He planned his life around Trudy, a thirty-two-year-old widow, whose husband died in a terrible car accident while driving up to Washington, D.C., for business. He was burned alive when his car collided head-on with a drunk driver in the wrong lane. Occasionally as they slept after making love, Johnathan heard her crying in her sleep, calling out his name. Still, he just couldn't get enough of her. She was kind and gentle with him, with soft full breasts that made him feel safe and warm in her arms. And so, he plotted out each day according to her schedule. He met her at her apartment at all hours of the day—early morning, late evening, whenever he could. She waited for him. And then they became bolder...

He threw her up against the wall of a broom closet at the hospital. Several times, they sneaked into an unoccupied room and made love in an empty bed. He stayed with Trudy until he graduated from high school, right up until the night before leaving for college at the University of Virginia in Charlottesville. He told her he'd call once he got settled in, but he never did. He did not want to hurt her. More important, he was smart enough to realize that Trudy would no longer fit into his life.

Chapter 2

Shabby Gentility

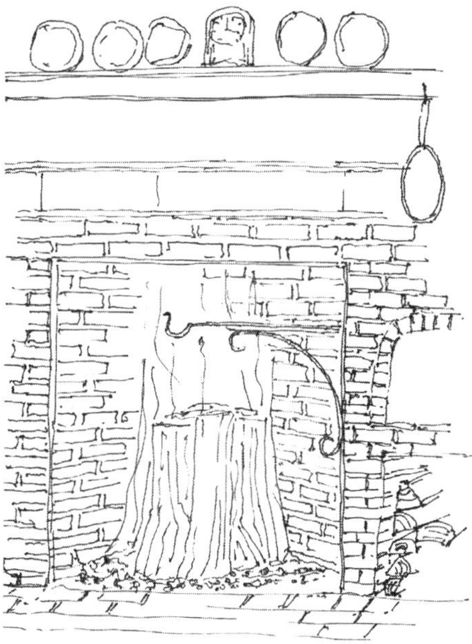

Johnathan and Isabelle first met at a cocktail party out in Middleburg, fifty miles west of the Capital in the horse country of Virginia. The quaint town and rolling green countryside surrounding it was home to a curious blend of politicians, lawyers, ambassadors, patrician farmers, and wealthy landowners on one stratum. On the other, there were struggling horsemen—trainers, riders, and equestrian teachers—trying to eke out a living as best they could. From time to time an occasional movie star like Liz Taylor or Helena Winkler came to town for the weekend, often staying in someone's private guest cottage. Still, until John Kennedy and his equestrian wife, Jackie, discovered the hamlet back in 1960, few people had ever heard of the place. Now, it was a mixture of the haves surrounded by the have-nots grooming their horses, mowing their fields, and raising their children.

The town also attracted the occasional writer and artist drawn by lush green fields, country dirt roads, and enough peace and quiet to create their work. Many residents were often accompanied by small, feisty Jack Russell terriers tagging along at their heels wherever they went, dinner parties included. Or maybe a pair of large, slobbering and smelly black Labradors, always waiting patiently in the bed of a pick up truck with racing colors painted discreetly on the door. Other family dogs waited in the back of an old station wagon or new Range Rover (that no doubt bore a vanity license plate with the initials of the owner). Residents ran errands, stopped at the post office or ate lunch in the village. The number of dogs they owned was directly related to how much money they had...one wealthy matron had fifteen dogs in residence in the main mansion of her decaying estate and it was said no man dared enter her bed for fear of rousing the half-dozen animals who slept with her every night.

High fashion was a glaring shade of sherbet colored turtleneck from a shop in Palm Beach, as opposed to the more conservative drab choice from L. L. Bean. Some women had been wearing the same long wool tartan kilt to formal winter dinner parties for thirty years or more. It was chic to brag how much one didn't pay for something, and new money could be smelled miles away with the bragging of how much something cost or how many acres they owned. Old family jewelry was coveted, new was considered vulgar. It was a place where it was equally as important to be seen out foxhunting, playing tennis, or praying in the old Episcopal Church.

Shabby gentility in all its splendor.

Isabelle hated any kind of party that had the word *cocktail* in it. It reminded her of her parents' parties in Raleigh when she was growing up. It was an antiquated way of entertaining. But then again, nobody ever said that things in Middleburg were au courant. To the contrary, in Middleburg, the older, the better. The joke was that it took four men to change a light bulb in Virginia: one to change the bulb and three to talk about how great the old one was. At cocktail parties, most people ordered dark looking drinks out of stemmed glasses with a small piece of fruit in it—an orange slice teetering on the edge or a bright red cherry on the bottom. They drank Manhattans and martinis, which were, in Isabelle's, opinion passé. And always they talked of the good old days: famous show horses, famous racehorses, famous steeplechase horses, famous former wives or husbands and famous love affairs.

The parents of Isabelle's best friend Tracy owned a small farm a few miles outside Middleburg and invited her out to the country for the weekend that summer evening almost ten years ago. She had other plans, but at the last minute decided to cancel and spend the weekend with Tracy, who was always telling her stories about the so-called Hunt Country. Isabelle thought it was time to find out for herself.

On Saturday night, they were invited to a party at a nearby estate. The hostess, Pauline Howard, was often referred to as one of the village's *grand dames*, a woman who enjoyed throwing parties. In addition to being slightly eccentric, she was one of the largest landowners in the county.

"You'll love it," Tracy told her. "You just won't believe how some of these people live."

Tracy was not exaggerating.

The two-and-a-half-mile gravel drive wound around some woods, which led to row upon row of apple trees, hence the name of the estate, The Orchard. The land cleared to reveal a circular drive at the front of the house. Three black men who normally worked in the stables and orchard provided the valet parking. The main house was a Federal period three-story brick home with a low-hipped roof and windows in a fan shape at the top.

"The original kitchen where Susie does all her cooking is still intact," the grand dame told her while giving the grand tour.

Everything was grand.

The beams in the kitchen ceiling were exposed and a large brick fireplace covered one end of the narrow part of the room. It had a large opening and the mantle had a decoration of carved oval patterns. It didn't take a genius to see that slaves once cooked right here. Still, it was a cozy and comfortable room, and Pauline Howard tended to every detail. Isabelle took mental notes. It was obvious this woman knew how to entertain and decorate.

There was a wooden bowl on the long pine tavern table in the kitchen. Instead of flowers or fruit strategically placed in the center, the grand dame put together an arrangement of summer vegetables. Isabelle thought it was just the right touch...red leaf lettuce, crisp-looking green beans, and plump plum tomatoes.

Susie, the maid, was busy arranging the platters for the buffet table, preparing to carry them up the narrow back staircase to the dining room above. It was warm in the kitchen, despite a ceiling fan and an open back door.

"The floor plan in this old house is outdated," Pauline Howard explained, then added, "There's no air conditioning down here, but we manage."

Mrs. Howard was the widow of the late Vernon Harrison Howard, whose family owned the first privately held utility company in the state of Virginia. After his death, Pauline's share of the family fortune amounted to less than twenty percent of the company. But the interest on the small fortune of $15 million sufficed for many, many, years to come. As one guest whispered, "She couldn't begin to spend it all, no matter how many parties she threw."

In the meantime, Pauline Howard tried to spend it. Nothing but the very best would do. Now in her early sixties, her clothes were of simple design and she often wore the same style dress on different occasions, varying the fabric according to the season. This time it was linen. Yellow linen. Lemon yellow. She preferred a loose fitting A-line design with longer sleeves to conceal her sagging upper arms. She always wore a designer scarf, her signature. Over the years, she amassed hundreds of scarves—mostly silk and mostly Hermes—from Paris. She wore them tied loosely around her neck or knotted off to one side.

Then there was the jewelry. Always gold. Necklace upon necklace and bracelet upon bracelet. Gold earrings...big ones. Everything about her reeked of old money and elegance, with the possible exception of her hands. They were large, almost man-sized. Her fingernails were bright red and polished weekly to perfection. No one could help but notice the huge ruby and diamond engagement ring and matching wedding band she still wore. On anyone else, the jewels would have looked vulgar and garish. On Pauline Howard, the grand dame of Middleburg, they were old and a perfect fit.

Isabelle looked around the kitchen and could see where some of the money had gone. The cabinet doors were glass, just the way they did it in the stately old homes in England. Every piece of china was on display. There was the French faience, the Sevres dinner service complete with dinner plates, luncheon plates, compotes, cake tazzas, bonbons, teacups and demitasse cups, each piece painted with a bleu celeste border and the gilt monogram of VHH; a set of original Flora Danica, hand molded and hand painted in Denmark; the everyday Spode; the Wedgewood for informal luncheons; the Spode Christmas tree pattern; the Worcester Hunting Scene pattern with the horses and hounds and a fox all running around the plates and saucers. And a divine set of china known as The Blind Earl, taking up one entire cabinet. Isabelle stopped and admired it and was told the story of how, in 1770, the Earl of Coventry had ordered from Tiffany a set of china to be decorated with a pattern of one of his own rosebushes.

"A tragic hunting accident caused him to lose his sight," Pauline explained, "but that didn't stop him. He ordered the set made with a raised design so he could feel it, like Braille. So you see, dear, that is how this china was named. This is one of the few complete sets. Isn't it grand?"

Isabelle, Tracy, and the grand dame took the expansive front steps up to the main floor, which emptied out into the main hall. Every light in the house was on and the place sparkled. A bartender apparently known to everyone as "Bean" was serving drinks at a sideboard set up as a bar.

"We couldn't have a party without Bean," Mrs. Howard said. "One has to plan their parties according to his schedule. Please girls, tell him what you want to drink."

With a vodka and tonic in a cut crystal tumbler wrapped in a delicate white linen napkin, Isabelle entered the more formal oval shaped living room on the left side of the hall. And then she saw him.

He was alone in the room, the rest of the dozen or so guests were in the drawing room, hovering around Helena Winkler, an old German movie star who was a weekend houseguest.

Johnathan's half-glasses were perched on the edge of his nose and he was leaning his elbows on an over-stuffed linen chair as he eyeballed a small painting. He looked directly into Isabelle's eyes and stared, just for a moment, thinking to himself he had never seen such a pretty girl in this house, or any other house for that matter.

"Ahh," he said, trying not to focus on Isabelle, "I love all your artwork. This is one of Rusty's isn't it?" He straightened up.

Pauline thanked him and explained that a local artist, a guest in the other room, had painted the small oil. He specialized in horse and dog paintings. "That horse won the Virginia Gold Cup for Vern. He was a grand jumper."

Very grand, thought Isabelle, who was trying to avoid staring at Johnathan while waiting for an introduction to this man who took her breath away.

After what seemed an eternity, the hostess made the proper introductions. But just as she said, "Miss Stoker," he leaned over and to give a kiss on each cheek to her friend Tracy.

"How's my riding buddy?" he asked.

"Good," Tracy answered, adding, "went on a great cross country ride at the crack of dawn this morning with the neighbors and mom. Dad had to go to work early," she continued, as if an explanation was necessary. "Oh, John, I'm sorry, this is my dear friend from college, Isabelle Stoker."

As she extended her hand, Pauline, ever the proper hostess and not one to be upstaged, continued the introductions. "Miss Stoker," she said in a commanding lockjaw tone, "I want you to meet Johnathan Douglas Dent." The way she said JOHN-Nay-Thin, made it sound so noble. *So grand.*

His hand was warm and his handshake firm. His eyes, over the half-glasses, stayed riveted to hers. "So good to meet you," he said. "If you are friends of these two ladies, then you must be okay. What brings you out to the country?"

"Oh, some fresh air and an overnight away from the city," she said, almost lost for words. "Tracy called and invited me out. We don't get to see each other much, now that she moved away on me." She was nervous and hoped it didn't show.

"Well, I know you two will have a great time," he said. "Are you going to the horse show tomorrow?"

"Oh, yes," she declared, "Wouldn't miss it."

Just then, Tracy's parents, Raymond and Smith Curtis, entered the front hall. Pauline excused herself to greet them. Isabelle, Tracy, and Johnathan stood chatting, about what, Isabelle couldn't remember.

More people entered the room, Randal McGrane, MFH (master of the hunt), was a regular on Pauline's A-list and reveled in his role. And, depending on the state of his marriage, his wife Madelyn, aka Maddie, would accompany him as she did on this night. They were an on-again off-again couple and some said that he was "over-mounted" with such a young wife. Since catching her in a rather embarrassing situation with a groom in the back of a horse van, he kept a tight rein on her. A waiter brought around a silver bowl filled with large fresh pink shrimp mixed with Thousand Island dressing. They each took one on a toothpick.

Another round of drinks was served and then dinner. The guests were seated at round tables covered with long pink cloths set up in the front courtyard. It was a cold dinner of sesame chicken and a variety of salads: rice, pasta and artichokes. The broccoli, raisin, and red onion salad was one of the best things that Isabelle ever tasted.

Coffee and dessert—apple cobbler, a Virginia standard—were served back in the main house. There were thirty-six guests, including the main attraction, Helena Winkler.

She was holding court and telling stories about each of her former husbands...seven to date, and counting. These included a well-known movie producer, a former football hero, a young soap opera actor (who had parlayed his marriage to her into a new career directing a top TV sitcom), an obscure count from Yugoslavia, and an auto glass salesman. Isabelle had seen Helena Winkler on television; bantering with Johnny Carson one night, and even watched a few of her old movies. She was radiant this night. It was the red hair. Red was her color. She drove a bright red Mercedes. She wore red clothes, red shoes, red everything. And her hair...her famous flaming mane poofed to perfection every day by her personal hairdresser. Her skin seemed flawless, until you got up close enough to see the tiny scars from three facelifts. Still, at her age—sixty-five, maybe seventy—she was still attractive, a definite asset at this point in her career. Helena Winkler knew that acting parts were few and far between at this stage in life.

Two years before, she was the front woman for a new cosmetic business. Her line of makeup, based on computer color customization to match skin, eye, and hair color, took off. Now, she spent most of her time traveling and doing promotions for the company. In between trips to shopping malls, she did "special appearances" for a fee, usually $5,000. This included just about any charity dinner, sports event, or political gathering. Her attendance tonight at Pauline Howard's was gratis, of course. It was no secret that Pauline had given Helena a "small loan" to get her into the cosmetic business.

Tom Taylor, the judge for the final event at the Upperville Horse Show the next day, was among the other guests. A tall, striking, and athletic man of fifty-five, he was a champion show jumping rider in his day and was very much sought after by women of all ages on the circuit. Helena Winkler obviously was attracted to him. They leaned into each other over coffee and they were undoubtedly going to mount up long before the horse show began tomorrow.

Isabelle glanced around the room, trying to guess which of the impeccably dressed women was Mrs. Johnathan Douglas Dent. She chatted a bit with Alex Carroll, a local veterinarian, who traveled from stable to stable around the countryside curing ill and injured horses and delivering foals. He had another specialty, as well: a stately Irishman with silver hair, he was especially favored by several women around town. His wife, Bunny, had endured at least four major and well-known indiscretions, each one resulting in the birth of a child. To date, the couple had four gorgeous daughters of their own, but theirs was a marriage hardly made in heaven.

Isabelle took her small cup of cappuccino and sat down in the pink drawing room on the other side of the hall. The sofa was stuffed with goose down. As she sat, she sank about a foot into it. An attractive woman came and sat on the edge of the sofa next to her, passing a plate of cookies to Isabelle. Her large glass of white wine was on the end of the table.

"Have one," she offered, "homemade I'm sure."

"No thank you," said Isabelle, adding, "I'm so full I don't know if I'll ever get up."

"Yes this couch is sooooo comfy," the woman said, smiling at her. "That's why I'm sitting on the edge. Oh, by the way, I'm Betty Dent, I don't think we've met." She took a sip of wine, but did not extend her hand.

"Oh...uh...I'm Isabelle Stoker, a friend of Tracy Curtis," she said, adding quickly, "I'm...uh...visiting for the weekend. Since Tracy moved to New York we don't get together very often."

"How nice," Betty Dent said. She had that same lockjaw accent as Pauline Howard. *So genteel.* "I know how important girlfriends can be."

Isabelle thought that remark was unusual, made note of it and continued to listen.

"The Curtises are good friends of ours you know," she said, this time leaning forward to take a cookie from the sterling silver tray in the middle of the hand-painted table before the sofa. "John," she called him *John.* "And Tracy's father, Ray, went to school together at The University. Of course, you probably already know that. Ray's family has lived in the area for many years. They're one of the reasons we bought a place out here."

Of course, thought Isabelle. *So...Johnathan was the old family friend...John, the one Tracy always was talking about.* Of course...everything was starting to fit together.

Isabelle and Betty Dent made small talk like long lost friends. Isabelle spoke about her family and some of the "events" in her life at college with Tracy. She casually mentioned her job in Georgetown at Michael Aldridge, *the* decorating shop.

"Oh, my yes," Mrs. Dent exclaimed, sipping more wine. "He did some work for me when we moved to the country."

Isabelle learned they had three children, including identical twin boys. They were twelve years old: Johnathan McClain Dent and Douglas Crane Dent. The third child was a daughter—obviously the apple of her mother's eye—Maude Hutchison Crane Dent, age seven. "Named for the maternal side of my family," she explained, adding, "four generations back."

Of course.

"Excuse me, I'm sorry to lean over like this," a male guest interrupted. "I just have to steal one of Susie's goodies," he noted. *Ah,* thought Isabelle, *of course homemade meant the cook had baked them, not the hostess.*

"Rusty," Betty said, "Have you met Tracy's friend?"

At that point, Isabelle knew that Elizabeth, aka Betty, Dent didn't even remember her name. So, she pushed up on the edge of the sofa and extended her hand. "Isabelle Stoker," she said, avoiding embarrassment for Mrs. Dent. Isabelle would never forget her name.

"Nice to meet you, I saw one of your paintings in the other room, I'd like to go back and study it," she said. Then, wanting to add a bit of credibility to her statement, "I work with Michael Aldridge, we're always looking for nice art." She didn't want to tell him her main duty was answering the phone for the decorator.

"Oh, John just loves his work," Betty said. "We have three..."

"I'm Rusty Stewart," interrupted the artist, leaning over even more as he took a cookie and completed the introductions.

"We have three of Rusty's paintings," Betty Dent continued. "Johnathan thinks his work is wonderful. Did you see the one of the May Day Dance in the other room?"

"Oh, Betty, you and Johnathan are always so kind to me," Rusty said, throwing back his head. He turned to Isabelle, "They have been so supportive and so gracious. This woman throws a mean dinner party. She has a real feel for Mulligan Stew."

"Not only is Rusty a fine artist," she said, "but he's also the extra man about town. A bachelor," she said, lifting her eyebrows to Isabelle. "All the women in town are crazy for him," she said as the artist flushed with embarrassment.

That didn't stop Betty Dent. She kept going. "Never married," she said, making both Isabelle and Rusty uncomfortable. They were both relieved when Johnathan approached from the other room.

She still didn't stop. "Oh, John, I was just telling Tracy's friend here..." *My gosh she still didn't remember my name...* "All about Rusty and his great art work."

"Yes, well..." he said, as he stood next to the artist looking down at the two women seated on the sofa. His attraction to Isabelle was instant. He knew it and so did she. He was having a difficult time taking his eyes off her.

"We have four of his paintings," he said, rubbing his nose. The pine scented Rigaud candles Pauline Howard used in each room always triggered his allergies this time of summer, along with all the fresh cut grass in surrounding fields. He continued, only to be interrupted.

"Three, honey," she corrected.

"No, dear. Four," he answered kindly. "You forgot about the one in my office downtown. Rusty is so good at capturing the conformation of a horse, and his colors are so perfect together. On the one in my office that he painted of my old hunt horse Tom Collins, the light chestnut color and the flaxen mane and tail come to life for me. He was my favorite horse."

"Now, I remember," Betty said, softly almost under her breath. She took another sip of wine and asked Isabelle, "Did you see the paintings Rusty did for Mrs. Howard?"

"Well, I saw the one in the other room of the racehorse, the one that won the big race." She was in a panic, she couldn't recall the name of the horse. Oh, well...it didn't really matter.

"Well, there's also..." Betty began.

"The one of her grandson on his pony in the leadline at Devon, I just finished it about two months ago," Rusty said.

"John, darling, show this young lady that painting in the other room and Rusty, dear," she commanded, patting the couch, "sit down here next to me and tell me what you're working on at the moment."

Blissfully, and with some sense of relief, Isabelle finished inspecting the paintings in the other drawing room that she studied before dinner.

Johnathan Dent's knowledge of artwork was a pleasant surprise to Isabelle. She didn't expect it from a lawyer, at least not a senior partner in a prestigious Washington law firm. He reviewed each painting on the lime green-glazed wall in great detail. There were three by Rusty, including the two horse paintings and another colorful scene of a garden party.

"This one here is the May Day Tea Dance," Johnathan explained, then added, "that's a charity event held every year for our local private school. Rusty did the watercolor for the cover of the program, then he donated it to the school to be sold at auction the night of the dance. Pauline always loved it from the time he first showed it to us, so she bought it in the auction. The colors are her favorites, all those bright pastels."

He moved along the wall to a painting by one of the well-known English horse artists, John Nost Sartorius; then to two unsigned paintings of horses in their stalls, also English. On the other side of the room a painting by Jane Gaston hung alongside one by Fleur Cowles and another by Valerie Poole, each in vivid glowing colors.

That night, Johnathan went on to tell Isabelle of his passion for artwork of all kinds. "My wife's family had a huge collection of folk art; some of it's in the National Gallery," he said casually.

He told her that he occasionally took an afternoon off and roamed around the museum. He liked to take one room at a time and often stayed in that room for as long as he could—an hour, sometimes two—focusing on the tiniest detail of every picture on the wall. He started with the very early Italian paintings in the old part of the gallery and was working his way through the vast building. He could name all the artists: Giotto, Duccio, Botticelli, Castagano, Raphael, Michelangelo, and DaVinci; as well as their works and details about his favorite paintings.

"I appreciate all kinds of art," he told Isabelle, just as Betty approached, apparently overhearing the conversation. "Next time you're downtown you absolutely must see that painting Rusty did for John's office."

Absolutely, thought Isabelle.

Isabelle and Tracy spent the rest of the weekend in the country catching up. They went to the Upperville Horse Show finals on Sunday afternoon and there, perched in the high rickety judge's booth sitting next to Tom Taylor, was Helena Winkler. Her presence was causing quite a stir among the spectators and horse show exhibitors, who were not-so-subtly parading by to get a peek. Later in the day, Ms. Winkler joined Pauline Howard and other officials in the center of the ring to present the blue ribbon and trophy to Don Stewart on Monday Blues, winner of the hunter class.

Isabelle wore a revealingly low-cut black sundress that accentuated her long legs, hoping to run into Johnathan. Instead, she came away with a beastly sunburn and not even a glance of him. Though Isabelle felt a definite attraction toward Johnathan, she was not quite certain he felt the same way. She decided not to confide anything.

Tracy's father, Raymond Curtis, was also an attorney. He and Johnathan knew each other since prep school and went through law school at The University together. That would be "THE" University of Virginia in Charlottesville, the school of choice for the state's native sons. Certain places were always referred to with *the* before it: THE University, THE Club, aka The Country Club of Virginia; THE River, aka The James River and pronounced as rivah; and so on.

Isabelle drove back into Washington late Sunday night. After the horse show there was yet another cocktail party, this one held under a modest yellow and white tent not far from the main ring. More ham biscuits, washed down with white wine. It was informal yet chic, and she met some of Tracy's horsey friends: a well-known rider named Rodney Jenkins, who'd won the Big Jump that day, and again the rider trainer from Jacksonville who won the blue ribbon named Don Stewart and his wife, Nancy. She also spotted the veterinarian Dr. Alex Carroll in the distance, walking back to the barn area.

As she drove east down Route 50 back to the city, Isabelle started to think about Johnathan. *What a sensitive man he must be to spend free time at the National Gallery.* All her life she loved to wander through galleries and museums. As a little girl she and her father spent countless Sundays looking at art. She studied art history to complete degree requirements in interior design. Since moving to Washington, she begged friends to accompany her to the latest exhibit at the Corcoran or Phillips Collection. When no one wanted to go, as was usually the case, she simply went alone. How could it be that someone else on earth—particularly such an attractive man—also shared the same interest?

CHAPTER 3

Doc Dalinsky's, The French Market & Neam's

By Tuesday at noon Isabelle had all but forgotten Johnathan Dent. Thirty-six cans of red enamel paint for a powder room belonging to a wealthy young couple living in the swishy Kalorama neighborhood had arrived in the wrong shade of red.

"It's supposed to be *Chinese Red*, Goddamnit!" wailed her boss, Michael Aldridge. "This job has already been delayed ten days. I can't stand it! Get those people on the phone right now."

Though she'd been on the job more than a year, Isabelle was still a nervous wreck when things like this happened. The first time her boss had thrown a fit, she thought she was going to be fired. She took it personally and it hadn't even been her fault. This time, she very calmly went to the files and got out the order form for the paint, even though her stomach was churning.

She looked for the letter she had written to Donald Kaufman in New York. His firm was the best in the business, custom mixing the colors with far more depth than regular paints. They usually mixed more than a dozen different pigments in a translucent base; most commercial companies—the Sherwin Williams of the world—only used two or three.

There, plain as day it was written:

36 gallons *Beijing Berry*

This batch was marked as *Wildfire*.

The entire time she was looking for the order forms and flipping through her Rolodex for the phone numbers, Michael stood over her desk. That made her discomfort even worse. She just had to get things right.

She put the order form on top of her desk—an antique Mr. Aldridge had identified as a George III style mahogany schoolmaster's desk. She sat at the back of the shop/showroom so she could see any customers coming in the front door while at the same time she'd be close to the private offices in the back.

"Yes, this is Michael Aldridge's office in Georgetown," she said to whoever answered the phone at the paint supply office in New York. As she spoke she turned the order form around and tapped the desk gently with the wrong end of her black Flair pen, indicating to Michael that she had, indeed, typed the correct information. He nodded to her.

"Yes," she said, "we need to speak with someone about our order number 3280. It seems you shipped the wrong color and we need this matter corrected immediately. We ordered *Beijing Berry* and the cans that arrived this morning are *Wildfire*." She was talking to the owner's wife and partner, Taffy Dahl.

"Tell them this just won't do," Michael said, interrupting. "I can't have this, I'm going to find someone else who can deliver the right goddamn color on time. This is wrong...wrong!"

Isabelle tried to cover the phone so Taffy Dahl wouldn't hear his ranting in the background. "You'll have to send us the *Beijing Berry* right away, we're late on this job," Isabelle explained, "Do you have it in stock?...Yes..." and she was put on hold.

Now another call was coming in on the line as Isabelle was holding. She put her hand over the receiver, leaned over the desk and quickly explained to Michael. "I'm on hold. I can't get that line."

He turned on his heel, still in a huff, and went back to his office to grab the telephone. He had an air about him that told the world he was above such menial tasks. Still, it could have been an important customer, an inquiry about new business. He'd definitely answer the phone.

Taffy Dahl came back on the line with Isabelle, apologizing for the momentary delay. "We do have twenty-four gallons of *Beijing Berry* in stock right now," she told Isabelle. "I can get the remaining twelve in ten days."

"That just isn't going to do. We have to have all thirty-six from the same mix lot," she said. "I'm going to check with Mr. Aldridge and get back to you."

Mr. Aldridge.

That's what he told Isabelle to call him the day she was hired. He wanted to be referred to in the formal manner when conducting business and their relationship at work had not gotten to the point yet where she felt comfortable or adequate enough calling him just plain *Michael*. *Mike* would never do. He just wasn't a *Mike* kind of guy. And he'd given her no indication that anything less than *Mr. Aldridge* would do.

His attention to detail bordered on the obsessive, a necessary trait in his line of work. But the same obsessiveness spilled over into other facets of his life including, of course, the way he dressed. He wore nothing but natural fibers—linen, cotton, and wool—right down to his patterned socks. A silk bow tie was his special signature.

He hired her right out of college. She drove five hours from her hometown in Raleigh on the recommendation of a friend of her mother's. It was her first and only interview. Michael Aldridge was a very well known and respected Washington decorator, though he preferred to be called a "designer." He helped "do" many homes of the rich, famous, and powerful in Washington, then went on to help them "do" their summer homes in Maine, Michigan, and the Cape, and their winter homes in Palm Beach and St. Barths.

When the formal rooms at the State Department were renovated, Michael Aldridge had been among a select few asked to consult on the project, an honor that gave a tremendous lift to his business and sealed his reputation as one of the very best in town. Still, the pay he offered was a pittance to what he took in every month, but she was happy to get the job and probably would have worked for nothing. He owned a small shop on upper Wisconsin Avenue, just on the edge of Georgetown, which was overflowing with furniture mostly antiques, lamps, fabric samples, side tables, and all kinds of expensive decorations and objets d'art.

There were four people working full time: Isabelle, Mr. Aldridge, Ruth the bookkeeper, and Gunther, the handyman, who did everything from hanging the draperies, making the deliveries in the shop's signature purple minivan (with a bow tie painted on each door), and anything else Mr. Aldridge asked. Gunther had been with Michael from the beginning. He was pleasant enough, rather quiet, and hard of hearing. You had to look right at him when you were talking. He'd lost eighty percent of his hearing in a flying accident as a Luftwaffe pilot during World War II. Nobody was certain of the exact details, and Gunther kept to himself and didn't say much about anything, let alone share war stories.

The shop was a fascinating place to work when business was going smoothly. But when there was a mix-up, like the paint fiasco, nerves were frayed all around. The deadlines were frantic, with little time to do anything other than the current job at hand. Isabelle often worked through lunch, sending Gunther up the street to the French Market for a sandwich on a fresh baguette or some vanilla yogurt. She never brought anything with her, it was just not her way style to carry a brown bag to work. This was supposed to be a semi-sophisticated job. Occasionally, she would skip lunch altogether and just roam around Georgetown, stopping at Doc Dalinsky's Pharmacy for a newspaper or magazine before she went back to the shop. The clients were always fascinating—political appointees, socialites, powerful government lobbyists and consultants such as Washington Post editor Ben Bradlee, Joseph Alsop, syndicated political cartoonist Art Buchwald and David Brinkley. Some would remember Isabelle by name, others would pretend they didn't know she existed—until something would go wrong, and the lady of the house would call anxiously.

"This rug is just not right, Isabelle," the wife of a powerful congressman complained by phone. "Is Michael in? I need to talk with him."

Clients called him *Michael.*

Then Mr. Aldridge would get on the telephone, smooth it over with the anxious patron and tell her he'd drop by the house around four o'clock. Then, over a tall glass of white wine, he'd convince the client that the $20,000 Aubusson rug was positively perfect.

No other rug would do for that place.

Positively perfect.

It was his favorite phrase and in two years, Isabelle had wished she'd kept count of how many times she'd heard it. She didn't resent it, because he was almost always right. The man's style and sense of color was not to be believed.

That summer they were called upon to redo the salon of a 103-foot yacht in Annapolis. It was the first such floating assignment for Mr. Aldridge. While it was hardly an enormous job, he found it challenging and somewhat tedious.

"I met a woman named Eleanor Hartley over the weekend," Mr. Aldridge announced the Tuesday after the fourth of July weekend. "I was visiting friends in Annapolis and she was a guest at a party we attended. Nice woman."

"Anyway," he continued, walking around the showroom and rearranging a set of Limoges oyster plates, "she said she has a boat, I mean a yacht, she wants me to come see. So...I thought I might take you along on Thursday afternoon and we'll see what we can do for her."

Finally.

It had been over two years since she'd been on the job and this was the first time he was going to take her to actually meet a client. It was definitely a big step. She could hardly contain herself.

"Oh, Mr. Aldridge, it sounds great. No problem, I'd love it."

As it turned out, the job was far more complicated than Michael had initially thought. Mrs. Hartley had convinced her new husband, a wealthy real estate speculator who formed partnerships and sold shares in his ventures, she had to redo the entire cabin area of the custom made Huckins. That meant not only the main salon and a dining room below, but also a small guest stateroom, the main stateroom and two "heads."

It also proved to be an enormous hassle. The bulkheads, decks, and cabinets had to be refinished in a burnished mahogany. The custom made elm burl tables had to be mounted on gimbals, very much like a ship's compass so that when the boat rocked the tables would remain stable. Isabelle later began to realize why Michael had asked her along. There were endless trips back and forth from Washington to measure and re-measure and to show samples to

Mrs. Hartley, who by then had become very demanding. Mrs. Hartley could only see someone midday during the week, as Mr. Hartley wanted to take his boat out on the weekend and insisted that nothing be torn up until everything was entirely ready to be installed.

The most exacting and challenging task of any decorator is coordinating. Getting the carpenters to complete their cabinets on time, getting the wallpaper shipped and the wallpaper hanger synchronized, and the painting crew on standby. So, what had seemed like a minor project began to look like it might not even be competed by Labor Day.

Particular rugs had to be ordered. Michael chose a deep hunter green industrial strength, because it was usually used in restaurants. Regular carpet would never last on a boat.

The furniture had to be made to order for a custom fit. The couches and chairs he planned to use in the salon were manufactured in High Point, North Carolina, and every July all the furniture plants closed down for two weeks. They had to have furniture that was smaller to be in scale with the room and not overwhelm the space—thirty-and-a-half inches high instead of the usual thirty-two inches. Each piece of stemware: the wine glasses, the water goblets, and the champagne flutes, was fitted into its own cubicle.

It was exacting work and Michael and Isabelle would be up late many night laboring in the office trying to anticipate every conceivable glitch. They didn't want to overlook any detail. Lamps normally purchased by a decorator at a big city showroom in New York or Chicago wouldn't do, they would sway too much. So Michael commissioned a very well-known company in Paris that had been making yacht fixtures for years to make new fixtures. That bill alone would come to $12,000. Even the tablecloths, shower curtains, and wallpaper had to have specific water-resistant coatings to prevent premature mildew from exposure to the sea and salt air.

Isabelle made countless seventy-mile round trips between Washington to Annapolis. The summer traffic east on Route 50 was unbearable at times. Her 1970 gold Ford Mustang was air-conditioned, but when the traffic slowed down to a crawl she had to turn it off to prevent overheating. Sitting in traffic one day, two thoughts occurred to her...

First, how kind of Michael Aldridge to ask her to assist on this yacht assignment, so he didn't have to schlep back and forth bringing all the samples to Mrs. Hartley.

And as her car approached the boiling-over stage for the third time that afternoon, her thoughts also kept coming back to...Johnathan Douglas Dent.

By the time Isabelle approached Annapolis one sweltering summer Wednesday afternoon, it was three-thirty. She'd been on the road for two hours. There was an accident outside Bowie and she sat in her car waiting and stewing. She had to go to the bathroom, she was sweaty, and needed something to drink. Anything.

"Oh, you poor girl," Mrs. Hartley said, greeting Isabelle. "I was wondering what had happened to you, I expected you at one-thirty or two. I called your office and someone said they thought you were well on your way."

Isabelle explained about the accident and politely asked to use the powder room, where she went to freshen up and use the *facilities*, as Mrs. Hartley described it.

Isabelle thought she was going to pop sitting on that road. She thought of anything but her current dilemma and discomfort. Halfway between Bowie and Crofton, she decided that she had to see Johnathan Dent again.

It was ages since she'd had a man in her life. She'd consciously eliminated any serious relationships ever since she'd broken up with Bruce, her college flame, a few months after they'd both moved to Washington. He found a job as an "AA" (administrative assistant) on the Hill a few weeks after she went to work for Michael Aldridge.

They dated and mated insatiably for two-and-a-half years before Isabelle discovered, quite by coincidence, she was not the only woman in his life. It was a startling experience. They made a conscientious decision not to live together, but spent as much time as possible with one another in their infrequent off hours. So how did he manage to have another girlfriend?

Isabelle decided one Sunday morning to get up and go to Neam's Market on P Street to pick up orange juice, croissants, and jam. She brought him breakfast in bed. She and Bruce had not spent their customary Saturday night together because he told her his aunt and uncle were in town. He wanted to have a family dinner.

"Sounds great, have a good time," Isabelle's replied. "Where are they going to take you ?"

"I haven't a clue, but I'll be thinking of you," was his answer.

"I'll talk to you tomorrow," she said, hanging up the telephone. That night, Isabelle went to the movies with three friends, then stopped at Nathan's, a Georgetown saloon and restaurant, for a couple of drinks. It was after midnight before she got home, washed her face, put on her nightgown, and got into bed.

She slept well but woke up before sunrise and decided to go over to Bruce's apartment, just up P Street near Dupont Circle, and wake him up with breakfast.

His car was parked in the space he rented in the alley behind his apartment building. She entered the back door as she'd done many times before, stepping up the aged wooden steps and into the kitchen.

And there they were: a girl who could have been Isabelle's twin (she even wore the same style flannel nightgown...Wait! Is was Isabelle's nightgown, the one she left in his closet) and Bruce in his frayed terrycloth bathrobe.

The other girl evidently knew about Isabelle and the confrontation was not as much of a surprise to her. Isabelle was thunderstruck. She said, "Oh,

I'm sorry," turned and walked out. She was still carrying the bag of groceries. She drove home, struggling to steer through her tears.

For two days Isabelle didn't eat. She went to work and didn't say a word to anyone. After all, who could she confide in, Ruth the bookkeeper?

Bruce didn't call her until Wednesday. He left a message on her answering machine. She played it back three times that evening: "Hello, Tinker," he said, calling her by her childhood nickname. "It's me, we need to talk."

We sure do need to talk, thought Isabelle.

She sat down in her lonely damp English basement apartment and stared at the drab pale green walls for two hours that night. She was finished crying over him. She had loved him. Her parents and friends all liked him and would be disappointed. But, by the time *The Tonight Show* came on TV, she had concluded that was the end of Bruce or any other man for a while. She'd immerse herself in her work and take on a new project. Maybe even repaint her dingy apartment.

She never called him back.

Now as she looked at herself in the mirror in Mrs. Hartley's powder room, she had far more important concerns.

Isabelle brought swatches of various styles of quilting for the bedspreads in the main stateroom. There were triangular patterns, scalloped patterns and rectangular configurations. They needed to settle on that today, so the fabric could be sent to the workrooms, along with the type of edge on the spread, and the final number of coordinating pillows and shams.

Michael asked Isabelle to show Mrs. Hartley the matching bed linen samples and the everyday bath and guest towels he chose in a new ultra-absorbent cloth. They also didn't take up as much space in a storage or linen closet. It was after five when they finally started on the choice of guest towels. Looking at her watch, Mrs. Hartley got up and asked Isabelle to stay for dinner.

"My husband's bringing home an associate from work, a nice young divorced man," she said.

Why was everyone so concerned with my love life? Isabelle wondered. Even Ruth was always asking questions when nobody else was around the office.

"I really can't," Isabelle said. "I need to get back to Georgetown and write up these orders tonight." She closed her red notebook, shuddering at the thought of the long drive back to town.

"But the traffic at this hour will be horrendous," Mrs. Hartley pointed out. "And I think you might enjoy meeting Dan Collins—he's a bright young attorney. Very good looking."

That was all it took. She was right and Isabelle would be delighted to stay, even if she wasn't really all that interested in meeting someone. She didn't want to sit in her car any longer than necessary. The commute had become unbearable.

The evening proved to be pleasant. Eleanor Hartley served paella, with warm twisted bread sticks, followed by a mixed green salad. After dessert of fresh strawberries, they sat outside on a patio that overlooked the Severn River. It was a sprawling open home that Isabelle noted needed absolutely no updating in terms of decorating. The conversation was light: the drought in California, recent movies they'd all seen, books—including Alex Haley's latest, *Roots*. No politics or heavy international issues, though Isabelle did learn that Dan Collins eventually hoped to get into some consulting work with Congress.

Right after coffee, the men excused themselves. Isabelle concluded that Dan Collins was pleasant and polite. But that was it, and he was no Johnathan Dent.

Mrs. Hartley seemed disappointed when the men left, but was accustomed to her husband constantly huddled in business discussions. She amused herself in other ways...like shopping and redecorating the yacht.

"Maybe he'll call you sometime," she offered as Isabelle stood up to leave.

"Not to worry," Isabelle said, "I'm so busy. Thank you for dinner, it was wonderful and I'll call you on Monday to set up another appointment."

Mrs. Hartley ushered her to the front door and ordered her to drive back carefully. She was such an attractive girl, she thought. *Why didn't some man grab her up?*

When Isabelle got home late that night, there was only one message on her answering machine. Mr. Aldridge had called, in a bit of a huff, as usual.

"Isabelle, it's *Michael*, what the hell happened to you? Mrs. Hartley called, it's about three o'clock and she hasn't heard from you. Hope everything is okay. I'll see you in the morning at about eight. Thanks, bye."

It was the first time he identified himself to her as Michael. By now he was more at ease in her presence. And of course, he also expected her to arrive extra early at work the next day, which she often did, more than willingly. It was late and she wanted to get to bed early. But she wasn't the least bit tired, even after yet another frantic trip to Annapolis and back.

She washed her face, just as she did religiously every night. She put on a stretch terry cloth headband before she splashed the water on her face in order not to get her hair wet. Her translucent skin didn't require any cream or astringents.

She flipped on the television set in her Lilliputian living room, now painted a cheerful shade of yellow, known as *Shasta Daisy*. She sat down with a tall glass of Coke with ice, the drink of choice for most southern girls. The latest edition of *Architectural Digest* had arrived in her mail that day. It was her Bible. All decorators strived to have one of their clients' homes in it. It was fascinating to see who had made it every month, not to mention a financial boon to any decorator mentioned on its glossy pages. The room was a bit stuffy, so she opened one of the front windows, barred to keep out potential burglars, even in swanky Georgetown. She was eye level with the sidewalk outside. She wanted to stay up a bit and read the magazine. She snuggled into the loveseat and flipped open to a middle page.

And there was Mrs. Vernon Harrison Howard's lime green drawing room in all its grandeur. The grand dame of Middleburg had landed in AD. Fresh flowers and the whole nine yards. And there on the far wall was the Rusty Stewart painting Johnathan Douglas Dent had been admiring the moment they had met.

As Pauline Howard would have said...*How grand.*

That was all it took for Isabelle.

Johnathan Dent was on her mind too frequently lately. She was determined to see him. He was married but she didn't care about that right now. All she could think about were those eyes and how he gazed at her that night over his glasses.

On the following Wednesday, she called him at his office. She had to get past two secretaries at the law firm, not to mention the receptionist who first answered the phone.

"Duke, Graves, Dent, and Coggin," she sang going up an octave on the last syllable.

"Mister Dent, please," Isabelle asked.

The first voice quickly transferred her to the second voice, who passed her on to a third, his personal secretary, without so much as a "Just a moment please."

"Johnathan Dent's office," said the third voice.

Now Isabelle's heart was racing. She was scared, she didn't know what to say but was determined not to turn back. "Is Mr. Dent in please?" she said, trying to stay calm in her best business voice.

"Who's calling please?" was his secretary's efficient question to her question.

"Isabelle Stoker," she said simply.

"I'll see if he's in" she said, implying to an unfamiliar name that he was not available as the hold button clicked on.

He came on the line quickly, "Isabelle, how are you?" he said, as if they had talked yesterday.

"Fine," she replied, trying to hide her nervousness. "I was going to the museum, it's open late in the summer." *Boy, I'm into it now, she thought.* "I thought you might want to join me, since you'd mentioned it was one of your favorite things to do."

It was rather brazen move, but Isabelle felt remarkably at ease, once she got past the first question. It just seemed so, so...natural. He was such a warm and gentle man. She wanted to know him better. And before they so much as even had lunch or dinner together, she knew she wanted to know him better than better.

First things, first.

"Tonight?" he asked.

"Well, yes," she said, never pondering that a busy lawyer like Johnathan might not be able to rearrange his schedule on only a few hours notice. She was in a momentary panic now. *What if he couldn't make it? What would she say?* She would feel so imprudent.

"Sounds great," he said, almost immediately. "I'll tell you what," he said, taking the lead now. "Why don't you come to my office and we'll go from here?"

"At about what time?" was all she wanted to know.

"After work, about five-thirty or sixish."

"Great," Isabelle said, "I'll see you then," and she hung up.

It was all over so rapidly she didn't know what to think. She leaned back in her chair. Everyone else in the office was still out for lunch or running errands. Her boss was on vacation in Southampton. She took a deep breath. How exciting. She wanted to call someone, a friend and tell them the great news...

She was going to meet Johnathan Douglas Dent and go to the museum.

Next question. What time did five thirty or sixish mean?

She would arrive at five-forty: not too early and not too late.

She was ushered into his office at five-forty-two.

Ohmygod, she thought, they all know who I am. What must these secretaries think?

That thought left her the instant she saw him. He came around his desk and shook her hand.

"What a pleasant surprise," he said, "have a seat."

His office was immense. Isabelle took note immediately of the decor. Beige. Everything was in beige and brown. The walls were covered in beige silk wallpaper. The couch was a darker beige linen. And the chairs, all club type with deep soft cushions were finished in a stripe fabric that coordinated, and was two shades darker. There were a number of needlepoint pillows in the chairs and one on the couch that said Lawyers Never Grow Old. They Just Lose Their Appeal. It was an unusual touch for an office. Isabelle wondered if his wife had stitched them? It added warmth to the space. She pondered the situation momentarily. And asked herself where he told his wife he was going that night.

There was a window. Actually it was more than a window. One entire side of the room was glass, floor to ceiling. There were no curtains or blinds and the view was an interesting angle that provided a glimpse of the intersection on L Street and a full view of Connecticut Avenue, now bustling with rush-hour traffic.

Someone buzzed on the intercom and he walked back to the large antique walnut desk to answer the phone. Isabelle continued to glance around the room, enchanted and not at all listening to his conversation.

When he hung up, he came back to the couch and pointed out the painting of his horse, by Rusty Stewart, the court artist of Middleburg. It hung on the large wall behind the couch with about thirty other framed works of art, photos, letters, and diplomas. It was odd, but Isabelle had pictured one whole wall in his office devoted to a large painting of his horse.

"Here's the painting I told you about," he said, adding, "It's really one of my favorites.

"And this one over here came from England," he explained, pointing out another painting. It was of a large, rather fat, and not very attractive bay horse. "I call him the 'big bay beer horse.' He came from a shop in London.

"You see here," he pointed to the lower left-hand corner. "It says 'Old Brown aged 35.' I just thought he was the cutest draft horse I've ever seen."

Isabelle had a difficult time looking at it, with all the other objects crowded around it on the wall. "It's lovely," was all she could say, looking to one side trying to read a framed letter with the logo of a major national corporation on the top. Next to that was a picture of Johnathan shaking hands with another man. In the photo Johnathan was wearing a traditional black tuxedo and the other man had on a dark green velvet dinner jacket.

He saw her looking, and explained that it was taken one night at a ball in the British Embassy with Ambassador Anthony Ackland. Above that picture was his law degree from The University and next to that a picture of Johnathan, in his cap and gown with his arm around another graduate, also in cap and gown.

"That was taken the day Ray and I graduated," he said, referring to his close friend, Raymond Curtis, the father of her best friend. Isabelle recognized the familiar face. It momentarily crossed her mind the picture must have been taken more than twenty-five years ago.

She didn't care.

They had an enchanting time at the museum, which wasn't at all crowded. He took her directly into the downstairs room in the main part of the National Gallery.

They started at the beginning: the Italian paintings of the thirteenth century...

Afterward they went to dinner at Blackie's House of Beef near her apartment in Georgetown. They talked about everything and the conversation was spontaneous. It was obvious he enjoyed her company, but Isabelle couldn't help it when her mind wandered on to other thoughts.

What did he think of her? Did he see her as a friend, or merely as a friend of a friend? Or as an enchanting woman who almost ached to be with him?

He hailed a taxi after dinner and delivered her home, walked her to the door, shook her hand and thanked her for "a very lovely time. It was great. Perhaps we'll do it again sometime."

When she went inside, she threw her purse down and wanted to cry. There was no doubt about it; she was falling in love with this gorgeous man. *How could he leave her like this? Not even a peck on the cheek.*

What would she do?

She took a shower, crawled into bed, and tried to sleep,

Impossible.

Her mind was spinning with thoughts of Johnathan Douglas Dent.

The next day, her friend Tracy called and invited her out to the country for the Labor Day weekend.

"Oh, gee," Isabelle said, lying, "I really wish I could, but we have this enormous project on a yacht in Annapolis and we're doing all the installation next week. I have to work overtime and make sure everything is coordinated."

It was sort of true.

"But I haven't seen you in ages," Tracy half-begged. "What are you doing with yourself? How's your love life? Anyone new?"

It was a logical question from one girlfriend to another, but it still hurt.

"Nonexistent," she answered, this time telling the whole truth. *Damn that Johnathan Dent*, she thought. She should have been smarter. She should have known.

"Well, listen," Tracy instructed, as she often did, "how about we make a firm date for Thanksgiving? Mom and Dad will be having their Hunt Breakfast that weekend and it will be a big time."

"Sounds great," was Isabelle's way of not making a commitment, "I'll call you soon." But the way she felt right now, she was not at all sure she wanted to risk a chance encounter with Johnathan in Middleburg, and certainly not with his wife close by.

Isabelle spent Labor Day weekend alone. She went to Georgetown on Saturday and roamed up and down Wisconsin Avenue looking into the windows of all the colorful boutiques, not buying a thing save for a few cards. She never missed a birthday or an anniversary. Picking out cards was one of her favorite things to do. She loved to surprise friends with funny cards that often made no sense. Just one of those "I'm thinking about you" cards.

She yearned to send one to Johnathan.

Saturday night she stayed home. All day Sunday she moped around, read the Sunday Washington Post and the New York Times and on Monday she decided to go to the National Gallery alone. Maybe somewhere deep inside she thought it would bring her closer to Johnathan, as if he would be with her in spirit somehow. She knew she would never run into him there, even if she did secretly harbor that hope.

It was the worst thing she could have done.

Something pulled her to the same rooms she had visited with him. She studied the paintings, recalling what he had told her about them. She missed him terribly.

She stopped at the Georgetown Safeway for a frozen dinner and went home. That night she washed her hair, put it up in rollers (something she rarely did) for lack of anything better to do and prepared for work the next day.

Chapter 4

The Southern Trail

The day after Labor Day, Isabelle woke with new ambition and aspiration—like starting a new school year. She was at work before eight on Tuesday.

Michael arrived shortly after her, with a Styrofoam cup of coffee from the nearby 7-11, and a bundle of fabric and wallpaper swatches under his arm.

They went over their checklist for the Hartley yacht. The Hartleys didn't want their boat out of commission for more than four days and Michael promised he could do it. He and Isabelle lined up a crew of seventeen workers to be at the basin the next morning no later than six. The Hartleys wanted everything re-papered, painted, installed, hung and finished, so they could take their boat out that next weekend. The weekend after that, they were entertaining twenty-eight guests for a formal dinner cruise aboard their newly redecorated yacht, The Southern Trail.

It would be an important business dinner, the better for Vernon Hartley's company to foot the bill for the entire redecorating project. It would be a very expensive tab, but that was of little concern to Mr. Hartley. He had major clients to entertain, and in the end, he had as much input into the decorating venture as Mrs. Hartley, who had overseen it.

"Now we have to make sure with the dock master at the yacht basin that those extra electrical lines are installed *today*, as promised," Michael said, emphasizing the word today. "We can't function without those lines. The carpenters need them."

"It's on my list of things to do," she said, thinking... *When is he going to believe I can get things done?* Isabelle spent the rest of the day on the phone.

"This is Isabelle Stoker at Michael Aldridge's shop," she repeated, all afternoon. "I'm calling to confirm that your wallpapering (painting, carpentry, rug laying, etc., etc.) crew will be at the Annapolis basin slip number thirty-eight and thirty-nine tomorrow morning at six."

By the time Isabelle got out of the office, it was almost eight o'clock. She was exhausted. *Another night, another Lean Cuisine.* By the time she zapped it, took off her clothes, and sat down to eat in front of the TV, it was almost ten. Tomorrow might be worse. She would have to set her alarm for at least four in the morning to get to Annapolis by five-thirty, and even that was cutting it close. But she had to be there to oversee the work, lay out the instructions for each crew, and probably provide coffee and donuts.

Things began badly even before the sun was up. There was no water pressure for the wallpapering crew.

"We can't work without water," the crew chief explained to Isabelle, who didn't have to be told. "It just won't work Miss..."

"Stoker," she reminded him. They had worked together many times, including an embassy project.

"I assumed that this would be a difficult job," he said. "But I didn't think it would be impossible."

"Don't worry," she said, trying to think of the dockmaster's name. "I'll get on this right away. Have some coffee and Danish. I'll be right back."

She could hear him mutter, "I've had enough coffee for one morning, we need to get going." The dockmaster was quick to solve the dilemma. He cut off the water supply to the north end of the marina, which in turn provided the needed pressure to the workmen.

Michael had arranged for two motel rooms in Annapolis so he and Isabelle would not have to drive back and forth during the four days of work on the Hartley yacht. He had forgotten to mention this to Isabelle, however and had not brought extra clothes.

"Why don't we go back to the motel and change and have a stiff drink?" he suggested.

"What are you talking about? What motel?"

"Oh, no," he said. "Didn't I tell you I'd gotten us two rooms?"

"No!" Now after another frazzling day, after a dinner with her boss, Isabelle got in her trusty Mustang and drove back to Georgetown. She was so worn out she didn't even bother to wash her face or brush her teeth. She set the alarm for four in the morning again and slithered into bed, aching from the day's work.

Her mind raced with details. The china she'd ordered from New York, with the name of the yacht on the border, had not yet arrived. She had to call tomorrow and check on it. They'd have to send it by air express. Michael wanted everything to be perfect. Mrs. Hartley needed this china for her dinner party...

It was an unseasonably warm fall that year, and Isabelle decided to splurge on some new clothes. After the Hartley yacht project was completed, Mr. Aldridge gave her a $2,500 bonus, even if the hand-painted china never did arrive on time. It was the most money Isabelle had received in one check, and she was flattered. She knew that Mr. Aldridge's final bill to the Hartley's was over $80,000, so she didn't feel even guilty about taking the extra money. She earned every nickel in gas mileage alone back and forth to Annapolis.

She went out one Saturday afternoon thinking she'd buy a new suit, something business-like and professional. She thought about the secretaries in Johnathan Dent's law firm, all dressed for success. Truthfully, though, she was also thinking about Johnathan Dent, who had never called her after their excursion to the museum.

A new suit. A tweed suit and a silk blouse, perhaps that would make her look older and more sophisticated. Maybe Johnathan preferred that look. She strolled up Wisconsin Avenue to a shop called Dorcas Hardin. It was a tiny, tasteful boutique on a side street in a narrow brick building where all the well-heeled ladies of Georgetown shopped.

As she stepped onto the plush carpet, a bell went off indicating to the saleswomen that a customer had arrived. An older woman approached and greeted her with "Hello, can I help you?"

Isabelle was not at all intimidated by the tight quarters or the woman hovering so close. She now was accustomed to small work spaces. "Well... yes.." she answered. "I was thinking about a new fall suit, about a size eight."

"Certainly," the woman said.

Certainly, thought Isabelle.

Two hours later, she walked out, the owner of not one but two new suits. The first a "daytime suit" according to the saleswoman. It was camel hair cashmere and she bought a brown turtleneck sweater to go with it. Then she also had to have an evening "cocktail suit" for "the theater and dinner and things like that" the woman told her. It was a black knit with large brass buttons on the waist-length jacket. Then the saleslady convinced her that she had to have the white silk blouse to go with it to "complete the look."

The bill came to $1,400, and Isabelle was beaming when she stepped on the uneven cobblestone sidewalk. She rarely went to the theater, and not since her parents visited over a year ago. But if she ever were invited, she'd certainly be prepared.

It was dusk as she made her way along Wisconsin Avenue. She was weary from trying on all those clothes. The pink plastic bags were hanging over her arm. The air was chilly now that the sun had disappeared, but Isabelle paid little attention, stopping for a moment in front of a jewelry store to look at the baubles in the window. The owner, whom she recognized, was starting to take things out of the display and put them in the safe for the night. In the reflection from the shop window, Isabelle could see the traffic along the street behind her and, across the street, a popular children's shop. Now, another woman joined her in admiring the jewelry display.

"Oh, I just adore the lapis," she said to Isabelle. "And the lapis with pearls back there," she tapped on the window. The owner looked up and smiled at Isabelle. "Isn't that lovely?" she said, pointing her red gloved finger toward the back of the display. Isabelle had heard that voice before, but before it could register, a man was speaking.

"See anything you like?" yet another familiar voice asked as he approached.

Isabelle froze for a moment. It was *him*. She looked up, past his wife, with whom she'd been half-conversing and hadn't realized it. He looked back, keeping his gaze intently on her eyes.

"Why...Miss Stoker, how are you?" he asked. "Betty you remember Tracy Curtis's friend, don't you? We met at Pauline's last summer."

Actually, Isabelle was unconvinced that this woman remembered her name. *What was her problem?*

"Of course, I do darling. How are you, dear?" extending her gloved hand and adding, "We're just on our way to a cocktail party up the street. I just have a hard time passing a jewelry store though, don't you?"

A cocktail party, thought Isabelle. She wanted now to burn the cocktail suit and Johnathan Dent at the same marshmallow roast.

"I'm in a rush to get home myself," Isabelle lied, letting her eyes drop and now inching away, clutching the pink garment bag. "Good to see you both, I'll tell Tracy I saw you."

And she was off up the street.

Damn, she thought. *Why did this have to happen today of all days?* She'd been feeling so happy with her new purchases and couldn't wait to go home to try them on again. And here they were, a happy couple on their way to a party smack in the middle of Georgetown.

Isabelle had a difficult time falling asleep that night and almost welcomed the sun. Soon after the early light sliced across her bedroom, she was up and out and to work early Monday morning. And, as usual, Mr. Aldridge was right behind her, a Styrofoam cup of coffee in hand and a long list of tasks she'd have to finish in yet another twelve-hour day.

At precisely two minutes after nine, the phone rang.

Isabelle answered on the first ring, her boss was standing over her. "Michael Aldridge," she said.

"Isabelle?"

Silence.

"It's Johnathan Dent."

"I know," was all she could say. Mr. Aldridge was still standing over her. He did it all the time, at the ready to take a call from one client or another. Ready to book a job or pencil in a luncheon on his ever-expanding social calendar.

"I thought we might go to the gallery again," he offered, almost whispering.

God, Isabelle wished Michael would move. She answered as briskly as she could. "Sounds won-der-ful," she said, dividing up the word distinctly as she said it. She was trying to let him know just how delighted she was that he'd finally called.

She was using her heart, not her head.

As usual.

They met at "about threeish" (his words, not hers) in the central lobby of the Hirshhorn Museum. "A different angle," he had said. "Modern art."

Downstairs was a work Isabelle would never forget. It was a geometric painting, rather large, about five feet high and six feet wide. It was done in primary colors... reds, yellows... in stripes. She stood in front of the painting, mesmerized by the powerful colors.

Then, Johnathan said, "Come over here." He took her hand and led her to the side of the painting, about four feet back.

"Look here," he said, pointing to the side. "Look at this painting sideways. It's a surprise."

To Isabelle's astonishment, the colors changed. When she leaned forward to look at it from the side, the colors were the same, but in completely different configuration. Then he led her around the front and over to the far side. He held her hand and didn't let go. As they walked, the colors changed again. The stripes were painted on triangular wood strips, with each side a different arrangement. The painting worked like a kaleidoscope.

"His name is Gene Davis," Johnathan explained, still holding her hand. "This is called *Planks*. His work is meant for sustained viewing. Here read this," he said, indicating the wall plaque alongside the painting.

They stood, motionless yet comfortable as they read: "Instead of simply glancing at the work, enter the painting through the door of a single color. And then, you can understand what my painting is all about."

They silently took an elevator down to the parking garage. He opened the car door for her and she got in. She never asked a single question about where they were going.

They ate dinner in a back booth at the coffee shop on the Virginia side of the Key Bridge. They talked about everything. He had mentioned that for three weeks in September, including Labor Day (since he had last seen her) he'd been traveling with a client.

"A developer. He's trying to buy waterfront property down around Norfolk," Johnathan told her. "He's my most important client and we've been back and forth many times looking things over and talking to some attorneys down there. I've met every member of the city council and the mayor, too. I'm sure it'll get done, but it's going to take a lot of time."

Isabelle told him about the Hartleys' yacht, how it had consumed most of her time all summer. She now had at least five assignments in the works. "It's the busiest time of year," she explained as a waitress interrupted them for coffee.

"I'd love some. High-test please," she told the waitress. Johnathan ordered decaf. "Everyone wants their house redone for the holidays; it's a mess."

The waitress brought their coffee and laid the check down next to Johnathan. They both leaned over for that first steaming sip. And Isabelle sat back.

She sat on an angle in the corner of the booth. "Well?" she asked, "Now what?"

"Now what?" he asked, glancing up from the bill over his half-glasses. "Now I want to make mad, passionate love to you."

Isabelle once thought this moment might never occur.

Now, they drove back into the city and up Constitution Avenue. Johnathan turned right near the Forrestal Building, then left up a cobblestone entrance to the front of the L'Enfant Plaza Hotel.

The doorman opened the car door as Isabelle slid out and walked silently inside the plush lobby next to Johnathan. The mauve carpet was deep and soft and everything seemed hushed. This was not a typical tourist trap, catering instead to conventions and consultants in town to do business with the federal establishment almost within walking distance. A huge fresh flower arrangement was placed in the center of a round marble table in the middle of the room. He gently took her arm and led her around to the bank of elevators. Isabelle could hardly contain herself. She was nervous and wished she had ordered a glass of wine with dinner. When they got to the room on the top floor, it was almost eleven o'clock. She flipped on the TV out of habit and nervous energy. She peeked out the windows at the Potomac River.

He took her hand and led her to the bed. They took their clothes off as if they had known each other for many, many years.

And then he drew her close, and for as long as she lived, Isabelle would never forget the moment Johnathan Douglas Dent entered her life.

Isabelle glowed for days after that first night with Johnathan. Even the people at work noticed it.

"Looks like someone's dating again," the bookkeeper had teased, and Isabelle couldn't help but smile.

He called one week later. It had been the most difficult week ever. She wanted to speak to him so badly, but she knew she'd have to wait until he made the next move. She picked up the phone at work and at home at least a hundred times. She put the receiver to her ear, thought about him, and then replaced it. Somehow she just knew he felt the same way about her.

Their lovemaking had been equal parts passion and poignant tenderness. Isabelle was so scared she might disappoint an older, more experienced man. Maybe there was something she hadn't done? But in the end, she just knew in her heart this had been something special for both of them.

It was almost five o'clock when the phone at work buzzed once more. She was still at her desk, typing orders. She expected to be there for at least another hour, even though the front door would soon be locked to keep the public out until the next morning. She had so much to do.

"Michael Aldridge," she said, cradling the phone on her shoulder and continuing to type. As soon as he spoke, she stopped

"Isabelle ?"

"How are you?" she answered softly. She knew she wanted him again... and again. *Thank God*, she thought...*he called me.*

"I've been over my head in work," he said. "Remember that real estate business in Norfolk? Well, we've been trying to close the deal. We finally got the approval from the town council and the mayor. It's been interesting. You wouldn't believe some of the people who serve on this council...one guy's a hardware store owner. I'll tell you all about it when I see you."

When you see me? "Well, I can't wait to hear about it." Of course, she didn't know one thing about real estate and, truth be told, she wasn't really sure she wanted to know. But she *was* certain of one thing...

If Johnathan Douglas Dent had anything to tell her, anything at all, she'd always listen.

"How about another museum and dinner on Wednesday?"

"I would...," the phone was ringing. "Just a second," she said, putting him on hold and not waiting for a reply while at the same time not believing she had done that.

"Michael Aldridge," she answered. "Can you hold, please?"

"Yes, sure," said the second caller, a female.

She flipped back to Johnathan, "I'd love it. I'm so sorry, no one else is here. I had to get the phone. So...where shall we go?" she asked, almost not taking a breath as she rambled.

"Well," he said, thinking out loud, "there are some special things at the Smithsonian I'd love to show you. Some folk art."

The collection of artifacts in the Crane Collection of Folk Art was charming. Most of the pieces were donated by Betty Dent's late father, a few were listed as "promised gift of Elizabeth Crane Douglas."

Johnathan explained the arrangement that had been worked out by gallery director J. Carter Brown. "Ten percent of each work of art has been pledged and a deed has been signed that promises the rest to the museum upon her death. For tax purposes it's wonderful and if she really wanted to, she can also bring these pieces home. The insurance is so high, they're here most of the time.

"I wanted to share this with you, Isabelle," he told her, "but I just wasn't sure how you'd react."

"React? I love it. It's great. How could anyone not love all of this?" she said, gesturing with her hands in the air. "It's so colorful."

"No...I mean, did you realize that this was Betty's family collection?" he asked cautiously.

"Well...no...I didn't" she said, thinking a bit and pausing. "But that doesn't matter. I love it anyway."

"I was hoping you would."

The collection featured more than three hundred objects of American Folk Art acquired by Elizabeth Crane Dent's family over many years. When her father died, half of his collection was left to the museum and the other half was sold at auction. Isabelle vaguely remembered reading about the auction in the past few years now that she thought about it. Betty Dent retained a few pieces and they were now in her home in the country.

There were all manner of pieces, some carved, others painted. There were whirligigs, toys, canes, walking sticks, and decoys.

A large canvas carnival banner featured a tattooed lady. A carved and painted wood figure of an Indian woman had been assembled by Miles B. Carpenter and was positioned next to a piece of primitive sculpture done by Steven Ashby.

"He was an old black man who hung out at the Delaplane Store," Johnathan explained. "Betty's father used to go out there and buy his pieces for a song. It's not far from Middleburg. I'd love for you to see the old store sometime."

A whimsical primitive painting done by Gustav Klump showed minuscule naked people romping in the countryside around a lake near a woods. "Oh, Johnathan," she said. "This is great: Wedding Dream in Nudist Colony."

They made their way back to Georgetown for dinner. "Where shall we go?" he asked.

"Well we could go to Martin's. Do you know that place?"

In the heart of Georgetown, the old tavern was her favorite. She was almost a regular, and most of the waiters knew her name and her preferred dish—crab cakes and fries—by heart.

"Perfect."

If Johnathan was at all leery about going out to a fairly well-known public place, he didn't show it. Anyway, the lights were dimmed, and it was almost dark in the pine-paneled back room filled with old sports pictures hung above the ancient wooden booths.

It took no time at all for Isabelle and Johnathan to fall into a routine. Soon after that first night, they were bedding down once or twice a week.

Sometimes they went to dinner, sometimes to the museum or to a movie. She was positively giddy, despite the grueling hours at the shop. When they went out, she hooked her arm in his, occasionally resting her head on his shoulder and squeezing him tightly. Once he took her to the Lincoln Memorial late at night and told her how much he admired the man and how he secretly aspired to be a politician.

"After all this work down in Norfolk, winding my way through the political system, I think I might actually like it," he told her as they stood, arm in arm looking up at the imposing granite statute.

Once in a while, they would slip off to an early movie. But each time, the evening ended the same. As time wore on, they learned so much from each other. She couldn't wait to absorb every part of Johnathan.

Of course, he was married and she did feel slightly guilty about that. She'd never been that kind of woman, and wouldn't be now if she didn't think he loved her and stayed with Betty for the sake of his children, not to mention appearances. Still, the weekends were torture. She would roam around Georgetown, go to dinner with friends, occasionally even accept a date that always ended with a handshake at her door. But she couldn't wait until Monday morning, when she could finally speak with him again.

Eventually she got up the nerve to call him herself. She simply could not stand the suspenseful agony waiting for the phone to ring. Sometimes she waited until noon to call, but most of the time they spoke between nine-thirty and ten. If he didn't call by nine-thirty, she had to wait until noon, because he had a staff meeting at ten-fifteen every Monday.

It became easier as time went on. They chatted about their weekends. He was careful not to mention Betty's name. He'd say *"Oh we had a nice time, we went to watch the foxhunters over near Upperville. And then we went to a hunt breakfast at the Fosters."* The fall social season was in full swing out in the country. He talked about his children a lot.

One thing Isabelle noticed was that he never asked her direct questions like: *What did you do?* or *Where did you go?* He would say, *"And you?"* Meaning, *What did you do all weekend?*

She wondered if he thought there was another man in her life. She could never dream of such a thing now. No one else would ever do. They hadn't really gotten around to talking much about their respective pasts, and she had never mentioned her one former lover, Bruce. From time to time, she did wonder if he'd ever been involved with someone else.

One particularly lonely weekend when Isabelle didn't feel like being around anyone. She went to the Biograph movie theater on M Street in the heart of Georgetown for an early show. She wanted to be out of there before all the Saturday night daters. She felt uneasy around couples. She wasn't jealous, but she hated to see other girls with full-time lovers or husbands. Quite a few college students from Georgetown University or the alluring rich girls from Mount Vernon College up Foxhall Road were out bar-hopping from

Clyde's to Nathan's to Champions. They were laughing and joking as they walked down the crowded streets, stopping to ogle the latest fashions in the windows of the numerous boutiques like the funky Off The Cuff, filled with gaudy costume jewelry and vintage clothes just up the street from Nathan's.

Isabelle decided to see Neil Simon's latest movie, *Chapter Two*. It was fun, she liked his work and it made her smile. Her fantasies led her to think about what it might be like for her and Johnathan to have a "Chapter Two"—a second marriage perhaps?

But she knew that was not about to happen anytime soon—if it ever did—so she quickly pushed such thoughts to the back of her mind.

When Thanksgiving arrived, Isabelle was in a foul mood. She wouldn't see Johnathan for another week. Instead, she traveled home to Raleigh to visit her family. It would be fun, she told herself. And she loved her mother's pumpkin pie and raisin stuffing. The two of them went shopping and had dinner at the Carolina Country Club one night. Isabelle saw some of her old friends and their parents, and for a while, she managed to put Johnathan out of her thoughts.

No sooner was Thanksgiving over and it was Christmastime. Things were popping at work. Women were frantic, they wanted to get things in order. *Now!*

"You know, I'm having eighty-five people here for cocktails in less than a week," one wife of a diplomat told her. "What am I supposed to do without that chandelier?"

Isabelle almost laughed out loud. What would that woman say if she told her to put her finger in the socket? She smiled at the thought of the old bat's blue-gray hair standing on end.

"Mrs. Quince," she said instead, politely, "please, I know you're upset, but the company has promised they shipped it out by UPS two days ago. As soon as it gets here, Mr. Aldridge will have Gunther rush right over and install it. Don't worry."

"Oh, sweetie. Everything has been so perfect. I love the new colors in my dining room. It's such a marvelous shade of yellow. And the seats on the chairs are beautiful. It must have taken that woman forever to stitch that needlepoint. But really, darling, how can I have this party without that light fixture?"

She kept talking, "You know I sent out over fifty invitations?" she said, not expecting an answer. "I'll be mor-ti-fied."

Isabelle just listened and once again reassured her that when the light fixture came in, she'd immediately be in touch. Nevertheless, Mrs. Quince called every day, sometimes twice a day once she learned that the UPS man made two visits to the shop.

"Has the delivery boy shown up yet?" she would say when Isabelle answered the phone, not even bothering to say hello. *"My party is two days away. It's Thursday. I'm getting desperate."*

"Yes, I know," Isabelle would reply, *"don't worry."* And then they went

through the entire thing again. About how much she loved the yellow and the eighty-something guests, etc., etc., etc., and on, and on, and on.

Finally, one day before the big party, the oversized box arrived a few minutes before five o'clock. She called Mrs. Quince with the glorious news and told her Gunther would be right over to install the fixture.

"Oh my dining room is going to be a mess," she declared. "Oh come right over, please. You are coming with him?" she pleaded.

"Of course," said Isabelle, who had never intended to do any such thing. But she knew this woman needed her hand held and she felt it was her duty. So much of the decorator's job involved what Michael called "stroking." At this point in the holiday season he was running all over town with last minute deliveries. His job at this time of year was not just decorating. Many clients ordered special gifts, wrapped and delivered personally by him to their friends. That would often result in another assignment later on. When Michael Aldridge arrived at the front door with a gift of antique English candlesticks or an unusual cachepot wrapped in his signature white enamel paper with white satin ribbon, ladies practically swooned with delight.

Isabelle went along with Gunther to Mrs. Quince's home off Foxhall Road to oversee the installation of the unwieldy brass and crystal light fixture. As it turned out, it was a good thing she went. Three of the glass globes in the box were broken. It was too late to call the company, so Isabelle would have to go in search of something to match.

"Not to worry, Mrs. Quince, I'll fix it..."

"Oh, I just knew it...," She stood with her hand over her mouth, staring up at the naked fixture in the center of her enormous dining room.

"No, I'll find something," Isabelle told her.

Her mind was working on plan B. She'd have to go to Hechinger's out in Virginia, or up on Wisconsin Avenue and buy something to make do until they ordered the correct custom glass globes. She had to get going. It was close to eight o'clock. She wanted to get this done. It was bitter cold and dark outside. Car headlights glared at her eyes, she was getting a headache. But there was no time for that. Everyone was going somewhere. Christmas was on Monday and today was Friday.

Isabelle drove up Foxhall to Nebraska Avenue past American University to the large hardware chain store. They didn't have a thing that would do. She rushed across the street to Sears, no luck there either.

It was past ten when she arrived back at her apartment. The traffic back down Wisconsin Avenue into Georgetown was horrendous. Her head was now throbbing and her eyes ached. Mrs. Quince insisted that she call her that night and tell her what she found.

The lady was near a breakdown. "A chandelier and no glass shades!"

Isabelle knew she couldn't suggest candlelight after all this mess. She would drive to suburban Virginia first thing in the morning and look at the Hechinger's out there. She would have to postpone her trip home to North

Carolina by one day.

By three o'clock on the afternoon of Mrs. Quince's big Christmas cocktail party in her new dining and living room the chandelier was complete...sort of.

Isabelle had saved the day.

After driving out to Tyson's Corner in the Saturday-before-Christmas rush, she had found eighteen matching globes that would fit over the tapered light bulbs in the fixture.

"Oh, sweetie, you're wonderful!" Mrs. Quince gushed as she walked Isabelle to her double front door. "I can never thank you enough."

Probably not, thought Isabelle.

Probably not.

Sunday morning, Isabelle was driving south toward home in Raleigh. It was a frigid day, but there was no snow in the forecast. She wondered what the Dent family was doing at this very moment.

She couldn't bear to think about it.

She spent a lovely Christmas at home. The Stokers went through all their holiday rituals: roast beef, opening one gift on Christmas Eve, the rest the next morning over coffee and cheese Danish.

New Year's Eve the family went to the country club with longtime family friends, the Blounts. She danced with her father and brother Adam and her brother's friend, Holder, who was visiting for the holiday. Cole Porter music dominated the dance tunes. And she ate black-eyed peas for good luck.

So much for 1977, she thought, *bring on 1978.*

Chapter 5

Michael Sussman & Willard Scott

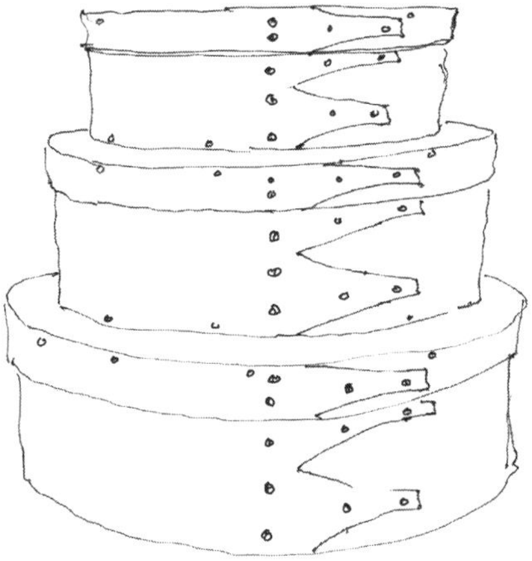

Isabelle was on the phone with Tracy quite a bit during January. It seemed that Tracy had exciting news of her engagement to a "fabulous man".

"You're going to adore him," Tracy informed Isabelle. "We had a party during Christmas at Mommy and Daddy's, I'm so sorry you couldn't be there."

Isabelle accepted with pleasure the invitation to be in Tracy's wedding as her maid of honor. What she hadn't planned on was how much time that would involve. Tracy's mother wanted to do everything "properly." All kinds of parties were to be planned, with special invitations sent, reservations made, and detail after detail.

First there would be a bridal shower, which was "usually given by the maid of honor," Tracy explained one day by phone. "But since you don't live out there, Mrs. Howard is just dying to give it. I told her I didn't think you'd mind and thought for sure you'd help."

"Sounds great," Isabelle told her, not wanting to upset the apple cart in any way. "What do you want me to do?"

"I think the best thing is for you and Mrs. Howard to get together on the date and the guest list, stuff like that," Tracy said. "Mom is driving me nuts with the guest list for the wedding and it's four-and-a-half months away. She wants to know how many invitations we need to order, so I have to fly home this weekend and meet her at Copenhaver on Connecticut Ave. and go over things. Maybe I'll see you?"

Isabelle felt ambivalent about it. If she went out to the country she might run into Johnathan. After all, the families were so close. In the end she decided to risk seeing her friend, and was glad she had. They had a marvelous time and stayed up late one night talking and eating Fritos, just like they used to do in college.

Tracy finalized the fonts and ordered over two hundred invitations to mail. Her mother's blood pressure was already soaring at the thought of four hundred people showing up for the at-home wedding reception planned for mid-May.

Isabelle met with Mrs. Howard again. They got on "famously" as the grand dame said later. They planned a tea party in early May for about thirty. They'd serve tea sandwiches of cucumber and asparagus. And "Susie makes the best red onion sandwiches this side of the Bull Run Mountains," Mrs. Howard told her. Everything, would of course, be *so grand.*

Isabelle would be in charge of sending the invitations, but Mrs. Howard's home phone number at The Orchard would be on it "for the gals to respond." Isabelle would be responsible for the cake and cookies. But that wouldn't be too hard, because she would simply go to the appropriately named Upper Crust, a bakery in town with a devoted clientele.

In addition to the shower, there would be a dinner dance in honor of the couple, the rehearsal dinner given by the bridegroom's family, and a luncheon for the bride and her attendants the day of the wedding.

"Mom has made appointments for all of us to get our hair done that morning," Tracy informed Isabelle the night they stayed up talking.

"The girl, Margaret-Anne, is actually coming to our house. She'll do mom's hair first, because she'll be in a tizzy. Well...actually...she's just going to do a comb out, because she's going to town on the Friday before to have it done for the rehearsal dinner. Then she'll do the six of us girls."

"Six?" Isabelle asked, "I thought there were four bridesmaids, plus you," she pointed out, "that would be five."

"Well...yes. But don't forget the flower girl."

"Flower girl?"

"Sure," Tracy said, "how on earth could I leave out little Maude Dent? She's seven years old, she's perfect."

Johnathan's daughter would be in the wedding with Isabelle, walking down the same aisle. *Perfect*, thought Isabelle.

Just perfect.

For most of the winter of 1978, Isabelle and Johnathan spent their weekly, semi-weekly or bi-weekly meetings at her apartment. They had never discussed these new logistics, they just evolved.

Whenever they went out together, they always ended the evening at her place... in her bed. Once in a while they would sneak off to a hotel for a change of pace and scenery. But that was difficult in Washington, where Johnathan could very likely run into a colleague in the lobby of the Jefferson or Madison Hotels. She was more than happy to have him in her apartment. He was the only man in her life. She had him all to herself. Well...part-time at least. Occasionally she caught herself thinking about what it would be like to be Mrs. Johnathan Dent and spend a glorious life on a farm somewhere in Virginia. But she also knew that was out of the question for now, and she was content to be a small part of his life. Their time together was so full of love and happiness, she told herself she'd make it last all week, until the next time. After all, she was only going to be twenty-four this April. She had plenty of time.

Johnathan was the first and only man Isabelle knew who truly understood her innermost feelings. She was a sensitive girl. She wanted to savor certain moments, and he liked to do the same. She appreciated the small things in everyday life. Part of her perception came from loving art: colorful and beautiful things. Her apartment reflected these affectations. A sofa covered in a French yellow and white checked fabric faced a fireplace. A chair in the same fabric was angled to face one end of the sofa, and a deep club chair in a yellow and white stripe was on the other end. Next to the club chair was a Chinese wedding box that served as a side table, on top of it a cobalt blue bowl Isabelle always had filled with fresh flowers. An old pine table in front of the sofa was washed in a pale blue, which matched the color of the ceiling and a number of key accessories. The top of the table was covered with antique Shaker boxes and brass boxes of all sizes and a larger brass cachepot held a violet plant. The colors in the room sang out that it was a happy place the owner cherished.

A pair of Wedgewood blue candlesticks that once had belonged to her great aunt stood on the mantle alongside an old wire basket that was filled with ceramic lemons. A large gilt edged mirror hung above the fireplace. On the opposite wall was a grouping of English botanical prints and a narrow pine table, a basket beneath it contained old magazines. On the far end of the room there were bookshelves from floor to ceiling. The front end of the English basement apartment faced the street.

She obviously adored her job and loved to help her boss search for just the right accent piece or accessory for someone's new house, office, or den. She'd often go to flea markets and antique shows in her spare time. Once in a while she would go to the flea market in Georgetown on Sunday mornings, up Wisconsin Avenue across the street from the "Social Safeway." The flea market was run by Michael Sussman, who'd started it while he was going to law school and kept it going even as he worked as an attorney at the Treasury Department. Sussman always gathered an eclectic mix of dealers. One dealer had displayed a chair by Gustave Stickley and sold it for what he thought was a healthy price of $150 only to later learn the purchaser had sold it for ten times that amount. So it went at the open air extravaganza each week. And every week Isabelle also managed to uncover some new treasure that might be suitable for her place, or one of Michael Aldridge's clients. If she saw something she thought Mr. Aldridge might like, she'd go to a pay phone and call him at home.

"Michael (her boss recently told her to call him by his first name) there's an old chair here, small with hip rests, walnut I think. It needs to be recovered, but it could be something we might sell in the shop," she told him.

"How much?" That was always his first question.

"They're asking $50."

"Give him $35, cash, and take it to the shop. I'll pay you back tomorrow."

Then he'd recover the chair in a piece of $30-a-yard flowered chintz, put it on display in the shop, and sell it for $400. And each time, he would give Isabelle a small finder's fee.

Isabelle had a keen sense for what would sell. She was able to pick the jewels from the junk. She could hone in on the only quality item at a garage sale, like the six tiny toile-painted tin trays she once found for a dollar each. Michael Aldridge sold them for $30 apiece, or the whole set for $150.

When Johnathan came to her apartment, usually Wednesday night, she'd often tell him about her latest discovery. He also was fascinated, and slightly disgusted, by Michael's markups, wondering how much more his wife had paid for all the pieces in the home they shared.

He would sit back in the club chair and listen to her stories and watch as she cooked dinner in her kitchen that was no bigger than the walk-in closet in his bedroom at home.

He felt totally relaxed in her apartment. They had a routine. He'd come in, just as if it were his own living room, take off his jacket and tie, put it over a chair and kiss her. Then, he'd sip a drink of bourbon and water. He drank the local brand, Virginia Gentleman. He wasn't one of those people who changed drinks with the seasons. She usually drank a large glass of Chardonnay, in a tall and elegant glass. She'd sip,talk and cook. She felt so close to him, warmed by the knowledge that they were now part of one another.

Isabelle wasn't the greatest cook, but she had loved to help her mother when she was a little girl and she learned how to do just about anything from any cookbook. She wasn't nervous cooking for him, because she would not try a recipe on Johnathan unless she had tested it before. Now the entire cooking process had taken on a new challenge for her. She enjoyed pleasing him with a new dish, a special soup, or a daring dessert.

On Saturday mornings she would find something new in a cookbook. Something she thought he might like, something half-simple but elegant at the same time.

Something like Chicken a l'Orange with Mushrooms from *The New York Times Cookbook.* Then she'd pick a white wine to go with it, make a list, and go to the Georgetown Social Safeway on Sunday after the flea market, and buy all the ingredients. On Sunday evenings she would make the entire meal by herself, just to make sure she could prepare it properly for Johnathan again on Wednesday. Sometimes on the second preparation, she changed ingredients to improve it.

She never told Johnathan about her cooking experiments. And each time he came to dinner, after about three bites, he told her how wonderful it was.

"Great chicken," he would say, taking a sip of wine, that time a chardonnay from Piedmont Vineyards in Middleburg.

They usually ate dinner off their laps in her living room, because there was no formal dining area in the apartment. Often, he'd build a fire, sometimes they'd watch the news or just talk.

"I've got to go back down to Norfolk again," he told her one Wednesday. "We still have lots of details to work out on that real estate deal. My client is anxious to close."

Isabelle looked up from her plate of Beef Stroganoff. She was disappointed he was going to be away. *Too bad*, she thought.

"Do you think you could get off work for a few days?"

She was just taking a large sip of Merlot. His question caught her off guard and a touch of red wine spilled on her blouse. "Gee...I don't know," she said, putting the wine glass down and trying to mop up the stain on her shirt.

Isabelle was in heaven as she sat beside him on the Piedmont Airlines flight to Norfolk. She was in heaven when they went to dinner, and in heaven in bed with him that evening at the downtown Hyatt, not far from the harbor. They stayed for three days and two nights.

The days were somewhat boring for her, but she looked in the yellow pages for antique shops and went exploring around town.

"You know," he told her over drinks before dinner, "if this deal goes through—and there's no reason why it shouldn't—my client is going to build quite a retail complex down by the water, with all kinds of shops and restaurants. You'll love it when he finishes. It'll be like Harborplace or the South Street Seaport. They're going to call it Waterside."

They were joined that night at dinner by Jim Russell, the mayor of Norfolk. Johnathan needed to tie down a few last minute details on the deal.

"I'll just introduce you as my assistant," he had assured Isabelle. "Don't worry about a thing."

Isabelle listened while Johnathan explained that his client, Sam Blackwell, was still working on the deal, but he thought the contract would be completed a few days after they returned to Washington.

"The problem here is that the seller, which you know is actually a corporation, wants us to pay an extra $100,000 since this deal was drawn up last year," Johnathan told the mayor. "They bought it to sell and didn't expect to ever have to make more than one interest payment on it before selling it to us. Well, now they may have to and we're still negotiating. I just need some kind of assurance from you that we can get all the permits and everything we need at the next city council meeting. We can't afford to wait until the next meeting."

"That shouldn't be any problem. No problem at all," Jim Russell said during dessert. "I'm sure this will do nothing but good for this town. You know you have permission for the project. All you need now is the final construction permits and then once the individual spaces are rented, each tenant will need an occupancy permit. We'll take care of all the details."

"That's great. I don't have to tell you how appreciative we all are," Johnathan said. He made a mental note to send a lavish gift to the mayor's home address.

"Well, it's been interesting," the mayor said. "If I don't run for office next term I'm thinking of putting a group together myself and doing some kind of a retirement community down here. I think we could really use it. And watching you maneuver through this maze has been enlightening."

"Well, I wish you luck. For us the hard work is just beginning. We have to negotiate the final phase of the purchase contract. These sellers stand to make a large profit. I know they're flipping it quickly. In the end, I think everyone will be happy."

After dinner, Isabelle and Johnathan drove around the old part of Norfolk. He showed her some of the charming old homes and nicer neighborhoods. Then they drove down to the waterfront to look at the piece of property they were talking about.

They sat in the darkness of the car and he pointed out where the new buildings would be and told her how some of the warehouses would be renovated for the food halls and restaurants.

They drove back to the hotel in silence, with her head leaning on his shoulder. They didn't say much on the ride up the elevator to their room, then quickly took off their clothes and stayed up half the night making love. It was the first time since Isabelle met Johnathan that they made love more than once. On this night, at least, he was insatiable and she was more than happy to oblige. She would take him any time, any place, she thought when he rolled over to her for the third time shortly after five o'clock the next morning.

Oh, please dear god, she prayed...*don't ever take this wonderful man away.*

It was back to reality on Monday morning, but she was on time at work and ready to go. Michael was late, so she got a cup of coffee and sat down at her desk to sort the mail. The *Washington Post* was on her chair and she picked it up to move it.

Isabelle noticed a small headline on the bottom of the front page of the Style Section: "Mellon Donates Four Paintings to Benefit British Museum."

Naturally, any time she read something about the philanthropist Paul Mellon who lived in Upperville near Johnathan, her thoughts turned to him. Oh, how she ached for him. He was always on her mind.

Someone came in the front door of the shop and her daydream was interrupted. An older woman, who lived around the corner above the Francis Scott Key Bookstore, wanted to re-cover a chair in her bedroom and wondered if she might look at some fabric swatches.

"Sure," Isabelle said, directing her to the back of the shop. "I'll show you everything we have. What color did you have in mind?"

"Pink."

"Well...exactly what shade of pink?"

Isabelle spent the rest of the morning in a flurry of activity. Michael called and said he'd be in later. He had last minute things to do before leaving the next day for Los Angeles on a buying trip. Isabelle juggled the phone, the lady looking for the pink fabric, and about ten other things.

By the end of the day, she was ready to drop. She had a pounding headache and didn't have a crumb of food in her apartment. She was in no mood, but she would have to stop at the Safeway for something to eat alone in front of the TV. A frozen dinner, or maybe just some fruit and yogurt.

The phone was ringing as she opened her front door. Isabelle dropped the bag of groceries in the chair and grabbed it. It was Tracy.

"Tinker?" she said, calling her by the childhood nickname only a few of her friends still remembered. "Where've you been? I've been trying to get you for over an hour."

"Just working a little late," Isabelle answered as she took off her shoes and sat down on the loveseat. She cradled the phone on her shoulder and proceeded to go through the mail as Tracy spoke.

"Just checking to see if your bridesmaid dress arrived yet. I had it shipped overnight mail."

And just as Tracy was asking the questions, Isabelle came across a yellow slip, indicating that the mailman had attempted to deliver a package. "I see they tried to deliver it," she answered. "But if I'm not here they won't leave it. Too much chance of it walking off in Georgetown. I'll have to go up to the post office in the morning and pick it up."

"Great, I'm dying to know if it fits. If not, you can find someplace in Georgetown to alter it, maybe where you said you bought those suits?"

"Sure," she said, now only half-listening as she flipped through the rest of the mail. "I'll let you know," she continued, hoping to end the conversation and get to unloading the groceries. No such luck. Tracy wanted to talk.

"Brian and I went down to pick out the gifts for the wedding party today," she began, "You'll be so surprised, they're just perfect. And his is just so won-der-ful. He's buying my parents a sterling silver frame with the date engraved, so he has something to give them on our wedding day. Isn't that just sooooo thoughtful?" she asked in a way that would elicit nothing but a positive response. She rambled on and on about the wedding and about Brian and about how *won-der-ful* he was. And about how much her parents liked him and what a bright future he had on Wall Street.

"I'm truly envious," Isabelle continued, this time meaning every word of it. Oh how grand it would be to have the love of her life around all the time. But it was out of the question and Isabelle was content enough to savor the precious moments she did have with Johnathan. Maybe one day...

Spring arrived with an abundance of invitations, including one to her best friend's wedding.

But the biggest surprise was an ecru-colored formal invitation.

MR. AND MRS. JOHNATHAN DOUGLAS DENT
REQUEST THE PLEASURE OF YOUR COMPANY
AT A SMALL DANCE
IN HONOR OF
MISS TRACY CURTIS AND MR. BRIAN HALL
SATURDAY, MAY 17
8 P.M.
RIDGE VIEW
RSVP BLACK TIE

Isabelle's stomach sank. Why hadn't he told her this was going to happen? How could she go to his home and look at the paintings and see their bedroom and watch his wife play hostess? Her gut told her it would be dreadful. Still, she was curious.

Maybe they slept in twin beds.

The dinner dance at the Dent estate was the first party to kick off Tracy's wedding. Isabelle and Johnathan discussed the possible problems the situation presented, then decided it was foolish to worry about it. As long as they were discreet, nobody could possibly notice that they were more than just casual acquaintances.

"Who knows," he told her on one of their Wednesday nights over dinner, "I might whisk you off into the boxwood." Then he kissed her on the neck.

Isabelle was staying at Tracy's parents farm in Middleburg for the five remaining days before the wedding. The Dent's party was on Wednesday night, *their* Wednesday night. *Wouldn't you know it*, thought Isabelle. She also was sorry her parents weren't arriving until Friday afternoon. She so much wanted them to meet Johnathan, even if she couldn't tell them about their relationship. Anyway, they were staying just two nights and Mrs. Curtis arranged for them to be guests of some other friends up the road.

Isabelle drove out to Middleburg early Wednesday morning. She had seen Johnathan the night before.

"I want to be with you," he told her. "I want you in every conceivable way and I want you to remember it while I look across the room at you."

He was more than good to his word. He arrived early, and they were under the covers by eight o'clock. Once again, they made love three times that night and he didn't leave to drive home to Middleburg until close to midnight.

"I told Betty I had to work late to get everything done so that I could take off for the weekend," he told her.

Isabelle did wonder how on earth he arranged to stay with her so late. He normally left her apartment by eight, or no later than nine, so he'd be home by ten, an acceptable hour for working late. Any time after that would, in his words, "raise suspicions."

As Isabelle drove west on Route 50 toward Loudoun County, she turned on the car radio and let her mind wander. He was so good to her, constantly asking her if she needed anything or if she was too cold. Together in bed, they were both insatiable. He couldn't get enough of her and she wanted to do everything she could to please him.

It was just before lunchtime when she got to the Curtises' farm. The day seemed ideal. It was surprisingly cool, it could be brutally hot or unmercifully wet with rain this time of year. It looked as if Tracy might get lucky on one count: the weather. But Isabelle wasn't yet convinced that Brian was *won-der-ful.*

Isabelle so much wanted to share her secret life with Johnathan with her best friend, but the timing never seemed right. Tracy was wrapped up with wedding and honeymoon plans. Isabelle wondered how she'd react.

As they dressed for the dinner dance at the Dent's, Isabelle was so excited and wanted so badly to tell Tracy, but this clearly was the wrong time and *definitely* the wrong place for it.

Brian sent a dozen white roses to Tracy and the maid brought them upstairs. *Can't wait to dance the night away with you. Love, Brian*, read the card.

"Isn't that just won-der-ful," Tracy gushed.

Just won-der-ful.

Isabelle was wearing a pink floral dress made of organza. It came just to her ankle and the skirt was wide and flowing. The top of the dress was bare with the shoulders dropping off her arms. She planned to wear a pearl choker, held together with a new clasp she'd bought just for the occasion.

"I need help with the necklace, too," she told Tracy. "This clasp is tricky."

She wore a pink grosgrain ribbon in her hair with a bow tied on the top, which she pulled around her head to one side. Her hair was full and flowing and she had a new shade of lipstick—*Beautiful Pink*—that was just two shades darker than the lightest pink in her dress. Since it was a very special occasion, she even wore eye shadow and when she stepped back to look into the free-standing antique Regency mirror in the corner of the room, all of the pieces fit splendidly.

She looked striking and she knew it. *The bridesmaid was about to upstage the bride.*

She couldn't wait to walk into Johnathan Dent's house.

There was a single white bow and two white balloons tied around the farm sign at the entrance to Ridge View, the Dent's farm.

"It's just something that people do out here," Tracy explained as she, Brian, Isabelle, and her date for the evening approached the house.

One of the ushers had been called in as an escort for Isabelle and it was a complete surprise to her. He appeared to be friendly enough, and when he first saw her, his mouth seemed to drop ever so lightly as he admired his date for the evening. His name was Van something-or-other and he was "pleased to oblige."

"Nobody ever refers to the roads by their proper name or number," Tracy babbled on in the front seat. "All the roads out here have nicknames like Frogtown Road, Zulla Road, or the Catholic Church Road. But all people will tell you is *'just take the dirt road just past the third chicken coop.'* If you don't tie balloons out nobody would find the party. And besides people out here don't like to announce things very loudly. If you do, all kinds of riff-raff might show up at your party."

The driveway was unpaved, which Isabelle later learned was also considered de rigueur by hunt country standards. It was a mile long. The house was brick, built in the Georgian style, thought Isabelle, sizing up the architecture instantly: the strong symmetry, axial entrances, hipped roofs, and sash windows of the three story Palladian design. She put out her hand to her date as she stepped from the car. Every light in the house was on. The place glowed. An attendant took the car and they walked through the front door, which was already open.

A maid, dressed in black with a white apron, greeted the guests and asked if she could take any of the ladies wraps.

"I think I'll keep mine," Tracy said, her attention span already limited to ten seconds as she nervously glanced around the house, searching for Brian. "In case it gets chilly, how about you, Isabelle?" She didn't even notice that Isabelle was carrying nothing extra, except a tiny pink purse with a long string of a strap.

Mr. and Mrs. Dent were in the center entrance greeting guests as they arrived.

"Tracy!" Mrs. Dent exclaimed, "I'm so glad you're here. Everyone wants to see you. Maybe you and Brian will join us here in the receiving line? Oh, here's your friend," she said, gesturing to Isabelle. It was obvious, she *still* didn't remember her name.

Isabelle stood in the entrance. She was radiant. Johnathan had his back to her and was talking to another guest. The floor in the entrance was black and white marble and an immense crystal chandelier hung in the center of the room. The place was twinkling with candles and lights everywhere. She could hear the orchestra playing out in the back of the house.

She was watching him.

When Johnathan turned and saw her, he had a difficult time maintaining his composure. He'd never seen her look so alluring. He tried to look straight into her eyes and held his gaze upon her for what seemed to Isabelle like an eternity. She put her chin up a bit and returned his gaze, winking ever so slyly. Now, Isabelle also was trying to listen to the conversation. Betty Dent extended her hand and for a half-second, Isabelle was slow on the uptake.

Betty Dent could light up a room herself. As much as Isabelle hated to say it, she was terribly becoming. She also had blond hair, with a warm smile that seemed genuine and sincere, even if she still didn't remember Isabelle's name.

Betty Dent was wearing an elegant pale lemon yellow, lace-edged crepe de chine that Isabelle recognized as a designer dress by Geofrey Beene she'd seen in Town & Country magazine. She wore pearl clip earrings that must have been twenty millimeters surrounded by yellow diamonds and a matching ring on her right hand that Isabelle noticed immediately as they shook hands. Other than her wedding rings, the only other jewelry she wore was a bar pin of white diamonds with one centered yellow diamond, which Betty Dent had placed just above her right breast. It appeared to be a family piece, and had to be at least fifty years old.

Her lipstick and nail polish of pale apricot color matched exactly. Like Isabelle, she also had blue eyes, and wore blue eye shadow. Her short hair curled gracefully around her ears, highlighting the gorgeous earrings. She was busy looking back at Johnathan, and clearly relishing her role as hostess.

"Good to see you again, Mrs. Dent," Isabelle said, "it was so nice of you to have a party for Tracy and Brian. And I'd like you to meet my escort, Van..." *Ohmygod,* she thought, *I've forgotten his name. I'm going to make a fool of myself right now.*

"Van Wilson," he said, saving the moment and sensing Isabelle's momentary amnesia. "So nice to see you, Mrs. Dent."

It was going to be an evening full of *So nice to see you*s but Isabelle was relieved. *At least Van was a gentleman, and a rather good-looking one, at that.* At another time, in another place, she might have been interested. But not now, not here.

Just then Mrs. Dent turned to her husband to continue the introductions.

Isabelle was about to be introduced to her lover.

"John," Betty said. "This Is Tracy's friend, Isabelle and her date, Van Wilson."

"Good to see you," she said, focusing on his eyes. Isabelle was so busy looking at Johnathan that she hardly had time to look around the room. She wanted to get a better look at Betty, too. She wanted to size her up and study the competition. Unfortunately more people were arriving and Isabelle and Van had to keep moving along into the party.

"Nice to meet you," Van said, as they headed toward the back of the house. "Hope to see you later."

As Isabelle turned to walk outside, Johnathan watched her out of the corner of his eye. He noticed that the back of her dress came halfway down her exposed back—nothing distasteful, but low enough. Her blond hair fell on her shoulders and a pink bow matched the one in her hair, accenting the back of the dress. It was all he could do to keep from going after her, taking her in his arms, and smothering her with his love. But not now, not here.

The flagstone terrace on the back of Ridge View was so expansive that no tent was needed. A balustrade that probably had been added after the original house was built surrounded the promenade. Ordinarily at one of these country dinner dances, a vast white tent was erected. But the terrace of this house went from one end to the other and was at least forty feet wide. It was the best part of the house and in the daylight, you could see miles away to the Blue Ridge Mountains, hence the name, *Ridge View.*

It was an old house that had been thoroughly renovated. Isabelle sensed that a lot of work had recently been done, just for the occasion. The black paint on the shutters was shiny and fresh. Isabelle stood looking up at the second story, trying to figure out the location of their bedroom.

"What can I get you to drink?" Van inquired, half-startling her.

"Oh...uh..I guess I'll have a vodka and tonic," thinking how difficult it was going to be to make it through the night.

Tiny white Christmas lights were everywhere in the back of the house, strung in the boxwood bushes and in the trees and around the edge of the patio that led down to the formal gardens. There was no pool in sight, but Isabelle felt sure there had to be one with three children in the house.

The gardens also were lit. A few guests wandered down the wide steps into the gardens. Round tables were set up on one end of the terrace. A few ladies had already parked their purses and turned the white wooden folding chairs over, assuring a good seat. The latest socially ambitions couple, Randy and Jane Hammer, to invade the area from Napa, were searching for a place to sit. Everyone there knew they intended to build a vineyard in order to impress the locals with their California knowledge, which would never happen.

Van returned with her drink.

"Thank you so much."

"My pleasure. Isn't this a marvelous house?"

"It really is something, and the weather is perfect," she said, straining to be pleasant while sipping her drink.

A waiter approached with a silver tray of cheese puffs. They each took one and said "Thank you." They stood, silently eating.

"Tracy tells me you work in Georgetown?" he asked. "Sounds like a fun place to be."

"Well there certainly is a lot going on," she said, hoping that Tracy would be finished in the front room soon and join them. She was definitely ill at ease and really didn't know what to say to this man.

"I've been there about three years now. And I do love my job. What about you?" She figured if she could get him talking about himself it might make the time go by faster.

"Well...after college, I took a job on Wall Street. I just—"

"Isabelle!" a voice from behind called. "Darling, is that you?"

She turned and was pleasantly surprised to see Pauline Howard, the grand dame.

"Mrs. Howard, how are you?" She answered as she put her hand on Van's arm to introduce him. There was no way she was going to forget his name again.

"I want you to meet Van Wilson," she said, stepping back a half-step to allow them to shake hands. "This is Pauline Howard."

They exchanged pleasantries, commented on the weather and the party's beautiful setting. Isabelle recognized the veterinarian Alex Carroll and his wife Bunny. Pauline reintroduced Randal McGrane, the master of the hunt, who was attending this evening without his wife, Maddie.

They also met Charlotte and Andrew Barcroft, both lawyers in the tiny town, who maintained a virtual monopoly on clients they had inherited from his father, the first lawyer in Middleburg. "He was almost the first *and last* lawyer in the village," Pauline Howard told an enraptured Isabelle and Van, as she chronicled the history of just about every guest. "Old Mr. Barcroft met an untimely death when his wife caught him in bed with her best friend and shot him. Mrs. Barcroft was acquitted when her own son defended her successfully on the grounds that she was overcome by the heat of the moment. Some people still say she would have done twenty years if she had shot and killed a horse. But she was tried right here in this county and that was that. She went on and it was life as usual. In fact, the two women remained friends when they both discovered during the trial he was cheating with his secretary, too."

Finally Tracy and Brian had broken away from the receiving line. The band had taken a break and food was being served.

The dinner was a summer offering of asparagus with vinaigrette (fresh from the Ridge View garden), cold roast beef, cold sesame chicken, and of course, the main staple at all Middleburg parties...ham biscuits. There were sliced tomatoes, a carrot salad with some kind of a Tabasco dressing, and a salad of romaine lettuce, radicchio, and radishes—*"For color, I'm sure,"* whispered one woman. The wine with each course was a selection from nearby Piedmont Vineyards, except the Veuve Clicquot champagne (referred to in certain circles as "The Widow" in honor of the French founder).

Isabelle counted the tables. There were eleven, most with ten chairs, a few with twelve. The tablecloths, which fell all the way to the ground, were in a pale peach color and the centerpieces had peach gerbera daisies mixed with baby's breath. There were v,otive candles on each table.

Isabelle, Van, Tracy, and Brian sat at an empty table after they went through the buffet line. A waiter came and filled their glasses with champagne, Mumm's. Soon, several other guests joined them at the table. They introduced themselves: Ruth Wilcox, recently separated from her husband, Charlie the headmaster at the local private school. She had her arm in a sling.

"A riding accident?" someone inquired.

"No," she answered firmly, with no further explanation.

"She was afraid to leave him for years," Tracy told them later. "She finally raised the money by breeding their Welsh Corgi and selling the puppies for $450 each. She's living above the art gallery in town now, happy as all get-out."

Then there was Brooke Kincaid and Tyson Michaels, both horse trainers. And Wilbert Morgan, who said he "dabbled in real estate" and his date, a leggy blond named Melanie Keach, who Tracy later told Isabelle was notorious as the one who had "completely" taken Randal McGrane under the table during last year's hunt ball.

"Maybe Wilbert Morgan thought she could do something for him," Tracy said later, "because the word around town is that he hasn't been capable of *performing* since his third wife left him five years ago."

Just as several white-coated waiters began clearing the tables, a clinking of glasses could be heard on the other side of the terrace.

Johnathan stood up to make a toast.

Isabelle took a big sip of champagne and sat back to watch and listen. *God, he's wonderful*, she thought.

"I want to make a toast to the bride and bridegroom, may they have a long and happy life together," he said as he held his champagne flute high in the air.

"Here, here," everyone said, not quite in unison.

Thank god he didn't bring his wife into it. He could have easily added something into the toast like *"May they have as long and happy a life together as Betty and I have."*

But that was it. Straight, honest, and directly to the point. Isabelle would later learn that Johnathan had been rehearsed on the subject of the toast by his wife, who instructed him that it was just the proper thing to do.

Small individual fruit tarts and coffee were served for dessert and the band started up again. Brian took Tracy out for the first dance. They were playing "I Love Paris."It was most appropriate since the newlyweds were planning a honeymoon in Paris.

Tracy's parents joined them, followed by Johnathan and Betty. Soon everyone else gathered on the far end of the terrace, where a temporary dance floor had been installed.

Isabelle sipped her champagne. She declined coffee. And soon, her tongue loosened by the bubbly, she actually found herself in a long conversation with her date. He told her he had nine brothers and sisters, all with interesting careers, families, and stories.

But the entire time she sat talking with Van, she couldn't help but keep one eye on the dance floor or the back doors to the main house. *When was Johnathan going to come over and ask her to dance?*

At one point she saw him on the dance floor with his seven-year-old daughter. She was adorable, with a smocked dress in a tiny floral print with a big bow tied in the back. She had on white tights and white patent leather Mary Jane shoes. Isabelle could tell they were having fun and she remembered what it was like to dance with her own father at the big parties at the country club.

Eventually she got up and danced with Van. He wasn't very agile and she was hoping that Johnathan didn't see them on the dance floor together. They stayed for about three dances and thank goodness two were "fast" songs.

She drank another flute of "The Widow," met more people, and danced with Brian. And then it was time to go home.

She never did get to dance with Johnathan, nor could she find him without attracting too much attention to tell him good night, otherwise known as "making your manners" in this part of Virginia. When she left, she was feeling just a little bit more than tipsy.

She woke up at twenty minutes after nine the next morning. It was dark outside and raining. *Damn*, she thought. *Today is the day of my luncheon for Tracy. Why does it have to rain?*

Originally Isabelle and Pauline Howard planned to host a shower for Tracy. Isabelle felt obliged, as Tracy's best friend and maid of honor. Pauline Howard took the task on as a social obligation and what one does with pleasure as a "close friend of the family." They tried to coordinate the details and eventually came to the conclusion that it was going to be too difficult to get everyone together months before the wedding. They'd have to have it one month before the wedding. Tracy would have had to fly home for the weekend. Isabelle would be too busy at work, and everyone's schedule was overbooked, what with so many parties and the Upperville Horse Show scheduled.

So they "compromised" on a lady's luncheon the Thursday before the wedding. Isabelle really didn't have a whole lot of choice in the matter, she found herself deferring to Pauline Howard on just about every matter. The older woman's seniority and social standing was one matter, but her haughty airs were quite another matter. There were fifty women and it was more than Isabelle bargained for. She fully intended to pay for half of the expenses, since she was the co-hostess with Mrs. Howard. But the Grand Dame would hear of no such thing. She had also added more and more names to the guest list, so she felt obligated to be responsible for the extra cost.

"Darling," she had said, *"I wouldn't hear of such a thing as accepting your hard earned money for this luncheon."* She just couldn't help but remind Isabelle she was still a member of the working class. *"You just be in charge of addressing and mailing the invitations. And you can bring some nuts and maybe some colorful napkins or something like that. Don't you worry about the rest, dear, I'll take care of it. I've got Susie to help, too."* Isabelle almost felt like one of the hired hands.

As expected, the luncheon was ever so elegant, even if it was pouring rain and the ladies feet got wet as they stepped from their cars up the front steps.

Mrs. Howard served a chicken and rice casserole, warm bread, and salad—and *lots* of Little River White wine from Piedmont Vineyards. A few of the out of town guests brought small gifts for the bride, which she opened before dessert.

"Just a little something for your honeymoon," said one longtime friend of her mother's, who had traveled from Ohio for the wedding.

Tracy was genuinely pleased when she opened the box to find a long, sheer white robe. "I just love it," she said.

Pauline Howard served those wonderful homemade cookies. Homemade by Susie, that is. And more white wine for dessert.

Isabelle spent as much time as possible that afternoon studying Betty Dent. *What was she really like?* She noticed she constantly had a full glass of wine in front of her. But Isabelle concluded she was a striking woman and seemed pleasant enough. Even though Isabelle wanted every reason to despise her, she hadn't found one yet.

In fact, Isabelle almost liked her. She went out of her way over lunch to speak with Isabelle and ask her about work. On this day, she'd even remembered her name. She took her by the hand at one point and introduced her to her sister-in-law, Irene Dent.

"Irene and Bob live down in Richmond," she explained to Isabelle. "We never get to see enough of them."

It was obvious to Isabelle that Betty Dent was close to her sister-in-law. She could tell by the way she put her arm around her when she introduced her to Isabelle. *They could almost pass for sisters.*

When Betty put her arm around Irene, Isabelle's eyes fell upon her wedding ring. It was one of the biggest diamonds she'd ever seen: square cut with baguettes on each side. She tried to avert her eyes and not think about Johnathan and how he might still be in love with his wife.

"I understand you and Tracy have been friends for some time?" Irene Dent asked.

"Oh, yes.. well. We went to school together. We've had some great moments. I'm going to miss her," Isabelle said, just now coming to the realization she just might be losing her only close friend. She had to tell her now...soon...about the new direction her own life had taken since Johnathan...

"Oh, now you know that's not true," Betty Dent answered. "I've kept in touch with lots of school chums. Some of us try to meet in New York each year and go shopping or something. Your school friends are forever. Trust me."

Maybe, thought Isabelle.

Maybe.

It was past three when the luncheon broke up. It finally stopped raining, yet the sky was still and dark. The talk was of the weekend weather. All the guests tried to reassure Tracy as they departed.

"Don't worry, Tracy," said the veterinarian's wife, Bunny Carroll, as they stood at Pauline Howard's front door. "I heard Willard on the *Today Show* this morning, it's going to be a grand weekend." Willard, who lived in nearby Delaplane, had a stake in the forecast. He'd been invited to the wedding as a longtime friend of the Curtis family, a fellow gentleman farmer.

Isabelle was standing off to one side watching as everyone said good-bye to Tracy and Pauline.

How grand indeed, thought Isabelle.

Absolutely grand.

Her best friend's wedding.

Chapter 6

Sex Secrets Husbands Keep

It was a five o'clock wedding and the church was filled.

At precisely two minutes before five, a limousine delivered the bride and her father to the church. They drove right up to the door, passing though a small porte cochere in front of the old brick building.

The mother of the bride was seated in the first pew on the left. They timed everything down to the minute and Mrs. Curtis was insistent that the one thing that absolutely had to begin on time was a wedding.

Isabelle was standing right inside the portico when she saw the dark grey limousine approach with the bride and her father. The driver jumped out of the car and practically fell over himself as he went around to open the door and assist his passengers.

Inside the church, the organist was still playing background music, killing time until the big moment. The guests had not been waiting long enough for there any muffled coughs from the crowd, like what might happen when anticipation turned to boredom.

The weather had definitely improved from the previous day's rain. The sun came out and the moisture had burned off, though the humidity seemed to be rising by the minute. The afternoon sunlight filtered through the massive stained glass windows on the bride's side of the church. It was a glorious day for a wedding.

"Oh, Tracy...you look beautiful," Isabelle said as she got out of the car and walked about five steps to the entrance alcove. She handed her a large bouquet, made up entirely of white dendrobium pompadour orchids tied with a large soft white satin bow.

As maid of honor, Isabelle knew she was in charge of the timing. It was exactly five o'clock.

"Okay, this is it," she whispered. She leaned forward to Maude Dent. "When it's your turn, don't forget to go very slow."

The girls fussed with their hair and pulled at the waist of their peach colored bridesmaid dresses.

The guests rustled in the pews, shifting and occasionally whispering. From the front of the church, the organist stopped playing.

There were ten seconds of silence.

Someone coughed and tried to muffle it.

Then the three chords in G-major were struck, indicating the start of Anderson's wedding processional, played at nearly all Episcopal weddings.

Isabelle stood on her toes a bit to look over the others and watch as precious little Maude Dent began walking down the aisle and dropped flower petals in clumps as she beamed at the onlookers. She tottered a bit on each slow step.

Tracy linked her arm in her father's arm. She had tears in her eyes and started to laugh at the same time.

Ten days later, Isabelle received a postcard from Tracy, postmarked "Paris." It was a picture of a typical sidewalk café.

> *Tinker,*
> *We took a lovely walk in the Tullieres this morning. Went to the Louvre, the Jeu de Paume, did the Galleries Lafayette, and we're going to Hermes tomorrow. Brian has already promised to buy me a scarf.*
> *Love, Tracy.*

Two years and two months later, almost the same exact crowd gathered in the same Middleburg Church for the christening of Tracy and Brian's first son.

August 22, 1980.

"I want to see you the night before the christening, just like we did before Tracy's wedding," Isabelle told Johnathan. "I want to stand at the reception afterwards and look at you across the room and hold you."

In just two weeks time, it would be almost three years since Isabelle began her marvelous love affair with this handsome man.

They continued their quest to be intimately familiar with each other's minds and bodies—in equal parts, of course—and they continued to become intimately familiar with every piece of art in the National Gallery. With the opening of the new East Wing, they visited the Splendor of Dresden exhibition. And although Johnathan enjoyed it with Isabelle he failed to mention to her that he had seen it at the opening night reception he attended with his wife, Betty. Since her family had donated so many priceless pieces of folk art, they were among the elite to be invited to dine with J. Carter Brown, the head of the gallery, and a number of other dignitaries, including the German Ambassador Peter Hermann and philanthropist Paul Mellon.

Johnathan and Isabelle took yet another afternoon off to view an exhibit called *American Light: The Luminist Movement.* They were now thoroughly at ease with each other. Isabelle knew there would never be another man in her life like Johnathan. She felt so safe and secure in his presence. He never talked about his family and she never asked. Still, their time together was the highlight of her week, everything in her life revolved around their weekly liaisons.

Early in the summer, during the Wimbledon Tennis Championships, Johnathan arranged to come over to her apartment on Sunday morning—a very rare happening. They made mad passionate love, then sat up in bed snuggled naked, ate strawberries and watched Bjorn Borg win the title for the fifth time.

On the August evening before the christening, Isabelle sat up in bed on her left elbow and put her right arm across Johnathan's chest. He in turn gently put his arm around her. She looked down at him and wanted to tell him how very much she loved him, but instead, just kissed him.

"I have not one thing to make you for dinner," she told him. "I really wasn't expecting that you could get over here on a Saturday night. Should we go out for dinner? "

"What do you say we order some Chinese?" he asked. "I haven't got all night, but we can stay here and watch the news."

"Sounds okay to me."

So, Moo Shu Pork it was. She opened a bottle of white wine and they sat up in bed eating out of the cartons with chopsticks, *"Just like something out of a Woody Allen movie,"* she told him. The television news was dominated by word of the latest eruption of Mount St. Helens that night, and Isabelle could only laugh at the analogy she could make.

The next day at the brunch following the christening, the talk once again turned to Mount St. Helens. Isabelle was careful not to talk with Johnathan too much, but she gazed up across the expanse of the back lawn of the Curtis home, took a sip of her Chardonnay, and smiled with her eyes to her lover.

Tracy and Bruce and their new baby boy, Malcolm, were staying in Middleburg for a few extra days following the ceremony. Then Bruce was going back to work and Tracy and the baby were going to spend some time with her family.

"Mom said she would watch the baby while I come into Washington one day, so we can have lunch," she told Isabelle. "How about next Wednesday?"

"Wednesday? Uh...as far as I know that'll be okay. But...let me call you on Monday." She wanted to first check with Johnathan and then inspect the calendar at work. With Labor Day weekend approaching, she was sure it would work.

Johnathan and his family once again were taking their annual ten-day summer-fall vacation over that weekend. It was a family tradition and they went to a different place each year. Isabelle's heart sank when he told her he would be away that long. She couldn't stand the thought of him being with his wife all that time.

She called Tracy and set up a date for Wednesday. "We'll go to Martin's. How does that sound?"

"Great! See you then."

As soon as she'd said *"Martin's,"* Isabelle knew she'd regret her choice of restaurants, even if she thought for a fleeting moment it might cheer her up. Instead, it made her miss Johnathan even more, and Tracy definitely sensed something was troubling Isabelle. For a change, she was quiet and Isabelle did most of the talking. At first, she told Tracy she was involved with a married man, but by the time dessert arrived, she'd held nothing back.

"You know him, Tracy," Isabelle finally blurted out. "It's Johnathan Dent, and I love him."

"How could you keep this from me all this time?" was Tracy's initial response. "I can't believe it. But now that you tell me about it, I guess I knew there was somebody else in your life. You seem so damned content. And I sort of half-figured he was married, but...*Johnathan Dent*? Do you know what you're getting into?"

Tracy had always been the first to hand out unsolicited advice, but in this case, she seemed genuinely sympathetic. She also seemed somewhat ill at ease, and Isabelle sensed her friend wanted to tell her something, as well. *Could it be that all was not well with Tracy's marriage?* Call it ESP or whatever, but Isabelle's gut told her Tracy wasn't as happy as she should be, even with the birth of her first child.

"Listen, Tracy," she told her. "I want you to know that um...even though I don't know that much about babies, I'll come up and watch Malcolm any time you want." After all, Tracy had asked her to be his godmother, a role Isabelle took terribly seriously. "If you two want to go away, just let me know. In fact, that'll be my gift to you—free babysitting for the weekend of your choice. But you've got to give me plenty of warning!"

Tracy just sat there. Her eyes practically welled up with tears. "How won-der-ful, how did..."

"Not to worry, Tracy."

Three weeks later Tracy and Bruce took a long weekend at a country inn in New Hampshire, and Isabelle found herself baby sitting in New York.

"Now don't forget. He gets cereal at eight in the morning. *Exactly*, or he'll start fussing. He has lunch at twelve and a bath at one and takes a nap at two until about four. *No later*," she ordered. "The phone number for the doctor is in the kitchen. Our phone number in New Hampshire is there, and my mother's phone number. Even my mother-in-law's phone number is there, if you get desperate.

"And he likes to get on the floor in the bedroom and crawl around and play with all those animals. And watch what he puts in his mouth. *Everything* goes in his mouth.

"You won't forget, will you Isabelle?"

"Isabelle...?"

Isabelle was too busy holding the squirmy baby boy, a blonde bundle of energy with a smile that wouldn't stop. "Not to worry, Tracy. I can handle it. Go have a good time."

That weekend, Isabelle didn't have two minutes to think of anything else but Malcolm; every waking moment was taken up by the baby. Tracy called three or four times a day. She called to check in the morning.

"Did he eat his cereal?"

Then she'd call again in the afternoon.

"Did he take his nap?"

"Oh, he's being so good, Tracy. Don't worry," she assured her.

Isabelle took Malcolm out in the stroller on Saturday morning. They went to a nearby store and picked up a few things for the night. Mainly junk food for Isabelle: popcorn, Coke, chocolate Häagen Daz. And a few things for the baby: bananas and cereal, which was just about all he ate.

Tracy and Bruce came home six hours early on Sunday. Malcolm was napping and Isabelle was collapsed on the oversized chair in the living room. It was her first "rest" of the weekend. She heard a noise at the front door.

They tiptoed in.

"We couldn't stand it," Tracy said. "How is he?"

"Just fine, taking a nap. How was it?"

"Oh fine, we had a good time," Bruce said, somewhat half-heartedly. "It was sort of a long drive and we decided to beat the traffic back."

"Well, listen," Isabelle told Tracy, looking at the clock. "I'm going to go to the store to buy some ground beef and sauce and I'll make spaghetti and meatballs for all of us. I want you to have a little more vacation."

"Oh, you can't do that—" Tracy started to object.

"Oh, yes I can."

They had a nice dinner. Malcolm woke up and seemed happy to see his parents and the three of them ate spaghetti and salad at a small table in the cramped little kitchen. Isabelle washed the dishes, scooped up the baby, and put him down for the night. He was so precious, and as she laid him down in the crib on his tummy and rubbed his back, it brought tears to her eyes.

For the first time in three days, she thought about Johnathan and wondered what it would be like to have his baby one day, even though she knew it would never happen. She thought about all the great moments in the nursery he and Betty must have shared, and what a joyous occasion it must have been when their twin sons were born. Isabelle wanted to hold the baby again, but he was all snuggled in now. The room smelled pretty and sweet with all the baby lotions and powder. Malcolm had crept toward one end of the crib, so his head touched the bumper pads. She noticed he wouldn't go to sleep until he had arranged himself just so, in a specific position. His head had to be touching something.

She was happy for Tracy and Bruce and hoped somehow they had a few good moments on their first weekend away. Tomorrow was Monday and she had to get back to work. She would rise at dawn to get back to Washington. She had to decide whether to take the Eastern Airlines shuttle or the train. Either way, it took over three hours. You took a cab out to La Guardia, waited on the runway for all the other planes to take off, flew to Washington, waited for the bags and then got another taxi back to Georgetown. It took about as much time as taking the Amtrak Metroliner from Penn Station.

Tracy interrupted her thoughts as she entered the tiny room. A slice of light from the hallway appeared on the floor and Isabelle turned.

"I can't thank you enough, Isabelle, you're such a special friend." She leaned over to look at Malcolm and pulled a cotton thermal blanket over him. Feeling his mother's touch, he unconsciously wiggled his tiny bottom.

"You've done enough, now come on," Tracy said, shooing her friend out of the room.

Bruce went to bed early so Tracy and Isabelle made a cup of tea and sat in the kitchen for a while. Tracy didn't say too much, but in no uncertain terms let Isabelle know she was now home all the time with the baby and missed her job. She'd worked at one of the large hotels in the city and had been in charge of special events sales. She helped coordinate weddings, business meetings, and conventions. And even though she majored in home economics in college, she was good at sales.

"Somehow, I hope I can maybe go back full-time or do something. I'm not sure yet. In the back of my mind I keep thinking about something to do with food, maybe catering or cooking classes at the hotel. You know, a lot of hotels have one-day cooking schools, I just don't know." She was rambling now, thinking out loud.

"You know, we do have a lady who comes in all day three days a week, and maybe I could do something then. But the cooking schools usually want someone famous and I'm not famous. I need to think and read the paper and get some ideas. Maybe I'll just take a course or two at NYU and brush up on the pastry or something like that. The bottom line, you know," she said, looking square into Isabelle's eyes, "is that I have to have a life of my own."

"We all do," Isabelle said.

We all do.

Isabelle was so tired the next morning that she decided to play hooky from work. She'd overslept and it was almost eight when she rolled over on the fold-out couch in Tracy's living room.

"Ugh," was her only response when she looked at the clock. Normally she'd have jumped out of bed and started to rush, in a panic to get to the airport.

"What do you say I call in sick or something and we'll take a day off together?" she asked Tracy, who came into the room holding the baby.

"Perfect, I've got Mrs. Oliver coming and everything. We can go shopping and have lunch."

"Then I'll just take a late train back."

When Isabelle called the shop, before nine, Michael wasn't in yet. She was relieved she wouldn't have to talk to him, even though she'd never called in sick before.

"Just tell him I won't be in today," she told Ruth the bookkeeper. "I'm sorry, I just can't make it. I'll see you all tomorrow." She quickly hung up, but she definitely had no guilt. She worked long and hard for more than four years and never gotten a raise. She loved her job, but she also learned to become less obsessive about it. If Michael Aldridge could find a better assistant, let him try. Besides, she and Tracy were going to have a big day on the town.

"How about we go to Macy's and do the whole store—every floor—and we can have lunch in the basement at P. J. Clarke's?" Isabelle asked.

"Well, don't you want to go somewhere better?" Tracy asked. "What about Saks, or Bergdorf's or Bendel's?"

"Oh, you go there all the time, I bet."

"You're right," she said. Tracy jumped up, still holding the baby. "Well," she declared, "let's get going."

Isabelle took a shower when suddenly, she could think of nothing but Johnathan. She usually called him on Monday morning. She couldn't call him from Tracy's even though Tracy knew all about it now. She just didn't feel comfortable talking with him with the possibility of someone hearing their very private conversations. She would call him after lunch, from a phone booth at Macy's.

They took a cab down to 34th Street to Penn Station, where Isabelle checked her bag. She decided to take the train back to Washington later, since the station was practically right across the street from Macy's. It was one of her favorite things to do. She'd get a big corned beef sandwich from one of the delis along 7th Avenue and have them wrap it in foil. Then she'd go downstairs to the train station and buy a couple of good magazines—*Cosmopolitan* or *Town & Country*—a copy of the *New York Times* and some M&Ms. On the train, she'd buy a Coke and some chips and settle back to read and eat her New York deli corned beef sandwich.

They arrived at Macy's just after ten. As they entered through the revolving doors at the corner, they found themselves in the men's department.

"So what shall we do?" Isabelle asked, wanting Tracy to have as much fun as she planned to have. "Shall we start on this floor and work up, or start at the top and go down?"

"Doesn't matter to me," she replied.

They spent the entire day "doing" Macy's. The two old friends roamed around all nine floors in a store that covered one square city block. It was like a museum. There were clothes and more clothes and furniture. And on the fifth floor, where they spent the most time, children's clothes and the pet shop. They gushed over the puppies and Tracy bought Malcolm a little red raincoat.

Isabelle bought him a pair of tiny swim trunks. "For this summer, when you come to Virginia to visit."

They ate lunch as planned in The Cellar, where an abbreviated version of the well-known bar/restaurant P. J. Clarke's offered Béarnaise burgers served on an English muffin.

By a little after five o'clock, Isabelle was settled into her seat on the Metroliner with her corned beef sandwich on the tray table. She suddenly remembered that she hadn't spoken to Johnathan in more than ten days. She looked out the window as the train passed through the Meadowlands of New Jersey. It was late fall and almost dark but the sky had an orange hue to it. The clouds were dark, and silhouetted against the ominous sky.

The door at the back of the car opened, creating a sound when the vacuum was broken. The conductor entered and announced "Tickets please."

Isabelle turned to the vacant seat next to her to get her ticket from her purse. She glanced down at the *Cosmo* magazine, which had the list of articles on the cover urging young women to buy it.

"Sex Secrets Husbands Keep" was one of the headlines. She settled back to see what she could learn, and before long they were pulling into Washington's Union Station.

Two days later when Johnathan came for his weekly "dinner," their lovemaking was as spirited as ever. She started dinner as usual and was in the kitchen sipping her white wine, as she put the lid on a pot of brown rice. She turned to go and join him in the living room. He was thumbing through a magazine, and hadn't even turned on the television, as he usually did while she cooked. He grabbed her wrist as she walked past "his" chair (she never sat in it any more).

She looked straight at him, and never said a word.

He later claimed she had a familiar smirk on her face. She took a big sip of wine and they never made it to the bedroom. She left her clothes in a pile and kissed him on the mouth and made her way down his body as he stood completely naked in her living room. She put her arms around his waist and sat on the couch while he stood and she never stopped in her desire to give him absolute pleasure. He was the most astonishing man she had ever known. She stood up and kissed him gently on the cheek and finished making dinner wearing just a pale peach pullover tee shirt dress that came to above her knee.

She drank more wine and he complimented her on the dinner. Then he set his plate on the table and leaned over to kiss her. He pulled her back on the couch and eased up the cotton dress. He started at the top and kissed her everywhere. They made love and then rested on the couch entangled in each other's arms.

When he got up and dressed to leave, Isabelle went with him to the door. It was freezing outside, but she walked to the front steps that went up to the street level as he left. He didn't kiss her again. Maybe he was worried that someone might walk by on the cobblestone street and see him.

At the top of the step, he turned and said, "Do me a favor, don't go away that long again, will you?"

Yet another, somewhat pleasant Christmas came and went for Isabelle and her family in Raleigh. More roast beef, more doings at the Carolina Country Club and more black-eyed peas from Dips Country Kitchen in Chapel Hill.

It pained her to think of Johnathan snuggled up all warm and cozy in the country with family and friends. He seemed to get a bit weird this time of year. If Isabelle tried to be warm, he became almost distant, to say the least. This year she had bought him a funny tie, with Christmas holly on it. It had been enough time, she thought, that maybe they could exchange gifts of some kind. She knew he would have a hard time explaining where the tie had come from. But she also knew that he had explained away bigger things to his wife. Maybe someone at work saved him the tie. *So what?*

In the end, Isabelle never did receive a gift from Johnathan. She wondered about it, but didn't dwell on it, because she cared for him so much, she just took it in stride.

Two weeks after New Year's they were together again, practically like magnets. All of Isabelle's melancholy over the holidays had lifted. He made it more than obvious that he missed her.

They once again skipped dinner and started right in on their "dessert." His sexual appetite was voracious and Isabelle bet that he hadn't slept with his wife while she'd been home in Raleigh. *A woman knew these things*, she thought.

He kissed her over and over again and they made love twice that freezing night before he got up to drive back to the country. Isabelle dropped her flowered flannel nightgown over her head so she could walk with him to the door.

As they opened the front door to say good-bye, it was a surprise to both to see that it was snowing outside.

"Be careful," Isabelle pleaded as she lifted her head up to him to accept a quick kiss as she usually did when he left.

She closed the door gently and leaned back against it with a sigh...

She never saw or heard Johnathan slip on the slick, snow-covered, uneven brick sidewalk a few doors down.

CHAPTER 7

Eljo's, The White Spot & Cabell Hall

Betty Dent remembered looking at the digital clock when the telephone rang. It was one-fifty-eight in the morning. She wondered who would be calling at this hour. *Probably a wrong number.* She slid across the bed to John's side to pick up the receiver.

"Hello."

"Mrs. Dent?"

"Yes." Her heart was instantly pounding.

John.

He was staying in Georgetown that night. She remembered the snow. She knew something was wrong. *Oh please dear God,* she thought to herself.

The voice continued. "This is Mildred Feeney, I'm a nurse in the emergency room at George Washington Hospital..."

Betty Dent braced herself.

"Everything is going to be alright," she continued. She heard the fear in Betty Dent's voice, she had to make this kind of telephone call all the time.

"What is it?"

"Your husband had an accident. He slipped on the ice and has a broken shoulder. Dr. Martell has set it and he's resting comfortably."

"Can I speak with him?" She wanted to rush right down there, but knew that would be next to impossible. The eleven o'clock news had video of the downtown Washington area. Snow had been falling since the rush hour. Now, in the middle of the night, it was approaching blizzard conditions, with eight inches already on the ground.

"Well, he's a bit sedated, but doing fine. You can try calling tomorrow morning. He'll be in room 687."

"Thank you so very much for calling," she said and hung up.

Now she was wide awake and knew as soon as she hung up that she had twenty other questions for the doctor and the nurse.

First and foremost: *How on earth could this have happened?*

When John didn't come home that night, Betty didn't really think much of it. They had talked earlier in the day and he told her of the impending storm and that he would probably stay downtown.

This was not unusual. With such a long drive to and from the country, he often took a room at the Georgetown Inn when he had to work late or be up for an early morning meeting. After all these years, the front desk clerks and the bellmen at the Georgetown Inn knew him well and getting a room had never been a problem, even when he called at the last minute.

So when it snowed, it didn't strike her as odd when he called and said he'd decided to stay overnight. He had to be in town bright and early the next day. He even talked to the kids; they were up late that night watching a special show about the life of John Lennon, who had been shot and killed two days before.

After he hung up with the children and before Betty could say good night, she remembered that she wanted to remind John that they were to have dinner the next night at Pauline Howard's.

She was entertaining longtime friends from Greenwich on an overnight visit on their way down to Palm Beach, and Pauline wanted John to meet them. She thought John might be able to do some business with him and she took great pride in helping her friends. She was very supportive of Johnathan and always told Betty, "He has such a very bright future." Even though he did not represent her, she had introduced him to several important clients.

Anyway, Betty had forgotten to tell Johnathan. She knew he didn't have the proper clothes at his office. So she was going to tell him she would send the housekeeper in with another suit the next morning. That way, he could change and come straight to Pauline's from work.

As soon as she hung up the phone and realized what had happened, she dialed the Georgetown Inn. By now she knew the number by heart: (202)333-4900. She even knew some of the night clerks, though she didn't recognize the voice of the switchboard operator that night.

They usually said, *"Georgetown Inn, this is Gail (or whoever was on duty)."* Betty could not remember who answered the phone. She asked for Johnathan Dent's suite and the voice said *"One moment please"*. The phone in his room rang seventeen times. She counted...seventeen rings.

Her stomach began churning as the operator came back on the line.

"There must be some mistake, could you please check again?" The operator was polite and checked again and said she was *"terribly sorry, but there doesn't seem to be an answer in Mr. Dent's suite."* Betty Dent remembered that moment and she thought it would stick with her for the rest of her life. She sat on the edge of the bed, she heard the phone ringing over and over. *Seventeen times.*

There she was in her huge bedroom with her three gorgeous children glued to the television. It was just after eight o'clock. The fire was warm and crackling, and she sat on the bed looking down at their heads and her eyes were filled with tears. Her mind was racing. The first thing she thought about was that she didn't want her children to know she was upset. She blinked her eyes and quickly wiped away any trace of tears. She remembered in a flash thinking, *Well if they see me crying I'll tell them how much I thought of John Lennon and that it was so sad he had been killed.*

She didn't really want to tell them that she was actually ready to kill their father. A woman's initial instincts were usually right. And Betty Dent knew something was terribly wrong.

She sat on the bed, took a deep breath and a sip of water, which she always kept on the bedside table.

She began to think about her next move.

She could wait until the children went to bed and in a couple of hours she would call back and check again. Maybe he hadn't come in yet, maybe he had called from work. She quickly dialed his private line and, of course, there was no answer. That tied her stomach in bigger knots, but she had to keep her cool.

"So what do you kids think about having some ice cream?" she asked, trying to stay calm.

"All right," Mac said, "let's go." He was always the more enthusiastic of the twins. She didn't know if it had anything to do with the fact that he was the first-born.

When they were younger she thought it was her imagination that Mac was just a tad livelier, but she was convinced now that it was true.

"Come on Doug, let's go," he said, pulling his brother away from the TV set.

They all went downstairs and ate ice cream. She knew it was the only thing that could possibly pull them away from that lousy television show. She never really thought much of the Beatles' music or understood all the fuss over these scruffy musicians from Liverpool. She guessed she was just a half-generation too early. Or maybe she was just a half-generation too late.

It was colder downstairs in the kitchen. So the four of them, bundled in bathrobes and slippers, sat in the bay window eating pecan ice cream and hot fudge. Betty sipped tea, made polite conversation, and tried to sort out her thoughts.

It wasn't easy. She wondered where on earth Johnathan could be?

"Mommy, do you think we'll have to go to school tomorrow?" Mac asked, peering out at the blowing snow.

"Oh boy, I hope not," Douglas answered.

Maude never looked up from her ice cream. At age ten, food was more important to her than whether or not she would go to school. Actually, she was a good student, usually got all As. But right now she was at that rather awkward age. She was not a little girl and not quite a teenager. She spent a lot of time reading, which pleased Betty, but not enough time playing with friends or riding the pony they bought her three years ago.

Once in a while she walked down to the barn after school. She took the pony out of his stall, brushed, kissed, talked, fed him carrots and sugar and put him back in the barn. Betty couldn't push too much, because with daughters of any age past six (maybe even five or four, if she were to think about it), any suggestion that mom made was a kiss-of-death *NO!* So, when Maude came back to the house or sometimes later after dinner, Betty would ask. *"How's the pony doing? Did you ride him today?"*

"Oh, he's fine," was the only answer she got. Maude never bothered to answer the questions completely.

But Betty always found out from Don, the man who worked in the stables, because he stayed down at the barn until after five each day. Part of his job was to clean the stalls and look after the horses and pony. They were only allowed to ride in the field behind the barn. That way Don could keep an eye on them but didn't have to hover. All of the children were proficient enough equestrians that they could ride without someone being right there. They'd had years of Pony Club and hours of lessons. Of course, Betty never permited them to ride without a hard hat and proper boots. And they could never go off in the woods or on a trail without Don.

Betty wanted to find a dance school for Maude. She felt if she could get some exercise after school she'd feel better about herself, instead of moping around every day. It was just something every little girl should do. Betty had been enrolled in dance class from the age of seven. She made a mental note to call Mrs. Hill, the secretary at school and ask her if she knew of a dance academy nearby in Manassas or Winchester. Maybe some other little girls were going and she could arrange a carpool.

Carpool, now that was the story of Betty Dent's life.

It was her only objection to living in the country. No, she took that back, it was not the only objection, but it ranked right up there in the top five.

There were no school busses to and from Country Day, the only private school for K-8 in Middleburg. So, unless you shared the driving duties or had help at home, you spent your life driving up and down the country roads. And, around Middleburg, the people drove like demons. She never forgot the story of the lovely teenage niece of a friend-of-a-friend. The girl was driving to meet her fiancé, hit a bad bump, flipped over and was in a wheelchair for the rest of her life.

But... that brought her back to the situation at hand. *Dear John.* After she finally got everyone tucked in, she went back downstairs to make another small pot of tea.

In the winter, it was one of her favorite things to do. She had an adorable tea cozy she bought at Fortnum & Mason a few years ago when she and John were in London. She poured the hot water and sat back down to get her wits about her. The solitude was sheer bliss. With three children and this big house and a farm to run, she rarely had time to herself. Just sitting down and reading the newspaper was a luxury.

John and Betty had met in the fall of 1959. He was in his first year of law school at the University of Virginia. She had finished two years at Marymount College just outside of Washington and had earned an Associate of Arts degree, studying fashion and merchandising. This included a two-month study program in Paris during her second year. It was a year she never forgot, for while she was abroad, her dear sweet father had died suddenly from a heart attack. The telephone call came in the middle of the night. Once the initial shock wore off, she immediately arranged a trip back home. She stayed for five days and returned to Paris to finish her studies. Looking back, it was all a blur. But in a way, Betty was fortunate.

Her father, a genius at investing in real estate, had planned for her future financial well-being with great foresight. A trust was established for her to be managed by his attorney in Washington. In addition to a large sum of cash there were numerous stocks and municipal bonds. Her father also collected a great deal of priceless folk art. It was his one passion in life and he had traveled all over the United States building a collection that was among the finest in the country. Betty always assumed that it would be left to her mother, so it was a surprise during the reading of the will that he left the entire collection to the National Gallery.

"Your father had a very agreeable arrangement with the gallery," the attorney told Betty. *"He had already pledged ten percent of the art and signed a deed that promised the rest to the museum upon his death. This saved you a significant savings on your taxes. And besides, it's such a nice way to share it with everyone."*

When she returned from her studies in Europe, Betty took a job at Lord & Taylor in the advertising department of their Seven Corners store in suburban Virginia. The suburbs around Washington, D.C., were booming. The land, once predominantly used for farming and raising horses, was being leveled by bulldozers into a sprawl of houses and strip malls. This included what was known as Seven Corners and it made Fairfax County one of the richest and most highly developed areas in the country.

Seven Corners had always been a favorite playground for Betty while she attended Marymount. It was close to the college and she and her friends often went down during the week or sometimes on a Saturday for lunch at the Birdcage restaurant on the third floor at Lord & Taylor. They roamed the store and usually traipsed home with bags filled with fancy underwear and stationary. Betty loved to order monogrammed postcards and informal notes.

She remembered the pink note cards with her initials in Kelly green, another set of powder blue with navy blue initials. All of it was engraved of course, for nothing else would do. Every piece of paper had "Elizabeth Laura Crane" across the top.

During the fall of 1959 one of Betty's college friends, Blythe Harper, invited her down to Charlottesville for a weekend. It was less than two hours from Washington, and Marymount girls were always driving down Route 29 for some occasion or another. This time it was a party at the Farmington Hunt Club and they were all invited.

That's when she met Johnathan.

She had been there for several hours when Johnathan and two of his friends arrived at the party. She was sitting with her back to the band—The Backstabbers, four local black musicians who were experimenting with a new type of sound that combined rock and roll with jazz. She was waiting for The Hot Nuts to come on stage next and was facing the front door when Johnathan and his pals arrived. She thought to herself that their late appearance was terribly rude.

She was about to lean over the table and ask someone who they were when John approached, greeted everyone else, then smiling down at her, stared into her eyes and said "We haven't met. I'm Johnathan Dent and this is Ray Curtis and Richard O'Brien."

She didn't extend her hand, but she was quite taken. His cheekbones were so wide and his eyes, oh...ok…she was immediately smitten. She always believed in love at first sight. And Johnathan Douglas Dent appeared in her life at precisely the right moment. Later that weekend she told her girlfriend she knew she was going to marry him.

Since it was late, they only danced a couple of times. He asked for her phone number and told her he hoped to see her again. He and his friends were off; the dance was just one of many stops that night.

It was eight days before he called. The longest eight days. She didn't go out one night after the weekend, just hoping that the phone in the townhouse she shared with two other girls would ring. Every time one of them got on the line to make a call she would jump up and ask "How long are you going to be?"

"Why?" they asked back, "Are you expecting a call?"

"Not really," she answered, lying through her teeth.

He finally called at almost ten o'clock one night. Betty answered the phone.

"Is Elizabeth Crane there please?" he asked.

"Betty," she answered.

"Betty?" he asked.

Oh, she felt like a fool. "No, this is Elizabeth Crane, please call me Betty."

"Betty, oh, I see, Betty," he said now, almost as confused as she was. "Oh, Betty, this is Johnathan Dent, we met in Charlottesville. I might be coming up to Washington next weekend with some friends and I was wondering if you were busy?"

And that was it.

He and Ray came to Washington. Betty set his friend up with one of her roommates and they had a fabulous time. They went to Georgetown for dinner, stopped at Blues Alley for a drink and some jazz, and they all went shopping on Saturday. Johnathan and Ray were on the polo team at school, though he wasn't playing that weekend. So they all went into W.H. Stombock & Son Saddlery on M Street and bought new riding breeches and other horse paraphernalia.

Sunday they went to brunch at the Georgetown Inn and every weekend after that Betty saw John. Either he came to Washington or she went to Charlottesville.

On February 14, 1960—Valentine's Day, of course—he proposed and on June 15, 1960, they were married.

Throughout the romance she kept one important secret, something her roommates didn't even know. She had inherited an enormous fortune. Upon her father's death, Betty inherited money that had been left to him by her grandmother, who died when she was fifteen.

When her father died, there were strict instructions that his only daughter, Betty, would receive seven million dollars, four in cash, the rest in art, stocks, bonds, and real estate. Her mother was left the house in New York and more than enough to live on forever. This did not even come close to Betty's share. She was definitely the favorite of a doting father, and never was that more obvious than on the day his final will and testament was read.

As she reflected on it now, she really didn't appreciate it at the time. Oh, she met with the lawyers and the bankers and they took her to lunch and gave her packets of notes and every month she received a thick envelope with updates. She instructed them to sell all the remaining real estate, which included her parent's winter home in Ft. Lauderdale, and a smaller place in Aiken, South Carolina.

The thought of dealing with all that money scared her. Betty didn't tell

John. She was afraid he wouldn't like her. Or maybe she was afraid that he would like her only for her money. Anyway, she had been told that it was vulgar to talk about money. For the first year-and-a-half of their marriage, she never mentioned it.

They lived a modest lifestyle in Charlottesville while he finished law school. They had a cozy one-bedroom apartment at the University Garden Apartments in a nondescript three-story brick building on Ivy Road. The rent was $185 a month. She took a job at Eljo's, a clothing store downtown. She was happy to get it because with so many students, there wasn't much work available. But the manager of the store liked Betty. He later told her he loved the skirt she had on that day, a Vested Gentress that was yellow with green silk-screened horses on it. The front of the skirt had the horses heads looking out of the stalls and the back of the skirt had the back side of the horses. It was one of her favorites and she had matching flat Pappagallo shoes on. Everyone in Charlottesville dressed in bright colors.

Her job at Eljo's was to assist in designing ads for the local paper, the *Daily Progress* and any other publications...*Keswick Life* and *The Piedmont Virginian.* Of course, since it was such a small shop, she had other duties. One of her favorite tasks was changing the window displays every ten days.

She occasionally pitched in and helped with the selling, too. It was exciting because it was the busiest shop in town. She was even asked to help design ties and scarves in the classic university colors of navy blue and orange.

As Betty looked back on this part of their lives together she had mixed emotions. Everything was new and exciting and she loved their evenings. Johnathan spent the day in class or at the law library, and was exhausted when he got home at seven-thirty. Betty cooked dinner and timed it for when he walked through the door—even then Johnathan was on a fairly rigid timetable. He'd study for a few more hours, and then they'd try to take a long walk before returning to their tiny bedroom to make sweet love.

Johnathan was considerate and tender. She responded as warmly as she knew how. Occasionally he became a bit more animated and Betty did her best to respond. She often felt self-conscious. She knew there was another side to Johnathan, the tattoo on his backside—"UVA" with a little Cavalier, the school mascot, just above it—told her that. It was the one thing about him that really bothered her, it was...*vulgar* and out of character. Yet, those thoughts passed quickly, especially when she considered how happy she was being married and in love. She devoted her life to John.

Betty had never faced running a house or planning menus. So she was perpetually reading cookbooks or food columns in the magazines. After work she walked up to "The Corner," to Mincer's Pipe Shop, for a pack of Marlboros and a newspaper. Then she headed to the grocery store before going home to make dinner.

Sometimes they went out. Johnathan would call her at work and tell her he was going to be late. He spent his life in the library or at St. Elmo's Hall, studying with other law students.

"I'll meet you later and we'll go to dinner." he would say. It was his way of making up for the fact that he wouldn't be home. A small form of bribery, but she was delighted to accept.

"What time," she would ask, knowing it would be late.

"Ninish."

"See you then," she said as he hung up.

Her boss at work, Al, didn't mind personal phone calls, but she couldn't press her luck. She had to get back to business.

It was understood that they would meet at the statue of Homer on the lawn near the Rotunda. Then they would decide where to go. Sometimes they went to Poe's Bar or the Virginia Café or the University Cafeteria, but that usually closed early.

Most of the time they went to The White Spot. This was a small greasy spoon: ten stools and a smart-ass, gum-chewing waitress with a beehive hairdo behind the counter. Their favorite waiter, Henry, knew them well and knew they would order two Gusburgers and two large Cokes. The Gusburgers were famous in Charlottesville: a hamburger with cheese and a fried egg. The White Spot also specialized in Pinto Bean Soup, which Johnathan occasionally ordered in the winter in addition to the Gusburger. The thought of pinto beans didn't do much for Betty.

Sometimes they dined at the ever-so-chic University Diner. They went there when it was going to be an especially late evening. The place was open twenty-four hours. Here she would splurge on dessert, which Ethel, their favorite waitress, knew she loved. A grilled donut with vanilla ice cream.

"Now are you ready for that dessert, Miss Betty?" Ethel asked as she cleared away the green plastic plates.

"You bet," she said.

Ethel was so skinny she looked anorexic but no one ever gave her a hard time. She worked the late shift, and was often confronted with football players and fraternity boys who had ingested far too much grain alcohol.

She could handle it.

"Those boys should know better than to come in here in that condition," she said one night as she placed the grilled donut in front of Betty. "I told them they couldn't leave here until they had three cups of coffee and a substantial amount of food. They need to sober up."

After dinner they strolled home, it was often past midnight. Betty knew she wouldn't get that much sleep. Johnathan was relaxed as they slipped into bed and snuggled up and one thing usually would lead to another... She got up before him each morning and washed her hair. She was eager to look nice at work.

When those glorious days in Charlottesville came to an end, Betty stood on the steps of Cabell Hall overlooking the lawn and the Rotunda during graduation ceremonies.

She looked over at the statue of Homer as an idyllic phase of their life concluded.

When John received his law degree in the summer of 1961 it was time to face the future. Some of his friends received immediate job offers. His best buddy, Ray Curtis went back to Washington to work for his father's law firm. The Curtis family was kind to Betty and Johnathan and made faint sounds about inviting John for an interview.

For the summer, Betty continued at Eljo's. John took a part-time job at a local law firm, doing title searches for real estate deals. That was to be three days a week, Monday, Tuesday, and Wednesday and frequently ran over into Thursday and Friday. In between he sent his résumé to every law firm between Charlottesville and Baltimore. Ever optimistic, he went on three interviews with the same firm in Richmond. They were excited, but in the end, they hired someone else. It wasn't that Johnathan wasn't bright, but the other candidate "knew someone" in the office and that was the clincher. As Johnathan later said, it was a competitive world.

So when Ray Curtis called one morning in mid-August and invited John and Betty up to Middleburg for Labor Day weekend, she accepted his invitation without first consulting John.

"We'd be delighted," she told him, then half-confiding, "I think it would be good for John."

"How's the job hunt going?" he asked her.

"Well he has a couple of good leads and just needs to get some time to pursue them," she half-lied.

Johnathan was delighted when she told him about the invitation. Betty was relieved, because they always promised each other they would not accept any invitation without first discussing it. She was concerned he might not want to see his good friend before he had settled into a job. But Johnathan was eager and they looked forward to the weekend.

They packed up Betty's little green Volvo (it had been a high school graduation gift from her father and was four years old at the time) and headed up the road. She packed some apples and a couple of beers.

They arrived in Middleburg at ten-thirty Friday morning.

Betty was immediately smitten with the tiny hamlet. The countryside around the town was a luminous green. The lawns (well you couldn't really call them lawns, because the farms and estates went on for miles) and the fields were mowed in immaculate geometric patterns.

Then, there were the fences. Betty adored them. Some were interrupted by an occasional "chicken coop" jumped by mounted foxhunters. Most fences were what the locals called "dry stone walls," dating back to the Civil War—which the locals referred to as the War Between the States. Tales of the "unpleasantness" were constantly told from the Southern point of view.

The stone fences were put together from old stones piled one on top of the other, lined up and strategically staggered. What she learned since living there was that there were only about three men—all of them old and black—

who could still do it properly. You had to wait for months before you could get your falling stone walls repaired or restored, at $100 per foot.

For the miles and miles of fences in this part of the country that were not stone, four-board wood fence was used, often for properties with horses. The fence was usually painted black with creosote, a tar based covering.

It always reminded her of the line from that Robert Frost poem, "Good fences make good neighbors." Some of the fences were split rail or snake, the type most people associated with the War Between the States. In the summer, along the back roads, day lilies bloomed in front of them; in the winter when it rained or got cold and snowed, the fences glistened with frost.

Betty loved to drive down the side roads during early summer, looking out over the fields beyond the black fences at the young horses sleeping in the sun or rubbing up against their mothers.

"It's only ten thirty Johnathan, we can't arrive this early," Betty pointed out. "I think it would be just a bit rude to get there before lunch. After all, it is a long weekend."

"What do you mean rude?" he asked, getting a bit defensive. Her compulsion for doing things precisely the right and proper way already was beginning to manifest itself.

"It's four days, Johnathan."

"They invited us for the weekend, didn't they?"

By now they were practically at the Curtises' driveway. Betty was mortified, worried their hosts would still be in their bathrobes sipping coffee on the veranda or whatever people in the country did on a sparkling summer morning.

"Why don't we drive into town?" she suggested.

Even though they hadn't been married that long, Betty quickly learned it was always better to make a suggestion, never a demand. She usually got her way by simply saying *"John, do you think we need to turn the mattress over and air it out?"* or *"John, does the car need some water in the radiator?"*

So, of course, he shrugged his shoulders, turned the car around and headed for the village. It was an appealing little town, a blinking light at the main intersection, bricked sidewalks and darling shops and boutiques.

"One of my dearest friends has a shop here," she told John. "Why don't we see if she's there?" It was somewhat of a surprise to him because she had never mentioned it before.

The gift shop on the main corner of the town was called Morgan's. They specialized in colorful dishes in white ceramic with painted pink and green flowers. Frogs also were in abundance—ceramic frogs, brass frogs, potholders shaped like frogs. Maybe Betty wasn't the only woman in the world who had a thing for frogs. She collected them and had them on shelves or tables all around the apartment in Charlottesville. When Johnathan brushed his teeth in the morning, he took his toothbrush from a frog mug. He put his razor in a frog dish. Even the spare roll of toilet paper was under a frog cover-up. The only advantage for Betty's frog fetish was that Johnathan never had to use much imagination on buying gifts. Anything "froggy" would do.

Morgan's also sold needlepoint canvases. Some were painted with flowers, some with horses, and others had a cute cliche. Betty bought one that said, "Lawyers Never Grow Old. They Just Lose Their Appeal."

The shop also displayed at least two dozen sets of ice buckets with matching glasses; and dozens and dozens of paper cocktail napkins with even cuter sayings. She bought some that said "Who invited all these tacky people?" and had them wrapped in tissue paper as a hostess gift to Mrs. Curtis.

"We simply must have some kind of a gift in our hand when we arrive," she explained to Johnathan.

She told the lady working in the shop to tell her friend, Franny the owner, that Elizabeth Crane had stopped by. Johnathan observed that girls like Betty who attended certain girls' boarding schools, always referred to themselves by their maiden names.

When they arrived at the weekend "vacation" it was two-thirty. They were so wrapped up driving the back roads they actually lost track of time. They ate the two apples and some cheese and never touched the beer.

"But my dears, you must be starving," Mrs. Curtis exclaimed, leading them through the front entrance hall, back into the kitchen via the dining room. "We just finished lunch, it's no bother."

The Curtis home was filled with relics.

The main house was white and made of wood. "It's fascinating because it has porches everywhere," explained Johnathan, a frequent guest during his college days. Up the front steps there was a wide deep front porch that ran the entire width of the house. There was also an upstairs porch right over the top of the downstairs porch. And Betty was later to discover that everything was exactly the same in the back of the twenty-room house. For reasons she could never explain, the porches on the back were referred to as *verandas*.

Every inch of wall space inside was covered with artwork or framed photos. There were all kinds of pictures of various members of the Curtis family out riding horses, including one of the entire family, with Ray's little sister in a basket saddle on a white pony and all the other family members mounted on bay horses. Mrs. Curtis was pleasant enough, but a bit intimidating. It was the first time in her life Betty actually felt as if someone were speaking down to her.

The first evening on the farm they had dinner at home. Ray, Sr., as he was referred to, cooked a pork roast on the grill. They sat outside after dinner on the porch talking until midnight. The Curtises seemed to enjoy one another's company, and everyone was curious to hear Ray, Jr. talk about some of the cases he was working on for his father in Washington.

"We're having a few friends out tomorrow night for drinks and then we're going to take everyone to the club for dinner," Mrs. Curtis announced as the maid brought out a tray for dessert.

"We have some lawyer friends we think you should meet, Johnathan," she said, serving fresh fruit from an oversized glass bowl as she spoke.

"Oooh, that sounds interesting," Betty said for Johnathan, who looked a bit surprised.

"Just a few friends, my dears, not to worry," she said, as she settled into the wrought iron cushion-filled chair.

The "few friends" turned out to be eleven guests, to fill out a dinner party of sixteen. Ray Jr.'s new girlfriend, Smith Howard, arrived at six, just before the others.

John and Betty were freshly showered and dressed ahead of schedule. They had taken a long walk on the farm that afternoon, then gone for a short swim. She wore a Lilly Pulitzer dress silk screened hot pink and Kelly green, with a coordinating pink cable-knit cardigan sweater—the kind with little round knots for buttons—and a new pair of pink heels. Johnathan wore his only navy blazer and khaki pants and the orange and blue UVA tie from Eljo's. He looked dashing; Betty was proud of him. They were chatting with Smith Howard, a recent graduate of Mt. Vernon College, a posh girls' school on Foxhall Road at the edge of Georgetown. She studied art, not to mention the art of attracting dashing young suitors, like Ray Jr. She recently took a job at the National Gallery giving tours and doing some work in the public relations office.

Betty Crane's heart nearly jumped out of her chest when she saw one of the other guests arrive. Among those entering the room was Arthur Morris, the lawyer who handled her father's estate and the man who sent her the updated accounting of her holdings each month. They were currently being mailed to her at work, because she still hadn't told Johnathan about her inheritance. How was she going to explain to Johnathan how she knew this man? And better yet, why hadn't she come clean by now? Still, she tried to remain calm. After all, her husband seemed to be in line for a position at the law firm of Duke, Graves, and Coggin. It would be just perfect for Johnathan.

Just perfect.

With the introduction and an almost embarrassing recommendation from Mr. Curtis, secretly seconded by Betty (who just so happened to be one of the firm's most valued clients), Johnathan was asked to start work at Duke, Graves, and Coggin on November 1, 1961.

That gave them just two months to find a place to live and pack up their things in Charlottesville. Betty was going to miss that town. Their lives had been so simple and uncomplicated, and somehow she knew that things would never be the same for either one of them.

Johnathan reacted rather calmly to the news of Betty's "hidden assets" when she eventually told him a few weeks after he'd been offered his new job. As Betty reflected, he didn't even seem surprised. Her fears were totally unwarranted, but clearly their marriage had gone from the honeymoon stage to real life. They became grownups overnight. They made a decision to buy a house in Middleburg.

"After all," Johnathan reasoned, "why not? We can afford it and you love Middleburg so much."

How could she deny such logic?

Arthur Morris called her just after Johnathan left his office for the big interview. Her father's lawyer was about to become her husband's boss.

`"Elizabeth, I want you to know that we're pleased that we're going to be hiring such an intelligent young man."

"Oh, Mr. Morris, that makes me so happy," she said as she blinked back tears and looked out the kitchen window of their Charlottesville apartment.

"I trust you're happy too?" he asked cautiously.

She was delirious and could hardly contain herself. Years later, she often wondered how long it would have taken him to find a job on his own, but that was not an issue in 1961. Friends helped friends, that's the way the world operated. In her heart, she knew Johnathan had a brilliant future as an attorney. He had the good sense to marry her, and her money had not been a factor. Or so she thought.

That night she splurged at the Safeway. She bought steaks, baking potatoes, asparagus, and strawberries and a bottle of "The Widow." (One thing her father had always told her was never to skimp on wine or champagne.)

It was eight o'clock when John returned. The potatoes were over baked and hard, but thank goodness she hadn't started the steaks. He was carrying a small box, wrapped in Kelly green paper with a purple yarn ribbon bow. It was from Morgan's, her friend's shop in the village.

John had driven out to Middleburg following his successful interview and bought her a tiny brass frog she'd admired. He was beaming. She didn't let on that she knew about the good news.

"But how did you know to go out and buy this fancy dinner?" he asked later in bed.

"Just a good guess," she sighed, still tingling from his touch moments before.

John and Betty both gave notice at their jobs the following Monday. Two-and-a-half weeks later they drove up to Washington and met with Mr. Morris. Later that day they opened a joint checking account at the Riggs National Bank with some of "their" new found money. They began the search for their first (and current) home.

Betty kept asking John if he was certain he wanted to commute that far to work. "Oh honey, I love it out here as much as you do and you know I love horses. Maybe I will play polo again one day." He put his arms around her right on the street in front of the bank. "Besides it's a great place to raise a family."

When they finally did find a farm in Middleburg they liked, it was November, time for John to start work. Still, there were a few problems. For one, the price exceeded what they had planned to spend; the sellers, an older couple planning to move abroad, were asking $350,000 for the 138 acres. They finally agreed on $338,000. Then the sellers said they needed at least until January to move out.

The money situation was easy to solve. Betty simply called Mr. Morris and he transferred more funds into their checking account. He agreed with John that it would be a good real estate investment. John said he thought the area would do nothing but appreciate in value.

"That boy has a sixth sense when it comes to real estate, Elizabeth," Mr. Morris told her. She felt reassured. "We have great hopes that he'll eventually specialize in this area—real estate that is."

To solve the dilemma of where to live for the two months before they could move into their new farm, they checked out the Georgetown Inn. They had very few alternatives; monthly rentals were rare in Middleburg.

John was close to work during the first few months and Betty ran around town buying everything needed for their new house. She was relieved to finally be guilt-free and able to spend money. She wanted everything to be impeccable.

She got a copy of the floor plan of their new home, known as Ridge View because of its magnificent view of the nearby Blue Ridge Mountains. She kept the plan in her purse as she visited the shops in Georgetown, trying to select the proper piece of furniture or light fixture. For the fabric in the drawing room, she went to a decorator on Wisconsin Avenue at the upper edge of Georgetown. She told him her problem, that she couldn't get in to the house yet, but wanted everything to be ready for just after the first of the year.

"Mrs. Dent," Michael Aldridge told her, "I have lots of clients out there. I'd be delighted to help you."

He did a smashing job. Not only did he measure the drawing room to hang the draperies, he also made the polished white chintz curtains that still hung in her bedroom today. Before they moved, the major decorating work had been completed.

Michael described it as "positively perfect." It was classic, and would never go out of style.

But now, twenty years later, Betty sat in her bedroom staring at those white drapes, wondering if her own marriage had gone out of style?

Their dog, Hobo, a long-haired Jack Russell Terrier, was dancing to go outside. If John were home, he'd take him. It was after eleven. She decided to call the Georgetown Inn one last time.

Once again, there was no answer in his room. Betty Dent was still upset until the hospital called as she tossed and turned in her sleep.

The nurse said Johnathan had a broken shoulder. Now Betty understood why he hadn't answered the phone in his room earlier that night. She walked to the bathroom, took a sip of water and got back into bed.

Just as she turned off the small crystal lamp on the nightstand, that old brass frog caught her eye. She hoped Johnathan wasn't in too much pain. She wondered how long he'd be in a cast, or even if there was a cast?

A broken shoulder...poor Johnathan. That explained everything. Almost.

Chapter 8

A Surge Of Passion

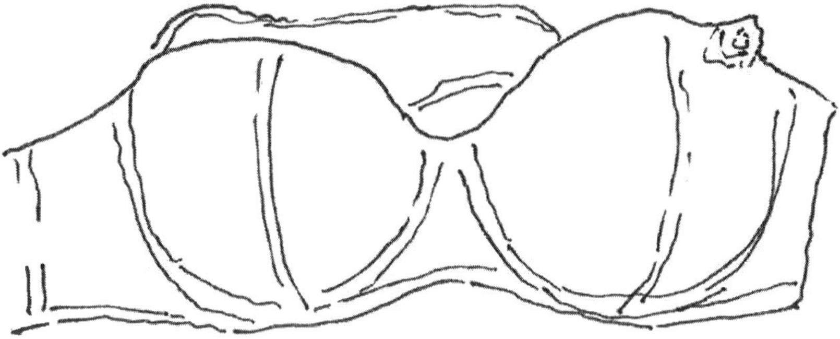

Betty was awake at five-forty-five, showered, and dressed by six-twenty. She was downstairs in the kitchen sipping coffee when Bertha, the housekeeper, arrived at eight minutes after seven.

She's always late, thought Betty, anxious to get going to Washington to visit Johnathan in the hospital.

"How are the roads," Betty inquired as she took an English muffin out of the oven. The toaster was still on the fritz. She put the muffin on top of the stove and stepped in front of Bertha to open the refrigerator for the butter.

"Well now, I had a hard time getting out my drive and down our road, Mrs. Dent," Bertha said, answering the question and explaining her tardiness at the same time. "You know the state road people don't come round 'til it's too late and all melted. But once I got out on the main road, well now Route 50 is fine, it's been scraped. And you know, the Zulla Road, with all its ups and downs, there's always slick spots..."

It suddenly dawned on the elderly black lady that there was a reason for the question and that it wasn't just idle curiosity. "Mrs. Dent, why you all dressed up?"

The room was silent for a moment and Mrs. Dent (as she was always referred to by the help) put down the muffin and took a deep breath.

"Bertha, Mr. Dent had an accident last night, he's in the hospital."

"Oh mercy, mercy..." Once Bertha got going on the "mercies" it was sometimes hard to stop her.

"He broke his shoulder. They called about one in the morning. They said he'd be all right, but I want to get downtown and see him right away."

Betty Dent didn't sleep well and the question of how and where John could have broken his shoulder still nagged at her. She needed some answers.

"We're due at Pauline's for dinner tonight, Bertha. Would you call her around noon and tell her John will not be attending but that I'll make every effort to return on time. Don't forget now?"

Betty Dent wouldn't miss a social function for anything. And as much as she loved and adored her husband, and as much as she wanted to know how he got into this mess, she would return for the dinner party. Some called it "saving face" at all costs.

She put the coffee cup, saucer, spoon, and muffin plate in the sink, wiping away any crumbs from the pine counter and eating space. She straightened the mail and put the catalogue from the White Flower Farm on the top of the pile. She had her day planned. She would drive into Washington, arrive about nine-thirty, visit with John until eleven-thirty, go out to lunch somewhere near the George Washington Hospital. The White House was only a few blocks away, and there were dozens of nice places to eat all around the area. She would return to his room at one and stay until one-thirty and be back on the road to the country and home at three. She was always punctual.

Between three and five she would bathe, do her nails, and finish looking through the catalogues and other mail that might arrive that morning. At five, she would have one short drink while dressing and at six-fifteen she would arrive at Pauline's, perfectly coiffed and suitably dressed for dinner. She prided herself on being methodical and always organized. She would answer the questions about John as soon as she could get a few answers herself.

At precisely nine twenty-eight Betty pulled into the five-story parking structure that adjoined the George Washington Hospital off Thomas Circle. She looked at the time on the ticket as she pulled it out of the machine in the lot as the automatic gate rose to give way for her navy blue Mercedes to enter.

She found a spot near the elevator, which pleased her. She feared these enormous, echoing parking lots, particularly with all the news of mugging and street robberies that was always shown on television. She inquired at the front desk as to Johnathan Dent's room number. Just to be sure he hadn't been moved since the nurse had called last night.

"He's in room six eighty-seven by the door," said a male volunteer, then added, "Your sister-in-law has already gone up there. She was here bright and early."

"You must be mistaken," Betty Dent answered. She was searching for the elevator and just half way into the conversation with the nameless man anyway. "I don't have a sister-in-law," she said over her shoulder as she walked to the bank of elevators. The man at the desk was relieved he didn't have to answer back.

"I knew that girl wasn't any immediate relative," he said under his breath. He was annoyed with himself that he been taken in by her charm and ravishing good looks.

"My brother was brought in last night with a broken shoulder," the young woman had told him less than two hours ago. *"I just want to stop in and say hello before I go to work. I'll just be a minute,"* she said, quickly taking the yellow pass from his hand. *"Thank you so very much."*

Isabelle had come and gone from the hospital even before Betty Dent ever pulled that parking ticket from the automated machine in the lot.

Johnathan was dozing, while the *Today Show* hummed in the background. A tray of breakfast awaited on an adjustable table along the side of the bed. The blinds were open and the extra bright sunlight slanted across the floor.

"Good morning, darling," she said kissing him on the cheek, adding, "how are you doing?"

Betty Dent, ever the efficient one, had the *Washington Post*, the *New York Times* and the *Wall Street Journal*, all purchased downstairs in the gift shop, in her arms. She put them on the chair as he opened his eyes. His face was drained of any color and he seemed groggy.

"What time is it?" he asked, pretending as if he didn't know. He'd been awake since before dawn. As soon as it was seven, he asked the nurse to dial the telephone for him. He told her he needed to make an urgent call. He spoke to Isabelle and told her what happened. It was the first thought he had as he smacked the icy bricks the night before. She insisted on coming right to the hospital.

"But I don't think you'll be able to get upstairs," he told her.

"Not to worry, darling," was her answer. *"I want to see you and I want to touch your face and know that you are all right."*

And that was exactly what happened. She tiptoed into the room, put her palm on his cheek and grabbed his good hand and kissed the top of it. She was gone by nine and John couldn't stop thinking about her. He knew now that she meant more to him than he ever intended. He could still smell her presence in the room...it was the Shalimar perfume. *"I wear a different perfume in the summer,"* she once explained.

"How about some breakfast?" his wife asked, waking him from his thoughts of Shalimar.

"What is it?"

"Well..." she said as she rolled the tray table over the bed and removed the stainless steal domes. "Scrambled eggs."

"That sounds great," Johnathan said as he maneuvered into position to try to eat with his left hand. "I'm hungry as hell." Which was true.

They had a pleasant visit, though Johnathan never did look directly into her eyes. Still, Betty Dent was able to chat with the doctor, who assured her that her husband would be out in another day or two. She plumped up his pillow before she left for lunch at a café a few blocks away. She returned for another brief visit, kissed him goodbye, and was on the road by one-fifteen, just as she planned. Four hours. She was back in her kitchen by two forty-five.

The dinner party at Pauline's was excellent as usual.

Every light in the entire house was on when Betty Dent arrived at six-fourteen. The fires were blazing and crackling and those green Rigaud candles with that expensive evergreen scent were lit throughout the downstairs portion of the house.

Her friends, the Holts from Greenwich, were on an overnight stay on their way to Florida. He and John would have gotten along so well, talking about real estate deals and prices and things like that. But, as Betty Dent explained to the guests:

"He took a bad step coming out of a restaurant in Georgetown last night. He had a business dinner and it ran late and he slipped on the ice and broke his shoulder. He'll be fine."

Franny Collins, her dearest friend, was there with her husband, Jake, and the two women spent most of their time talking about the annual May Day Tea Dance, a charity event for the school. Franny was chairman for this year's event and was frantic that she was behind schedule with the printing and other details. Betty promised to meet her at the country club the next day for lunch to go over things. Betty thought about whether to tell her about John not being in his room at the hotel last night. And how there was a small little something still nagging her about his broken shoulder. *Maybe I'm wrong*, she said to herself. But… she had read somewhere that a woman's intuition was usually on target.

Everything about Pauline's dinner party was timed to the minute. Cocktails starting at six-thirty until seven forty-five. She did not tolerate guests who were fashionably late. Her guests knew they were expected to be on time. The cold hors d'oeuvres were set out. And she never served cheese—too much fat and cholesterol. This time she had crudités—raw celery, carrots, and cauliflower with a yogurt dip. This was followed promptly at seven twenty-five by the hot hors d'oeuvres: bacon and leeks wrapped in phyllo pastry. They were divine, not to mention full of fat and cholesterol, a fact that eluded the hostess.

The guests were the usual group...the Collins, the Jaspers, both generations of Curtises, Holly Hawk (a friend from Upperville, whose husband was out of town—wasn't he always?), and Betty. Just a dozen people for what Pauline called an informal "do."

Susie, her right hand, "did it all" according to Pauline, who took credit for the genius of hiring Susie, planning the menu, ordering the flowers, choosing the china, setting the mood, and of course, selecting the guest list.

During dinner that night, Betty decided she would do the same thing when Johnathan came home. She would definitely set the mood.

When John did arrive home from the hospital to Ridge View two days later, Betty persevered with her well thought-out plan.

Say nothing; pretend all was right again in their cozy corner of the world.

Still, that first night, something came over her, and she didn't exactly know why. As she walked into the warm room and looked at John tucked in and seemingly so at home, she felt a surge of passion. After dinner on TV trays, Betty went to the walk-in closet and got her nightgown and laid it on the edge of the bed, pretending she was absorbed in the news as she undressed. Though she was close to forty and had produced three lovely children, she still had an exceptional figure.

She got down to her beige lace underwear and asked John some silly question about a story on the hostages in Iran. She took off her bra and laid it on the bed.

She had specifically asked the doctor about his recuperation. He told her John should take it easy at home for the rest of the week and that he could return to work the following Monday.

"Is there anything else I should know," she casually asked. "What about any special diet, sex, things like that?"

"No restrictions on either one," was his answer, with just the trace of a sly smile.

And so on his first night home, she continued with her plan. She watched the news as she undressed. She made a comment about Alice Roosevelt Longworth, who had died that day.

"She really was a legend, wasn't she?" she asked, at the same time, now stepping out of her panties. John looked up, just as she was about to drop her sheer pink nightgown over her head.

There was just enough chill in the air so that her body demanded his attention, and she fully intended to get it that night.

They had made passionate, and for Johnathan, somewhat uncomfortable love that night. Betty moved into positions she'd never tried to ease the pressure on his damaged shoulder. But all his other parts were working nicely, and after forty minutes, they fell asleep on top of the covers. It was three-thirty in the morning when Betty woke up, freezing cold and stark naked. The fire had died out. Johnathan had a pair of flannel pajama bottoms on with a drawstring waist. He was sleeping on his back because of his taped shoulder. Betty woke him up for a surprise second round and again he responded. When she finally rolled over to go back to sleep, she convinced herself there couldn't possibly be another woman in his life. She felt warm and full of energy.

By the time Betty met Franny at the Country Club the next day, she had forgotten that she was concerned about Johnathan's whereabouts when he slipped on the ice.

"Now tell me, where do you stand on the invitations?" she asked Franny as they sat down at a small round table for lunch. They both decided to splurge (on calories) and have cheeseburgers, something she didn't order very often. *But I need my strength back*, she thought.

Franny Morgan (that was her maiden name of course) and Betty had been best friends since boarding school in southern Virginia. Their first year in the ninth grade, they each were stuck with dreadful roommates. Franny's was a sickeningly sweet southern belle of belles from Nashville who was also crazy about Tennessee Walking Horses. This was something Franny absolutely despised because *"Those trainers work those horses hard to make them shuffle that way. It's so cruel."*

Betty's roommate that first year was Sarah Goodwin, a girl she often described to other girlfriends as "a slut from San Diego." All Sarah talked about were boys, and her knowledge was extensive for a young girl of fourteen. The very first night at school she had asked Betty Crane if she had "done it yet."

"Done what?"

"You know," she said. "IT."

"Are you kidding?" Betty asked. Then added emphatically for the record, *"Absolutely not."*

Franny and Betty found each other on the third day of their second year. They were in first period geometry class in the basement of the dormitory. Franny had pulled her blue jeans on under her flannel nightshirt, her hair was unbrushed, and she wore sheepskin slippers. Geometry was definitely not going to be one of her best subjects. Nor was it Betty's. Franny sat down at the one and only rectangular table directly opposite Betty.

The teacher began, *"Since some of you girls live in this building I can see where it would be very easy to just slip to class wearing some of your more comfortable clothes. And, while we do not have a dress code here at St. Margaret's, it would be nice if you could wear street clothes and not night clothes."*

Franny couldn't look right or left toward the teacher. Instead her eyes glanced up at Betty. And they were instant allies. After class, they walked down to the field house and bought Cokes. The small ones in those eight-ounce, green glass bottles. They were immediate best friends.

"I can't believe what a bitch she is," Franny said as they walked back toward the center of the campus. "It makes me sick to have geometry first period.

"Hey, what do you say we meet later and sneak a cigarette?" she asked as she ran off in the other direction. "I'll meet you right there at three-fifteen."

"Sure," Betty answered before realizing that she didn't even smoke or want to smoke.

They went through four glorious years of boarding school. Franny was a horseback rider and a good one. Betty went along for the fun of it and they had many memorable times after school and on weekends at the stables. It was the ideal place for Franny to sneak a cigarette, because of the lack of strict supervision. The riding instructor was just a few years older than most of the girls and a smoker, too.

During the first semester of their senior year, Franny met Jake Collins. He was standing in the warm-up area at a small indoor horse show at the Foxcroft School in Middleburg.

"My god," Franny said upon returning to school that night. "When I saw him standing there when I went into the ring, I forgot which way I was supposed to turn. I felt like a fool. He's soooo cute."

Two weeks later, Franny saw Jake again when he came to a horse show at St. Margaret's. It was a fundraiser for the senior class. Franny was in charge of the food booth that day. She ended up giving Jake free hot chocolate, free lunch, and would have given him a free dinner if he had stayed that late.

He seemed to be just as absorbed in her. And before that day was over he invited her to Lynchburg for the annual Thanksgiving weekend hunt and dinner dance.

"What am I going to tell my parents?" she pleaded with Betty one day during lunch. "They'll never let me go down there with some horse trainer. He's so cute, I can't stand it. What am I going to do?" she rattled on.

"Just tell them you're coming home with me," Betty offered, thinking she had no other choice.

"Oh, I was hoping you'd say that Betty. I'm so excited, I can't stand it! What am I going to wear?"

When Thanksgiving rolled around, Franny went south to Lynchburg. And she ended up calling Betty at her house at least fourteen times, to make sure her mother hadn't called to check on her.

"No problem, yet." But by Saturday afternoon of that weekend Betty's own mother was getting quite curious.

"Why is Franny calling you so much, dear," she casually asked.

"Oh nothing mom, just something to do with a school project we're trying to work out."

Franny pulled it off beautifully. The day after graduation, she and Jake Collins ran away and got married.

Betty was delighted that her old school chum now also lived in Middleburg. Her husband Jake was teaching Betty's daughter how to ride.

Franny and Jake were heavily into horses. He was often away on buying trips or judging a horse show. Franny confessed she was suspicious of his fidelity, but couldn't put her finger on anything particular.

"You know," she said one day. "There are a lot of young things that swoon over him, just like I once did." She took a bite of hamburger.

The two women had a lot in common. Both had inherited a great deal of money. Some people wouldn't believe it, but it wasn't always so easy when the woman had more money than her husband. Franny solved the dilemma by having $100,000 transferred into Jake's account each January 1.

"I turned most of the financial and legal things over to his brother Dan.

He's a lawyer in Washington," she told Betty one day. "It's much easier that way, I don't want anyone to feel uncomfortable."

Franny hadn't changed much since prep school. Her chin-length hair was cut in a blunt style and she still wore the same style of clothes—cotton turtle necks, blue jeans, and a cable-knit sweater. She had freckles, which gave her a youthful look, and a narrow, angular nose.

Even though she didn't always dress for the occasion, meaning that she often underdressed, she wore diamond earrings and a diamond tennis bracelet every day.

The only thing different about her was that now, as they went over the invitation for the tea dance, she wore glasses. Tortoise shell glasses, big round ones.

"I've got the cover design and I've sent the rest of it to the typesetter, so we should get a proof by next week."

"Do you have a copy of the artwork?" Betty asked.

The waiter interrupted "Would you ladies care for some coffee?"

"No thanks, not now," Betty replied.

"Oh, it just so happens I have a copy of it," Franny said, leaning over to search her oversized L.L. Bean canvas tote bag that carried her life. "I've got it here somewhere.

"Oh, you're going to love it," she said still fishing in her bag. "He did a great job," she continued, referring to artist Rusty Stewart, who had been doing the artwork for the May Day Dance for as long as anyone could remember. "He's looking for more commissions to do paintings of dogs and horses. His animals are wonderful. I promised him we'd give him a write-up in the program and two free tickets to the ball. Oh...here it is!"

"Wait a minute." Betty said, wiping off her hands. "This is fabulous."

"We have one of his paintings. I must say this work is entirely original." It was hard to tell about the colors of this painting since the two women were looking at a Xerox copy in black in white. It was a watercolor of a giant May Day pole with children and animals dancing all around. In the background up on a hill was the Country Day School, which would receive all the money raised from the dance toward the building fund for the new library.

"My only problem is that Jake and I leave for Florida on Tuesday, if it isn't ready by then I'm sunk. We're going to be gone for ten days and then if there are changes that will take another three days."

Betty knew instantly that she had to offer to proofread the copy for her friend. She was always getting Franny out of one jam or another, just like at St. Margaret's. Betty also knew she was resigned to the fact that she would probably end up finishing off whatever needed to get done so the invitations would be out with plenty of time to spare.

Franny was her best friend, but she always had ten irons in the fire and was constantly in a panic to complete her tasks. She just didn't know how to say no. Whenever anyone asked her to serve on a committee or sit on the board for a charity event, she never refused. She had worked on the May Day

Dance for as long as she had lived in the country.

In addition to four children aged two to twelve, Franny also owned Morgan's, the shop where Johnathan and Betty first stopped to buy a gift for the Curtises years ago. It was right on the corner in town and she carried a vast array of gifts, clothes, and jewelry. She was a busy woman, but dearly loved and very thoughtful. She never forgot a birthday or anniversary and continuously gave precisely the accurate gift on each occasion.

"Not to worry, Franny," Betty promised. "I'll do whatever I can."

"Oh, Betty, you are so dear, I couldn't live without you," she said, pushing her plate away and putting a file folder on the table. "I've made a list of what needs to be done and when. If you could just oversee things while we go away, I'd be forever grateful."

"How long will you be gone?"

"Not quite three weeks," meaning, *at least* three weeks, maybe longer.

Franny and Jake were going to Florida for the winter horse shows that took place at Wellington, near Palm Beach each winter. No way was she letting him go without her. Many locals made the same trip and some of the kids even had a tutor while they were gone from school. Franny got the children's schoolwork ahead of time and took all the books and workbooks along, insisting her children study for at least three hours each day. She said it wasn't easy, because most of the other children were out riding their ponies or swimming or riding those infernal three-wheeled motorbikes. Nevertheless, it was three weeks of warm sunshine, and Betty envied her friend.

The file folder was chock full. Franny must have known Betty would offer to take over. She had samples of the paper that was to be used for the invitation, a handsome eggshell color in a matt finish. The typeface was called Gothic Tudor. She left a check from the dance fund account made out to the postmaster for the stamps with instructions that read: *"Be sure not to use generic type stamps, buy something colorful and commemorative."* Franny Morgan Collins didn't miss a trick. Then her note went on: *"When the envelopes are ready, call Claudia Jasper, she volunteered to do the addressing."*

Claudia. She was another one of Betty's oldest and dearest friends. She and her husband, George, a reporter for the *Washington Post*, lived in Upperville. They had one daughter, Lisa, age ten, the same as Maude Dent. The two women become friendly because their daughters were in the same class at the Country Day School since first grade. The little girls were just months apart in age and constant companions.

Claudia was one of Betty's favorites. Unlike most of the women around town, she was no gossip. Her husband, the reporter, told her that was a surefire way of making enemies, and there wasn't a mischievous bone in her body. Unlike Franny, she wouldn't dream of smoking or drinking. Claudia had studied art and was quite talented, particularly in pen and ink and watercolor. She also loved animals and often took long walks down the dirt roads near her house just to "take in everything." She met her husband, George Jasper at

Clyde's, the M Street tavern, one Sunday afternoon during her second year at Georgetown. Not only did Clyde's serve the best chili in town, the place was filled with students or young trendy types who populated Washington.

George was a waiter at the time, studying journalism at George Washington, and even though the help wasn't supposed to fraternize with the patrons (much less flirt), he asked Claudia out on a date. She was just what he needed, a sweet, demure, good looker. He was a friendly, inquisitive fellow with a delicious sense of humor and a sarcastic way of looking at the world—all prerequisites for what would later become his life's work. More important to Claudia, he was fun, attractive, and hard worker—definitely a man who would support her.

Claudia was the product of an upper-middle class Catholic family of six children. She had grown up in the Chicago suburb of Mt. Prospect. Coming to Washington was a big step and if she hadn't met George, she probably would have ended up with a job as an administrative aide on Capitol Hill along with countless other women her age.

Ever since they married, George was her life. After she had her first child, they hoped to have more. But her pregnancy had been rough. She was in bed for five months. One wrong move and she would have lost the baby. She adored her little girl and from time to time would get tears in her eyes and tell Betty how much she wanted another. But finally they knew it could be too dangerous for mother and child and they silently gave up. Claudia accepted this and the three of them would go off on special weekends to Hershey, Pennsylvania, Annapolis, or Colonial Williamsburg.

Claudia was tall and rail thin. Her clothes hung on her, something other women envied. Her legs were long and she covered the tennis court from one end to the other effortlessly in just a few strides.

She had short hair that brushed her shoulders. It hadn't always been that way. In college it was long, and she held it up in the back with a large clip. Then one day, after her daughter was about five months old, she had it all cut off. At the time, she also went from having it frosted to bleaching it. Betty hated the way it looked—a nasty, yellow color that almost made her look cheap. Betty had tried to tell her that in a nice way, and didn't want to hurt her feelings, but Claudia—ever the nonconformist artist—loved it. She told Betty it made her feel good.

"No hassle," she said. "All I have to do is wash it in the morning, I don't even have to blow it dry. And once a month I put a new bottle of color on it."

"But Claudia, I liked it so much the other way," Betty told her. "Why don't you let it grow out and redo it that way."

"Oh, I've tried. It made me look sick, it was too dark and besides, this is a whole new me."

End of discussion.

Claudia had gorgeous handwriting, almost like calligraphy, and she was always asked to do the "addressing," which she did willingly. Her husband now traveled frequently for the paper on various assignments and she had a lot of free time each evening to do the work. Her card table remained set up in her living room with stacks of envelopes.

The two of them addressed and stuffed the envelopes, proofread the copy, oversaw the printing, sorted through the mailing list, licked the stamps, and finally put them in the mail on Thursday, March 28, a few days ahead of schedule and the April deadline. Franny's note reminded: *"You must have them in the people's mailboxes by April 1st. No invitation should go out later than four weeks before the event."* This year the May Day Tea Dance was set for Saturday, May 19.

Franny returned from her winter sojourn to Florida, and was busy ordering Christmas items for her shop. She didn't have time to stop and deal with the final details for the dance.

Claudia and Betty again took over, happy to bail out their friend once more.

Occasionally they'd meet at one or the other's house for an early dinner. George Jasper was off in Iowa covering the caucuses for the upcoming presidential election and John no doubt had to work late and stay in town.

"I'll tell you what," Betty said, the morning the invitations were in the mail. "How about you and I have a celebration dinner tonight? John's brother and my sister-in-law are coming here next weekend and I need to try out a new recipe. I'll splurge on a leg of lamb and you and Lisa come over at about five. We'll eat by six."

"Sounds great to me," Claudia answered.

They sipped white wine while Betty finished the final dinner details in her massive country kitchen. The news on the television provided background noise and the two little girls went off to play upstairs.

"So," Betty asked, "How did you do today?" referring to her tennis game in the winter tournament, which Claudia had played that afternoon.

"Well, it was postponed. One of the other gals called in and said she had a cold and couldn't play. I really think it's just the sniffles or she's got her period or something. So now we have to reschedule the whole damned thing."

"What a shame, but I'm sure it will work out."

"You bet, it just gives my partner and me more time to practice. No problem."

Claudia was addicted to tennis. She went to the country club as often as possible. She was almost there as much as the handsome young tennis pro, Steve. If Betty didn't know her better, she would have thought something was going on between them, as many lessons as Claudia took. But her friend was clearly not the type to fool around.

"Oh, turn it up," Claudia half-shouted, looking at the television. "I think I see George there in that swarm of reporters. Yes...yes...there he is!" she said, jumping up and pointing to the television a second too late. By the time her finger reached the tube she was pointing at the reporter finishing his story.

"Oh, well, I saw him," she said, returning to the stool at the kitchen counter and taking a big sip of white wine. "What kind of lamb are we having?" she asked.

"Butterfly, with soy sauce, ginger, and honey, and curried rice." Betty's cooking abilities had greatly improved since the Charlottesville days. No more Gusburgers.

The phone rang. It was Franny.

"Oh, Betty, how can I ever thank you girls?" she gushed. "I just found out the invitations are in the mail—and three days early! You're Wonder Women!"

"How did you find out?" Betty asked.

"Lucy Douglas told me it was in her afternoon mail," she answered.

"She got hers already?" Turning to Claudia and putting her hand over the receiver Betty whispered, "It's Franny, some people got their invitations this afternoon."

"Well, we had a good time doing it, Franny. Claudia's here now. We're just having an early dinner."

"Oh great," she said. "That'll save me a phone call. Listen I want you two girls to be my guest at a luncheon next week. It's the big Cancer Society Fashion Show downtown. They're doing Chanel this year. It should be fun. Please ask Claudia, right now, and please say you'll both come. We can go to Georgetown afterward and do some serious shopping, just the three of us. Now come on, ask her."

That's how it usually went with the three women...their life in the country revolved around children, charity work, tennis, horse shows, riding lessons, hunt breakfasts, point-to-point races, and tailgate picnics.

A trip to Washington for a luncheon and fashion show was a great diversion.

CHAPTER 9

Horses, Riders & Foxhounds

It felt good to get out of the country and into the city. Most of the women at the luncheon were dressed elegantly. Wool suits, hair perfectly done, and almost every woman had a quilted Chanel handbag over her shoulder.

There was a cocktail hour before the lunch. No name Champagne. They met some of Franny's friends from Washington: B. B. Baker, a decorator, and Norma Solomon, whose husband was a well-known plastic surgeon.

It was well past three o'clock by the time they got down to Georgetown to go shopping after the fashion show. Betty wanted to look in Stombock's Saddlery on M Street to buy Maude a gift for no reason whatsoever. Then she hoped to head up Wisconsin Avenue to Little Caladonia for some fabric to cover a chair. Franny wanted to stop at dressmaker and designer Dorcas

Hardin's shop for a new cocktail dress for a horse awards banquet she and Jake would be attending. They parked behind People's Drug Store up on Wisconsin.

"I'll meet you back here in forty-five minutes," Franny said. She always ran behind schedule. "I'm just going up the street to Dorcas Hardin to look for a print dress."

"Now wait a minute," Betty interrupted. "Let's rethink this. I wouldn't mind looking at the clothes, too. Let me think...why don't I give John a call and see if I can't meet him for dinner and we'll go home late. Why don't you call Jake and tell him you'll be late and we'll all have dinner together? Claudia can call George and maybe he can meet us, too."

"Oh no way. No way. Jake would have a blue fit if I came home late. He can't feed four kids and do the horses, too. He wouldn't even know what to feed the children."

"Oh come on. Let's try, let's call him. I'll talk to him."

"We'll be home before ten o'clock," Betty promised.

Of course Betty made all the plans before even calling her own husband. She had forgotten that it was Wednesday and he had mentioned something about a late meeting.

"I'm not sure what his plans are Mrs. Dent," his secretary told her. "He's in with a client right now, can I have him call you back?"

"Well, no, I'm at a pay phone in Georgetown. Just tell him I called and that Franny and Claudia and I are in town and we want to meet him for an early dinner, if possible. When should I call back?"

"Why don't you try back in about forty-five minutes?"

It was difficult for Johnathan to explain to Isabelle that he couldn't make it for their Wednesday night together. He ached for her. But there were times when he had no choice, not if he wanted to keep Betty from becoming suspicious. He did not like confrontations, anyway, who did?

John rearranged his meetings that night, and told Betty he would meet her for dinner in Georgetown at Martin's Tavern. It just so happened to be right around the corner from the shops the women were visiting.

A few hours later, the country friends were together in the city. Johnathan ordered a bottle of white wine and talked with George Jasper about his work. He told his friend about a real estate project he was working on in central Virginia.

"Actually, it's between Orange and Charlottesville," he said. "These clients want to build a sort of self-contained community centered around sports—golf, tennis, even equine sports. You know, Fran (he called her Fran and was one of the few people to do so), we might be able to use Jake's expertise. Sign him up as a consultant or something."

"That would be interesting," she said, "What do you mean?"

"Well, they want nothing but the best. The best stables, the best riding ring, the best spectator facility—a setup to attract their clientele. And then they want to have horse shows and tennis matches and maybe even a professional golf event. It's all in the working stages."

Betty was proud of John and hoped it would work out with Jake and Franny. It had been difficult for Jake to make money in the horse business. This might be just the thing. They talked late, the place was empty, except for two other couples in separate booths in the main room. They had two cups of coffee each and it was time to go.

Betty had assumed John would drive back to the country with her since he had been able to rearrange his schedule. So it was a surprise when he said: "Where did you ladies park? I want to take you to the car."

"We're over in the People's lot. We didn't want to have to walk very far."

Betty didn't let on to Franny that she was surprised. She couldn't understand why John would be staying. But as they stood at the front door of Martin's putting on coats, he offered a vague explanation.

"I had to reschedule that meeting tonight for tomorrow morning. We're meeting for breakfast at seven-thirty at the Madison Hotel. I'll just stay in town if you don't mind too much. It'll give me a couple of hours more sleep, and I've got to go over some papers before I see these people. Now I want you all to drive carefully. It's late."

She felt somewhat reassured with his explanation. He did work so hard. And on the way back to the country driving down the lonely stretch of Route 50 just before Gilbert's Corner, Betty said to Franny. "You know, I can hardly blame Johnathan for not wanting to make this drive late at night." It was almost as though she felt she had to explain.

"I can't either," Franny agreed. "It's a long haul."

By ten forty-five Betty Dent was back safely at home getting ready for bed.

Johnathan Dent made the short walk to the other side of Georgetown and gently knocked on the wooden door at Isabelle's apartment.

She was waiting for him.

Johnathan's brother Bob and Irene, his wife, were coming to Middleburg for the weekend. The tenth meet of the foxhunting season was going to be held at Ridge View, a tradition the Dents had inherited from the previous owners. They'd never even thought of changing the date, not in this part of the country, where people thrived on what once was and what had always been. Tradition also dictated that the field was invited for a breakfast that followed the hunt.

Bob Dent had a new airplane and was due to fly up from Richmond on Friday morning.

Betty Dent liked to say that if you were going to cook for two, you might as well cook for two hundred. "It's just as much trouble," she'd say. So she got on the telephone and invited a few extras to the hunt breakfast, which didn't start until three or four o'clock when the riders finished their outing. She enjoyed the preparations, it was a marvelous midwinter break.

She called Claudia. She and George told Betty they'd be happy to attend. Franny and Jake also would be there.

Holly Hawk said her husband was out of town.

"So why don't you come without him?" Betty offered. So many women just assumed that if their husband couldn't attend, the invitation was no longer valid.

"Really?" she asked.

"Sure, why not?"

"Is there anything I can do?"

"I can't think of a thing. Just bring yourself. I'll figure out the rest."

"But are you sure?" Holly asked.

"Of course, you know better." Betty said, jotting down the names of those who had accepted as she talked. "I thought I'd also ask Spencer O'Brien." Spencer was a vice president at the bank, in his late fifties, never married, and always a standby extra man at every dinner party. There had been rumors about his sexual preferences, but no one had ever been able to confirm them.

"Whatever," Holly answered. "I'm just glad to be included. With Hank gone all weekend, it'll be good to get out of the house."

"Okay, I'll put you down."

The guest list grew longer. When she picked up Maude at the Country Day School, she managed to invite two other couples as she waited for school to let out. The Douglases, who lived right in town, had invited them to a Christmas cocktail party and said they'd be delighted. Theodora Crist, the mayor, and Bunny and Alex Carroll, the vet, also joined her ever-expanding list.

Naturally, she included Pauline Howard. Then there was the Curtis family; Ray, Jr., who would probably be out with the hunt that day anyway, and his wife, Smith, who was Spencer Howard's sister. Add to that Mr. and Mrs. Ray Curtis, Sr. Betty quickly calculated more than two hundred people coming for breakfast at four in the afternoon.

She called the local market and increased the size of her order. Tradition also dictated that she serve Brunswick Stew, warm spiced peaches, salad, and mandatory ham biscuits. Then she called the club to see if she could get Bean the bartender to come and asked if they knew of an extra woman to help serve. Bean was available, but they didn't know of anyone else.

"Bertha," Betty said to the maid over her usual lunch of soup the next day. "I'm in a real bind. I've gone and invited all these extra people for the hunt breakfast and I know it's short notice, but we need extra help. Do you know anyone else who can help serve? We'll probably need two or three more."

"Oh, Mizz Dent, you know I can handle it. I'll get Susie from over at Mrs.

Howard's and her sister. What time should I tell them to come?"

"I think two o'clock would give us plenty of time to get things organized and ready. There'll be a lot of last-minute things to do, but that should be about right."

Betty felt relieved to have Bean, because nobody had a party without him. He was almost seventy now, but as soon as a guest walked into the room, Bean already had prepared his or her favorite drink before they headed toward the bar. With Bertha in charge of the kitchen, she knew she'd have no problem with the food or the service.

"I've told the other guests to come about three," she told Bertha.

Betty went over a list of things to do: "Get out chaffing dishes, wash wine glasses, make sure napkins are ironed." She was constantly repeating herself with Bertha. Despite the Dents oft-repeated offer to get her tutoring, Bertha still couldn't read, and Betty feared she would forget something.

Then she flipped to a pad of paper and made a list of the things she needed at the local market. She also jotted down a timetable. Bertha refilled Betty's cup of soup as she continued to write herself reminders.

"Bertha, please check and make sure we have those imported peaches?" she asked, still making notes. "If we don't I'll have to call the importer in Dayton."

Warmed spiced peaches were one of her favorite things to serve, some would even say her specialty. These peaches were divine, but very hard to find. Over the years, she ordered them by the case from Reese's Fine Foods in Dayton. They would ship directly to the farm.

"There are two cases, far as I can tell, Mrs. Dent," Bertha reported.

"Let's see," Betty said, flipping over a piece of paper to figure it out. Two cases held twenty-four cans each...

"That should be fine," she said aloud.

As she fiddled with the piece of paper, another thought crossed her mind. She'd been writing on the back of the Xeroxed paper of the artwork for the May Day Dance. She simply must remind Rusty Stewart that she expected him. He was a regular at all the hunt breakfasts. Even though he didn't ride, he normally followed the hunt by car, taking the back roads to get as close to the action as possible. Often he carried a Nikon camera and would be strategically positioned by a coop as the riders came galloping through the field and over the jump. He had been standing next to a split rail fence years ago when Jackie Kennedy took a fall. Marshall Hawkins, the photographer standing next to him, captured the moment brilliantly, then rushed to Washington. He sold the picture to *Life* magazine for enough money to keep him in film and extra lenses for ten years. Rusty used his photos as a reference when these same people frequently commissioned him to do portraits of their beloved horses.

"Mr. Stewart, this is Betty Dent calling."

"Oh yes," he said, "How are you?"

"Franny showed me your artwork for the dance program. I can't wait to see the original, But, of course, you know I adore everything you do..."

"Why thank you, I'm more than..."

"Anyway, the real reason, I mean the *main* reason I'm calling is to remind you to be sure to stop by our hunt breakfast on Saturday. My in-laws are coming and we have quite a few of our dearest friends..."

"I'd love it, about what time?"

"I've told everyone about three."

"I look forward to seeing you then," he said and hung up.

Betty spent the next two days running around preparing for the gathering. It wasn't just the hunt breakfast she had to worry about, with house guests there was breakfast food and lunches and she had to make sure the guest rooms were in order.

On Thursday, she drove the twenty-five minutes to the large grocery store in Warrenton to get white raisins, which would go in the salad. They didn't have any at the mom and pop market in the village and she knew if she didn't buy them now, it wouldn't get done at all.

After dinner that night, she went to the front closet to pull out the china and serving dishes she'd be using. She put them out on the dining room table, counted the silverware, arranged the silver serving pieces and counted out the napkins. It was close to ten and John just arrived. He told her he'd been working late.

"Hi darling. What are you up to at this hour?" he asked, leaning over for his usual, obligatory kiss on the cheek. He took off his coat and loosened his tie at the same time, all the while avoiding his wife's eyes.

He thought about what a sensible woman she was. So organized in looking after the house and his children. He admired her generosity, especially with her money. It was an ideal situation...almost. He thought about the woman he just left back in Georgetown. The hunger and the intensity of his craving for Isabelle was beyond definition.

"Just trying to get organized for the weekend," she interrupted his lascivious train of thought. "Do you want some dinner? I kept a plate warm."

Even though he was late, Betty always had a nice dinner waiting for John. She loved being a busy wife and mother and tried to wait up for him. He was often very late. He took comfort that she appeared to be content. If the children were awake they all gathered in the kitchen. If they were in bed, then John and Betty would go into the library in the front of the house and he ate dinner at a side table. He kept a bottle of white wine cold in a small refrigerator under the bookshelves.

Betty automatically poured him a generous glass of wine and settled down in the loveseat. The conversation was light.

She told him about the hunt breakfast, what she was serving, the dilemma with the white raisins—now solved—and who was coming.

"And, oh, I invited Rusty Stewart too. We haven't seen him in ages."

After driving to the nearby Winchester airport to pick up Bob and Irene Dent, they returned to the farm for a quiet family dinner in the kitchen, the first night of the long weekend. Johnathan built a fire and they sat and had drinks. Betty put out cheese and crackers, nothing fancy. For dinner, they had quiche (which Bertha made up that afternoon) and a salad.

It was during the dessert of sliced bananas and apples that Betty learned of the pending airplane ride.

"Uncle Bob," Maude interrupted. "Tell mommy about the plane ride." She was clearly excited.

"Well..." Bob started to explain. "We thought we could kill two birds with one stone, so to speak. Everyone could have a ride in my new airplane. And we can fly down toward Culpeper to see the piece of land Johnathan's clients want to develop."

"Sounds..." Betty began.

"Oh, mommy, *please* say we can do it," Maude begged.

"...great to me," Betty finished. "When did you have in mind?"

"How about early tomorrow morning?" Johnathan interceded, adding quickly, "That way we can be back by lunch and tend to all the details for the hunt breakfast."

"Well, you know, I have so much to do."

"Oh mommy," Maude begged again, "we'll all help you later. Don't worry."

"Oh...all right," Betty said, not telling anyone how much she abhorred flying in small airplanes.

The following morning they loaded into the station wagon and headed for the nearby airport. Betty couldn't eat a thing for breakfast, but nobody noticed. She downed two cups of coffee and her stomach was doing flip-flops. It was a clear and crisp morning.

All Betty could think was *Thank God John is driving.* She was worried about going up in that airplane, but she didn't want anyone to recongnize her fear, especially Maude. After all, she was still curious about the land John intended to develop.

They turned off Route 50 just before coming to the old town of Winchester, where George Washington often stopped to sleep. He'd hardly recognize the place now, what with all the fast-food restaurants up and down Route 50, not to mention a K-Mart and a J. C. Penny that anchored the Apple Blossom Mall. The airport was two miles off the main highway. They parked in the small lot in front of a red brick building.

"If anyone has to go to the bathroom," Bob announced, "there are facilities inside."

Betty took Maude's hand. "That sounds like a good idea," she said, knowing instinctively that Maude would protest. She never wanted to go on demand.

"Oh mommy," she said, wrestling away from her mother's firm grip.

"And put your hat on your head," Betty ordered. "Let's go inside for a minute. I need to make a stop anyway. Just come with me." She was half-pleading and half-ordering. The little girl obliged.

After the short detour, Betty and Maude walked out to the airfield and looked at Bob's new Beechcraft Bonanza. The white paint glared in the sunlight. And the red stripe from front to back was just the right touch.

Bob was on a pay phone, just inside the hangar, calling in his flight plan to the regional FAA office.

"This is three-five-romeo-zula, V-F-R," he said, giving the registration number of his plane and indicating that he'd be flying under visual flight rules. "B-E three-five, alpha, one-hundred-sixty knots, sixty-five-hundred feet, Winchester, Culpeper, Winchester," he continued, indicating that he was flying a Beechcraft airplane that could travel 160 knots at 6,500 feet and would go today from Winchester to Culpeper to Winchester.

"Forty minutes, three hours of fuel, four souls, white with red stripe, alternate airport is India, Alpha, Delta," he concluded, which meant that the trip would take about forty minutes, that he had three hours of fuel, that his new plane was white with a red stripe, and his alternate airport would be Dulles International, the FAA airport code for which was I-A-D, translated as "India, Alpha, Delta."

"Okay, I think we're ready to roll," he said, hanging up the phone. "It's not really necessary to call in our flight plan, but I like to do it, if I have time. Now how about we go for a ride?" he said, patting Maude on the head.

Bob and Johnathan untied the plane and Betty and Maude settled into the two seats in back. The brothers sat in front. Since there was no control tower at the modest airport, Bob tuned his radio to what he called "Unicom," a universal frequency for all airplanes at uncontrolled airports.

They headed west, gathering speed down the runway. Betty tightened her grip on the arms of the seat, though no one seemed to notice.

They were off the ground.

The car dealerships along Route 50 on the edge of Winchester slipped away. The golden arches at the interchange of the Interstate got smaller and smaller. Betty took a deep breath, they were climbing quickly...out, up and out and up, and out and up.

Maude had yet to speak one word. She was mesmerized, alternately watching out the window and looking at her Uncle Bob as he flipped switches and guided them over the rolling Virginia countryside. They headed south and slightly east toward Front Royal, climbing at six hundred feet per minute. They passed over the Paris Mountain and above the most stunning valley in the entire Virginia countryside.

Bob sat back slowly. Piloting a plane was always stressful, even in good weather. But he had been flying since he was eighteen. It was something he always wanted to do. He once said he wanted to be a professional pilot, and later added "just liked to be up in God's skies taking all of life in."

Johnathan was sitting in the copilot's seat. He had headphones on and was listening to the radio. He knew nothing about controlling an aircraft and never had the passion for it like his brother.

"Look over here, Maude. There's the horse show grounds in Warrenton."

"Oh, wow!" she exclaimed, "There's the ring and there's the green barns, and I see the food stands too!" She was smiling at her mother, who still had a death grip on her armrest.

After passing over the horse show grounds and above the truck stop out of town near Opal, the outskirts of the county spread out like a smooth soft quilt. There was a patch of rich brown earth, soon to be planted with corn in the spring, and then a graceful blanket of gently sloping fields. Every now and then, a house would appear. Not a fancy mansion, but a house on a working farm. One would be a white frame structure with a wraparound porch. And the next would be a smaller version, this time painted green, with a row of stone steps leading up the front and a small wooden set of steps on the much more used rear entrance.

They swished over a country store, which Betty recognized as a halfway marker to Culpeper. She was all too familiar with the road below. It was Route 29, on which Betty had just driven the boys farther south to their boarding school in Orange, Woodberry Forest. She liked to stop for a Coke and potato chips at that country store after she picked them up for the weekend. They loved to go inside. Betty always refused and sat in the car while they ran inside. She missed them right now, and oh, how they would have loved this plane ride. She made a mental note to call them later in the day and report on their trip.

They continued along the other side of Culpeper. Bob was descending. They hadn't hit one bump yet and Betty was actually starting to relax a bit. Johnathan was leaning forward looking out the front of the plane.

"Now go to the left, just about twenty degrees," he said, pointing. "It's down that road three point six miles. You see there? Right by that country store?"

Bob guided the plane in that direction.

"Okay everyone, this is it," Johnathan announced. He was pointing at the windshield of the airplane in front of Bob's view.

Betty held her breath. She wanted to say something, but couldn't. Johnathan interrupted her racing mind.

"You see that old store there on the corner?" he asked. "That's called Payne's Grocery and that bridge there is called Payne's Bridge. And this entire area is known as Payne's Corner. The Payne family owned all of this at one time. We bought up the original four-hundred-eighty-seven acres from four different families."

They passed the grocery, and were above the farmland.

"I guess the Paynes were a fixture in this part of Virginia, fought in the

Civil War. Anyway, the community's going to be called 'Payne's Corner.'The group of investors call their corporation, Payne, Inc. As in P-A-I-N," he said, laughing and shaking his head.

Bob was guiding the plane lower and making a steep banked turn to come back around for a closer look. At the same time he asked, "So what are they going to do? The developers are your clients, I assume?"

"Yes, I represent them, but I don't have any financial interest in it. It's the same group that did the complex down in Roanoke. I guess about seventy percent of my practice is with the head investor, Sam Blackwell. Before we bought this—"

"Daddy, daddy, look!" Maude said, interrupting. "Daddy, look at the horses!"

"Oh, yes, we're...or I mean *they're* going to have horses here, Maude," Johnathan said to her, then turned back to his brother. "We bought the property contingent on specific zoning. Some of the preservationist types fought it, but we have zoning for a recreation community with eighty-eight percent single-family homes and twelve percent townhouses. We were able to appeal to the zoning board on the basis that many of the people who would buy here would be weekenders, even though I suspect a lot of them will commute to Washington and Charlottesville from here."

Bob Dent made a second three hundred and sixty degree turn, this time in the opposite direction. They were taking one more close look at Payne's Corner when suddenly, with no warning, they hit an air pocket. The bump, roughly akin to a sudden drop on a roller coaster, started Betty's stomach churning once again.

"I've asked Jake Collins—you remember him Bob, he's a horseman and Betty's friend's husband—to oversee the design of the stables and riding rings. They're planning to have horse shows here. They'll also have a tennis center with indoor and outdoor courts and indoor and outdoor swimming pools, too. We have a retail area planned too," Johnathan told them.

"We're going to pattern it all after an English village and design the shopping area like Covent Garden in London."

Everyone was silently looking at the lush countryside below. Betty was worried about her party the next day. Johnathan thought about dear sweet Isabelle. And Maude just took everything in. It was near silence except the steady purr of the engines.

Bob broke the quiet. "Well if that's all, I think I'll head back to home base," he said, pushing the throttle in and climbing back up to altitude, picking up speed. They were soon headed back to Winchester.

Maude Dent peeked out her front bedroom window the next morning, just before ten. The front yard, driveway, and the side pasture of the Dent's farm was filled with horse trailers, horses, riders, and foxhounds. The hunt was due to depart.

She spotted her father passing a silver tray with small servings of sherry in miniature silver cups for what was known as the "Stirrup Cup." Horses nickered back and forth. And the people did the same...trilling "Good morning" to one another.

Randal McCrane, the master of the hunt, was resplendent in his "pink" coat standing in the center of the circular drive, smoking a cigarette and greeting people. Some were mounted and others stood waiting for their grooms to pull up, driving a pickup truck with horses trailing behind.

Rusty Stewart stood off to one side, camera in hand and a tiny sketchbook in his back pocket. The minister, Andy Mayhaw, made his rounds bidding everyone a good morning and wishing them well.

"Andy you look divine!' someone hollered in jest.

The vet, Alex Carroll, wearing his customary olive green wax raincoat and rubber boots, was running his hand down the leg of a grey horse, while a young woman held the bridle. He would have preferred to run his hand down her leg instead.

"I think he's just fine," Alex said, looking up at the young rider. "I don't feel any heat in it. But, let me know how he goes today."

"Thank you so much," she said, looking deep into his enchanting blue eyes.

A shining silver goose neck trailer with big red letters spelling out "DORCET STABLES" came down the long drive being pulled by a blazing red, oversized pickup truck.

"Who the hell is that?" Roberta Dutch asked the huntsman, Wilber Kaller.

"The Klingers," said Betsy Drain, Roberta's live-in lover. "They're new. They just bought the old Wright Place. Didn't you know that? Very rich, you know. And very Jewish..."

"Oh, yeah..." Roberta said. "Tacky trailer...don't you think?"

A near vintage drab green Ford pickup truck followed the tacky Klingers up the drive. The bed of the truck had been remodeled to accommodate the hounds. The sides and top were enclosed, except for the circular windows that allowed the hounds to poke their heads out.

It was considered a sacred moment when the hounds arrived for the start of the hunt.

Maude bounded downstairs. She stood watching in the front doorway with Betty as her father followed along on his big black hunter, Chester. The little girl dreamed of the day she would join him.

Wilber Kaller, the professional huntsman, guided the hounds down the gravel drive around the house down toward to barns and the wide, open fields. He took a short brass and copper horn from between the second and third buttons of his pink coat. He spoke to the hounds, half-hollering, calling each by name. Jake Collins was with him, serving as a whipper-in, helping to keep the hounds in order since they were easily distracted.

Behind them, Randal McCrane, cigarette in one hand, was almost casually directing his horse with his other hand on the reins. He was chatting with Ruth Wilcox and Betsy Drain. He reveled in his role.

The rest of the field, which included a former First Lady and an ambassador's wife, were among the seventy or more riders. They all followed dutifully behind.

Soon, they all broke into a trot and were off down the lane.

The riders started to trickle in to the breakfast around two-thirty.

Cynthia Jordon was the first. "I can only take so much of that," she said, taking a sip of her first drink of the day. "I actually prefer horse shows."

Maddie McCrain, the wife of Randy, the master of the hunt, was among the early arrivals along with Franny Collins, whose husband Jake was guiding the hounds. Johnathan, still in his riding breeches, came in and went upstairs to change from the more formal black riding coat to a tweed jacket as he prepared to greet their guests. He removed his spurs, considered a no-no indoors. He stopped quickly to dial Isabelle's number in Georgetown. It rang six times. No answer. He had no idea where the rest of the family was. The party was now gaining momentum.

Claudia and George Jasper came in through the kitchen as most close friends did in the country. She put her purse and dark brown wax raincoat on a chair. She paused to chat with Bertha. Then they proceeded to the front rooms.

Johnathan was just coming down the circular staircase as Rusty Stewart came in the front door.

"Johnathan" he said extending his hand.

"How are you," he said. "Good to see you. Come right in. Can I help you with something?"

Johnathan wasn't necessarily referring to his perfectly fitted Burberry raincoat. He was eyeballing the large leather case Rusty had under his arm. The artist explained, "I came early, or rather I should say on time, but I know that's early for some folks around here. I brought along some of my latest work to show Mrs. Dent."

"Oh," Johnathan said. He hesitated a minute. "Oh, yes, of course. Let me take your coat and get you a drink and we'll have a look."

Johnathan handed the coat to a butler he did not recognize, though it hardly mattered. He knew there were always a number of servants imported for the day for a party like this.

Betty walked into the front hall. "What are you all doing in here? Johnathan have you offered Rusty a drink?"

"Hello darling," he said evenly, thinking about how often she attempted to manage his manners. "He just got here. He brought some things for you to see."

Rusty Stewart pulled out his artwork and leaned the oversized watercolor up against the leather loveseat. He stood back.

The colors were exquisite. And it was so much better than the black and white photocopy. All sorts of pastels: pinks, more pinks, and bright green and rocket blue. The May Day pole was the central attraction and the school was behind up on the hill, with a festive atmosphere just oozing off the paper. Ladies in hats with big bows, men in navy blue blazers.

"You've captured the essence of our event perfectly," Betty gushed. "It's just fabulous, don't you just love it Johnathan?"

"It's magnificent, you have a keen eye Mr. Stewart," Johnathan said. Still, it was difficult to know whether he really liked it or if he was just being polite.

"Now what's going on in here?" Betty heard from the front hall. It was Pauline Howard, ever the proper guest, she would never be more than ten minutes late. Franny and Jake Collins joined them.

"Mr. Stewart's brought along some of his artwork, including the art for the May Day ball."

Pauline extended her hand to him. "Oh how delightful," she said, stopping for a moment to admire the painting.

Pauline stepped aside and Franny extended her hand, too.

"So good to see you again," Jake Collins said to Rusty. It was a greeting that should have worn out years ago. They shook hands and momentarily paused.

"Yes..." Rusty said. "Good to see you, too." And the handshake ended.

Pauline Howard turned. "Oh my, this is lovely. It's just wonderful—Oh, I just can't tell you!" She was bubbling. It was obvious she meant it. "And the colors, oh the colors..."

"Thank you so much Pauline. You must know how much I really appreciate it." he said. "You've always been so supportive."

"Now, what else have you brought?" she asked, getting right to the point and practically unpacking his case. She peeked inside.

"Just a couple of horse and pony portraits," he said, pulling them out.

More riders arrived. Some were joined by their spouses and others came alone. Many of the riders left the horses and the grooms off in the field to make their way home while the owners gathered inside. The fireplaces crackled softly. An air of contentment enveloped the room. The conversation was entirely horse-oriented, with everyone commenting on the magnificent run they had down near Thatcher's Thicket.

Newcomers Daphne and Ariel Klinger, both tanned from their midwinter vacation in Miami, where he managed his real estate empire, had arrived. She had changed into a tweed coat, adorned with a diamond horseshoe pin on the lapel.

"It's beautiful," Cynthia Jordon whispered to a friend. "But it's… new." She said the word "new" with an air of disdain.

Bloody Marys were the drink of the afternoon. A waiter passed a tray of ham biscuits and guests made their way to the dining room for Brunswick Stew and salad. The general rule was to have a small bite to eat, chat a bit, and head home. The hunt breakfast was not to be a long and drawn out affair. Most people would go home, check on the horses, shower, rest a bit, and probably go out to a dinner party of some kind later that evening.

Betty was pleased as she looked around. Everyone seemed happy and comfortable. She prided herself on running an orderly household, and putting on a fun party. She looked around for Johnathan. Most of the guests had departed and she wondered if he had gone upstairs. She hoped not, it would be rude to disappear before everyone left.

The waiters were picking up the dishes and ashtrays. She asked someone, "Has anyone seen Mr. Dent?"

"Yes ma'am, I think he's in the library."

"Thank you," she replied, turning to find him.

She walked across the front hall and opened the right side of the double door, just as Johnathan was saying:

"Yes, well I'll talk to you Monday." And there was a pause...

Then: "Right...me, too." As he replaced the receiver and turned his expression never changed. "Betty, is something wrong? I had to talk with a client."

"No nothing, dear," she said. "I just wanted to know where you were. I hate to see you work on the weekend. Was it something important?"

Well, yes, was his first thought as he visualized Isabelle alone on a Saturday afternoon in Georgetown. "No, not really," he said, putting his arm around her waist and guiding her out of the room.

Pauline Howard was standing alone in the front hall as they came out of the library. She was the last to leave.

"That Rusty is just wonderful," she said, as Johnathan held out her black mink coat for her to slip into. "I am so glad to talk with him. Although I will say, I had to practically tear him away from your friend, Claudia. And I heard Jake Collins ask him to paint one of his show horses. But I have a surprise for you. I commissioned him to do a painting of my grandchild in the leadline at the Upperville Horse Show this year."

"That's wonderful," Betty told her, wondering why she thought she would be so happy about that.

"No, no, no, my dear." she said as if reading her thoughts. She put her hand on Betty's upper arm, "He's agreed to donate that artwork of the May Day Dance to the school. We can sell it at auction the night of the dance. He did that years ago and the school made lots of money. I know...I bought it. I have it hanging in my front room. The money will go to the new library building this year."

"You're kidding. That's wonderful! Oh, what a perfect idea."

"I knew you'd think so," she said somewhat haughtily, as only Pauline Howard could. She was walking toward the front door, then turned for a final word. "But I also want you to know something else. Even though that young artist was talking to me, I could feel a bit of wandering in his attention span now and again. And I want you to know, I caught something, I'm not quite sure what. But I felt some chemistry in the air..."

Johnathan Douglas Dent knew all about chemistry.

His attraction to Isabelle was almost beyond his control. He studied her that first night. Indeed, he couldn't take his eyes off her the first time they met years ago at Pauline Howard's. She had a way of moving effortlessly across a room. And the way she sat on the loveseat next to his wife that night had intrigued him. Johnathan instantly noticed the difference between the two women. Isabelle sank back into the cushions and seemed so relaxed, so at ease, so natural. Her long tan legs were crossed and she wrapped her right foot around her left leg in a position that looked so uncomfortable (Johnathan had since learned of the woman's incredible flexibility no matter which way she contorted her body). Meanwhile, Betty was positioned on the edge of the sofa, knees tightly together, trying not to rumple the cushions, or herself for that matter.

Isabelle was casual, yet elegant. Her clothes clung to her body in what Johnathan thought was the sexiest way he'd ever seen. Actually she preferred the same style clothes Betty had worn for years. But Isabelle's blouses fit perfectly over her square shoulders and hugged her brests. There was just a hint of her taupe lace bra. In the summer, Isabelle often wore a cotton and lace teddy with no bra. Johnathan adored that look more than any other. He went wild when she peeled off her blouse and then took off her lace undershirt over her head. Johnathan longed to pull her to him.

Chemistry.

It wasn't that his life at home was miserable or that his wife didn't understand him—an excuse most men used for their various dalliances. His moments with Isabelle were desperate, as if he couldn't get enough of her. His sex with Betty at home was warm and he certainly cared for her and was singularly devoted to Maude and the boys.

He was torn.

In equal parts.

Chapter 10

Bond Street To Payne's Corner

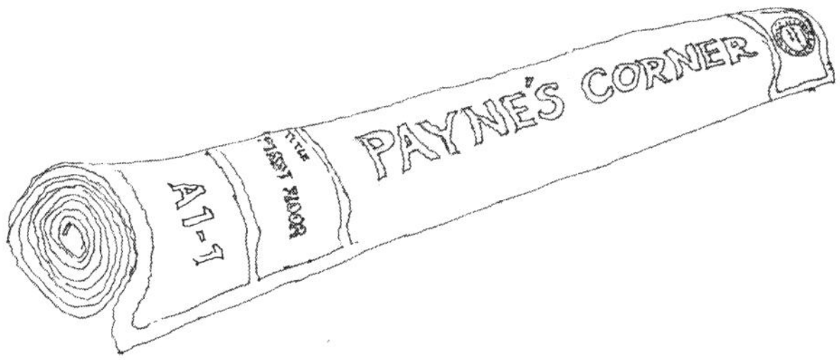

Johnathan shared the plans for Payne's Corner with Isabelle. He wanted her to see the sketches and the blueprints and to hear her opinion on the entire concept. Still, he had not intended to share as much about the development of the project as he did.

Over dinner one night he caught himself saying, "We want to pattern it after an English village and shopping complex. We don't want it to be hokey. And while this really isn't my area of expertise or my job description, I agreed to help see this project through. We're going over to London next month to get more ideas."

"Oh that sounds wonderful," she said, adding innocently, "I've always wanted to go there, I've heard about all the wonderful antique markets. Oh, Johnathan, I'm so jealous."

"But Isabelle...I want you to come along," he said, surprising himself more than it surprised her when the words came out.

"Are you kidding?"

"Of course not," he said leaning over and kissing the small of her neck. There was just one small problem: Betty was already planning to make the trip too.

Johnathan had a hard time concentrating on what Isabelle was talking about. As soon as he told her about London she jumped up from the couch where they were having dinner in her apartment. She went in the other room and came back carrying a file folder.

"Look I've been saving all these travel articles out of the Sunday Times. This one is all about the flea markets in London," she continued, unfolding the yellowing newsprint. "And here's one about Thomas Hardy's cottage in Dorset. I know this doesn't have anything to do with antiques, but the picture of the country roads and the thatched roof looked so neat. Oh, Johnathan, this is wonderful. But how will I get off work? What will I tell Michael?"

"Not to worry," Johnathan lied. "It'll work out." His mind was racing and he didn't have the foggiest notion how he could juggle the two women in his life.

She took the plate from his lap, threw the napkins on the floor, and kissed him. As she leaned over, Johnathan caught a glimpse of that bit of lace and the familiar smell of her summer perfume. . . L'Air du Temps. That was all it took for Johnathan to forget his dilemma.

It was mid-April by the time the details of the London trip were finalized. Betty and the three children were taking off with Johnathan and staying one week. Their TWA flight back to Dulles airport outside of Washington would return eight days later at 4:27 p.m.

Isabelle was going out on the very same TWA plane at 9:00 p.m. later that night.

Johnathan timed it to the minute—seven days with each woman. Equal time. Time with Betty, Maude, and the boys, Johnathan and Douglas.

They saw all the attractions, foremost among them the Tower of London and Buckingham Palace.

"When the flag is flying, it means the Queen is home," he informed his family. He took them to high tea at Brown's Hotel, lunch in the Georgian Room at Harrods, Madam Tussaud's wax museum, and to the theater to see *Cats*. Everyone was smiling as he kissed them goodbye in front of the immigration officers waiting to check their passports.

"I have lots of things to do," he said, explaining why he was staying behind. *Which was mostly true.*

Johnathan arranged a number of business meetings during the day while Isabelle was in London. He tried to schedule them over breakfast as often as possible, so they could spend the afternoons together exploring.

Still his plan got off to a rocky start. Howard Barth was waiting in the lobby of Dorchester Hotel in the Mayfair section of London when Johnathan arrived almost twenty minutes late. Barth had been there a half-hour and some of the bellmen were starting to look him over. He was carrying two bulky briefcases filled with architectural sketches he'd made after ten days of traveling around the countryside getting ideas for the Payne Corner project. He was staying in a bed and breakfast not far from the Dorchester and he and Johnathan decided it would be a good meeting place.

The appointed time had been set for nine-thirty.

"Jesus Howard, I'm sorry," Johnathan said as he approached. The two men shook hands quickly. "I had no idea the traffic would be this bad, we're... uh...I'm staying just around the corner."

"No problem," the other man said, but you could see he was peeved. Howard Barth, like most architects, was thoroughly organized and did not tolerate tardiness—not from his wife, his children, and certainly not from hotshot Washington lawyers used to getting their own way. But now there was nothing he could do about it.

"Why don't we order some coffee and I can show you my sketches?"

"Good idea," Johnathan answered, leading the way.

For the next hour and forty minutes the two men drank three cups of coffee each. Johnathan ate three croissants; Howard had one piece of dry toast. Howard was from Richmond, Virginia and his firm had been chosen by Johnathan's clients to design the homes, offices, and shops. He was a good friend of Johnathan's brother Bob and had done part of their previous project in Norfolk. That was a pavilion on the waterfront that housed a number of both fine and fast-food restaurants. His designs were state of the art, and there was no question he'd be the architect of record for this job. He was extremely qualified, almost born for the project. After all, his mother was British and he spent nearly every summer of his teenage years with her visiting his grandmother in Brighton. He had a sense of the country and it was evident from his designs. As a fellow graduate of the University of Virginia, Johnathan felt close to Howard and liked him, despite his rather persnickety ways.

"This is from a row of shops down in Brighton, which they call The Lanes," he told Johnathan. "Needless to say, the town itself is not what it once was. It's rather seedy now. And when I walked out on the pier I swear it was moving."

"I've never been there," was Johnathan's answer, making a note to cross it off his list of possibilities with Isabelle.

"Now here are some sketches for the restaurants."

"Well, now," Johnathan said. "As far as I know there will only be two."

"Right, I'm well aware of that," Howard answered, adding a bit curtly, "but the development partners need to have more than two drawings from which to choose."

Barth had captured the essence of the English pub perfectly, yet without overdoing it. One of his sketches showed a stone building with a large bay window in the front looking over a stone courtyard with tables and a sign that read "The Wagon and Horses." He drew a white stucco building and called it "The Seven Bells," the sign for which was adorned with seven mounted bells. One establishment was named "The George and Dragon," another "The Swan," and yet another "The Black Rabbit."

The drawings and sketches for the houses and townhouses were charming. The townhouses were attractive and looked like nothing that Johnathan had seen back in the states. So many of the American housing projects looked cookie-cutter institutional, stamped out with little thought toward pleasing aesthetics, green space for children to play, benches, or playgrounds. Howard's drawings had them all. Once Johnathan studied them, he began to realize the Rose Quartz color on the window shutters Howard painted in watercolor brought them to life. He even sketched in the lace curtains everyone in England had in their windows. The window boxes were dripping with vinca, geraniums and petunias. Yes, the windows he chose were just picture-perfect. The bay window had a seat. The railings on the front steps were made of wood, painted white like the steps. Back home, Johnathan thought most builders would simply slap up some cement steps and an iron railing—if even that.

"The colors are great," Johnathan said to him.

"Well, I thought I'd suggest the colors...Northampton Putty, Shelburne Buff, and Yarmouth Blue. I think it's important. And, the window boxes are built in. All you have to do is drop in a metal liner. I've included them on the second floor windows front and back."

"Well it's just flawless. You've done a grand job."

"I'm not finished. They wanted me to have some tentative plans for the second phase. It's supposed to be English, but they want a different look from these. So, I'm going out to Bath for two days to get some ideas there. I'll take an extra day to rest up and do some shopping for my family, then I'll head back to the States."

"Well, I'm sure all the rest of them will be pleased," Johnathan told him as he laid a 20-pound note on the table to pay for the coffee and pastry.

It was close to eleven thirty and Johnathan was anxious to get going now. He had seen the sketches. He liked them. Barth was on the right track, but now he wanted to be on his way.

"Oh, okay," Howard said. "That's it, huh? Well then, I guess we'll get going?"

That was evident, because Johnathan was standing. The other man seemed perplexed at the hasty departure. He had allotted until noon for this meeting. He was almost lost for something to do. Johnathan barely noticed. They shook hands and Johnathan was out the door and into a taxi. He headed to Bond Street; he'd told Isabelle to meet him there in front of the Gucci Store at noon.

He arrived a few minutes early and strolled along the fashionable street. At the largest jewelry store on Bond Street, Garrard, Johnathan bought his sons matching gold cuff links. He knew it was a bit extravagant, but, after all, they were graduating from the Woodberry Forest all-boys boarding school soon and this gift would serve a double purpose. They were simple gold balls that would reverse to gold and royal blue enamel. They were something Johnathan would have picked for himself, so he liked them. He had the lady quickly gift wrap them in small boxes, and stuck them in his suit pocket.

Once outside on the street again, he stopped and gazed in the massive windows at all the antique jewelry and sterling silver centerpieces. A sterling silver desk set caught his eye. There was a blotter, letter opener and a ballpoint pen, displayed ever so elegantly. Maybe the boys would have liked that better, he thought. How often did they wear shirts that required cuff links? It brought to mind how much he didn't know about his sons. But the cuff links were exquisite and he could only hope they'd get some use out of them.

He stood and looked in the windows at the gold and silver jewelry. Maybe he should buy a gift for his wife. Guilt? He knew any piece of jewelry would do for her. Maybe he should go back inside and look. That had been stupid. He knew she'd love anything he gave her, particularly since the store had the royal seal— the Queen's logo and the words "By appointment to her Majesty the Queen." Translation: "The Queen Shops HERE." The store had received quite a bit of publicity just last year when Lady Diana received her sapphire engagement ring from this very same jeweler.

Johnathan gazed in the windows at Gucci. Betty might like a new purse, he thought. But no, she could get that back home. He wanted it to be something from England.

He was gazing at the shoes and purses when he caught a faint whiff of that familiar perfume... He turned, and there was Isabelle.

She said simply, "Hi." They didn't greet with a kiss. Even though they were far from home they were mutually conscious of public displays of affection. Their eyes caught and froze for a fleeting moment. Then, they turned, without further conversation and continued up Bond Street.

They were at the end when something on the other side of the street caught Johnathan's eye. It was a painting of a horse and rider. The shop, Arthur Ackerman, was a bit imposing. They rang a buzzer to enter. Once inside, they appeared to be the only customers. It was very still and dark, except for the discreet picture lights over the oil paintings. You could hear yourself breathe. A salesman in an exquisitely tailored double-vented suit approached.

"Are you looking for anything in particular, sir?" he said in a rather haughty tone.

"Well, uh...not really," Johnathan answered. He noticed the antique paintings of horses and hounds did not have any price tags. He started to walk around and look, and then he noticed another painting in the next room. There was a large fat bay horse standing in a stall. He moved toward it.

The salesman moved with him.

The painting was of a large draft horse. He had a white stripe on his face and two white stockings behind. Johnathan couldn't make out the signature of the artist on the lower left hand corner.

"It's a Sartorius, sir," the salesman explained.

Johnathan was familiar with his work. John Nott Sartorius was the son of

Francis Sartorius and was the most prolific painter in the family, well known for his many horse paintings. Johnathan had seen one at Pauline Howard's, a racehorse crossing the finish line at an English course.

But this painting intrigued Johnathan. At first glance, he thought the horse was standing in his stall, but upon closer examination, he saw that the horse was in front of a barn. He was an imposing looking animal.

"I assume, sir that you are familiar with his work," the salesman said, not waiting for an answer. He wanted to inform Johnathan, without Johnathan having to admit to any lack of knowledge. Johnathan was aware of this.

"John Sartorius had a number of well-known patrons, sir. The Prince of Wales, the Earl of Derby, Lord Foley, and Charles James Fox. He also exhibited at the Royal Academy, the Free Society, and the Society of the Artists."

Johnathan didn't want to commit to anything. He was sure the price would be astronomical. "Very interesting," was all he would say.

"We have some others over here sir," the salesman gently noted as he walked around the room. "If you and the Mrs. like the draft horse types, here we have a shire horse in a landscape inscribed 'Hereford 1886'. This one is signed and dated W. A. Clark 1911."

"Well," Johnathan did admit. "I'm not really looking for any particular painting. And I am not particularly looking for draft horses."

"Very well, sir. But do take your time and have a look."

There were other very respectable paintings. One, a primitive study of a gentleman on his horse, unsigned. And another of a grey carriage horse. But Johnathan was still enamored with the big bay. He also took his time.

He glanced back for one more look, and then returned to the front room with the salesman. He was almost to the front door, when he decided to ask.

"By the way, what is the price on that painting?"

"Six thousand pounds, sir."

"If you like him dear, why don't you buy him," Isabelle said with just a bit of a smirk on her face. It was the first time she had spoken since they entered the shop. But that was all it took for Johnathan. He had to have it.

He would hang it in his office. Twenty minutes later, the transaction was complete. He wrote a personal check, arranged for the shipping and was told his painting would arrive within two weeks.

Back along Bond Street, they got sidetracked and looked in the window of another jewelry store. This one was called Hancock. It had antique jewelry in the windows, including some of those crystals they had just seen up the street. Johnathan, now familiar with the protocol, approached, buzzed and entered.

Again, they were the only customers in the small shop. He was head-on with the display cases and had nowhere to turn. The ever-present salesman approached. They all seemed to be the same after a few hours of shopping... discreet, yet eager. Johnathan knew he had indulged himself with the painting, and now more than anything he wanted to buy something very special for the beautiful woman with him.

"Can I show you something, sir?" the man asked.

"Well, I'm not sure."

"Very well then, sir. Do have a look around."

Something immediately caught his eye. Isabelle had taken a seat in front of one of the antique showcases. The salesman instinctively pulled out a number of stickpins.

"These are something unique to England, sir, antique crystal stickpins." He put three of them on a dark blue velvet pillow. One of the three was a liquid pink rose in full bloom. Isabelle looked at them as the salesman explained. Johnathan listened with her.

"Each piece is an original work of art. The crystal is etched in reverse, then hand-painted. This one is about eight millimeters across. The history of this art goes back to the era of Queen Victoria, when many a beautiful carving was borne of a royal commission. Today the same procedures are followed as were used by Thomas Cook and other pioneers of the craft."

Johnathan was watching Isabelle as she listened intently. He knew he would buy it for her, no matter the price.

The salesman continued, "Only the purest form of quartz can be used. It's found in Brazil and Madagascar. After a flawless piece is cut, it's carefully polished before the artist applies his imagination. The drilling and carving takes months. The coloring process is next. They have to use needle-fine paint brushes for each layer of highlight. Then the crystal is finished and is placed over a thin piece of mother of pearl and set in an eighteen carat gold frame."

The rose inside was beyond full bloom. It was open to its fullest, just the point of the petals dropping off, but not quite.

"The detail is exquisite, sir," the salesman noted.

Johnathan agreed. The color wasn't red, but an intensely potent pink.

"Any woman would adore this sir," he said looking at Isabelle.

"You are so right," Johnathan answered, handing the man his American Express card. He leaned over and stroked Isabelle's cheek with the palm of his hand and whispered to her, "Something to remember our trip to London."

It was the first gift he ever gave her.

She showed her appreciation for it later that afternoon. And they ordered room service for dinner.

She also wanted to give him something to remember their trip to London.

"It's just amazing to me Johnathan, how you've gotten everything accomplished in such a short time. All the permits, the designs and then the matter of the drain fields..."

A buzz interrupted the conversation taking place in Johnathan's Washington, D.C., law office.

He picked up the telephone intercom and his secretary told him, "Mrs. Dent is on the line. She said she has a quick question before she leaves home and for me not to interrupt if you're too busy."

"That's all right, Miss Wickwire, I'll take it," he pressed the blinking button. "Betty..."

"I just talked to Michael Aldridge's office and they're sending over some carpet samples. I wanted to ask you to bring them with you this afternoon."

"Bring them where?"

"To your office, dear. A runner will drop them off before you leave, and you can bring them when I meet you later."

"Oh, I see. Well, Sam Blackwell and I were just going over some last minute details and we'll be on our way. I'll see you there. Drive carefully." After years of marriage, it was his way of telling her he couldn't chat. She understood.

The past eight-and-a-half months were hectic for Johnathan. He was in complete command of the development project in what Virginians called the "central Piedmont region" near Culpeper. He hired a number of assistants, among them...Isabelle. She was in charge of decorating the model homes and townhouses. When Betty had seen the sketches, she in turn decided that she needed to "freshen up" her own kitchen, mud room, guest bath, and part of the dining room. It was too much for Johnathan, with his mistress now working with his wife. He adopted a certain mind set.

He compartmentalized everything.

First, there was the Isabelle he knew intimately. The Isabelle who was standing demurely in his kitchen in Middleburg, when he arrived home for dinner one night. He saw the ever so slight smile on her face when his wife announced, "Johnathan, I liked Isabelle's plans for your project so much I asked her to come out and give us some ideas to freshen up the kitchen."

"Sounds lovely, dear," he answered, taking quick leave and begging off to the other room with work he'd brought home.

He sat in his library thinking about his wife and his mistress out in the kitchen examining fabric samples. He didn't know what to think. He poured himself a drink. Things were getting complicated.

Payne's Corner proved to be Johnathan's most challenging project. Preservationists engaged in a much-publicized battle over the use of the land. It seemed that an area not far from this site had been one of the more important cavalry battles in the Civil War. A group had been formed to oppose the development and there was a morass of litigation soon to follow.

In the end, Johnathan Dent prevailed, but it hadn't been easy. Even his old friend George Jasper, the columnist for the *Washington Post*, was critical of the project in a lengthy op-ed piece on the history of Payne's Corner. He had ended his piece by saying *"Sites such as this are important for future generations. We must preserve our heritage, because if this generation doesn't, who will?"*

But Johnathan's brother Bob, ever the marketing and advertising genius, helped him turn it around. Once all the permits were in place, they launched their own public relations campaign through Bob's offices in Richmond. They decided to turn the negative into a positive with their campaign: *"Preserve a piece of Virginia's Heritage as your own at Payne's Corner".* The advertisements appeared in slick magazines all over Virginia and Washington, D.C., and in the *Washington Post*, the *Richmond Times* and the Charlottesville *Daily Progress*. Johnathan Dent's name was in all the papers. He now had what his brother called, "name recognition." The highly publicized ground-breaking ceremonies were scheduled for this afternoon, with a lavish, catered hunt tea following the ceremonies.

Johnathan and Sam Blackwell, the majority stockholder in Payne's Corner, made the eighty-minute trip together. Isabelle and Michael Aldridge were there as the decorators of record. Betty and daughter Maude drove down together. Jake Collins and his wife Franny, Betty's best friend attended, because Johnathan had hired him as to consult on the equestrian facilities.

As the final event of the day, Jake was scheduled to parade his horses and foxhounds up through the field and past the party tent. Steve Moffett, the tennis pro at the club in Middleburg, currently ranked number one in the Mid-Atlantic region, was tennis consultant for the project. The top attorneys from Johnathan's law firm traveled by limousine and a number of other guests including the local council members who had eventually approved the project were on hand. About one-hundred-seventy-five people gathered.

The final coup was to be the guest speaker. Somehow Bob Dent dug up a distant cousin of J. E. B. Stuart, commander of the cavalry that claimed victory at Payne's Corner. He was to speak on "The Future of Our Past" or "The Past is Our Future."

Damn, Johnathan thought as he and Sam now eased onto Route 29 heading south toward Culpeper, *that brother of mine did good.*

It was a gorgeous late August day, warm, but not blistering hot, as it could be this time of year. For that, he was thankful.

Once off the highway, Sam's sleek black Jaguar eased onto the secondary road that led to Payne's Corner. It was two lanes through lush farmland. An infrequent large old brick home would pop out of the countryside from time to time, but mostly it was farmland—expansive open fields filled with row after row of billowing corn stalks. Johnathan went over the afternoon's activities with Sam. They had become good friends as well as business associates and Johnathan had learned to regard and admire the man. This development at Payne's Corner was just one of five different projects he had in progress, all in various stages of completion.

The shimmering green fields stretched out for miles and the luxury car handled the gentle hills effortlessly. They came up over the last small ridge and edged into the area of Payne's Corner. There was a small corner store just on the right, a white wooden clapboard structure with a five-foot-high Coca-Cola sign on the edge of the road that read: "Payne's Store."

There were two working gas pumps out front and six steps up to the creaky wooden porch. The store was dark inside, offering everything from work boots and khaki pants to homemade sandwiches and, of course, ice-cold Coca-Cola in six-ounce, green glass bottles. In fact, all the "sodas"—as the local people called soft drinks—sold here were in glass bottles. The "drink box" had a bottle opener on the side of it. Johnathan loved the old store and hoped the owners would do well as new people moved into the area.

A few yards past the store was a battered wooden trestle bridge that crossed Nelson Creek. This had been a source of contention for the local activists opposed to the project. They wanted the bridge to remain untouched, just the way it had been when Union and Rebel forces lost hundreds of men trying to cross it so many years before. Finally, Sam Blackwell relented, agreeing to leave the bridge alone and add several roads and a new structure 500 yards away to handle the traffic heading to Payne's Crossing. Sam and Johnathan said nothing as they crossed what the locals called "Payne's Bridge."

Payne's Corner came into view, just past the old bridge on the left. Mile after mile of new fencing, made to look old, had been installed. Old-fashioned, split-rail, snake fences had been put up around the perimeter of the four-hundred-eighty-seven acres. It was made to resemble the old fences from the Civil War era. The topography of the land had been altered to accommodate the houses, shops, and restaurants that would soon be built.

The entrance was redesigned with a three-foot-high dry stone wall, the kind with large stones stacked evenly one on top of another. A small unobtrusive navy blue sign with white lettering was mounted on the right side of the entrance and read: PAYNE'S CORNER. There were purposely no other large commercial-type "For Sale" signs. This was an intentional marketing ploy, and yet another idea from Bob Dent, who explained, *"This is an exclusive community, we don't want just everyone with ears driving in here off the road. We've got to Gucci-ize this product. These homes are going to start at $450,000 for a townhouse for Christ's sake. Let's do it up right."*

The dedication proceeded just as planned, to the minute. Bob Dent's agenda and the entire ceremony was scheduled to end at five o'clock. It was, in fact, five-ten by the time the speeches were finished and the guests slowly flowed into a vast blue and white tent erected for the reception.

A group of country and western musicians played in one corner of the tent. Blue and white flowers were on the four oversized round tables in each corner, each draped in red and white checked cloths. At one table, cheeses and fruits were displayed on antique-looking cutting boards in three tiers. The second table had meats with the main attraction being home-cured ham. *"We want to keep the old Virginia flavor for this party,"* Bob Dent had instructed the caterers. A black waiter was stationed at this table to hand carve the meats. He was clad in all white, with a long white apron and tall chefs hat. The third table was overflowing with desserts featuring Virginia Apple Betty and homemade vanilla ice cream. Two full service bars decorated like the antique split-rail fence flanked each end of the tent. The bartenders were serving wine from a local vineyard, but most people were ordering bourbon or vodka.

"Daddy you were great," Maude said after her father finished greeting the guests.

"Thank you darling," he said kissing her on the cheek.

Betty was now at his side and also giving him a kiss. "It was nice," she said simply.

A number of people approached Johnathan, shook his hand, and made comments. Three attractive girls in their early twenties—models Bob hired from a Richmond agency—roamed the tent, wearing navy blue linen dresses, with white sashes. Each had an armful of slick brochures. On the cover, the image of a gallant cavalry officer, and above, in embossed navy blue letters the words, *Payne's Corner*. Below the rider was the phrase, *"A piece of Virginia's heritage."* It was each girl's duty to see that all the guests received a brochure and to point them toward the food and drink.

Johnathan watched Isabelle on the other side of the tent while he listened to one of the local council members discuss the possibility of a late summer drought: *"We"re just about even with last year's rainfall..."*

She was wearing a beige linen dress. It was straight and longer than what she usually preferred. It came to about mid-calf, but from the knee down there were kick pleats. She wore white stockings and matching beige shoes. A small coordinating purse hung on a long chain over her left shoulder. Three long strings of faux pearls hung around her neck and she wore her signature headband of beige grosgrain ribbon. Her hair hung loosely over her shoulders. She glanced his way while chatting with someone Johnathan didn't recognize.

"...if the weather continues as it has all summer we'll be all right." the man with Johnathan continued.

Sam approached. "It seems as if we can call this a success," he said to both men.

"Indeed," the politician/farmer agreed.

Johnathan felt obligated to introduce the two men. At a loss for the politician's name he began, "Sam Blackwell, I don't believe you two know each other."

Sam extended his hand "How are you?...Sam Blackwell."

The man reciprocated, "Gary Durden...nice to know you."

Johnathan added, "Gary's a member of the local council that passed this project Sam. We wouldn't be here without him."

He blushed a bit. These men didn't know that Gary Durden's lifelong friend was one of the four people selling out to the developers. "Well, now Mr. Blackwell, Mr. Dent here did a fine job. He did his homework well. We all have faith it will be a beneficial project. It had to happen sooner or later. Mr. Dent was very calm and diplomatic with his dealings with us, not at all pushy, like some can be. Why he'd make a great politician himself."

"Well, you know Mr. Durden, we've been thinking that ourselves. It's something I've been wanting to discuss with you Johnathan."

Ugh. Johnathan was watching Isabelle. She was leaving with Michael Aldridge. He wasn't going to get to say good-bye to her. *Oh well,* he would talk to her tomorrow. He wasn't paying full attention here. *What did Sam say... something about wanting to discuss something. Did he say the word...politician?*

A short staccato of a hunting horn in the distance signaled the hounds were approaching for the grand finale, Johnathan was straining to pay attention to the conversation, while watching Isabelle leave and at the same time trying to feign interest in Jake Collins equestrian exhibition as horses and hounds galloped up the field and toward the tent.

The three men turned to watch. Jake, in full scarlet regalia, was on a large bay horse leading the field with the hounds in front. He knew all the hounds by name. He was standing in the stirrups, cracking the whip. The rest of the riders, about a dozen or more, all wore black and navy blue jackets. A mutual friend and neighbor, Holly Hawk, was riding sidesaddle. She was one of those snobby types who thought riding to hounds was so chic. Jake had once said of her that, "she couldn't ride in a box car with both doors shut." *It was a good thing they weren't galloping at full tilt today,* thought Johnathan.

As the group moved closer to the tent they slowed down, first to a trot, and then to a walk. They were all gathered in a bunch, almost like a rugby scrum. Jake brought the hounds up to the tent so everyone could see them. They were a rare English breed, very tall and of a regal red color. The other riders watched Jake herd the hounds, like cows.

He cracked the whip with a *swish-crack.* "Bess, Angie, whoa, now."

Johnathan felt he should approach Jake and thank him for his marvelous exhibition. He was just excusing himself from the other men, when all hell broke loose. Johnathan remembered that the band had stopped playing "Sitting By the Dock of the Bay" and there seemed to be a split second of silence. He heard a shriek across the tent as half the pack of hounds broke loose from Jake's holding pattern. Three of them instantly made their way to the carving table and one leaped on top. He started to devour the home cured ham, eating it up as quickly as he could. The hounds were everywhere. Women were screaming and one little boy—no more than six years old—was crying, clinging tightly to his mother's leg.

Johnathan caught a quick glimpse of Maude, who was laughing uncontrollably and pointing at one hound who was taking care of business right in front of the band. Of course, every other hound was lifting his leg, marking the table or chair or whatever was available. Hounds did this every chance they got.

Bob Dent was in a frenzy and immediately commanded Jake to get off his horse and *"Get these hounds under control!"* It was lucky he hadn't said *"Get these goddamn hounds under control!"* But Bob was thinking about all the press people on hand, who, by now, were having a field day. The cameras were running nonstop, clicking and whirling.

Jake Collins jumped off his horse and flipped the reins over his head to ground tie him. He made six easy strides to the middle of the tent. Like a circus ringmaster, he stood on a white chair in the middle of the tent and cracked his long English hunting whip in the air. "*Wup, wup,*" he said sharply two times. Within fifteen seconds, the six hounds were sitting at the base of his chair, looking up at him. It was magic. "Whoa now, pups. Here, here." he said, stepping down from the chair. He walked slowly out of the tent, the whip dragging behind him, and the six hounds all in a single-file, military-style parade. The entire gathering was in awe.

"Here, here!" said one of the onlookers, raising his glass of Virginia wine.

"Here, here!" the other guests joined in. One lady plopped down on a chair, still shaking.

"A toast to our huntsman, a job well done!"

And the guests broke out in applause.

"More wine for everyone!" Bob Dent announced. His face was by now a flush somewhere between rose quartz, fuchsia, and magenta.

The throng of reporters and photographers had followed Jake out of the tent. The hounds were now waiting for their next instructions. Jake returned to remount his horse. The reporters surrounded him, barking out questions about his background with horses. It was like a scene on the courtroom steps following a major verdict.

"Where did you learn to ride, sir?" one asked.

"How old are you?"

"How do you spell your name? Where are you from?"

They were frantically writing on their narrow steno pads when Bob Dent saw an opportune moment. "Why don't we let Mr. Collins take the horses and hounds back to the vans and he can return to the tent for a brief press conference," he instructed the swarming members of the press. "I think everyone could use a drink."

Leave it to my brother to figure a graceful resolution to this disaster, Johnathan thought.

The next morning, a three column wide photo of Jake Collins standing on the chair in full riding attire with the six hounds gathered around him—their noses in the air and their deep, dark eyes looking up at him—appeared on the front page of the *Washington Post.*

The caption read: *Master horseman Jake Collins saved the day—and the ham—at the ground-breaking ceremonies of the historic Payne's Corner development yesterday near Culpeper. Details page D3.*

The photo would do wonders for Jake Collins's equestrian career. Not since Civil War times had more attention been focused on Payne's Corner, and this time without a single drop of blood having been spilled.

It was the best publicity money could buy, thought Bob Dent as he reviewed the stack of press clippings.

Yes indeed, the best publicity money could buy.

Johnathan considered it a miracle they came out of the hound disaster unscathed. He thought it would doom the project and that an avalanche of negative publicity would follow. Instead, the media had some fun with the story, and no harm was done.

Bob Dent's Richmond advertising and public relations business was swamped with telephone calls from writers wanting to tour Payne's Corner. The development was written up in the *Wall Street Journal* and as a result, five of the most expensive pieces of property were sold. A three-acre site, without a house on it, was purchased sight unseen for more than $700,000. Still, the hound episode marked one the few times in his life Johnathan Dent felt helpless. He prided himself on being in control. He had been this way since his father died when he was ten years old. He told himself he wouldn't cry at the funeral and he didn't. His mother, whom he adored, congratulated him for being so strong. From that moment on, he worked hard at hiding his emotions. He also worked hard at making money.

After his father's death, his family's financial position deteriorated badly. They weren't poor, but every penny counted.

His grandmother would tease him. "Johnathan, I want you to grow up and become a rich lawyer AND marry a rich girl." He always remembered those words.

It was no accident when he met and married Elizabeth Crane.

CHAPTER 11

A Novel Idea

Throughout high school in Richmond, Johnathan studied hard to get good grades. He had a one-track mind when it came to college. It would be the University of Virginia, or nothing at all. Once he completed the essays and sent in the application, he rushed home day after day and week after week to see if there was any news in the mail. When the letter finally did arrive in mid-April, his hands were shaking so much he could hardly open the envelope.

He sat down at the kitchen table and tore it open. He knew immediately it was welcome news.

He thrived at the University and never minded the strict dress code that required men to wear a jacket and tie to all classes. He cultivated a number of friends, male and female, and managed to do well enough in class to make the dean's list after his sophomore year. One of his earliest acquaintances was Raymond Curtis, who lived down the hall in their freshman dorm. They were fast buddies from the time they were "first-year men" in Charlottesville.

One weekend, Ray Curtis invited Johnathan to visit his family in Middleburg. That first visit to the area made an enduring impression. The Curtis home was vast and welcoming. Family photographs covered the tables; luxurious draperies hung from floor to ceiling ; needlepoint rugs and needlepoint pillows accented the rooms.

Yes, Johnathan told himself, *this is the way to live, with a lot of hard work and little bit of luck.*

Johnathan and Ray became best friends. They studied together, double-dated together, and traveled in tandem. One summer they drove cross-country to California and had a grand time sightseeing and meeting pretty girls.

In the fall of his senior year, Johnathan discovered a sure-fire method to meet the girl of his dreams. He and Ray went to a party and met some girls at the Farmington Hunt Club. Later that night, Ray mentioned something that sparked an interest in Johnathan.

"That was a fine group of girls Johnathan, old buddy," Ray said.

"Yeah, not bad," said Johnathan, who was driving the car back along the country road outside of Charlottesville.

"No, no...you don't understand," he restated. "I mean they were *fine girls*. The kind your mother wants you to marry."

"What do you mean?" Johnathan asked.

"Well, you know I recognized one of the names. The girl...Crane. Very well-to-do, if you know what I mean?"

"What do you mean?" Johnathan asked again.

"I remember when her daddy died, it was in the paper. My mother always reads the obituaries. She said, that so-and-so Crane, you know I can't remember his first name. Well...this guy Crane, when he died my mother told me he had only one daughter. I remember she told me the girl went to school in Washington. I'll just bet that's her. Her family donated lots of money to the National Gallery in Washington. You know the Crane Wing?"

"Oh, come on, there are lots of girls with that name."

"But I can tell, old buddy. I can tell. And I'll tell you what. When we go home to Middleburg next weekend, I know how to find out."

"Okay. How?"

"We can look her name up in the Blue Book. For sure, it'll be listed in there."

"What the hell is the Blue Book?" Johnathan asked as they were coming up on the outskirts of town. They were right in the area called Pantops.

"Want to stop for a burger at The White Spot?"

"Sure."

"But before we get there. Tell me, what's the Blue Book?"

"Oh, that. Well, it's a society register. No, I think they call it the 'Social Register.' Anyone who's anyone is listed in it. That girl Crane will be listed under her mother's name. Even if her father has died, her mother will be listed. The children are all listed until they finish college. We can look it up."

"Sounds like an intriguing idea," Johnathan said, parking the car at the all night hamburger joint.

The Blue Book never left Johnathan's thoughts for the next week. He didn't want his friend to know that he was anxious to glean the financial and ancestral lineage of potential girlfriends. So he decided to file the information away and use it at the right moment.

He went to the Alderman library and looked up "Blue Book" and "The Blue Book" and "Social Register" in the card catalogue.

Nothing.

But Johnathan had another idea when he visited Ray a few weeks later. It was late one lazy Saturday afternoon and everyone in the house was either taking a nap or out on a long walk. Johnathan stayed behind.

"I have some reading to catch up on," he said. "I think I'll just go into the library and read for a while if that's okay with you Ray?"

"Sure," he said, "I'm going to take the dogs for a walk."

As soon as Johnathan was sure he was alone, he began his search in the library. All four walls were lined floor to ceiling with books.

Well now, this can't be too difficult, Johnathan thought. *The Blue Book...it's got to be here somewhere.*

Johnathan's search in the stacks told him a lot about the Curtis family. There was a complete set of Charles Dickens bound in red leather. Then a vast array of what Johnathan knew must have been Book of the Month Club editions of Somerset Maugham, Ernest Hemingway, and Rudyard Kipling. Then a selection of cookbooks.

Cookbooks, Johnathan thought, *they don't belong in a library. The Joy of Cooking, The Middleburg Life Cookbook, The Way to a Man's Heart, Complete Curry...*

There was of course, the Encyclopedia Britannica. And three full rows of books on horses and foxhunting: *Hounds and Hunting through the Ages*, *The Will to Win*, and a book by Dick Francis called *The Sport of Kings*.

Suddenly the telephone rang. It startled Johnathan. It rang three times... four times...five times.

Wasn't anyone going to answer it?

Six times. Johnathan decided to pick up. After all, everyone was either outside or asleep and he didn't want them disturbed.

"Curtis residence," he said, thinking quickly. He didn't want any caller to think he was presumptuous enough to answer the telephone with a simple "Hello."

"Ah yes," said a deep British voice, "Gary Noble here. Is Mr. Curtis available?"

"I'm sorry sir, Mr. Curtis is unavailable right now. Can I take a message?"

`"Why yes, you can. Would you be so kind as to tell him I phoned. I was wondering if he'd like to play tennis tomorrow afternoon."

"Yes, yes, of course. I'll give him the message Mr. uh..."

"Noble."

"Noble. Right. I'll give him the message sir. Certainly. Thank you."

And the caller hung up.

Without even a "By your leave" thought Johnathan. *He probably assumed I was the butler. Oh well,* he thought *I'll write it down, so I don't forget. Now where can I find something to write on?*

He opened the drawer of the small telephone table. Surely there would be a pencil and paper in there.

Oh yes, here it is, a simple white note pad and perfectly sharpened number two pencil...

And also a copy of the small local telephone book, which always amazed Johnathan—it was only about five by seven inches—and a small leather bound book with red letters with the title....

Well what do you know, Johnathan said to himself. *The Blue Book. Why on earth would they call it that? Why don't they all it The Black Book?*

He picked up the hardbound *Social Register.* He noticed it was a few years old. He began to thumb through the pages.

"*Well, now,*" he said almost aloud. *Crane...that would be under "C."*

He spent the rest of the afternoon taking notes from the Blue Book.

It listed her late father's business address in New York at 200 East 72nd Street and the name of his business, REH, Inc. (After a few more trips to the library, Johnathan would later discover from the Dun & Bradstreet directory that REH Real Estate Holdings, Inc. had assets of over $20 million.)

Johnathan also learned that Douglas McClain Crane was a graduate of Columbia University and had belonged to a number of exclusive clubs, including the New York Athletic Club, the Knickerbocker Club, and the Union Club in New York, as well as the Green Boundary Club in South Carolina and the Jupiter Island Club in Hobe Sound.

Mrs. Douglas Crane served on the board of directors of the Kip's Bay Boys House, the Ladies Committee of the National Horse Show Association, and evidently had not attended college.

Elizabeth Laura Crane was listed, too. Right below her mother's name it said in italic letters: *at Marymount College, Washington, D.C.*

So, she was the only child of a very well-to-do family.

Yes indeed, Johnathan would have to give Elizabeth Laura Crane a telephone call...very soon.

The sooner, the better.

Chapter 12

Politicians, Tycoons, Media Stars & Sports Aficionados

The Payne's Corner project was well under way and Johnathan's daily involvement continued. He was on the phone with Sam Blackwell about some legal aspect or another two or three times every day.

"This is giving me an ulcer Johnathan," Sam began one Monday morning on the phone, before even saying hello. Johnathan had just arrived at the office. It wasn't even nine o'clock yet.

Miss Wickwire entered as he stood talking. She handed him coffee in a china cup and saucer, with the exact amount of cream she knew he liked. She left the office briefly.

"What's up?" Johnathan asked, sipping the coffee. Still standing, he moved behind the massive desk.

"These goddamn well drillers, it's taking forever. They told me last night we're going to have to relocate one of the two wells. It just isn't working. Some of these houses are ready to be hooked up and this holds up everyone. What does their contract say? I don't have a copy of it. Is there a completion date set? Any kind of limit? What can we do to get them to move faster? Seems like some of these rednecks move like goddamn molasses."

He was rambling now. But Johnathan knew he was angry. This was not a man who normally cursed.

Johnathan needed to hold his hand. "Where are you now?"

"I'm in the goddamn Madison Motel. It's a goddamn flea bag."

"Well, let me..."

"It takes these people forever to make a long-distance phone call here, I can't even dial it direct."

"Now, listen, Sam...get a hold here. I'm going to have Miss Wickwire look up the well drilling contracts. I can't—"

"How long will that be?"

"I don't know, you have to tell me the name of the firm. I can't remember who you contracted to do the drilling. What is their name?"

"Blue Ridge."

"Blue Ridge what?"

"Uh...the Blue Ridge Drilling Company, they're out of Hornchurch. See what you can do, would you Johnathan? We've got to light a bomb under these people. And this one guy, the head man, he's like a bull—what he doesn't break up he messes on. The place is a disaster."

"Okay," Johnathan said, "I'll call you back as soon as I can."

What a way to start the week.

Johnathan glanced down at the day's agenda. He wrote a note in the margin: "Blue Ridge Drilling."

Staff meeting at ten. That would last until God...

The intercom buzzed, again it was his secretary. "Miss Stoker is on line four." He took the call.

"Hi," she said.

Johnathan wished he could be as happy as she seemed. She called him each Monday morning before their weekly staff meetings. She was so faithful that it worried him at times. *Maybe it was guilt*, he thought momentarily. *After all, what kind of a life could this be for her? But then again . . . she seemed happy.*

"How are you doing?" he asked.

"Well, we're getting in lots of boxes of paint and wallpaper. It's stacked almost to the ceiling in the back room. The UPS man just came with more. When are we going to be able to get in to do all this work?"

She was singing the same song. *This project was more than anyone had bargained for*, Johnathan thought. *First Sam, bitching about the drilling. And now Isabelle, who had been contracted to decorate the models.*

"Gee, I don't know," Johnathan answered as noncommittally as possible. "Soon I hope, how was your weekend?"

"Great," she said, upbeat as ever. "I had some friends for dinner Sunday night, a great new chicken with sour cream recipe. Can't wait to make it for you."

She never told Johnathan whom she entertained. It was always "some friends." From time to time he wondered if there was another man or maybe several other men? But deep in his heart, he knew better. He knew he was the only man in her life. She was deeply devoted and he felt as devoted to her as possible. This was her way of asking the simple question "Will I see you on Wednesday?"

And he would always reply, as he did on this Monday, "It sounds wonderful. I'll bring the wine."

"Super, what time?"

"About sixish, but it might be later. We're swamped with work."

"Okay, whatever. I'll see you then."

Johnathan looked at his watch. *Damn, it's after ten.* He was late for the meeting.

The session offered little that was new or exciting. Each partner reported on the status of their cases. It was the usual mix of divorces, business settlements, real estate transactions, one ongoing case involving alleged unpaid income tax due to the IRS, and the most pressing case a $6 million medical malpractice suit that was three days away from the statute of limitations. There was a mountain of papers to be organized and it looked as if they would meet the deadline. The meeting broke up at eleven-twenty.

It was eleven-thirty by the time Johnathan returned to his office. The morning was all but shot. He hadn't even glanced at the mail.

"Any calls Miss Wickwire," he said on the intercom.

"Only Mr. Blackwell, sir."

Oh no, he still hadn't looked into the drilling company.

"Miss Wickwire, can you come in here a minute, please."

She entered quietly and gently shut the door. She stopped to straighten the pillows on the couch.

She was a lovely lady. More to Johnathan than a secretary, she was his right hand. She was in her late-thirties, divorced, with two teenagers. He was lucky. Most could not, or would not, put up with his demanding life. She often offered to bring his lunch, pick up gifts, even take deposits to the bank.

If she had a clue as to his relationship with Isabelle, she never acknowledged it. She was very attractive, ever so slim and always wore straight skirts. Her hip bones were wide and high, Johnathan had noticed this and fantasized about the possibility of a fling some years back. That was before he met Isabelle.

His mind drifted to the many women he had known. He was proud that he had been so adept at precisely matching the woman to the moment. He considered it a feat of discipline, though some would argue this point vehemently. Betty Crane was the perfect choice. He aspired to the grand lifestyle to which she was accustomed. He had done his homework. Once he started to date her, he was discreet yet continued to see a number of other girls throughout their courtship. He would drop Betty off at eleven p.m., then go on another date. Johnathan called those post-midnight adventures "real dates" with a number of eye-catching girls who were more than willing to indulge him in the greatest of pleasures, as often as he desired.

But, he was cautious. As he was with Thelma Wickwire, his secretary now standing before him. He had caught himself and thought twice about it. *Yes*, he told himself, *he had discipline*. She was more valuable to him as a secretary then as a lover.

"I need you to look up the details of a contract we have for the Payne's Corner project. It would be with...let me see," he was trying to find his notes. "Oh, here it is. Blue Ridge Drilling. I can barely read my own writing. It seems there are some problems. I need to know if there's a completion clause, any penalties for delays, etc. They told Sam they were going to have to re-drill somewhere else and he's having a fit. Also, see if you can find a copy of the geological survey."

"Well, then," she said. "I'll call him back and tell him we're still going over it. I think that would help. He sounds very anxious."

"Oh, that would be a great help."

"Is that it then?"

"Not unless you have any other messages."

'No, you do know you have a twelve-thirty lunch date at Duke Zeibert's with your brother?"

"My brother? Oh, hell, how could I forget? Monday. Right, right." With that he popped up from his chair, signaling to Miss Wickwire that their meeting was adjourned for now. She left the room as he went into his private bathroom to freshen up for his lunch date.

It was a long three blocks down Connecticut Avenue to Duke's, one of the most popular spots for a power lunch in a town famous for them. The affable owner, Duke Zeibert, a former waiter with a penchant for pretty girls and the ponies, was well known to everyone in town...politicians, corporate tycoons, media stars, and especially sports aficionados.

He was always at the front door to greet people, mentally assigning the tables and thus doling out the guest's importance, at least for the day. He did not take reservations, so it was of utmost importance to be prompt, if not a bit early for the first of the two lunch seatings.

Johnathan and Duke had known each other for years and shared a mutual passion for the local pro football team, the Washington Redskins. In fact, as Johnathan entered, he spotted the team owner at one of the front tables where Duke always parked his preferred customers.

Duke put his arm around Johnathan's shoulder, as if to tell him a secret. "Listen, I just want you to know, I got the inside poop. There is absolutely no truth to that story in the *Post* that that dog-ass kicker is going to be replaced."

"Well, Duke, I don't know if that's good news or bad news," Johnathan said, now shaking the older man's hand warmly. "He sure did mess up yesterday in Philly, didn't he?"

"Yeah, but the big man over there," Duke said, nodding in the direction of the owner, "well, he tells me he has all the faith in the world in this kid. They're going to put in a few extra sessions with him this week. And they should be able to beat the spread against the Jets."

"I hope so," Johnathan said, noticing that sports columnist Mo Siegel was now stopping by the owner's table for a chat. Siegel specialized in table-hopping, hilarious stories, and outrageously dirty jokes, and had been doing it for close to thity years. "Maybe Siegel will have some scoop for us tomorrow."

Talk show host Larry King was deep in conversation with Leonard Shapiro, one of the sports columnists at the *Washington Post.* At a table by the window. Eunice Kennedy Shriver was lunching with one of the priests from Georgetown University, who Johnathan didn't recognize, no doubt talking charity work of some kind, perhaps the Special Olympics.

Former Democratic National Committee chairman John White and Bob Strauss were heavily into conversation with another man, whose name eluded Johnathan at the moment.

And in the middle of the room, not far from the team owner, Rudy Maxa, a "people" columnist for *Washingtonian* Magazine, was holding court. Kevin Chaffee of The Washington Times was lunching with Chuck Conconi from The Washington Post. Power journalists were out in full force, including John Arundel.

"Oh, who knows what that SOB will dig up," Duke said, now moving to his podium, behind which he kept his seating chart. Casually he asked "Who are you meeting?"

Johnathan knew he was trying to determine where to seat him, whether to give him an up-front table of prime importance or stick him out in Siberia with GS-14s and the tourists. Johnathan also knew when to pick his spot. He didn't want to wear out his welcome in the inner circle. He also knew he might need it another time.

"Oh just my brother, we're going to have a quick lunch," he said looking at his watch. "He's a bit late. I'll just wait for him, no bother."

That was Duke Zeibert's clue that Johnathan didn't mind a seat in the back of the room. And, as it turned out, it was a good thing. Bob arrived fifteen minutes late and with a reporter in tow.

"Johnathan," he said extending his hand as he came through the glass doors. "Do you know Marc Leepson?"

"No, I don't think we've met." Johnathan answered aloud, cursing his brother under his breath for bringing along a nosy reporter.

Johnathan had so much to do, and not much time to do it. The last thing he needed was a two-hour lunch, with a lot of snoopy questions.

"Marc writes for *Regardie's*," Bob told him, lifting his eyebrows. "He's doing a story on Payne's Corner and I thought you might be able to fill him in on some of the details."

"Sure," Johnathan said, thinking: *You know you couldn't have gotten me here if you had told me this was the purpose.* "Let's go in the dining room and have some lunch."

Regardie's magazine focused on real estate in and around Washington, covered all important business matters and touched upon politics in the region. The owner, Bill Regardie, usually in a shirt open at the collar and a neck dripping in gold chains, was a regular at Duke's, and Johnathan was actually surprised he was not here this day.

The three men ordered their first round of drinks and the waiter brought a stainless steel bowl of plump, Kosher pickles and a basket full of onion rolls that were baked fresh in the kitchen every day. They chatted briefly about nothing important, then ordered lunch. The restaurant was packed, and the constant hum of conversation interspersed with laughter filled the immense room.

"I thought maybe you might be able to give Marc some insight into this project, John," his brother said. "We took a drive down there yesterday afternoon so he could look around..."

"It's a lovely area," the reporter said.

"Indeed," was all Johnathan wanted to say at the moment. He knew he had to be guarded with his answers to any reporter's questions.

"Tell me a little bit about this development." he asked.

Christ...where do I start? Johnathan thought. "Well now, let's see. What specifically do you mean?"

"Oh, you know—when did it start, who's involved, how many acres—things like that." he said, sipping his drink.

The waiter interrupted. "Would you gentlemen care for another drink?" Johnathan and the reporter said no. Bob wanted another scotch and splash.

Johnathan tried to be thoughtful with his answers to the writer. He didn't want to lie, but he did want to tread lightly on his legal problems with the locals trying to preserve the countryside. Instead, he tried to accent the positive aspects and tell the man how the principle partner involved, Sam Blackwell, saw the opportunity to "add to the integrity of a historical piece of property."

The waiter brought the lunches. Chicken in the pot for Johnathan, a large Duke's salad the writer, a vegetarian, and Bob ordered the crab cakes, and another drink.

The reporter took short quick notes on a small pad throughout the meal and during coffee. The conversation, at least as far as Johnathan was concerned, seemed to be going well. He told him about the life-sized bronze statue of J. E. B. Stuart they commissioned from a well-known Virginia sculptor for the entrance to the country club and about the man contracted to build the fences.

Johnathan decided to tell him briefly about the water situation. He thought it might be good if he brought it up before being asked.

"We've had to be very cautious about where we're putting both of the wells," he told him. "We were specific about their placement, we know exactly where the very important battlefields were located and we're working hard to preserve these. So, to tell you the truth, we're running a bit behind schedule right now because of that. But, you know," he said, leaning over as if he were sharing some secret, "we figured even if it did hold us up a bit, it would be for the best."

"That's interesting," the reporter said. "Um...I wonder, who is doing that drilling?"

"Gee," Johnathan said, still leaning on his elbow, "I can't quite remember. I'll have to look it up. Just call me later at the office. Now, can we order you some dessert? Duke's has the best cheesecake in town."

The three men had another cup of coffee, devoured the cheesecake, and departed as the second group of Washington movers and shakers arrived for the one o'clock seating. Bob Dent paid for the lunch.

The three men exited through the revolving door out onto the bustling sidewalks of one of the busiest intersections in Washington, Connecticut and L streets. The sun was glistening off the brass and copper jewelry of a nearby street vendor.

"I want to thank you both for your time," Marc Leepson said, extending his hand to Bob. "And thank you for the lunch. I've got to go back to my office now."

"Well," Johnathan said, "anything we can do to help you with your story, just let us know." He had forgotten the earlier frustration with his brother at putting him in this situation.

"Oh, I almost forgot, Mr. Dent," the reporter said, "my editor did want me to ask you one other question."

"Sure, what was that?"

"He wanted to know if there was any truth to the rumor that Sam Blackwell wants you to run for Lee Blair's seat in the Senate."

Johnathan feigned surprise. "Oh, really," he said, smiling. "Does he? That's news to me."

Back at his office, Bob was curious.

"Well now, brother John, you've been holding out on me," Bob said as he took his coat off and put it over the back of a chair. They had walked back up Connecticut Avenue without saying much, each immersed in his own thoughts. The question from the reporter caught both of them off guard.

Well, not exactly. Bob Dent had absolutely no clue about the possibility that his brother would run for political office. But it was an intriguing idea. His mind was racing. Naturally his firm would work on the campaign. He could already visualize the print advertisements: "Johnathan Dent: Preserving and Serving the Future of Virginia." *God, it would be fabulous, but why hadn't Johnathan even mentioned it?*

Johnathan removed his suit jacket, too, and sat down at his desk. He was going through his phone messages. "I'm not really holding out on you. I don't know what the guy is talking about. I hope I answered his questions correctly."

"I guess you did right. A little non-denial denial never hurts."

"You know, I've been thinking," Johnathan said. "The day of the ground breaking Sam was just about to say something to me, when we were standing there talking to one of the local councilmen. And then all hell broke loose with those goddamn dogs. I guess he never really finished his sentence. Or at least, I never heard it. But I do remember him saying he thought it would be a grand idea if I were to get into politics, or something like that."

"Well?"

"What do you mean, well?"

"Well, what's your answer? I got the campaign all planned."

"You do, do you?"

"You betcha."

"I'll tell you how I answer that. Do you want my honest answer?" Johnathan asked, not waiting for a reply.

"Doesn't everyone secretly yearn to be in politics or acting?"

"Aren't they the same thing?"

"Don't be funny, Bob."

"Well, maybe...but not everyone," Bob said. "What about Miss Wickwire out there? She certainly wouldn't want to be in politics or acting."

"How do you know? Anyway, you want to know what I think? I think it's something I've been waiting for all my life. I wish it were true. I'd love it. I'd love every minute of it. It would complete my lifetime plan."

Bob Dent was taken aback for a moment. He had not seen his brother so animated, so enthusiastic, in a long, long time. "Well what's the next step?"

"I'm not sure. What do you think?"

"I knew it!" Bob said, slapping the desk. "I just knew it! Already you're a natural. You're turning the question back to me. 'What do I think?' Hell—what do I know? Well...I guess I would ask Sam Blackwell. He's your man. Certainly you must know how to approach him?"

"It seems like such a touchy subject, doesn't it? What do I say? 'Oh, by the way Sam, are you going to back me for the senate?'"

"Well, yeah. Something like that."

"There are so many complications here. What about my law practice? What about my family?"

And what about Isabelle? he thought to himself.

"No problem," Bob said. "What you have to do now is, sit down with Blackwell—have lunch, have dinner, I don't know what. But I do know...have some good stiff drinks and ask him, goddamnit, ask him!!"

Johnathan put his head in his arms on the desk. His voice was muffled for a minute. "You're right, I know it. I'm excited just thinking about it." He brought his face up and looked at Bob. "How about I just tell him just like it happened. By the way, Sam, some reporter just asked me the strangest question the other day. He wanted to know if it was true I was going to make a run for the Senate..."

"Perfect!" Bob gushed, always the PR man. "Absolutely perfect. Right to the point. I knew it. You're a goddamn natural!"

"So what's the bottom line here on the drilling contracts?" Johnathan asked his secretary as soon as his brother departed. "I need to get back to Sam, what did you find out?"

"Well, as far as I can see here, the contract calls for two wells to be completed on or before ninety days. I think this clause will save the day." She walked behind the desk to point out the important paragraphs to Johnathan. She put the papers on his desk and leaned over to point.

"Paragraphs twelve and thirteen, right here," she indicated.

"It is specifically agreed that Blue Ridge Drilling, Inc. will drill a total of two wells, and no more, in the above outlined areas. This drilling is to be completed on or before ninety days from ratification of this contact.

If said drilling is completed before the ninety-day period, a bonus for advance completion of one half of one percent will be paid to Blue Ridge Drilling, Inc. for each day the work is completed and has passed the necessary state and local inspections.

If Blue Ridge Drilling, Inc. is unable to complete the above drilling by this date, except due to an act of God, they will be penalized one half of one percent for each day that the drilling of the two wells goes beyond the aforementioned completion date."

"That's it, that's what we're looking for. Okay, we've got them. I was sure I, uh, *we* put this in here, but I wanted to be positive. Now, I need to talk to Sam, get him on the phone...would you, please?"

She picked up the receiver on the left side of his desk and was through to him within seconds. She handed Johnathan the phone and left the office, this time leaving the door slightly ajar.

"Sam, sorry to take so long to get back to you."

"I've been pulling my hair out down here, what's the story?"

Johnathan explained that the drilling company would be liable for any extra work to be done and would be financially at risk not to finish on time. The ninety-day expiration date was still forty days away.

"I think if I call them we can straighten this out."

"Great. Listen Johnathan, I'm going to head back to Washington now. Any chance you could meet me for dinner? I have some other things to go over."

By eight that evening, Sam and Johnathan were sitting down in a back booth of Martin's Tavern having a drink. Johnathan called home to tell Betty he was in town late and probably would be staying over. Then he called Isabelle and told her he'd see her "late, late tonight." The problem with the well at Payne's Corner was solved. Johnathan felt like he had accomplished a great deal that day.

"Johnathan, I'm glad we got to sit down and have this drink," Sam Blackwell began. "I'm sorry we've had such a horrendous day. I feel bad when there's a goddamn crisis like this, but there's something else I've been meaning to discuss with you."

His brother Bob would love this when he told him. All that discussion about how Johnathan would subtly bring it up, and here Sam Blackwell was making it so much easier.

"Now I don't want you to make any snap decisions here, Johnathan, because I haven't. But you know I've been deeply involved in politics for years. My daddy was a state legislator, you know?" He was almost talking to him like a son, even if he was just eight years older than Johnathan.

"No, I didn't know that," Johnathan said, trying to stay calm.

"You probably know that Lee Blair is planning to retire?"

"I heard that just today," Johnathan replied.

"You've pulled me out of so many fixes and you've worked your way around so many tangles with this project and all the others that I can't imagine there could be anyone better qualified to run for his seat."

"Well, Sam," Johnathan began, setting his drink on the table. "Please, please forgive me, but I'm not going to take a lot of time to think this over. And please, don't think that this a snap decision. Because I have thought about this for a long time. And there is nothing I would love more than to represent the state of Virginia in the Senate. Nothing."

Chapter 13

Ambition & Obligation

It was past midnight when Johnathan tapped softly on Isabelle's front door. She opened it immediately and turned to sit in the living room. The television was on. She was wearing a red silk oriental kimono, the belt tied tightly at her waist. Johnathan could see the soft outline of her breasts. He was so energized after his dinner and conversation with Sam Blackwell. On the way to Isabelle's apartment it pleased him to think he would give her the news before anyone else. He was euphoric as he walked the four long blocks from the restaurant to the Georgetown Inn and then to her apartment. He was cautious on the uneven brick sidewalks. He checked into the hotel, despite the fact he knew he'd spend the night with Isabelle. There was always the chance his wife would call for one reason or another.

Isabelle lived for these moments. There was not a single day, not even a single hour that she did not think of Johnathan in some way. Her life revolved around him, even if he really didn't know it. If she went into a Hallmark store, she could hunt for an hour or longer for the appropriate card to give him. If she was in the grocery store, she thought about what she would cook for his weekly visit. When he called her late that night to announce that he wanted to see her "much, much later," well, she was ecstatic. But at the same time she also wondered if this would mean she wouldn't see him for their regular Wednesday dinner.

What if I hadn't been home? she thought. *Oh, god, my hair is a mess.*

She quickly got in the shower, washed and dried her hair and put it in hot rollers. She had no idea what time he would show up. Only that it'd be late. So she primped her hair, redid her nails, and curled up in the front room waiting for him. When her friend Tracy called, she kept the conversation short, in case he wanted to get through.

She had a light on behind the chair, where she'd been reading while waiting. He took off his jacket and dropped it on the chair. She stood almost in the middle of the room, with her hands behind her. She looked like a little girl...almost innocent.

"Hi," she said, finally.

He leaned over and turned off the light, the room was in low light with just the glow of the television screen. He slipped both of his arms inside her robe and around her bare body. He looked down at her dancing eyes and kissed her. And the sheepish little girl was instantly transformed into an eager and willing woman.

Now...she had every intention of showing how enraptured she was to see him. She relaxed into his arms and kissed him in return and kissed him again. They stood holding each other.

So much went unsaid, she thought. *They just had to grasp each moment.*

She stepped back and so did he. The robe fell loosely just off her bare shoulders. Her hair was disheveled and sexy. She unbuttoned his shirt and he unbuckled his belt. They both knew what they wanted.

He started to lead her back to the bedroom.

"No, no..." she said kissing him and backing him up to the chair where she had been reading. Isabelle most of all savored making love to Johnathan in different places in her apartment.

She dropped her robe from off her sholders and it slid to the floor. She helped him take off the rest of his clothes. Then sat him back in the chair and took in every part of him. Johnathan stroked her head as she depleted him of any energy that may have been left after such a momentous day. She stood up, took his hand, walked him into the bedroom, and they slid into her soft, soft bed. Johnathan was exhausted. He wanted to reciprocate her love. He wanted to tell her about Sam Blackwell, and the Senate, and how they planned to have a grand fundraising party to make the big announcement at The Red Fox in Middleburg. He wanted Isabelle to somehow be a part of all of this... he wanted to share this with her...but he was just too sleepy.

Johnathan was at work at eight-ten the next morning. He slept well and felt good. He wanted to get a jump on the day. There were so many things to do now. And there were phone calls from yesterday that he had to get to.

His private line rang.

"Hello."

"Well, Johnathan," the female voice said, "what on earth are you doing at work so early?"

It was Betty.

"Just trying to get things in order." He was concerned that she had tried to call him at the hotel.

"Well, I tried to call you last night and then first thing this morning and they said you were already gone. I guess you're like a ghost in the night."

"Not really, how's everything?"

"Just fine, nothing unusual, just wanted to know when to expect you."

"Well, I hope to get home in time for a late dinner," he told his wife. "I've got some exciting news to tell you."

"What?"

"Oh, I want to tell you in person."

'Oh, Johnathan, that's so mean...you know I hate that. What is it? Tell me," she begged.

"No, no, I'm not going to, just trust me."

"Have you gotten a raise? A new case? What is it?"

"Bett—", he started to say her name.

"I know—someone's quit—is that it?"

"Look, don't ask me to tell you. I'm not going to. How's Maude?" he asked, hoping that changing the subject would work.

"She's fine. I'm taking her over to Jake's for a late riding lesson. I'll be back in time for dinner. I was going to take her out to The Coach Stop or something, if you were going to be late. But, now, I'll be here. Hurry home, I want to know what this is all about." *I'll have to go to the Safeway and get something special for dinner*, she thought.

"Okay, I'll see you later."

Johnathan sat back in his chair. How the hell could he have forgotten to call home? He always tried to call Betty first when he spent the night in Georgetown. He aimed to touch base and so she wouldn't call the hotel and not find him in. It was risky, and it made him nervous, ever since he had tripped on the ice and broken his shoulder. But that was then and this was now. He never worried about what might have been. Still, it had been stupid not to call her. It was five in the morning when he returned to the hotel, took a long steamy shower, shaved, and ordered some coffee and Danish. He read the morning paper: the national news, the local news and then the Style section, quickly reading the "Personalities" column for the gossip before he arrived at the sports section, checking to see how UVA's basketball team had done. He was going to call home, but figured it was too early.

There was a soft knock on his office door.

"Come on in," he said loudly.

"Well, good morning Mr. Dent," his secretary greeted him. "I guess you're here early to start making your campaign plans?"

He was stunned. *How the hell did she know.* He knew she was efficient and always anticipating his every move. But this was ridiculous.

"What...what do you mean?" he stammered.

"What do you mean, 'what do I mean'?" she asked him. "I read it in the paper today. There's a note in the "Personalities" column of the *Post.*"

"What?" he shouted. "How the hell could that be? " They only had the conversation last night. Now he started thinking out loud. "I didn't see that in my paper."

"Well, I'll go get it."

By this point Johnathan was actually pacing back and forth. He was trying to take a mental accounting of all the ramifications. There were so many details to contend with before such a thing was reported in the paper.

For Christ's sake he hadn't even told him family yet. And what about the people in his office? He had to ask permission for a leave of absence... And then there was Isabelle...

"Here it is," she announced, walking to the desk and folding back the front page of the Style section.

"It seems that young handsome Johnathan Dent, attorney extraordinaire with the firm of Duke, Graves, and Coggin, has decided to do a bit of running—and we don't mean the kind of running the horses do out on his estate in Middleburg. Mr. Dent was seen having dinner with his major client/patron Sam Blackwell at Martin's Tavern in Georgetown last night. And the topic of conversation according to an unnamed source...the upcoming Senate elections. Mr. Dent just might be running for the seat that longtime Virginian Lee Blair will vacate after 18 years in office. More later."

"I need to see the front page...I need to see A-1," he said looking up at his secretary, while searching for his bifocals. "And I need to talk to Sam Blackwell."

"Do you want some coffee?" Miss Wickwire asked, handing him the entire copy of the paper.

"No, no, thanks. I've had some already. I don't need it," he said as he meticulously poured over the front page.

"Ah! You see here?" he said pointing to the top, near the masthead. "This is the final edition. It says so right here near the index. The paper I read must have been an early edition. This item was not in my paper."

"Well, yes...you know that, sir. We always have a special delivery brought to the office of the final edition, Mr. Dent. The final edition of the *Baltimore Sun* is also delivered."

"Yes, yes...I know that. I was just trying to figure this mess out," he said, folding the paper over and putting it down.

Simultaneously, two lines on Johnathan's phone rang. Miss Wickwire answered one, quickly put the first caller on hold and answered the second.

"Yes, Mr. Blackwell, he's right here. He said he wanted to talk to you, too."

Sam and Johnathan concurred that the tidbit in the morning paper wasn't all that bad.

"Granted...it caught us off guard, John," he said. "But, you know, in politics it's always good to get your name out there first. So we can work around it. But we need to get your ducks in a row."

"I'm planning on talking with Bud Duke, the head of the firm, as soon as I can—this morning, if possible. I'll bet this phone is going to ring—"

"Oh, Johnathan, sorry...but now I've got another call to take, how about we get together this weekend or something. I'll call you?"

"Good."

Betty Dent tried all morning to think what surprise Johnathan could possibly have in store. She finally decided that it just had to be some new client.

The phone rang.

"Hello."

"Betty, oh Betty...I'm so glad you're home." It was her good friend Claudia Johns. "George just called me. He said he's been trying to call Johnathan all morning. He told me to get a hold of you and see if you were home or if you knew where Johnathan was." She sounded anxious.

"Well, he's at work. I talked to him early this morning."

"Well, George can't get through. The secretary said he's not available for comment."

"Comment?"

"Yes, he wanted to get Johnathan's reaction or some kind of quote. He wants to write a column about this."

"What? What are you talking about?"

"Betty, don't be funny! It's *me...Claudia...*your *best friend.* You don't have to be coy with me."

"I'm not...what the hell are you talking about?"

"You really don't know?"

"No, I don't. Do you think I'd try to fool you?" She was put out with Claudia now. How could she doubt her?

"There was an item in the *Post* this morning that Johnathan is going to run for Lee Blair's Senate seat."

"Oh, my God." She put her hand to her cheek. "That's it. That's what he has to tell me," she said, thinking out loud.

"Oh, no...you really didn't know?"

"No. No...but he said he had some important news to share. I thought he got a new client or something. I had no idea. Oh, I can't imagine...where would we live?"

"Well I don't know about all that, Betty. All I know is that George wants to talk with Johnathan. He wants to be the first to write a column about it. Any idea how he can get through to him?"

"Well, I'll try to call him and then call you back. Where will you be?"

"I'll be here the rest of the afternoon. Then I have to go out to my art class. But that's much later. Call me back as soon as you can," she said, almost ordering. "George has a deadline. He can stretch it a bit, and he'll be late. But, he *needs* to talk to Johnathan."

"Okay, I'll do what I can."

Betty Dent was thunderstruck. She hung up the phone and stared straight ahead. Johnathan only once before in all their married life had even casually mentioned this possibility. And even then she didn't take it seriously.

But now...

She called his office and talked to Miss Wickwire. She told her he was in meetings all afternoon and that she would try to get him to call her.

"But he's up over his ears, Mrs. Dent. The place is buzzing."

"Oh, yes, well...I guess it is. Just tell him I called and that I had a few minor questions," she said, smiling to herself.

Betty called the local beauty shop, Polly's. "I need to come in this afternoon," she pleaded. "I hate to call at the last minute, but I'm desperate."

She was back home "poofed and boufed"—as Polly referred to a shampoo and blow-dry—by four-forty. Maude was dressed and ready to go to her riding lesson.

Betty breezed into the kitchen, where Bertha was unloading the food from the grocery store.

"Mr. Dent called you. He said he would be home as planned."

"Is that all he said?"

"Yes," she said, opening the door to the walk-in pantry to put the canned dog food away. "That's all."

"Shoot! I wanted to talk to him," she said half under her breath.

She stopped to daydream a moment. It would be so grand...and exciting. A senator's wife...the parties....the receptions... And who knew what other political ambitions Johnathan may be harboring. Oh, she knew it was true. She didn't have to talk to Johnathan. If there was something in the paper and Johnathan wanted to come home and tell her about it, then this was it.

She quickly negotiated her car along the back roads to the stables in Upperville. She was late and didn't want Maude to suspect she was nervous and anxious. She turned into the dirt driveway that led up to the barns. The dark creosote-painted fences lined each side of the drive. There were ponies turned out in the paddock on the right side and jumps in the field on the left. Jake Collins stood in the center of the ring, watching one of his pupils guide a big bay horse over a series of three brightly colored fences.

"Oh, good, we're not late," Maude said. "Jake is still out there with the open jumpers."

"That's a relief." her mother said, pulling up on the small area of blacktop near the barn where the clients parked. "Look, I want to make a quick run back to town. I just remembered that I need to get some wine. So I'll do that while you have a lesson and then I'll be back."

"Okay," she said, bouncing out of the car. Betty could tell Maude was happy now; she had finally outgrown that brooding stage she had gone through at age ten. She was obsessed with horses. That's all she talked about.

"Oh, wait, Mom," she said, just as Betty started to pull away. "Let me get my book, it's in the back of the car."

"What's that...your homework?"

"No, just a book I'm reading about how to groom your horse. I'll read it in case you're late."

"Well, what about your homework? Don't you have any?"

"Just Spanish."

"Well, why don't you take that, just in case. I'd rather see you get your homework done if I run late. Your Dad will want to see you tonight and it would be nice if you got it done."

She took both books and her black velvet helmet and headed to the barn.

Betty turned back down the dirt drive and made the seven-mile drive straight down Route 50, back into the village. She was giddy enough to buy a bottle of champagne. If this was such a joyous occasion, it deserved more than wine. She wanted to share the news with Maude, but decided it would be better if it came from her father. And she wanted Johnathan to be the one to tell Maude—she would be so delighted and would probably want to call all her friends tonight.

She found an appropriate and very expensive bottle of champagne at the Safeway, the familiar orange label Veuve Clicquot. They carried a good selection for a grocery store. But after all, this was Middleburg, where the lighting in the food emporium took the form of chandeliers and the windows were decorated with heavy velvet draperies. One entire aisle consisted of dog food of every variety, both canned and dry. After all, one must have priorities.

The checkout line for "ten items or less" was seven people deep. She spotted her friend Claudia ahead of her.

"Hey," she said knowing she'd identify her voice.

"Hey what are you doing?" she asked, then added, "Well I see. Champagne? It must be true?"

Betty sensed she was annoyed.

"I didn't hear back from you," her friend continued, talking over the other people in the line as if they didn't exist. "What's the word? I told George what you said—he said that wasn't much news."

"I didn't hear anything, Claudia. No more than what you told me," she was explaining now, trying to convince her friend she didn't know anything more. "I just thought I would buy this," she said, displaying the dark green bottle, "just in case."

The line moved forward as the next person checked out. Betty noticed that her friend was buying a bottle of local white wine, brie cheese, and Carr's table water crackers.

She couldn't resist. "And so..." she said, looking down at the items. "What are you celebrating?"

"What?"

"The wine?"

"Oh, that."

"Yeah."

"Oh, uh...it's for the class. The art class."

"Oh, that's right. Well, listen," Betty said as her friend paid for the items and was about to leave. "I'll call you tomorrow, first thing."

Maude was waiting inside the barn. She was still grooming her pony, Jackpot, when Betty pulled up.

She got out of the car quickly and said to Maude, "Hurry honey, we're late. Put the pony back in the stall and let's get going. I'll be in the car."

Maude sensed correctly that her mother had no time to spare tonight. So she put the pony in the stall and got in the car. It was dark outside and the mid-fall air was brisk.

They chatted about her lesson and about her pony named Jackpot. Then, just as they started to wind back up their own long driveway Maude said, "Mom...mom, you won't believe this." She sounded worried.

Betty half wanted to hit the brakes, but she continued cautiously. "What's wrong?"

"My homework. I forgot my books." This time she did hit the brakes, right in the middle of the driveway.

"Oh, Maude," she said trying to hold her anger. *How could she be so irresponsible?*

"I need it mom," her daughter pleaded. Betty glanced at the clock in the car. It was after six. She had no choice. She had to go back.

"Okay, okay, I'll do it. I want you to go inside. Tell Bertha what happened. Take your boots off, take a shower, and put something nice on. I'll let you eat with us tonight, I think that might be special. Tell Bertha to put the potatoes in the oven, and I'll be right back."

"Okay," she said, getting out of the car quietly. She knew she had to behave. She needed the Spanish book. But she really wanted to stay up late and read about grooming ponies. She had her flashlight right under the bed. She hurried along, the dog greeting her at the garage door and now leaping up to her.

Betty guided her car back on to Route 50 one more time. She hated to think how often she'd driven up and down this road, just today. It was pitch dark now as she glided along the Zulla Road toward the main highway.

The traffic was steady as she reached the dual intersection waiting to turn west toward Upperville. The commuters were heading home. She waited a minute, drumming the steering wheel with her fingers, her impatience growing moment-to-moment. She wanted this dinner to be perfect...

She reached the entrance to Jake Collins's farm in twelve minutes.

Not bad for this time of day, she said to herself, driving up to the barn.

There were no lights on and just two cars in the tiny parking area. *Damn*, she thought, *how am I going to see?* And Maude forgot to tell me where she left her books.

The moonlight was bright. Farmers called it a Hunter's Moon. Once your eyes adjusted you could see, if you were cautious. First she looked on top of the tack trunks. She tried to feel inside of Maude's grooming box, where she kept her precious sable brush for her beloved Jackpot. The horses were all content. They'd been fed and the water buckets were topped off. Most of the horses were wearing their first winter blanket of the season—a lightweight sheet that horse people called "fall coat." One of the horses coughed and startled Betty. She inched her way toward the other end of the barn. She could see now that the door was open to the tack room, which led into the pine paneled trophy room.

She opened the screen door and stepped inside. She couldn't find the light switch. She tiptoed around the room and found the second door, which was open. Something smelled familiar. She sniffed the air, it wasn't horse or hay, it was sweet, almost...

Aha, she said to herself, *here it is.* And as she flipped on the light she wasn't quite sure who was more surprised: her friend Claudia, who was astride Jake Collins in the middle of the floor, or Jake Collins himself.

Betty gasped for breath. She wanted to ask, *"What's going on here?"* But she knew damn well. The empty wine bottle and the white paper from the brie cheese were on the desk.

"Oh, oh, oh!" she said. She immediately started apologizing and explaining. "I was just..." Then she knew...the smell...Claudia always wore White Shoulders perfume.

Claudia stood up and wrapped a plaid horse blanket around herself. It was actually now sort of amusing, because in doing so she left Jake Collins lying face up, completely naked. There wasn't even one tiny piece of clothing, horse blanket, or rub rag within his reach. He instinctively covered himself with his hands. He had no choice. Then he sat up. He was speechless. The momentary humor failed to reach him.

"Betty, what are you doing here?" Claudia demanded indignantly, now stuffing one corner of the blanket inside the other as one would do with a bath towel. She hadn't even bothered to look down at her companion.

"Oh, God...I am so sorry," Betty said, walking over to her to try to console her. Her friend backed away. She could see the intense anger in her face. "I was just looking for Maude's books."

"Shouldn't you be home celebrating with your husband?" she inquired.

Betty started to say *"Ugh"*, and then thought, *"What do you mean? 'Shouldn't I be home with my husband?' What about you?"* But she held back; she felt sorry for Jake Collins, who had stood up and was trying to edge around the desk as the two women growled at each other. The box of Carr's crackers toppled to the floor. She caught a glimpse of his backside, as he finally fell into the chair. Now, at least, he was concealed from the waist down.

"Look," Betty said, trying to stop shaking. They were both shaking. "I'm sorry. Forgive me. I wanted to look for a book, I had no idea. I've got to go. Forget the book."

She turned and left.

She made it back home in a record nine minutes.

Johnathan was in the kitchen when Betty arrived.

"What's wrong?" he asked, walking toward her to kiss her on the cheek. "You don't look well at all." She was visibly shaken, her face drained of color.

"Mommy," Maude asked, "Is Jackpot all right?"

"I'm okay," she said, taking her old orange coat off and putting her purse down. She knew Maude needed some kind of explanation. "I couldn't find your books dear, it was too dark. We'll deal with that tomorrow, will that be all right?"

"Sure Mommy."

"What I really need is a Coke, a big glass of Coke with lots of ice."

The three of them sat down at the table in the kitchen. Bertha had gone home, the dinner was in the oven, and now it was time for Johnathan to tell her what she already knew. Betty took a long drink from her tall glass, caught her breath and tried to stay calm. She would tell Johnathan about the barnyard frolic later. If she ever told him at all. But now they had to hear his news.

They ate dinner on their laps in front of the fire and even ended up allowing Maude to have a sip of champagne to celebrate. And, of course, the little girl was delirious about the news.

"I can't wait to help you make posters, Daddy!" she told him.

There were many details to work out, but this run for office couldn't have come at a better time as far as Betty Dent was concerned. Wife of Senator, or at least, Wife of Candidate, was a role she'd prepared for her entire life, and knew she could play it brilliantly. So did Johnathan.

So much often went unsaid between them, Johnathan thought as they climbed into bed that night.

Soon she had pulled her nightgown over her head and he methodically began to kiss her on the neck. It was an obligation he knew he had to fulfill.

Another obligation, he told himself.

Bertha and Betty had talked about the big news during lunch the next day.

"I guess things be changin' here just a bit?" Bertha half-inquired.

"Well, I'm not sure how," Betty told her honestly. She was idly opening the mail and making various piles. She wanted to read the paper, too. She knew it would be so important to follow current events now. She glanced at the index on page two, then unfolded the paper on the countertop. She would start on the front page and go through it all. She turned each page and tried to look at the headlines and not read the ads—her usual habit from her days of designing advertising.

She came to the end of the first section and looked over the editorials. One of them was a tribute to Norman Rockwell and his art, which celebrated life in America. But something on the op-ed page caught her eye. It was George Jasper's column.

Oh, I Can't Imagine… Where Would We Live?

"The word is out now, although it is not yet official, that attorney Johnathan Dent will make a run for the Lee Blair's seat in the Senate next year. He's being backed by his number one client, developer Sam Blackwell. Mr. Blackwell's latest venture is the Payne's Corner community near Culpeper, where the average price of a home hovers somewhere in the $500,000 range.

And while Mr. Dent is clearly concerned with bigger and more important matters, his wife, the heiress Elizabeth Crane Dent, was worried about where they will live, should he get elected.

Mr. Dent could not be reached for comment yesterday, despite repeated efforts to call him.

Mrs. Dent was reached at her Middleburg estate. She was unable to confirm the rumors about her husband's aspirations, of which he has many. However, she did say, "I had no idea. Oh, I can't imagine...where would we live?"

Well, if Mr. Dent does indeed run and if Mr. Dent should by some odd chance win, he'd better be more concerned about lower income housing and how the other half in Virginia lives."

It went on and on.

"How could he do this?" Betty Dent asked aloud, slamming her soup cup down. "That no good, dirty—. This is horrible," she continued ranting. "And to think ..."

Bertha was astounded, in sixteen years she had never heard the lady of the house say a bad word. "What is it Mrs. Dent?"

"Well, that so-called friend of ours, George Jasper, has just written the most despicable things here," she said, pointing to the article and the headline, neither one of which Bertha could read.

Betty tried to call Johnathan.

"Out to lunch," she was told.

Then she thought about calling Claudia, they needed to talk and they needed to talk *now*. She picked up the phone, then put it down.

No, she thought, *I need to calm down, I want to plan this out. That woman and her jerk of a husband were going to have to answer for this.*

Betty had no idea everything she'd told Claudia would be for publication in her husband's column. And to think that Betty hadn't even breathed a word of last night's unexpected meeting.

Already Betty Dent was thinking like a politician's wife, and somehow, she'd get even. She wasn't quite sure how.

Not yet.

Chapter 14

R.I.P., Run & Replace

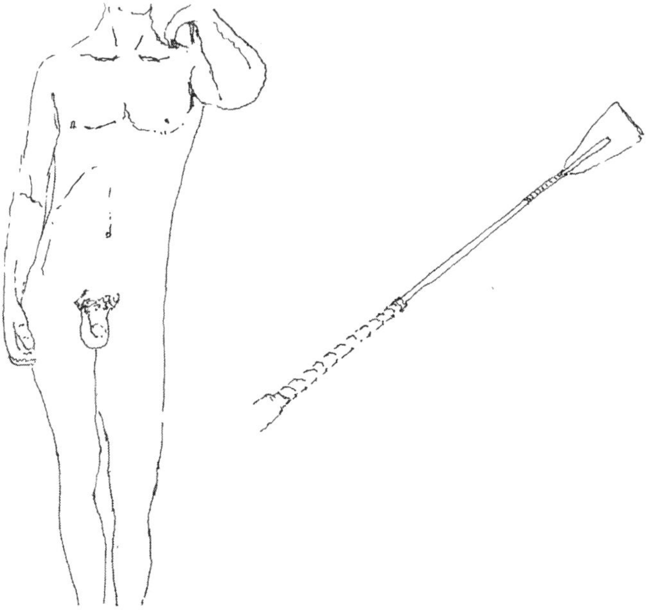

For Isabelle it was an entirely different kind of Wednesday. She didn't read the *Post*, or any other newspaper for that matter, during the week, only on Sundays. She had no idea how the life of her lover was changing since she had seen him late, late Monday night.

By the time she woke up the next morning, he was gone. She could still smell him on her pillow when she rolled over a little after seven. She still wanted him, but he had fallen asleep. She was content to know that she was able to please him, and more content it was mutually agreeable…

Johnathan.

Tonight was their night...Wednesday. And although she hadn't heard from him in two days, she assumed he would visit her apartment as usual. She was at the shop early to get her work completed. She left thirty minutes early to get to the Safeway for the ingredients for her new recipe.

She was making her list for chicken with sour cream:
boned skinless chicken breasts
1 pint sour cream
bread crumbs
salad stuff
carrots

She heard the back door open. It was Michael. He had his cup of 7-11 coffee in one hand and the mail under his arm.

"I've got great news," he told her, putting the paper cup on the edge of her desk. He was dressed in a bow tie and navy blazer and today had a trench coat over that. "I got an exciting letter today..." he continued.

Isabelle was listening, but not paying much attention. She was wondering if she should buy some wine, just in case Johnathan didn't have time. "Great news...what's that?" she asked, not looking up from her notes.

Butter, she wrote.

The back door opened again, this time it was Ruth the bookkeeper and Gunther the handyman, arriving at the same time.

"Ohhhh," Michael said, waving his hands for them to come into the front room. "Now, everyone is here to share this exciting news. I'm so happy."

"What is it Mr. Aldridge," Ruth inquired, as she put her purse down on Isabelle's desk, knocking over the coffee.

"Oh! I'm so sorry Mr. Aldridge. Forgive me." She went to get a cloth. She knew he'd be furious if anything got stained.

"No, no, Ruth...come back," he ordered. "It can wait. I want to tell you all," he said, waving a letter. "I've just been invited to do a room at the Symphony Show House."

"Oh, how wonderful!" Isabelle said, knowing much better than the other two employees about the prestige such an invitation brought. "Which room?" she asked.

"A guest bedroom," he answered. "Oh, we can make this sooo yummy. And it will be such great fun. I know exactly which colors we'll use...melon. I just know it's the next thing. All shades of melon." And he waved his hands in the air.

Isabelle could visualize the colors. She worked well with her boss and admired his enthusiasm. But her heart wasn't in it today. She was concerned about Johnathan. She hadn't heard from him in two days.

She went about her daily routine of opening the mail, answering the phones, and delaying anxious clients whose fabric, light fixtures, and furniture hadn't yet arrived.

She would say something like, "Oh, Mrs. Baxter, I'll bet you're calling about those sconces?" as she did around noon. Then, not giving the distressed woman a second chance, she continued. "Well they haven't arrived yet, maybe tomorrow. Why don't I give you a call around noon. I know you must be soooo upset. So am I, I was ready to strangle that UPS man when he didn't bring them."

By one forty-five, she couldn't stand it any longer. Isabelle hadn't eaten lunch. She wanted to stay by the phone in case Johnathan called. And there was no one around to mind the store while she ran across the street to The French Market for a sandwich. Michael was in the Kalorama area of the city to visit with a potential new client. Ruth had taken the ledgers to the accountant to review a few things and Gunther was out making a delivery up Wisconsin Avenue.

She dialed Johnathan's number quickly. She was afraid he wouldn't be in or wouldn't want to talk to her. Or worse yet,that someone in her office would walk in and hear her.

"Johnathan Dent, please," she said quickly.

"One moment, please."

"Johnathan Dent's office."

"Yes, ah, is Mr. Dent in please?"

"Oh, just a moment, I'll check," said Miss Wickwire. By now she no longer asked who was calling. *She must know*, thought Isabelle.

She came back on the line. "Oh, I'm so sorry," she said, almost apologizing. "Mr. Dent is in a meeting and says he will call you back late today."

"Okay," Isabelle responded, not showing any emotion, especially disappointment. "Thank you." Her heart was pounding.

Did that mean he didn't want to talk to her or wasn't going to see her tonight? Was the message *"He'll call you back late today"* some kind of code? She stood up and went into the workroom and poured herself a cup of half-stale coffee. She would have to wait the afternoon out until he called. It was going to be a long day.

By five-twenty she still hadn't heard from Johnathan. *How could he forget? Why didn't he call?* Now she didn't know what to do. Should she call him back before leaving? What if Miss Wickwire answered the phone again? She would think Isabelle a nuisance.

Isabelle picked up the phone anyway and dialed the number.

"Duke, Graves, and Coggin," the cheerful voice answered.

She hung up.

She decided to proceed as usual. Go to the Safeway, get the groceries and cook dinner. She grabbed her purse and a few notes and a shopping bag of samples she had to deliver the next morning. She hadn't eaten all day and felt weak.

Johnathan usually arrived at her apartment by six-thirty. So she hurried. She ran through the Safeway, systematically gathering what was needed, and was home by six-seventeen, which was cutting it close. She liked to take a shower and be fresh for Johnathan, but there was no time tonight. She had to get the chicken going and wash the lettuce. Oh, there were a hundred things to do.

She left the front door unlocked when she was expecting him. Though Johnathan knew it, he never just walked in without knocking first. She had given him a key. "In case you get here before I do," she told him long ago.

She put the dinner in the oven and opened a package of dill Havarti cheese when she heard a soft knock on the door.

Oh, thank God, she thought, a wave of relief sweeping over her. *Why do I get myself in such a state?*

But as she opened the door, she knew.

This gentle man, for whom she yearned night and day, was holding a bottle of champagne.

"What's the occasion?" she asked immediately.

"Oh, a big surprise," he said, "In case you haven't heard." He leaned back on the inside of the door to lock it. "I'm being asked to run for a seat in the Senate."

Isabelle was flabbergasted. *"Senator?"* she wanted to say, *"what's this going to do to our relationship?"*

It did not take long to find out.

"Isabelle," he said, snuggling into her bed after dinner. "I want you to know that this isn't going to change things between us." He began kissing her neck, working his way down and then gently took her right breast in his warm mouth. He rested his chin on her chest and looked up at her. She felt like crying, but didn't. "We might have to be a bit more careful about restaurants and things like that. But nothing will change."

"Just a bit," she said, holding his head to her body. "That's no problem. You know I love to cook for you." *You know I love you*, she thought.

The next two and a half months were wild. Thanksgiving and Christmas were always the busiest in the decorating business and this year was no exception. Frantic last-minute calls for dining or guest room redos flooded in to Michael Aldridge's office. As always, Michael and Isabelle came to the rescue.

``I'm thinking about redoing my dining room," the lady of the house announced in a begging tone. Or ``I've just found out my in-laws are coming for Christmas and I simply have to fix up our guest room. It's a mess." Isabelle decided to stay in Washington for Thanksgiving since there was so much work to be done. On the Wednesday night before the holiday, Johnathan made his usual visit.

"This wasn't easy," he announced as he plopped down in the chair, a glass of wine in one hand. "I had a hard time saying where I was going."

They usually didn't talk about such things. It was a subject Isabelle tried to ignore.

"Well, you know, it's the night before Thanksgiving and the entire family is coming for dinner tomorrow and *she* wanted me home early."

Isabelle walked across the room, glass in hand, and sat on the floor by his feet. She still didn't say anything, she let him go on.

"My brother is going to be the campaign manager. He and Ray Curtis are going to be co-chairmen. So we're going to get together and iron out the details."

Isabelle listened as Johnathan shared the plans he'd made for the campaign. "I'll tell you what," he said during dessert, "that brother of mine is a marketing genius. We've already planned lots of radio spots, and Pauline Howard is throwing a fundraiser and bringing in her foxhunting pals. To top it all off, I'm going to make my formal announcement at The Red Fox."

Isabelle agreed, it was very smart. His first campaign speech at The Red Fox in Middleburg would add even more color to the ceremony. This was one of the oldest taverns in Virginia; during the Civil War they'd used the bar in the back room as a surgery table. And everyone knew John Kennedy had held his weekend press conferences there when he and his horse happy wife came out to the country. She loved to foxhunt and ride. Johnathan would drop Kennedy's name into his speech, of course, and had no reservations telling people JFK was one of his heroes. Everything was falling into place. He was so enthusiastic and Isabelle found this bubbly, effervescent side rather intriguing. It was definitely an improvement over the proper corporate attorney image he had cultivated.

She also couldn't help but ask herself, *what if he does win the election?*

But first, he had to get nominated.

On December sixth, Isabelle received an ecru envelope. It was hand-addressed in calligraphy to "Miss Isabelle Stoker."

MRS. VERNON HARRISON HOWARD
REQUESTS THE PLEASURE OF YOUR COMPANY AT A
HUNT TEA
IN HONOR OF
JOHNATHAN DOUGLAS DENT
TUESDAY, JANUARY 6, 3:00 P.M.
THE ORCHARD
MIDDLEBURG, VIRGINIA
RSVP

"Mizz Howard, Mizz Howard," called Bean. The black bartender, who was busy slicing lemons and limes, preparing for the onslaught of guests set to arrive momentarily, stopped what he was doing to try to get the hostess's attention. Almost seventy, and still the most sought after bartender in hunt country, Bean was so named because he was "as long as a bean pole" when he was a youngster.

Bean was in the kitchen two flights below the master suite where Pauline Howard was getting ready to put on her tweed suit. She was in a full-length slip and had just put on her stockings. The old man was trying to get up the two flights of steps as fast as he could.

He was calling her name every two steps.

"Mizz Howard."

The old pine steps, especially those in the back part of the house, were slick. They had just been perfectly polished by Susie. Since they were "original," Mrs. Howard never dreamed of covering them with a carpet or runner.

"Mizz Howard."

He didn't bother to knock, he threw open the door.

"Mizz Howard."

"Oh," she said at the top of her lungs, unnerved that a servant would enter without knocking.

He didn't bother to apologize. "Mizz Howard, it's Susie."

"What is it, Bean?" She grabbed her silk robe draped on the bench at the end of the large mahogany four-poster bed. The room smelled sweet, like the powder she used.

She gazed at him, "What is it, Bean?"

"It's Susie, Mizz Howard. She's had a seizure or something." He spun around to go back downstairs and she followed him with her robe billowing behind her.

The kitchen was sweltering and jam-packed with extra servants and massive amounts of food. At the far end of the room, in front of the enormous fireplace, Susie was flat on her back on the floor.

She wasn't breathing.

"What happened?" Pauline asked matter-of-factly.

"She just started shaking, Mizz Howard," Bean said, kneeling down behind Mrs. Howard, who was hovering over the large woman who had served her so faithfully all these years. She put her hand under Susie's nose.

She felt nothing.

"I think she had some kind of a seizure," Bean repeated, moving closer to the lady of the house.

He wasn't aware that she was dead.

The rest of the staff in the kitchen was crowded together about ten feet away. Some of the women had their hands over their mouth. One young black woman was praying, another started to cry, and a third suggested, "I think we should call the rescue squad."

"That won't be necessary," Mrs. Howard ordered curtly. "Let's get her up on this sofa, Bean. Help me."

Together they hoisted all two-hundred-fifty pounds of Susie onto the sofa that faced the fireplace. Her big body bounced and jiggled as it hit the cushions.

"It's a bit warm here, someone open the back door," she ordered to anyone who would listen. Two of the women obliged.

"Now I need a blanket," she commanded.

Bean left the room and took a pink mohair cover off the back of the chintz sofa in the upstairs drawing room. He returned hurriedly, but he was perplexed.

"Hadn't we ought to call for help, Mrs. Howard?" he inquired holding out the soft blanket.

"That won't be necessary, Bean." she said, standing up tall and addressing the group gathered in the kitchen. "Susie is dead. There's nothing we can do for her now. And I'd prefer not to call the rescue squad just yet. If our guests saw an ambulance coming down the driveway, they wouldn't be able to get up here. This party is too important."

She laid the pink blanket over the woman's body. "Susie would understand. Now please, a moment of silence and then let's be getting ready. Susie will be fine here. Let her rest in peace. I've got to go upstairs and finish getting dressed. Bean, we'll handle all this later."

The servants couldn't believe what they just heard. They were aware there really was nothing they could do for dear sweet Susie. They looked at each other, shrugged their shoulders and went on about the business of Pauline Howard's party, almost as if nothing had happened at all.

Almost.

The party went off without a hitch. A few minutes after the last car departed, a rescue squad ambulance pulled up the driveway and parked behind the house. It took four men to carry Susie out. Pauline Howard put an extra $20 in the pay of each servant, and pledged $250 over her usual contribution to the rescue squad as they prepared to depart.

"Poor Susie," Pauline Howard said to Bean shortly before he put on his coat and left. "Everyone just loved her butter cookies."

On Wednesday, January 7, Isabelle read the following account in The *Washington Post*:

Johnathan Douglas Dent, long regarded as one of the area's more liberal attorneys, announced yesterday that he was seeking the Democratic nomination for the U.S. Senate, standing in the same room where John F. Kennedy often made significant history.

Among those crowded into the J. E. B. Stuart room at Middleburg's Red Fox Inn &

Tavern were his wife, the heiress Elizabeth Crane Dent, his daughter Maude, and his twin sons, Johnathan McClain Dent and Douglas Crane Dent. Numerous newspaper reporters, radio correspondents, and television crews also were on hand for what seemed like a press reunion to some of the members of the media.

The Red Fox Tavern was the sight of numerous press conferences held by the late President John Kennedy. "At one point the arm even came off the end of one of the chintz sofas that one of the reporters sat on," recalled Gwen Dobson, a reporter for the Washington Star in the Kennedy years and now the owner of a fashionable boutique in this chic hamlet.

The arm of the chintz sofas did not come off at a very large celebration following Dent's announcement yesterday. At The Orchard, the home of Pauline Howard, the Grande Dame of the Hunt Country, a traditional Hunt Tea helped the novice politician kick off his first run at elected office.

Among those attending the gathering were The Honorable and Mrs. Averill Harriman, major democratic fundraisers on both national and state levels, who also maintain a home in this exclusive enclave.

More than 300 invited guests and members of the media mingled in the large main room of the federal period brick mansion. A buffet of turkey and Virginia country ham were served, along with salad, warm spiced peaches, and a variety of homemade butter cookies.

Dent will face three other challengers for the Democratic nomination to succeed retired U.S. Senator, Republican Lee Blair. Former national Democratic co-chairman Harrison Scott, and State Senator Phillip Rees will oppose Dent in his quest, as will Winnie Milton the well known assistant district attorney from Norfolk, who seeks to become the first female Senator of Virginia.

A number of issues will face the candidates during the campaign, including the proposed Panama Canal treaty which has already become an issue in a very crowded race. The Democrats will hold their convention in Richmond, June 2-4.

Asked yesterday his opinion on the treaty, Dent hedged and said, "We have plenty of time to talk business. Let's discuss that tomorrow."

There was no mention of Susie.

The first couple of months of the new year, Betty Dent felt as if she'd been on a treadmill. There was a constant whirl of fundraisers and campaign events. All this in addition to her usual carpooling duties. She was a wreck. She was constantly shuttling Maude back and forth to school, horseback lessons, and everything else, from doctor appointments to visits to Polly's to get her hair poofed.

Johnathan took a leave of absence from his law practice to devote every minute to the campaign. Betty had a hard time keeping up with him. When he did come home it was often ten or eleven at night. He was in Lynchburg in the morning, Roanoke later in the afternoon for another round of meetings with even more delegates. He frequently flew with his brother, Bob in his Beechcraft Bonanza. Sometimes he traveled by car with a driver.

Today they were in Fredericksburg. This much Betty knew, because no matter where he was, Johnathan always called each morning around seven.

As if all the events suddenly in her life were not enough, Betty was this year's cochairman for the May Day Dance to benefit the Country Day School. The board of directors asked her to take on this task with her friend Holly Hawk. They wisely decided since Mrs. Dent was in the limelight this spring, it added to the cachet of the function. In turn, it possibly could bring in more money for the exclusive private school.

They were right.

Betty jumped into the project with great enthusiasm. First, she engaged her friend and neighbor Willard Scott as the guest auctioneer. The popular television weatherman lived in nearby Delaplane, often doing his *Today Show* segments from his front lawn. He told her he'd be happy to participate. Old Willard really was a good friend.

She kept a leather bound Filofax notebook with list after list of all the tasks to be done: program, publicity, decorations, etc., etc. She asked a friend or a friend of a friend to lunch at the club gently pleading for their time and money. She chose her committee carefully, picking women she thought capable to take on particular jobs—like decorations, advertising, printing, artwork, publicity. She wanted to start digging in to this at a month sooner than any previous chairman had dared. Flattered to be named chairman of a committee under the direction of the wife of a future Virginia senator, the team of volunteers eagerly undertook her requests.

Betty and Holly met weekly to deliberate the specifics and pour over her infinite "to do" lists. On this particular Tuesday, they gabbed about the artwork.

"Rusty Stewart did that painting a few years ago and it turned out so well," Holly said, "I thought we might ask him again."

"Yes, but I hate to have the same person twice," Betty said, sipping a large glass of white wine while waiting for lunch. "It's not very original on our part, is it?" She was trying to be polite, but Betty felt that they should make an all-out effort to be innovative.

"Well, ah, I can see your—"

"Why don't we look for some other local artists?" Betty asked, trying to change the subject. "How about that red-headed girl from over in Warrenton. I can't think of her name, but her stuff is good. I saw it at the Neighborhood Art Show last year."

"Oh, I saw it too, but—"

"Hey ladies, how are you?" It was Claudia, Betty knew without turning around, and she fairly bristled. Ever since that unfortunate night six months ago, when Betty "intruded" on Claudia and Jake Collins, the two women barely spoke. They'd been to many luncheons together and a number of dinner parties, yet they always managed to avoid extended conversations, save for a bit of harmless small talk. They were both good at faking their emotions, so none of their friends knew anything was amiss. Neither one had uttered a word about *the incident.*

Betty couldn't figure out how on earth Claudia could possibly be upset with her, when it was hardly her fault she found them naked in the barn. But Claudia chose to be icey and Betty made every effort to adjust. Still, she felt deeply betrayed and hurt. Especially since, on the heels of the entire "affair," her husband wrote an article about Johnathan and made Betty out to be a spoiled, rich, country housewife. *If her husband only knew,* thought Betty. Nonetheless, Claudia was one of her best friends, and Betty yearned that somehow, someway, things would settle. At the moment though, the relationship was strained.

"How are things going," Claudia chirped, knowing full well the massive amount of time involved in planning the dance, since she had been involved many times. She stood momentarily at their table, but did not sit down.

"So far, so good," Betty said, not turning to look at her.

"And we're counting on you to do the addressing," Holly half-asked, hoping to get a confirmation.

"No problem," Claudia said, "See you girls later."

The waiter brought lunch and the two women continued. Holly was trying to figure out how to tell Betty that Rusty Stewart had sketched a sample for this year's program. She decided to come right to the point.

"You know Betty...about Rusty. I had no idea that you wouldn't want to see what he had done."

"What do you mean?"

"Well a few weeks ago I asked him to do a mockup And before you say anything I'm here to tell you that it is *the* most divine and charming thing I've ever seen."

"Well...uh...," Betty Dent realized working on a charity event with other women, the best thing to do was not to make any waves. "Tell me, what is it?"

"You know, I think it would be fabulous for you to see it. I just know you'll think it's picture-perfect," she said, brimming with boundless enthusiasm. "Just give him a call later today and arrange to see it."

That settled, they went on to the topic of printing. The lunch ended and they all went along their merry way of afternoon chores: the post office, the market and, most important… the liquor store.

Betty was scheduled to take Maude to her riding lesson in Upperville. She tried to call Rusty when she got home. Since he lived nearby, she could stop by later.

"This is Rusty Stewart, I'm in my studio today until three or four when I'll break for tea and return your call, please leave your name and number after the tone."

Perfect, thought Betty. She would pay him a visit.

It was after three when she drove up the long paved driveway at The Fields, the O'Brien estate where Rusty Stewart rented a log cabin and a shed that served as his studio.

She stopped at the log cabin first, thinking he must be inside having his tea. There was no car, but she tapped on the wood door anyway. No answer. She went on to the studio.

There was no car there either. She got out and knocked. A friendly black Labrador nudged her hand as she waited for a reply. He rubbed against her leg, leaving a bit of drool on her skirt. She checked the door and found it was unlocked. She did not want to prowl and look for the painting without him—especially after what happened at Jake's barn last fall.

She went inside and to find a piece of paper and leave a note. She felt uneasy. She quickly left a message.

The dog followed her inside.

She left the door ajar.

There was a large workspace with canvasses stored at one end, filed on edge vertically. The table faced an imposing window that looked out over an endless field of cattle. There was nothing else in sight. Just immeasurable splendid green fields and immense black cows.

The shed was two stories high. A loft covered half of it. On the other side of the room was a second work area. An oversized canvas that must have been six feet high was propped up against an easel. Betty couldn't see what was on it. The aroma of turpentine and oils filled the room. There was a cot in the far corner and a door that led to what she presumed to be the bathroom. There were a couple of other canvasses propped up against the center beam of the loft.

She found a pencil and paper on the work table and jotted down a note:

> Rusty,
>
> So sorry I missed you. Holly said you've done a fabulous piece of art that might work for this year's dance. I'm just dying to see it. Call me.
>
> Betty Dent

She left the note in the middle of the table and started to leave. She noticed that the dog made himself at home and curled up on the cot.

"Come on boy," she said, patting her thigh, "let's go. Come on." He wouldn't budge. She was almost going to leave him there, but thought better of it. What if he got into some canvas and ripped it up? Or what if he ate some paints and got sick? Those Labs could be mighty destructive.

"Come on," she said, walking over to him. "Outside," she commanded. But as she reached the cot and saw the other side of the tall canvas, she froze.

Oh my God, she thought. Her fists clenched.

She held one tight hand to her mouth.

The painting was so lifelike, it was eerie.

For there stood Jake Collins, wearing nothing at all.

His face was contorted in what, at first, appeared to be torment. His eyes were clenched shut tightly and the lines around them were deep. His head was tilted back.

He was holding his penis with his right hand. Strong and full, the color of deep, profound pink was vivid. The tip of his uncircumcised penis was just visible as he was a gasp away from culminating his self-indulgence. Betty trembled. She couldn't take her eyes off it. He held a riding crop in his other hand.

She wanted to get the hell out of there before she was discovered. She glanced again…the hair on his legs and chest looked so real.

She gasped and shook her head to bring herself back to her senses. She hastily turned, walked out, closed the door and left.

CHAPTER 15

Byrd And A Plane

The Washington Post, June 1, 1978

The largest gathering ever of Virginia's Democrats is expected to converge on Richmond tomorrow for a state convention that will nominate a candidate for the U.S. Senate.

The Democrats are faced with two very important issues. First, the process of deciding who will run should prove to be a very tight contest. They were all very strong candidates and have been campaigning hard for the past six months.

As they head into the convention, Harrison Scott appears to have a slight edge in delegates over Johnathan Dent, with Winnie Milton right on his heels.

The Democratic nominee will run in the November election against the Republican candidate nominated at their state convention in Williamsburg later this month. The seat being sought is that of retiring Republican Senator Lee Blair, who has served in the Senate for 18 years.

The opportunity for the Democrats to fill the Blair vacancy is wide open since his career has been viewed politely by most as "lackluster." The state faces a number of important issues at this time, among them, legalized gambling—an issue that will also face the voters in November.

Scott, a former national party cochairman, has a large following and a deep loyalty among many of the 7,500 delegates—one reason he is regarded as the front-runner. Many of those attending this convention will view him as a party leader and are expected to step in line with others.

Dent, a relative newcomer to politics, has worked vigorously on the campaign trail leading to Richmond. He's spent well over $3 million on a media campaign orchestrated by his brother, Bob Dent, a principal in the Richmond-based Martin Advertising Agency.

Johnathan Dent, a long time resident of Middleburg in the heart of Virginia horse country, is a strong supporter of gambling in the state, especially "if it results in horseracing".

Governor Samuel Cook, who made history two years ago when he became the first black governor of the state, will deliver the convention's opening address at the Coliseum tomorrow morning. His endorsement of one of the three candidates is expected later in the day.

Johnathan Dent and his swelling entourage checked into Richmond's Jefferson Hotel three days before the start of the formal sessions. A pre-convention rally was scheduled that first afternoon after he arrived.

Betty and Maude made the two-hour drive from Middleburg and checked in to the hotel before noon. Maude was fascinated with the bronze alligator in the middle of the historic lobby.

"Well, young lady," a bellman explained. "Not so long ago there used to be real alligators here. This guy here was made to take their place."

The large hotel was decorated in the rococo style, with hand-carved gilded moldings framing the large high ceilings. A mezzanine surrounded the lower lobby that was one floor below the main reception area. Formal luncheons and afternoon tea were served on the mezzanine at tables draped with crisp white linen.

The bellman took their luggage on a rolling cart to Johnathan's suite on the sixth floor. The double door was open, leading to an expansive sitting room.

Bob Dent was on the phone at a small dining table at the far end of the room. He motioned his niece and his sister-in-law to come in and winked at Maude. Betty tipped the bellman and they looked around. There were two bedrooms and a small kitchenette. Johnathan was on one of the telephones in the larger bedroom. Another woman Betty didn't recognize was on a phone in the other bedroom.

Johnathan hung up the phone when they came in. He greeted them warmly and hugged and kissed them both.

"How's it going?" Betty asked.

"It's close. I'm trying to make as many calls as I can."

"Daddy can I help?" Maude begged, climbing up on the edge of the bed next to him.

"Sure you can, honey," he answered.

Betty was delighted he took a few minutes out to talk with her. She missed him so much recently. They were all passing strangers in the day and night. At least now, thought Betty, she'd find out what's what. The thought of Johnathan possibly losing the nomination never occurred to her until she read the morning paper.

"I couldn't believe them saying that Scott was ahead," she told Johnathan.

"Well, I guess it depends which paper you read," he answered. "But that could be very true. We just have to keep plugging away. Say, what time is it?"

"It's time for lunch, Daddy. Did you see that alligator in the lobby ? Why don't we go back there?"

"Oh sweetie, I wish I could, but I've got to keep calling people. I'll tell you what..."

"What?"

"Why don't you and Mommy go down there and have lunch on the mezzanine and bring me something back."

"Can we mommy?" she pleaded.

"Of course, darling," Betty said, stroking Maude's head. "What do you want Johnathan?"

"Oh, anything."

"Maude, go wash your hands and let me talk to Daddy."

"I'll be right back."

Betty leaned in close, "Now Johnathan, tell me the truth. How's it really going?"

"Well," he said, folding his hands and looking down for a moment. "It really isn't as bad as I thought, but it could be better. That Scott plays dirty pool."

"What do you mean?"

"Well when we got here this week, we found out that our special order for extra phones at the hotel and at the Coliseum had been canceled. We put that in months ago, and nobody from our side would do a dumb thing like that. I know I can't prove Scott's people did it, but Bob said that's how this guy operates. Just little things you know, anything to keep us off balance and waste more time that we really don't have."

She rubbed his back. He kissed her on the cheek.

"Thanks for just being here," he said. He looked worn out. "And the thing is, we know he has a few skeletons in his closet and there isn't one damned thing we can do about it."

"What do you mean?"

"Mommy, did you see the kitchen?" Maude interrupted, returning to the master suite.

"No, honey, but I will in a minute," she said, holding up her index finger. "Daddy wants to tell me something. Where's your case of Barbie dolls?"

"I don't know, I don't want them now. Let's go," she whined.

"Just a minute, Maude," Betty said, sternly.

"Come here," Johnathan said, extending his arms. He knew it would work. He held his daughter on his lap, while he continued his story.

"Well, you see Scott maintains membership in a very private shooting club down along the James River. It's not much of a club by most standards—no fancy clubhouse, just a broken down log cabin. Bob went down there to check it out. Well, first of all, not only is it a shooting club, but they specifically bar all black people.

"Which reminds me, Betty. Do me a big favor and do it right away would you, please?"

"Sure. What do you need?"

"Call my office and have them send a messenger out to Middleburg right away. I want them to hand deliver my resignation to the club, effective immediately. This is important. I don't know where any one else is, or I'd have them do it. Can you do that?"

"But..."

"Betty, I just don't want any problems right now, you understand?"

"But you know they don't discriminate there?"

"I know, but just for now. We can always rejoin after the election."

She made a mental note to do as he requested.

"Mommy, I'm hungry. Let's go," Maude said, pulling and tugging on her mother's hand.

"Okay, sweetie," she said, giving Johnathan a look that said *we'll talk about this more later, but I've got to go now.*

He understood, "I'll see you later," he said quietly.

An official welcoming ceremony for Johnathan Douglas Dent was scheduled to be held at the hotel at four-thirty. This was another carefully staged event, courtesy of Bob Dent, who pointed out, "It'll just be in time for the five o'clock news. They should be able to get at least one decent sound bite."

A brass band—trombone, French horn, tuba, and trumpet—was assembled on one side of a long red carpet. The musicians were dressed in white pants, white shirts, and navy blue blazers, and all wore identical navy blue baseball caps with "Dent for Senator" stenciled on the bills.

A bevy of attractive young ladies, courtesy of the Young Democrats at the University of Richmond and the College of William & Mary, were also dressed in navy blue. They wore navy blue skirts with matching blazers white blouses, topped off with more Dent caps. Their main job was to distribute buttons that read: "Johnathan Dent—Serving the Future of Virginia." Johnathan's original slogan had been "Preserving and Serving the Future of Virginia," but his brother Bob had wisely advised against emphasizing the issue of preservation given the nature of some of his property development projects.

The courtyard of the hotel was packed at four-twenty. The band played "Old Abe Lincoln,"a campaign song made famous in the presidential election of 1860. The tune was from the old spiritual "Ol' Gray Mare Come Tearing out de Wilderness" which most identified as "The Old Gray Mare, She Ain't What She Used to Be."

At four-thirty-five, Johnathan Dent, wife Betty, and daughter Maude, along with sons Johnathan and Douglas, stepped out the front door onto the red carpet and up to the podium.

There was raucous applause, whistling, and cheering. The band stopped playing. The motor drives on the still cameras whirred and video cameras were silently switched on. Johnathan momentarily basked in the adulation and began.

"Good afternoon ladies and gentlemen and children..." and he leaned over to pick up his daughter Maude.

More applause.

"My family and I welcome you."

Betty was momentarily surprised when Johnathan picked up Maude. He rarely showed that sort of public affection for the children. She also had been stewing all day about how she might be able to slip away to make a very important phone call. She worried about it since talking with Johnathan before lunch. She had to get to a phone. The deadline was approaching, it was almost five o'clock. She leaned over to her son, the oldest of the twins.

"Tell your dad not to worry," she said inching behind him. "I have to be excused for a few minutes," holding her stomach as if she had a problem. The young man turned and nodded to her and she slipped away.

Betty made her way through the lobby past the bronze alligator toward the ladies' room. She stopped at the telephone booth, a plush oversized enclosed closet, with what appeared to be a soundproof glass panel in the door.

She quickly dialed the number of her friend Claudia. She knew the number by heart after years of being the closest of friends. She was nervous. She punched in the numbers and waited for the tone to indicate that she should then punch in the number of her calling card.

An automated voice came on the phone, "I'm sorry but the number you have entered is invalid, please hang up and try again."

Her mind was racing.

Had the card expired? I'll just charge it to the house. No, that would take too long. Maybe I punched it in wrong, she thought, trying again.

Then, one ring...two...three... Good. No recording...but now there were four rings...five...six.

Oh damn, she thought, *don't let me get the answering machine.*

"You have reached the Jasper residence, I'm sorry we're not in right now..."

Betty was in shock. *How could this happen?* She had to get in touch with Claudia. She was the only one who could help. Just then, she heard the familiar voice.

"Hello. Hello?"

"Claudia?"

"Betty?"

"Yes."

"Is something wrong? Where are you?"

At least she's speaking to me, Betty thought to herself. *That's a step in the right direction.* Oh where should she begin, there wasn't much time.

"Claudia, I need a favor."

At six-forty-six the next morning, there was a light rap on the door to their bedroom as Bob Dent entered. Johnathan was in the shower and Betty was in bed.

She was startled as he sauntered into the room unannounced. She rolled over toward the door. He did not apologize about entering without permission.

He looked at Betty and asked curtly, "Where's Johnathan?"

"In the shower."

"Get him out quick, the governor's on the line."

"The governor? At this hour?"

"Yes, he's a very busy man. Quick, this is crucial."

Betty knew what this meant. The governor surely was preparing to endorse Johnathan. And while he wasn't the most popular man in the state, his approval could be pivotal for Johnathan. Since becoming governor less than two years ago, all manner of rumors and innuendo plagued him. It was said—both in the press and in corners of the ever-so-exclusive Country Club of Virginia—that he was spending much too much time in the company of Mrs. Edgar Winthrop Minot.

Dolly—as friends, acquaintances, enemies and anyone who vaguely knew her, called her—was the soon-to-be former wife of the legendary Edgar Winthrop Minot, one of the ten richest men in America. The Minots were strong financial supporters of the governor during his election, and the word was now that Mrs. Minot was continuing her full support. There was no scandal to date, but lots of talk.

"I'll get him," Betty answered as she rose out of bed quickly and headed to the bathroom.

"Johnathan," she said, as she opened the door to the steamy bathroom. "The governor's on the phone, Bob said to come quick."

He immediately turned off the water, grabbed a towel and wrapped it around himself as he headed to the phone beside the bed.

The governor asked Johnathan to join him for lunch at the Commonwealth Club at about one, right after his opening address at the convention.

"That'd be fine," Johnathan said, adding, "I'd be delighted."

Bob and Betty anxiously awaited for him to relay the conversation, as Johnathan stood dripping water on the carpet.

"Well?" they said almost in unison.

"Well," he said, now tightening his towel around his waist that Betty now noticed was expanding ever so slightly.

Oh well, she thought, *he'll lose it during the campaign.*

"...he wants me to join him for lunch."

"Oh, Johnathan, that's great," Betty said, instinctively reaching to put her arms around his wet body, then thinking twice and pulling back.

"That's it," Bob said, clapping his hands. "I knew it. You've got it made in the shade." He extended his hand to his brother for a high five, another rare occurrence for the usually reserved Johnathan Dent.

"Well, I better get dressed," Johnathan said, turning back to the bathroom.

"I'll say...you've got a busy day," Betty added.

"We need to get down to the Coliseum right away," Bob reminded him. "The governor will give his opening address at about nine-fifteen, right after the convocation. And oh, by the way, it goes without saying we can't let this get out until you've had lunch. We don't want to steal the governor's thunder. Meanwhile, we've got to keep plugging away, work the delegates, get our volunteers on the phone, and not get too smug."

Johnathan was dressed and gone within ten minutes. Betty said she'd shower and get a quick breakfast and meet him at the convention center, with Maude and the boys, within the hour.

She ordered room service. Ten minutes later, she poured a large glass of freshly squeezed orange juice and was going to sit down and wait for the others when suddenly she remembered she needed to check George Jasper's column in the *Washington Post.*

She hurriedly put down the glass and thumbed to the back of the first section, the editorial pages. She was sure it would be there. She read the headline of his column: "Summer Jobs Program: Boom or Bust?"

Damn, she thought, *it didn't work.* She'd been certain Claudia would pull through for her.

Their conversation had been brief. Betty told her that she was so sorry about what she'd seen in the barn, how badly she felt that they grown apart, and how much she dearly loved Claudia, would do anything for her, and had never and would never breathe a word about what happened with Jake. Claudia cried on the phone and told her how much she loved her and how much she missed her and would do anything for her. So Betty promptly launched into how Harrison Scott had disconnected all of Johnathan's phones and it put Johnathan behind. She told her about the club Scott belonged to down on the James River. The shooting club that specifically banned blacks, hardly something a politician would like to see become common knowledge.

Claudia took down all the information and promised to call her husband right away. She knew he was on deadline and would do her best. Betty thanked her friend, and repeated how much she loved her and trusted they'd get together "real, real soon.

"And by the way, this information won't do one bit of good if it doesn't make the paper tomorrow. It's the opening day."

"I understand," Claudia replied. "I'll talk to you soon."

So when Betty opened the paper that morning and saw nothing about the information she passed on to her best friend, she was deeply disappointed. She pondered for a minute that perhaps Claudia had second thoughts and wasn't really her good friend after all. Then, something on the left hand side of the paper caught her eye.

It was a cartoon, by the nationally famous Woodberry, who Betty knew had gotten his name while a student at Woodberry Forest School in Virginia. He'd been expelled in his junior year when he was caught drawing naked doodles of his teacher during biology class. He had since gone on to make a fortune drawing doodles.

There was his daily cartoon, right on top of the page. It was a caricature of Harrison Scott. He was all dressed up in shooting attire. He looked as if he'd just gone shopping at Abercrombie & Fitch. He was standing in front of a lean-to type log cabin, the name of the club, Frogtown was over the front door. Scott was pointing his rifle at a black man with a caption that read: *"Stand back, we don't take your kind in this neck of the woods."*

Betty beamed and smiled ear to ear. Claudia had pulled through after all. George Jasper must have passed the information to Woodberry. *How clever,* thought Betty. *That way no one would tie George and Johnathan, neighbors and old friends from Middleburg, to the accusation.* It also was no secret in Washington that the wives of the columnist and the attorney also were longtime friends. She folded the page back and shoved it in her bag. She couldn't wait to share it with Johnathan.

The driver stopped the rental car in front of the dark green canopy at the Commonwealth Club on West Franklin Street. It was precisely one o'clock. Betty and Maude were in the back seat and would continue on up the street to have lunch at Morton's Tea Room. Not only were they not invited to lunch with the governor, but until recently women (not to mention blacks of either sex) were not even allowed inside the elite club. But times had thankfully changed.

Johnathan entered the main foyer. The striking black-and-white tiled floor was set in a diamond pattern.

"Be sure to check out the decorating very carefully," Isabelle informed Johnathan when they spoke secretly earlier. "My good friend Bitsy Kurkendall did all of it."

Johnathan noted that it was, indeed, splendid. He told the white-coated black man in the lobby that he was there to meet the governor.

"You can wait for him in the Grill Room downstairs, sir," the man noted.

As expected of an ancient Virginia gentlemen's club, the place was creaky and musty. It reeked of old traditions laced with old money.

The two men dined at a small table in front of a bay window overlooking a distinctive garden area on the east side of the red brick building. They each ordered "The Old Dominion," a popular open-faced sandwich of fresh crab on an English muffin with seafood sauce on the side. A green salad followed and two glasses of Greenhill wine accompanied the meal.

They spoke of the weather, end-of-summer vacation plans (Johnathan, of course had none—just in case and family. The governor finally got around to the main topic of conversation.

"Young man," he began. Johnathan put down the glass of wine and wiped his mouth with his napkin. He felt as if he was back sitting in the headmaster's office in grade school. He knew this was a big moment. He looked the governor straight in the eye and did not respond.

"I want you to know I feel you have a very bright future and I have every intention of making my opinion public this afternoon."

"Thank you very much, Governor. I am delighted." Johnathan said carefully. He did not want to use the word *honored*. He knew this would certainly be a boost to his cause and told the man as much, adding that he was most appreciative.

They had a dessert of homemade vanilla ice cream with white chocolate sauce and one more glass of wine.

There were a number of stories in the *Washington Post* and the *Richmond Times* the next day.

A two-column-wide, three-inch short in the *Post also* caught Johnathan's eye as he scanned the papers at six a.m. He had not been to sleep the night before.

Shooting Club in James River
Sued after Barring Blacks

An exclusive Virginia club that includes former national Democratic co-chairman Harrison Scott among its members will be sued in federal court in Richmond later this month by a black physician and his wife who allege they were denied membership in the club based on their race.

Dr. and Mrs. Charles May will ask for a U.S. District Court order in Richmond barring discrimination by the the club known as Frogtown and the Tidewater Game Society and will seek $350,000 in compensatory and punitive damages.

Their decision to file suit was formally announced following publication in the Washington Post of an editorial cartoon based upon Scott's membership in the secretive enclave located in the James River area of the state.

Scott is one of many prominent figures in the club, where members have available to them over 2,000 acres of hunting and shooting facilities as well as miles of freshwater streams for fishing. Scott was also one of three candidates nominated to run for retiring Senator Lee Blair's seat at yesterday's Virginia Democratic Convention in Richmond.

The Mays' announcement came late in the day on the heels of a press conference by the governor endorsing Scott's leading opponent in the race, Johnathan Dent. A final ballot was not expected until very late last night.

Another item appeared on the front page of the *Richmond Times*.

Virginia Governor Samuel Cook late yesterday announced his endorsement of Johnathan Douglas Dent, a Democratic candidate for the U.S. Senate race in November.

Cook said he was making his announcement after "many hours of consideration" and that he had the "utmost trust in Johnathan Dent. I feel confident that he will be a strong leader with firm convictions."

Many Democratic delegates at the state convention yesterday expressed similar beliefs and others felt especially committed to Dent following disclosure of the news that his leading opponent, former National Democratic co-chairman Harrison Scott, was a member in an exclusive Virginia club that barred black membership.

As Johnathan Dent read these words, none of it was news to him. The Frogtown-Tidewater Club scandal had broken across the floor of the convention early in the day. As he sat now in the twilight of the cool Virginia ambiance on the hotel balcony, something came over him. This vast press coverage was no accident. This was carefully composed. This news and these stories on the morning of what was the "Big Ballot" were no coincidence.

His brother Bob spoke of the Big Ballot for months. He calculated the campaign down to the minute. He charted radio spots, newspaper stories, and interviews over five diagrams mounted in his Richmond office. This smacked of his labor and Johnathan was proud of him. He was more than willing to play this game with Harrison Scott. The man had thrown murky roadblocks for months.

Johnathan got up from the chair on the balcony and walked into the living room of his suite. His daughter was sleeping deeply on the cream-colored couch. He still hadn't seen the original cartoon in the *Post*, and now he wanted to dig it out of the stack of papers and have a look.

He quietly sifted through the one large stack of day old papers on a side table. He could not find the "A" section of the paper where the cartoon normally appeared in the back of that section. He found every other section and eventually gave up. It was time to shower and change and get down to the convention center early...For the Big Ballot.

Betty rolled over just as he was putting on his suit jacket and getting ready to depart. She inquired about the time and his schedule.

"I'll see you over there," he said, leaning on the bed to kiss her good-bye.

She mumbled and reciprocated. "Um," she said, waking from a sound solid sleep. "Okay, we'll be there right away." She was anxious to get going, too. "Good luck!" she called out, as the door shut.

Johnathan walked to the Coliseum alone. He felt confident after yesterday's endorcement. He savored a few blessed minutes of solitude.

He headed up Franklin Street toward the Convention Center on Fifth Street. He moved swiftly past such southern retail institutions as Miller & Rhoads department store and Woolworth's. He stopped for a red light on a corner near Cokesbury Bookstore, a pay telephone around the corner caught his eye. Through it all, he missed Isabelle. He yearned to share this with her. His moment in the warm Richmond sunlight seemed bittersweet.

He turned the corner, headed to the pay phone, and instantly dialed her home number. If he was lucky she'd still be home. She picked up the phone on the second ring.

"Oh, Johnathan," she said, in a pleading voice. "I miss you so much. It's so strange to read all this in the newspaper. I just know you're going to win and I just know I'll never see you again. And I know you don't want to hear that right now. Can you forgive me?"

"Of course." he said with similar emotion. Yet, he'd never say it. "I'll tell you what."

"What?" she asked as she held the phone tight to her ear while also attempting to dress for work.

"I've got an idea. Look...I want you to beg, borrow, or steal a car. Rent one if you must. I'll pay for it. I want you to come down here. I'll have Bob get you a room." He spoke quickly, with authority.

"Johnathan, that's much too risky. Don't you think?"

"No, listen," he said loudly. Traffic in downtown Richmond was picking up. He saw the early delegates heading toward the vast round convention center. "No, I know Betty and Maude can't stay tonight. They have to be back home for early school registration. If all goes well, and I don't see why it wouldn't, they'll leave around sixish or no later than sevenish. And then, Isabelle, if I am indeed the lucky man, there will be a big reception tonight. You can be there and see it all and I'll be with you late tonight."

"But how will I find you?" she asked. She knew there was not one iota of doubt she'd join him.

"Listen," he said. "I don't care how you get here. Just drive to Richmond. Take a bus if you have to. Come to the lobby of the Jefferson Hotel. Right off the lobby there's a small, dimly lit bar, I can't remember the name of it. Just plan to get there about eight or nineish. Things might run late, you understand. I'll find you there. There might be a number of votes tonight."

"Okay," she said, knowing she'd somehow be able to borrow her boss's car. She would make up some story. "Okay," she said again, "I'll be there."

"Oh, Isabelle, you are divine," he said.

He looked up and noticed a delegate waiting for the phone. He was sure the man hadn't heard his conversation. But he also was positive he'd been recognized. "Oh, okay," he said, changing to his business-like tone. "That sounds fine. Someone's waiting for the phone, I need to get going."

"Oh, I understand," Isabelle said. "I get it, someone's listening, right?"

"Right. So I'll see you."

"Okay, but one other thing, Johnathan."

"Yes," he continued in his business mode.

"Good luck. I love you."

And he hung up.

The entire morning session consisted of officially placing the three candidates names in nomination. Each nominating speech was to last no longer than eight minutes, followed by a no more than a twelve minute demonstration. The order of nomination was determined by lot, with Johnathan drawing the first slot, Winnie Milton in the second position, and Harrison Scott in the final and most desirable place.

Following the opening convocation, everyone was settled in for what promised to be a long day. (And what also later proved to be a long night.)

Johnathan Douglas Dent's final victory total was 1,579 votes and came fourteen hours later following six ballots.

Through it all, Johnathan was constantly thinking about Isabelle. As planned, she was waiting in the bar at the hotel. It was a problematic moment for Johnathan when he returned after eleven o'clock. A scrum of reporters was now attached to him. He turned to his brother as they entered the lobby. The doorman held the door open and hotel employees haulted and stared, several bellman asked for an autograph.

Was it really less than twenty-four hours ago that he strolled through this very same lobby unnoticed?

"I need a favor," he whispered to his brother.

"Oh, sure," he said as they continued to walk. They passed the bar, an intentional move on Johnathan's part.

"There's a girl in the bar."

"What?"

"You heard me. Please, Bob, don't ask questions and please don't get judgmental."

"No, no...you know better," he assured his brother. "But do you know her?"

"Yes, yes. Listen..." They were at the elevators now.

Bob turned to the flock of news hungry reporters and announced: "As you all may know, there's going to be a celebration reception that will begin at midnight in the courtyard of the Linden Row Inn. It's located just west of here on the edge of the Fan district. I want to extend an invitation to all of you to come over."

"Now then," he said sticking his hand in his pocket. "These blue and white tickets," which he held above his head, "will admit each of you. Who wants to attend?"

The reporters reacted predictably. It would be a chance to see the new candidate up close and personal—maybe even get fresh material for their stories and the personality profiles their editors would surely be demanding for the Sunday papers. The tickets were gone in a matter of minutes, and so were the reporters.

"Johnathan, you go on upstairs," he ordered as he distributed the tickets. "I'll be there in a bit." Johnathan knew that Bob would carry out his wishes and bring Isabelle upstairs.

Without any description from Johnathan, Bob identified the one woman in the bar he knew his brother wanted to see. He approached Isabelle quietly and with no fanfare. She wore a monochrome beige linen suit with bold gold earrings and a single strand of pearls. She was sitting alone at a table in the center of the room. Bob considered that was rare for someone having a clandestine meeting. He also deemed she was drop dead gorgeous.

He moved swiftly toward her table. "Excuse me," he said quietly, "I'm Bob Dent." He knew instinctively if he said his last name he would get a positive reaction.

At first he didn't. She said simply, "Yes?"

So he repeated himself, "I'm Bob Dent."

"Oh,oh, yes," she said, standing. "Johnathan's brother. He's spoken of you."

The television above the bar simultaneously flashed Johnathan's picture on the late news with the word of his nomination.

They shook hands awkwardly. "Johnathan asked me to come down and get you," he said.

"Oh fine," she said, opening her purse to pay the check. She left a ten-dollar bill and followed him.

The three of them went together in a cab to the midnight reception. Isabelle mingled among the more than three hundred guests and intermittently her eyes would meet Johnathan's across the courtyard.

All of Johnathan's volunteers were at the party. Isabelle chitchatted briefly with one of the men she'd met in Culpeper at the ground-breaking ceremonies for Payne's Corner. She also spoke with Sam Blackwell, who never thought to wonder why she was at this party. A number of large contributors were also on hand. The former First Lady put in a twenty-minute appearance and got all the attention. There was a steady swirl of people surrounding her and Isabelle watched and admired how she handled the crunch.

At just past two-thirty in the morning, Bob Dent came and took Isabelle's arm and they left. Johnathan joined them minutes later for the brief cab ride back to the hotel. Isabelle felt comfortable and they laughed and joked until they were back inside the hotel suite. She and Bob hit it off quickly. She saw he was certainly the more outgoing of the two.

Johnathan suggested one last nightcap for the three of them. They settled down in the sitting area

"This is a good idea," Bob began, "because we need to go over a few things for the morning. Now I plan to leave here bright and early. You won't have much sleep."

Isabelle just listened.

"What time are we talking about?" Johnathan inquired.

"I want to be at the airport and ready to go just before seven."

Johnathan didn't look Isabelle in the eye. He knew he couldn't. He wanted to spend some time with her, just a few brief hours.

"I'll tell you what," he began, "Isabelle has rented a car." He put his hand gently on top of her thigh. "How about I sleep in? I really need it and I'll meet you back in Washington later in the day."

"Hey, you're the boss. I'll just take Don and Pat back with me," he said, referring to his top two aides. "Why don't you call me when you get back. It won't be a problem will it?"

"No," Johnathan answered. "No problem."

"Well, in that case..." his brother said as he stood up. "It's been a helluva day and I think I'll retire. Nice to meet you Isabelle, hope to see you soon."

And he disappeared into the next room.

As the door closed, Johnathan leaned over and kissed Isabelle. He laid his hand in her lap and clutched the inside of her leg and drew her toward him. He'd been drinking straight bourbon and his mouth tasted soft and warm. She put her drink down on the table and they never made it into his bedroom until past five in the morning.

Bob Dent and the other two men left just after six. The sky was dark and ominous as they drove out Hanover Street to Byrd airport. The Beechcraft Bonanza was standing by when they arrived.

Bob stopped in the offices of the Aero Services to call the toll-free number for the FAA in Leesburg and give them his flight plans to Winchester. The phone answered automatically and he was put on hold. He stood waiting for someone to answer while elevator music filled his ear. He looked at his watch, he was eager to get going. He hung on while Barry Manilow first sang "I Write the Songs" and then, "Can't Smile without You."

Once they reached Winchester, he'd still have a one-hour commute into Washington. It was becoming late. Someone finally answered his call. He methodically repeated the information: "This is three-five-romeo-zula, VFR, B-E three-five, alpha, one-hundred-sixty knots, fifty-five hundred feet."

He continued, by memory, "Richmond, Winchester, forty minutes, three hours of fuel, three souls, white with red stripe, alternate airport India Alpha

Delta." The voice on the other end said he would record the flight plan and hung up.

The three men buckled in and Bob tuned to the ATIS frequency for the pilot airport weather briefing, mentally noting the wind velocity and direction.

Bob was on the radio speaking to ground control, "This is three-five-romeo-zula, we have ATIS. VFR to Winchester, Virginia. We are a Beech Bonanza at Aero Services."

"Three-five-romeo-zula cleared to taxi to runway two-zero."

He glanced at the digital clock, six forty-eight, and then spoke to the control tower. "Ready to go, two-zero."

"Cleared for takeoff runway two-zero, winds one-hundred-eighty degrees at seventeen knots.

They flew north from the state capital. Just south of Fredericksburg they made a thirty-degree left turn to a new heading of three-hundred-thirty degrees to continue along the western side of the Blue Ridge mountains, roughly the same path as Interstate 81, which was barely visible in the now constant rain.

It was seven thirty-six when a vicious choking vacuum of wind swept across the top ridge of the mountains, sucking the light aircraft into a steep dive, nose first. Seconds later, the airplane hit the treetops and exploded in a raging ball of fire, scattering debris across a one-mile radius.

Word of the crash hit the morning news in time for the eight-thirty local broadcast during the *Today Show*.

Betty Dent watched television in the kitchen as she and Maude ate scrambled eggs. She realized what was happening. She grabbed the little girl's head and held it to her, trying unsuccessfully to cover her ears. They stood and listened.

"A single-engine light Beechcraft private plane that left Byrd airport in Richmond early this morning and was headed for the Winchester regional airport has crashed in the area of Toms Brook, Virginia, at seven-thirty this morning. Details are still sketchy but the plane belonged to Bob Dent, brother of Virginia Democratic senatorial candidate Johnathan Dent, who may have been aboard. Though there has been no confirmation, it is believed that the two brothers were traveling back to Washington together to begin formulating campaign plans for the upcoming election. Johnathan Dent was nominated to run following his victory at yesterday's state Democratic Convention in Richmond. Stay tuned for further details."

Before Betty Dent could cry or shriek, the phone rang...

Chapter 16

Let Us Pray

Isabelle opened her eyes and assumed it was close to dawn. The curtains were open and it was still dark outside. Then she realized it was raining. She watched the rain and didn't move or turn toward Johnathan. She felt him curled up in a deep solid sleep. She recognized he was exhausted. She slid out of bed to the bathroom. When she padded back, his eyes were open.

"What time is it?" he asked.

"I have no idea," she said, searching for a clock. "I'll call the desk."

"Ten-twenty."

"We've got to get going," he announced, jumping out of the bed. "Order some coffee and juice and whatever you want. Tell room service we're in a hurry and have them rush it."

They showered (separately, for a change), dressed, and savored their togetherness as if they'd been a couple for years. They each pored over the morning papers, combing the columns for the details of Johnathan's victory and the party afterwards. In one paper, Johnathan was pictured air kissing the former First Lady.

They never turned on the television. They assumed there was no more morning news at this hour, when Oprah and Geraldo dominated the airwaves as a prelude to the afternoon soaps.

They rolled out of the hotel and headed north for the two-and-a-half hour drive to Washington. Isabelle drove so Johnathan might catch up on his reading and make notes for a meeting with his brother that afternoon.

Before they left the city, Johnathan directed her on a brief tour around the historic district. He narrated a history of the statues on Monument Avenue and how each one was either facing north or south according to their allegiance during "the great unpleasantness," otherwise known as the Civil War. They passed the Virginia Museum of Fine Arts.

"Maybe some day we can come back," he said, recalling their special days in the museums in Washington.

On their final loop through town, Johnathan pointed out the Hollywood Cemetery filled with the graves of fallen Confederate soldiers and loved ones of some of the FFVs—the First Families of Virginia. He told the old joke often repeated by locals that when they died, they wouldn't go to heaven, they'd head for Hollywood. A few minutes later, they eased onto the interstate. Johnathan noticed how sexy Isabelle appeared as she was driving a car. The seat belt came across her front so that the outline of her breasts was revealed. She had hiked up her khaki skirt to above mid-thigh, her right leg extended to the pedals and her left leg propped up against the seat. She occasionally rested her left hand on her left leg. Johnathan read a bit and observed as she maneuvered in and out of traffic.

Halfway to Washington, they stopped in Fredericksburg at McDonalds and ordered hamburgers and Cokes at the drive-through. He leaned over to kiss her as they waited in the line.

They never thought about turning on the radio. They had so much to say to one another.

They arrived in Washington just before the afternoon rush hour. Isabelle moved the rental car into the heart of the city up K Street to Connecticut Avenue. The streets at this hour were eerily empty. It was the calm before the storm, when some of the main thoroughfares became one way motorized marathons to the Virginia and Maryland suburbs. She pulled over to the far corner. There was always that mutual thought—never spoken—that someone might see them.

She put the car in park and turned to him. He touched her hand, said thank you, and got out of the car with his briefcase and an extra armload of manila folders under his arm.

He leaned into the window. "I'll call you later."

Congress was out and everyone was headed in all directions.

Washington was quiet in the summer. And very hot. The mirage on the sidewalks caused him to sense he was walking in a shallow pool of sweltering, brackish water. He was wearing a beige khaki suit, the unofficial men's summer uniform of this city. As soon as he entered the lobby of his office building, he felt relief when a rush of icy air conditioning hit his body as he swished through the revolving doors.

He was mentally making a list of things to do this afternoon as he rode the elevator to the eighth floor to the suite of offices occupied by Duke, Graves, and Coggin. He shoved open the right side of the French doors of the reception area.

Mildred, the receptionist, was on the phone and looked up and just gave a little nod. Johnathan didn't notice that she disconnected her call and unplugged her headset to follow him back to his office.

His secretary, Miss Wickwire, also was on the phone. He nodded to her and this time he saw her just hang in mid-sentence with someone.

"What are you doing here? My God. Mr. Dent," she bellowed. "What are you doing here?" She put her hands on his chest and put her arms around him. She kept inquiring... "What are you doing here?"

The receptionist came up from behind and said, point blank to Johnathan "I thought you were dead! My God—we've got to call the papers." Her headset was dangling from her ears.

A crowd gathered. Someone ran in the direction of Budd Duke's office, ushering the head of the law firm in Johnathan's direction.

Johnathan had no clue what was going on, thinking it was some sort of office prank. "I'm sorry Mildred, I'm very much alive." He was smiling, near laughter when Budd Duke approached. "Hey Budd, what's all the fuss?"

It took Miss Wickwire forty-five minutes to get through to Betty Dent. This followed a one-hour-and-twenty-minute discussion with Johnathan, in which he learned of the plane crash. His brother and the other two men were dead.

A wave of nausea instantly came over Johnathan as Budd expounded "the fuss." Johnathan broke out in a sweat and become queasy. When he started to get up to go in the bathroom, he knew halfway across the room it was futile. He tried to reach the hand painted wastebasket beside his desk. He streatched out his left hand to brace himself and leaned over. He missed his target by two feet. It was a beastly mess and he was embarrassed when the janitor arrived to clean up. The smell from the rug shampoo lingered for the rest of the afternoon.

Johnathan laid his head back on the beige sofa and put a wet rag on his head. He ruminated how he wanted to talk to his brother. Bob would help him out of this mess. Over and over again reminded himself, *Bob is gone.*

Bob is gone. Oh, Lord how could this happen? He died helping Johnathan pursue a dream that was now an outlandish nightmare. He hated himself one minute and the next minute he thought about Isabelle. Certainly by now, she had heard this horrendous news. It was all over the radio and television. He made a mental note to call her when he was alone later.

The immediate dilemma was how to manage this chaos Budd Duke never came right out and asked Johnathan where he was or how it happened. However, Johnathan did offer a simple explanation.

"I needed some extra rest and so I drove back in a rented car. I never turned on the radio."

Budd asked his secretary to bring two large Cokes and lots of ice. He recognized that Johnathan needed to settle his stomach. Like any lawyer, he was jotting down notes on a long yellow legal pad.

Things to do.

Call Betty.

Newspapers?

Television and Radio?

Should we do interviews?

He accepted the circumstances. He never questioned Johnathan any further than the details he offered throughout the afternoon. They reviewed the list of problems and how to tackle them.

Johnathan immediately issued a lengthy statement to the press and did not grant any interviews. Budd Duke distributed his own press release after repeated editing and rewriting.

Upon returning to Washington, D.C. by car, Johnathan Douglas Dent, the recently nominated Democratic candidate for the U.S. Senate, confirmed this afternoon that the passengers in the tragic crash of the twin engine plane near Toms Brook, Virginia, included his beloved brother Robert Dent, an advertising executive from Richmond, Virginia, on leave to serve as campaign manager for Johnathan Dent.

Donald A. Edwin, of Greenwich, Connecticut, an electronic media specialist with the J. Walter Thompson Agency in New York, and Patrick William Donovan of West Caldwell, New Jersey, an analyst with Moody's Investment Services, also were aboard the plane.

Funeral arrangements are pending. Mr. Dent will be taking some time off to mourn the death of his brother before resuming his campaign.

Budd Duke put in a phone call to Ben Bradlee, the editor of the *Washington Post.*

He explained to the secretary screening Bradlee's calls that he was the head of the law firm where Johnathan Dent was a partner and that it was of the utmost importance that they speak "in the next twenty minutes."

His call was returned eight minutes later.

"I'm sending over a statement by messenger, Ben," he said to his well-known acquaintance. "Johnathan Dent just returned to our office. It seems he was over-tired and drove back to Washington later in the day. He was not a passenger on that plane. I don't know if they've identified the bodies yet, but as you can imagine, Johnathan is distraught to lose his brother like this and just cannot talk to anyone right now."

"Well, Budd, this is incredible," was all the editor said.

"We'll be in touch soon. Thank you."

Timing was of the essence at this hour—with the six p.m. TV news and early edition of the paper approaching—and Budd Duke knew it. He sent messengers simultaneously to deliver the statements to the local television and radio stations as well as UPI, AP, and the Washington bureau of the *Richmond Times*. Then he finally reached Betty Dent. The two men had decided that if Johnathan were to call his wife at this point in time, she might just faint dead away.

"Betty? It's Budd."

"Oh, Budd, it's so nice of you to call. This phone has been ringing off the hook. How on earth did you get through?"

"It wasn't easy," he explained, adding, "Listen, Betty, I have some news for you."

"News?" she asked. "What news, I've watched the television all day. It's been just horrible. I saw them lift the bodies out in bags. Oh, Budd, I just don't know what I'm going to do..."

He knew she was about to cry. "Now Betty, please, please calm down. Listen to me. I want you to sit down. Are you sitting down?"

"Yes, oh I'm..."

"Betty?"

"Oh, okay..." she sniffed.

"This is important Betty. I want to tell you something, okay? Do you have a grip here?"

"Yes, Budd." She sniffled again.

He visualized her wiping her nose.

She took a deep breath. "What is it?"

"Betty...Johnathan wasn't on the plane."

"What do you mean?"

"Well, I mean, he wasn't..."

"Then where exactly was he, Budd? Please don't fool me. This is..."

"No, no, no. He's right here Betty. He's okay. He was tired so he drove back to Washington alone." Budd didn't actually know this for a fact, but added it because he suspected some skepticism in her voice. "He never turned on the radio. He was just as shocked as we were when he walked into the office. He had no idea. He's very upset about his brother and the others and feeling quite badly. He wants to talk to you."

She was stunned. She plopped down on one of the tall kitchen stools, put her elbows on the counter and sifted through it all. First he was dead, now he wasn't. She let out a deep breath.

The sound on the kitchen television was off. Betty wanted and needed a drink. She looked at the clock. It was almost five. Just a bit earlier than usual, she thought. She poured a large wine goblet with some Piedmont

Chardonnay. It was ice cold.

Just perfect.

A special dinner was obviously in order.

Oh my God, she thought...*the children.*

She hadn't called them. She had no idea if the boys had heard anything. And Maude. In the swirl of things it didn't dawn on Betty to call the school with the initial report of the crash—much less the correction that her father was alive and well. It had been quite an afternoon…more wine.

She made a list for dinner and had Bertha run to town and pick it all up at the small market.

Roast beef. No, there wasn't enough time. Broiled steaks would be faster and easier.

Steaks - 2 large, one small 1 1/4 inches
potatoes
butter
broccoli
rolls
lettuce
tomatoes

She continued to write her list and sip the wine. She didn't hear the visitor enter the room.

Andy Mayhaw, the much-admired Episcopal minister, stood near the end of the counter.

"Betty," he said opening his arms.

Her elbow was on the table, the glass of wine was in her left hand and her pen in the other.

"Andy?" She looked at him blankly.

"Betty. Oh, Betty," he continued stepping closer across the room. "I came as soon as possible."

She put the glass down and came off the stool to embrace him.

"I'm so sorry," he repeated.

"Oh, Andy don't be," she said.

"I know this is a difficult time."

"You have no idea what I've been through today."

"I'm sure," he said, looking down at her while still holding both her hands.

"Andy...he's not dead."

"Oh, Betty, I know this is difficult," he said, ever so sympathetically.

"No, really, Andy," she pleaded, "he's not dead. He just called here."

"Oh...?"

They sat down on the sofa and Betty told the clergyman the whole story. How Johnathan decided at the last minute not to fly, but to drive back to Washington. *How he hadn't turned on the radio and didn't know about the accident was still a mystery.*

As she told the story, she offered Andy a glass of wine. He joined her.

For his one glass, she drank three. She sat and rambled and concluded that it sounded stranger than fiction. She would get details from Johnathan when he got home. Maude arrived and the clergyman excused himself. He embraced Betty and suggested that they might see one another one Sunday very soon.

Bertha left the essentials for the evening meal on the countertop. She washed and dried the lettuce, peeled and sliced the cucumbers and cut up carrots, and celery. Before she left for the day, she washed the potatoes, poked them deep with a sharp knife and put them in the oven. She did not bother to ask Mrs. Dent if there was anything else she should do. The woman knew it was a incomprehensible day and she did her very best to stay out of the way.

Betty walked over to the counter and dispensed another glass of wine. She shifted to the other side of the room and took the phone off the hook. She faced Maude with the day's bizarre incidents.

"How was school?" she began.

"Okay."

"Do you have any homework?"

"Not much."

"Well, why don't you come sit down with me?"

"Why?"

"Oh, no reason, just to talk."

"Well, I promised Sarah I'd call her."

"Well, you can call her later. I've got a story to tell you."

By the time Betty finished her story to Maude. She had her fifth glass of wine for the evening and Johnathan was home. After recounting the episode to her daughter, she felt shattered. She didn't even jump up with open arms to greet him. Rather she sat on the loveseat and watched him take off his jacket and tie and lean over and kiss her lightly on the cheek.

He started.

"It's been a helluva day."

"I'll bet it has," she answered. She put her hand on his shoulder and looked at him, then put her arms around him and clutched.

"I think I'll join you for a drink," he said finally, crossing the room to pour a cool glass of wine. She stood up and prepared the steaks for broiling and put some water on to steam the vegetables.

His eyes started to well and he put his glass down to wipe his face. "What a goddamn mess. Just when things were going so well, there have been a thousand times today that I wanted to turn to Bob and ask, 'How should we handle this?'

"I keep going over and over it in my mind. How did this happen? And now what happens? Should I drop out? Stay in? I keep thinking Bob would have wanted me to stick this thing out. But right now, I'm not sure I've got the stomach for it. I just don't know. I really don't know what to do."

He was clearly distraught. Betty thought now was not the time to interrogate him about the specifics of driving back from Richmond. She just couldn't doubt him at a time like this. She took him in her arms again, and tried to reassure him.

"Of course you'll stay in," she said. "Of course that's what Bob would've wanted. Don't even think about getting out now."

They ate a quiet dinner in the kitchen with their daughter. Two hours later, after watching an hour-long special about the accident and its political ramifications, they climbed the steps upstairs, together.

Almost as soon as he was under the covers, Johnathan Dent fell asleep in his wife's arms. She held his head tightly to her chest. She still loved him dearly, even if she was slightly suspicious about his trip north in a rented car. She kissed the top of his head and he slept, breathing shallowly.

Later, she said to herself.

Later.

Three days after the crash, Johnathan Dent buried his beloved brother in a family plot at the Hollywood Cemetery in Richmond, not far from Monument Avenue.

The irony did not elude Johnathan that just a few days before he and Isabelle had driven by this spot and laughed at his little joke about the cemetery and "heading to Hollywood".

Johnathan Dent gazed off, over the mass of mourners. He was too numb to cry. He was oblivious to the people. He shook his head quickly, as if there was something in his ear. He put his chin up. He felt the cool, crisp air that signaled the onset of autumn. He sat in the front row of seats set up under the small, dark green canopy near the grave where his brother's casket was about to be lowered. The monotonous words of the Episcopal minister hardly registered in Johnathan's mind.

O God, whose mercies cannot be numbered: Accept our prayers on behalf of thy servant...

Yes, his brother would want him to kick on, he told himself. His brother would want him to campaign harder than ever. He'd have to find a new campaign manager, and soon. He'd start interviewing people tomorrow.

Oddly enough, Isabelle hadn't heard anything about the plane crash when she returned to Washington that afternoon with Johnathan. She was tired—a good kind of tired—and went straight home, took a hot shower, and slipped into her nightgown.

She found a frozen lasagna dinner, put it in the oven and poured a glass of red wine. She sat down to read the Post's version of Johnathan Douglas Dent's stunning nomination in Richmond. She ate the dinner, had another glass of wine, and fell asleep on the couch.

She awoke at six-thirty the next morning. She showered again, washed her hair and prepared for work. She walked through Georgetown, and stopped to get a toasted bagel and a cup of coffee along the way.

There was a stack of mail on her tiny desk in the back of the shop. She propped open the front door in case some clients stopped by early. She began making the various piles as she opened the letters to be answered—bills, sample catalogues, junk.

Gunther let himself in the back door. It was early, not yet eight-thirty.

He must have deliveries to make, she thought.

"When you get a chance would you sweep out front and maybe run the hose on the sidewalk, I noticed it was a bit messy."

"Oh, no problem," Gunther replied.

Michael and the UPS man followed one another through the front door. Michael was carrying his usual cup of coffee from the 7-11, along with a sack full of carpet samples, a briefcase, and the Washington Post was tucked under his arm.

The UPS man had three large boxes. He could hardly see where he was going as he weaved to the back of the shop, past the furniture, end tables, vases, and a pair of antique stone greyhounds that someone might use at the entrance to their estate. He cautiously bent down and lowered the boxes at Isabelle's desk. She automatically stood up, moved around the desk and signed for them. Not a word passed between them, until she simply said "thank you" and bid him a good day.

Michael put the bag of samples on her chair, deposited his briefcase, paper, and coffee on her desk and started going through the mail. He was always anxious to look it over, hoping to find a check or two. His habit of taking over her desk each morning had irritated her at one time. She now accepted it as part of Michael's routine. He was the typical, disorganized, slightly scatterbrained artiste, and always said that "sloppiness was a sign of genius."

"I've already started to make a list of things to be done," she noted.

"Great," he said absently, still leafing through the mail. "Any calls?"

"Not really."

She picked up the bag off the chair and retrieved his briefcase and walked them back into his office. *That might get him out of my way*, she assumed.

It worked. He followed her. She returned to her desk and the phone was ringing. She was scheduling an appointment with a client, talking and leafing through the mess on the top of the desk at the same time, when the folded newspaper fell open and her eyes caught the headline:

Three Members of Johnathan Dent's Staff Killed in Light Airplane Crash

Just below the headline another line read: *"Brother of candidate among victims."*

Isabelle continued to read:

STRASBURG, VA—A light Beechcraft Bonanza airplane carrying three members of newly nominated Democratic senatorial candidate Johnathan Dent's staff were killed during a violent midday storm along the edge of the Blue Ridge Mountains here yesterday.

Robert Dent, brother of the candidate who played a major role in his brother's recent nomination, was the pilot of the plane, which slammed into a mountain.

Donald A. Edwin of White Plains, New York, and Patrick W. Donovan of West Caldwell, New Jersey, both consultants to Mr. Robert Dent, were also among the victims.

Johnathan Dent, who was scheduled to be among the passengers, but canceled at the last minute, preferring to drive north from Richmond. Mr. Dent's office issued the following statement late yesterday...

For Betty and Johnathan there was a fortuitous lull following the funeral. Their political life was on momentary hold until the Republican convention concluded in a few weeks in Williamsburg.

It gave them a much-needed opportunity to regroup and mourn their loss at the same time. Johnathan had never been a brooder and felt it best to try to lose himself in his work. He continued to go into the office every day and left early to get home for dinner with the family.

Betty knew this was the calm before the storm of the campaign as the summer wound down and the fall elections lay ahead. Often, she felt like she was living in a movie, going through the motions of maintaining the house while dreading the path her life was about to take. She had a terrible fear of public speaking. She had no problem jabbering with her friends on the phone or in line at the Safeway, but in front of a group of people...well, just the thought of it made her skin crawl.

Still, she knew that as "wife of candidate" she would work to aid her husband in appearances around the state. She realized winning the Senate seat was the aspiration of a lifetime.

Poor Johnathan, she thought one day, sitting alone in her bedroom. *He never even had time to grieve the death of his brother.*

She observed Johnathan closely when he arrived back in Middleburg each evening. He seemed calm. Yet, he was distant. He was attentive and always took time out to talk with Maude. He spoke about looking forward to the boys coming home for a long weekend. Yet, Betty felt that something else was on Johnathan's mind...something he was not willing to share.

Still, he seemed tender enough in bed. In fact, Betty was surprised by a recent *Donahue* show, which featured a psychologist who explained that it was not at all abnormal for a married couple's sex life to drop off for a short time after the death of a family member. Apparently it was all part of the depression period. It was short-lived and normal relations would resume soon.

That had not happened to Johnathan. If anything, their sex life had taken on new warmth, especially since she discovered that having a few glasses of wine before and during dinner often heightened her pleasure in their bedroom.

She glanced at her watch: three-fifteen. She had dinner planned, so she stayed upstairs until Maude got home. She finished going through all the mail-order catalogues and marked the pages for Christmas gifts. She figured since they would be traveling on the campaign trail, it would make things easier this year.

Perhaps an early glass of Chablis with lots of ice would help her relax a bit. She buzzed downstairs to Bertha and asked for some wine.

"And, oh," she added, "would you do me a favor and answer the phone if anyone calls?"

"No problem, Mizz Dent, I'll be right up."

She began her Christmas list on one of Johnathan's long yellow legal pads. She wrote down the names: Johnathan, Maude, John Jr., Douglas, Bob... She caught herself promptly. The notion of her brother-in-law brought tears. They always celebrated Thanksgiving and Christmas together. Maybe it was a blessing that Johnathan would be so busy this year.

She sat back in the deep floral chintz covered wingback chair, it was hard to think ahead to what Christmas might bring this year. *Where would they be? Would Johnathan be a member of the United States Senate by then?* She wondered what that might be like.

No time for that, she thought, shaking her head and draining the last bit of wine from the tall crystal goblet.

She continued to make notes on her legal pad.

Johnathan: L.L. Bean wax raincoat, wool socks, rubber boots. She wasn't really too sure about the rubber boots. She thought twice about them, then scratched that off. *Not enough warmth in winter.* She searched for something else.

She made a memo in the margin to call The Papery and order their usual Christmas cards. They sent the same red engraved card with "Season's Greetings: Elizabeth and Johnathan Dent" for years. All she needed to do now is give the woman in the stationary store her order over the telephone. They usually sent about two hundred, but this year she was certain they'd need at least five hundred.

After all, there were so many people already involved in the campaign, with more being added for the fall campaign every day.

They'd all have to be on the list, particularly the people who contributed time and money to the effort. She wrote down the number "500" with a question mark. She would ask Johnathan later.

It was after five when she finished, combed her hair, put on some lipstick and went downstairs. She bid Bertha good-bye and poured another glass of wine.

"Mrs. Jasper says to call as soon as you can."

"Okay, Bertha, thanks a bunch. See you tomorrow. Oh...wait. Where's Maude?"

"She's over at the Morris house and said she'd be home by dinnertime."

It was always a chore to get messages out of Bertha, since she was unable to write them down. The more she relied on her memory, the less reliable it was.

"Okay, thanks again."

Betty looked over the ingredients Bertha put out for dinner. The chicken breasts were laid in a glass casserole dish and brushed with butter, and seasoned with salt and pepper. There was a colander full of fresh vegetables—broccoli, cauliflower, and carrots—to be steamed. Three baking potatoes were scrubbed and poked with a knife and ready to go in the oven. She opened the refrigerator door to search for a package of rolls to bake. They were on the shelf by the door, she took them out and put them on the counter and then returned to take out another bottle of local wine.

The phone rang.

"Where have you been?"

"Nowhere, why?"

"Didn't Bertha give you the message I called and that it was urgent."

It was Claudia. Betty sat down on the high stool next to the phone and poured a glass of wine and continued the conversation. It was five-thirty.

"Well, she said you called and that it was rather important. She didn't say it was urgent. Why, what's up?"

"I need to talk to you."

"Well sure, go right ahead." She settled on the stool, leaned over the counter, and hunched over the phone, as if to get closer and more intimately involved with her friend on the other end.

"Oh, Betty, I know you have so many problems right now. I'm so sorry but I just don't know what to do."

For a moment Betty was perturbed. Why was it that her dearest friend was constantly apologizing for everything she did in her life? "That's okay, tell me."

There was no sound on the other end. Betty knew it was serious. She thought to herself, *I hope someone else hasn't died.*

Claudia was weeping. She took in her breath and her voice cracked. "Please Betty, don't get mad at me."

There she goes again, thought Betty, as she sipped on the wine, and then said,

"You know better."

"Well, I mean...don't get mad at me for saying this, I know I don't have to but you must promise. No...you must *swear to God* you'll never tell anyone. I know you won't..."

"You know I won't. Go ahead." She was losing patience. After all, she didn't have all night, she had dinner to think about. Then she heard Maude coming in the back door. The dog was making noises.

Betty waved to her as the voice on the other end of the phone announced. "Jake has AIDS."

"How was your day?" Betty whispered to Maude who was unloading her books on a chair.

"What?" said the voice on the phone.

"What?? Betty said.

"I said, *Jake has AIDS.*"

"Oh my God! How do you know?" Betty asked as she watched Maude reach for a Coke in the refrigerator.

Betty shook her finger back and forth to tell her "no" to the soft drink right before dinner. The little girl made a face as if to plead please. "You know better," Betty whispered to Maude, but Claudia thought she was talking to her.

"*Of course*, I know better. But Betty, it's too late for that. You know, you're the only one I can talk to about this. You're the only one who knows. And you know that's why I love you. That night you walked in on us, well...I knew you'd never tell anyone, not even Johnathan. I knew I could trust you with this."

Betty had no idea what to say, how to react. What could she do? She turned away from Maude, as if her daughter couldn't hear her, though she obviously could. "Well, listen...what can I do? Have you been to a doctor? Anyway, just because he has it, doesn't mean you do, too. You do know that, right?" she whispered.

"Have what mommy?" Maude asked.

Betty turned toward Maude. "Listen, honey...can't you see I'm on the phone? Now please, take your drink and go up to your room, do your homework, and stay there until I call you. Do you understand?"

She added, as if an order, "And, don't spill anything."

"Yes ma'am," Maude said, and turned and left the room.

"Well, he called me yesterday morning," Claudia continued. "He wanted me to meet him in this hole-in-the-wall diner over the mountain. We've met there before, but never during the day. He told me he wanted to talk and maybe have some lunch. So, naturally, I went through contortions at home and rearranged my schedule—which I always do when he calls—and I headed over there."

Betty didn't say a word.

"My imagination went crazy driving down the road. You know, I'm always assuming he's going to dump me or something. Then I thought, *no, maybe he just can't stand not being together for a few days and maybe we'll check into a motel over in Winchester for the afternoon.* We've done that a couple of other times. So we meet and order a sandwich. We're sitting there drinking iced tea and he just blurts it out. God, Betty...I'm scared to death. What am I going to do?"

"Well, damn, I haven't got a clue. What else did he say? Did he tell you where he got it himself?"

"Oh, hell, I don't know. He told me he has no idea, but he wanted me to be the first to know. I can't remember it all."

"You mean to tell me he hasn't even told his wife yet?"

"Well, no, I guess not. Well, I mean...by now maybe he has. I don't know. He was going to tell her last night. You know the strange thing Betty?" she continued, not waiting for an answer. "He doesn't even look sick. And the craziest thing is, after all that, I still lust for him in the worst goddamn way."

Betty was puzzled. "Did he have any symptoms at all?" she asked. "I can't understand what made him go for the test in the first place?"

"Oh, Betty, I don't know. I couldn't think. Everything is just racing through my head. I'm not like you. I can't think of those things at the right time. Now I've got to figure out what to do. I can't let George find out about this. It would ruin our marriage."

"Well," Betty said, sitting up straight on the stool now. "What makes you think he has to find out?"

"What do you mean?"

"Well, if you were to go downtown, I know a place in the city that gives the test and they don't ask your name. I think I read about it in last month's *Washingtonian.* I think before you make any other decisions, at least let's go and find out if you've got it, too."

All Betty could think about were Claudia's precious children. *How would she ever be able to explain that to her family? What an unmitigated disaster.*

"You know, Betty. I was hoping you'd say that. I've heard about that place, too, but it's not in a real good location if I remember right."

"Well the neighborhood's not great. It's Adams Morgan—lots of blacks and Hispanics. But who cares? It's the only way to go. Why don't I call? I'll make an appointment and I'll go with you next week."

"You mean you'll take me?" Claudia said, incredulously. "Oh, Betty...you are a dear friend."

"Yes, yes," she assured. "Don't worry, everything will be okay."

Don't worry.

Chapter 17

Testing News

"I had an interesting conversation with Pauline Howard this morning," Johnathan began during dessert in the kitchen several nights later.

Betty knew from his tone of voice that it meant something good, something positive. Whenever Johnathan began a sentence with, *"I had an interesting conversation with so-and-so,"* good news was certain to follow. She remembered when he told her he would run for the Senate, *"I had an interesting conversation with Sam Blackwell..."*

Betty merely responded, "Oh, really?"

"Yes," he said, taking a last bite of the fresh peaches Bertha peeled for dessert. He sat back. "Well, actually it was an interesting conversation with the First Lady."

Betty knew that this did not mean the current First Lady, but actually a very well known socialite who was very private. Pauline Howard, as had already been established, had impeccable connections.

Johnathan continued, "It seems that she recommended someone who sounds like he'll be perfect for the job."

The job was as media advisor for Johnathan's campaign. They both knew replacing Bob would be gut-wrenching under any circumstances, but it was the most important decision facing Johnathan right now.

"He lives in the area and he was a top advisor to Jimmy Carter during his election. Of course, he was just starting out at the time and he was a junior member of that team. In the years since, he's built a great reputation. One of the people he was working with dropped out because he had a heart attack—you know, Governor Harris from Montana—so he had an opening, and we're going to fill it. And Pauline said he gave a preliminary okay when my name was mentioned. It's going to cost the campaign a lot of money, but I think it's important."

He left his last comment hanging for just a moment. Money wasn't usually a touchy subject for Betty and Johnathan. She invariably gave him whatever he wanted or needed in the way of funds. But Johnathan Dent would never ask. He always waited for her to offer, and she forever obliged.

"You know Johnathan, that's never been a problem. You know you don't even have to ask—especially now," she said. She wanted her husband to be the next Senator from Virginia. "So please Johnathan don't keep me guessing any more. Who is it?"

"Dennis Harris."

"*Denny* Harris? You mean the guy who's always on *Good Morning America*? Len Hirsch's good friend ?"

"Yep," Johnathan said, proudly. "That's right."

"Wow... You're right, I'll bet that'll be expensive," she said adding "but it will be worth every dime. I thought he just did national stuff?"

"Well," Pauline said, "he also takes on one or two other small campaigns, and this year he doesn't have any one else for the fall elections. You know he doesn't take on just anyone."

"But wait," Betty said, "he's got a pretty tough reputation, doesn't he? Wasn't he involved in the campaign for governor down in Texas that got so nasty?"

"Well yes, he was. And yes, he does have what could be called...how shall I say this...well, let's just say he plays hardball. Okay? And besides I'm not even certain he'll consider this. I've got to call Pauline back to see if she'll set it up."

"Sounds wonderful," Betty said, standing and picking up the dessert bowls. She filled her wine glass one more time, finished clearing the dishes, and put them in the sink. Then she quickly wiped off the countertops, turned off the lights, and followed her husband upstairs.

Johnathan admired Betty in many ways. Deep inside he knew she had unique insecurities and that she'd always wonder if he married her for her money. He did everything he could to assuage her doubts. She'd made a nice home for him and he adored his children. But, like many men, he knew there never was, and never would be, that fire in the bedroom. He tried over and over again to direct her, hoping time and again that she'd take the initiative to please him the way dear, sweet Isabelle did.

There was no point. It would never be likely, and he came to accept it. The train had left the station.

In the past few weeks, Betty boldly undressed with the lights on. Yet, she stopped to fold them neatly over the chaise in the far corner of their blue bedroom. The moment vanished.

Tonight she did the same thing. Johnathan felt sorry about her attempts. It was like watching one of his children ice skate for the first time—wobbling and skidding along the way. You knew they were getting bumped and bruised, but you had to laugh anyway as they struggled to get their balance.

He went into the bathroom to brush his teeth and put on a robe. There was no question in his mind that they'd make love that night. Or attempt to make love. Johnathan was uneasy, since he had just seen Isabelle during lunch that afternoon. He wasn't sure he was capable of a repeat performance. He'd have to try. In fact, the idea of such a thing was rather arousing in its own way, making love to his mistress and his wife on the same day.

Betty was standing in the middle of the room, naked. She turned out the lights, except one by the bed. He walked over and bit her gently on her now erect nipples. He felt her quickly inhale and momentarily hold her breath.

She held his head and he sucked as hard as he could on each breast, first one side and then the other. He wanted her to *know* he was making mad passionate love to her. He wanted her to be sore tomorrow. He sucked harder and then laid her back on the edge of their bed and kissed her slightly round stomach and listened to her, softly purring with desire, as he continued...

Oh yes, he thought, *this will be no problem.* He could feel his excitement swell. He was going to screw the hell out of her, he thought. He would let her know once and for all what all of this was about...

"Bertha, it's Mr. Dent, is Mrs. Dent available?"

It was noon the next day and Betty asked not to be disturbed. "Well, let me check Mr. Dent, she's upstairs. I'm sure she'll talk with you. One minute now."

"No problem," he said, "I'll wait." He was sitting in his downtown Washington office.

He skipped a formal lunch at Zeibert's in favor of a quick sandwich at his desk. The campaign was swinging into high gear and he was more energized with each passing day. He felt as if everything was going to be just fine, both in his private and public lives.

"Johnathan?" Betty said, picking up the receiver on the upstairs telephone.

"Yes."

"How are you darling?" she asked.

"Well. I wanted to tell you Denny Harris and I have an appointment in Middleburg at the Red Fox on Thursday for lunch. Very hush, hush. I've talked to him and we seem to get along but he felt we should have a personal meeting to finalize things. I really want you to be there."

What he really wanted was for her to hear that it was going to cost him close to $50,000 just for openers. That was the retainer. Johnathan knew it would be to his advantage to have her there.

"Oh, sure, I'd love that."

"Great," he said, taking a silent breath of relief. *That would be a big help.*

"Now when did you say?"

"Thursday at noon," he answered, adding, "at the Red Fox, I've already made the reservation and I've asked to be downstairs in the back room. I told them three people and I used your maiden name—I don't want anyone there to call the press and tell them ahead of time. They love to do that in Middleburg, you know. We've got to keep this quiet until it's firm."

"Oh, sure," she said rather blankly, "I understand. Thursday at noon?"

"Right."

"Thursday at noon. Gee..." she was thinking now. "Oh, no, Johnathan... you won't believe this."

"What?"

"I can't make it."

"What do you mean you can't make it?"

"I can't make it. I just can't. I have other plans and I just cannot change them."

"What the hell can't you change?" he was almost indignant, but he caught himself.

"Johnathan, I can't tell you exactly why. I just can't make it. Anyway, I really do think it would be better if it were just you two men alone. If I could, I would, but I promised someone I'd help them out of a jam."

It was the first time he could ever remember Betty refusing a request, and now it was his turn to wonder what sort of a jam Betty was talking about, and which friend needed her help.

"Okay, not much I can do about it," he said. At least he tried, he thought, and that could end up being a point in his favor down the road.

"Thank you for understanding, Johnathan. You know I'd be there if I could. Now, tell me, when will you be home tonight?"

"Um, I'm not sure," he said. He hoped she wouldn't ask. "But don't hold dinner for me. Why don't you and Maude go out? Take her to The Coach Stop, you know she loves it."

"Okay then, I'll see you later." She replaced the receiver and glanced down at her appointment book. *Thursday ten a.m.*—it was marked in black pen—Claudia, Washington.

Johnathan replaced his telephone immediately and quickly picked it back up to dial Isabelle at work.

She answered on the first ring. She too, was having lunch at her desk.

"Hey," she said in that sultry southern drawl he so loved. "What's up?" she added, smiling at her own double meaning of the phrase.

"Not much, right now," he answered knowing full well what she meant. "Are you busy later? I can be home late."

"Oh sure," she said, "I mean no...I'm not busy. What time?"

"Sixish. I'll be there."

"Great."

Johnathan felt supremely confident of his chances for election after being nominated to run for the Senate. He realized Denny Harris was the man to assure victory. Now, as they sat at lunch in the back room of the popular old tavern, he wanted to convince him to take the job.

Harris had a clean-cut, boyish demeanor, particularly for a man with such a ruthless reputation. He was in his late thirties, with short blond hair, and gained his lean physique by running five miles a day plus nautilus work in the YMCA down at 17th and Rhode Island—the "upscale Y" many called it because so many members came from nearby law offices and the corridors of the Old Executive Office Building next door to the White House.

He was wearing an olive poplin suit on this steamy day, a yellow tie, and Italian loafers—definitely a Washington power look. Johnathan was far more conservative, in a dark blue suit and black wing tips. They ordered bloody marys, followed by crab cakes, iced tea (they agreed that one drink was the limit at all business lunches) and white chocolate ice cream for dessert.

As the conversation proceeded, Harris did the selling, not Johnathan. He explained his philosophy. *"Hit 'em hard, right from the start and never let up."*

"I'm not just offering a consulting arrangement. I don't operate that way. I'm talking about molding an image of the candidate throughout the campaign and perhaps beyond to higher office. I'd need to have access to you twenty-four hours a day."

Over coffee, he brought up his fee: "$50,000 retainer, plus expenses."

The two men walked out into the bright sunshine of the charming village and stood on the brick sidewalks in front of the historic tavern and shook hands.

Johnathan agreed on every point. "I believe we'll get along just fine," he told Harris. "I'll have a check to you in two days. I hope we can get going right away."

"I'll look forward to it," Denny Harris said, smiling.

Betty Dent and Claudia Jasper, the wives of a prospective senator and a highly-regarded Washington journalist, traveled to inner-city Washington that day. They purposely wore what they called "barn clothes"—faded jeans and old shirts. Betty borrowed a pickup truck from the stable manager at her farm, and explained that she needed to pick up some large items for a charity event. They bounced along the interstate and eased into the Adams Morgan section of the city around noon. They'd hardly spoken during the hour-long drive. Betty waited outside in the truck, reading a couple of magazines she'd brought along to occupy the time, while Claudia went into the clinic. It took an hour-and-a-half until Claudia returned to the truck.

"Well?"

"They said to call in for the results next Tuesday," Claudia said. "I didn't have to give my name. They gave me an anonymous ID number."

Denny Harris dug in on Johnathan Dent's campaign the day he received the retainer. He was a man totally devoted to his work. Each client presented a diverse test. Johnathan Dent would be fairly easy to get elected, as long as he cooperated. Over the years, Harris perfected his methods. He began by ordering a complete undercover investigation of the client and the opponent.

He'd been burned once too often. He always asked new clients one question: *"Do you have anything in your past or present life that you do not want the world to know?"*

Johnathan, like all the others, said *"No."*

One former client, after answering no, divulged three weeks before the election that he had a "minor" problem with the IRS. This "minor problem" was a series of audits on his returns for six straight years in the early 1960s and a substantial fine. Once that leaked out to the press, his candidate had no shot, losing by a margin of 75 to 25. *"There is no such thing as a minor problem with the IRS,"* Harris told the client. Never again did he allow himself to be associated with a potentially disastrous situation. After all, he had his own reputation to consider.

Denny Harris knew how to read between the lines of the exhaustive investigation report prepared by a private firm with impeccable credentials and a field staff of former CIA operatives. This time he was both happy and concerned.

He was pleased with what he read about the newly nominated Republican opponent, James Alexander Russell.

Russell led a fairly nondescript life. Born and educated in Virginia, much like Dent. Married with two children. Never divorced—not that it much mattered these days, but it helped. His previous political experience was as a member of the city council in Norfolk for six years, and most recently he served as mayor of Norfolk.

In that office, he led the way for major development along the city's waterside. One of these projects, Tidewater Place, Johnathan Dent actually helped put together. Denny Harris wondered if the two men had ever met. The fact that Harris had publicly favored development would be an issue here. The majority of voters in Virginia were against any such thing. Harris would use that information to his best advantage.

The most recent residential development in the Norfolk area, a fairly small planned community targeted to low-income senior citizens, was a disaster. The community consisted of small one-story condominiums and a cluster of three-bedroom apartment houses. In the apartment houses, the residents had their meals together in a dining room three times a day. It was precursor to assisted living, much like a nursing home, but the staff of the community was not obligated to provide any medical care.

In his investigations, Denny Harris discovered three important facts. First, one of the residents had choked to death while eating some pickled beets. It was later discovered the man was highly allergic to anything with vinegar and the family was suing. It was still under litigation and with a bit of luck it would drag on forever, or at least until after the election.

Second, James Russell's mother was a resident of the community. In order for him to help sell the idea to the city, he purchased her a condo. She lived alone and had been robbed—not once, but twice—since living there. The second time, she lay unconscious on her living room floor all night after being knocked down by the intruder. She was not seriously injured but the thief entered and stole all of her family's silver. Denny Harris discovered this after having his investigator sift through the records of crimes in the community. All of these things would make excellent advertising copy, Harris thought.

And third was the well-known that a ship had accidently spilled some medical waste in the harbor and the cost of the cleanup absorbed by the city of Norfolk was prohibitive. That debacle, and several other expensive projects, ran up huge cost overages approved by the bureaucracy, when Harris left office, the city's budget was in total disarray.

And what about Johnathan Dent?

The background check disclosed the usual...born and educated in Virginia. One marriage, three children, including twin sons. Brilliant lawyer and brilliantly married. His wife was an heiress. They lived on a rather large estate in an exclusive section of Virginia hunt country. The report outlined some of his larger cases and his clients, including Sam Blackwell, the well-known developer. Harris knew he could work around that.

The report continued. Harris and his private investigators managed to obtain copies of Johnathan Dent's personal and business telephone bills as well as copies of his credit card bills. Those always proved to be very interesting. This time was no exception.

It revealed frequent and consistent telephone calls to a Miss Isabelle Stoker.

Early the next Tuesday morning, Claudia Jasper went over to visit her best friend, Betty Dent. "I wanted to call the clinic from here," she explained while they sipped coffee in the kitchen.

"Oh, I'm glad you came over," Betty said. "That's fine, I understand. Do you want me to call them for you?"

"Well..." she thought it over. "No, I can do it. I just need you to hold my hand. And besides, I don't want it to show up on my phone bill. What if George asked me why I called there. He never looks at the bill, really. But with my luck, this would be the one time."

"Okay, now do you want some more coffee?"

"No, God no, I'm nervous enough."

At ten-fifteen Claudia called the clinic. She gave them her ID number and they put her on hold for what seemed like an eternity.

Finally a young man came back on the phone.

"Can I have your identification number again, ma'am," he said.

God, this was demeaning, thought Claudia, *I'll be glad when this is over.*

She repeated her number, "Two-six-three-six."

"I just wanted to make sure, ma'am," he said, talking slightly down to her. "I want to tell you a few things before I give you the result, please listen carefully. You must understand that all of our test results are completely confidential. You must also understand that they are 97 percent accurate. We therefore recommend you retake this test. It's come back HIV positive, but there is always a very small chance that might not be correct. Do you understand, ma'am?"

"Ma'am...?"

"There are a number of things we need to go over," Harris explained to Johnathan at their first meeting since he received the reports.

They were sitting in Johnathan's downtown law office. The move across the Potomac River to the official campaign headquarters in Alexandria would take place early next week, after Labor Day.

"Hey, no problem," Johnathan said, getting up from behind the desk. "Can I get you anything? How about if I ask Miss Wickwire for some coffee and Danish?"

"That would be great," Harris said.

Denny Harris outlined his plan. He told Johnathan how he would attack Russell's "old folks' project," as he called it. And about the medical spill and other points he viewed as negative. By next week the first of their television commercials would go on the air.

"We want to put them on the defensive," he said. "I've got a crew working on the commercials right now. We're going to get footage of his mother and then the voiceover will say, *'James Russell's own mother was robbed and assaulted. She was unconscious for ten hours in her own living room at the Tidewater Place Community Retirement Center, unable to call for help. Is this what you want for your family? Is this how you would treat your family?'*"

"Quite an ad," was all Johnathan could say.

"Well we're not really accusing him of anything. We're just raising a few questions for everyone to ask themselves." Harris went over the advertising plans for television, radio, and newspapers.

"And we need to outline our other strategies. I think I've defined the areas where you'll be most vulnerable," he said. "Russell will try to play on the fact that you were the counsel of note on the waterfront development in his own city. We will counter this with the fact that as mayor he led the city council into approving the project. We hope he doesn't get onto the fact that Sam Blackwell is your biggest backer."

"How did you know that?" Johnathan asked.

"Oh, I have ways, but doesn't everyone know that?"

"Oh, well...I guess so," Johnathan said. "What else?" They had been talking now for almost three hours.

"Well, we need to redefine part of your lifestyle."

"Like what?"

"Well the social image, you know—the private clubs, the horses, the foxhunting. That elitist image is not an asset."

"I see," Johnathan said.

"So, I have a plan," Harris said. "We'll make an asset out of a liability. It's always the best thing to do."

"Oh, by the way," Johnathan said. "You know I resigned my membership in the country club? I did that even before I was nominated."

"Yes, I knew that."

Johnathan just looked at him. The man had done his homework.

"No, that is not a concern. It's the foxhunting thing. So I've devised a plan. We'll stage a big reception-type fundraiser on your farm in late October. We'll bill it as a hunt breakfast. We'll invite every member of the press we can think of, along with some big schmoozers and boozers, and a number of FFVs.

"FFVs?"

"Sure....Certainly you know who they are Johnathan?"

"Well, no...not really."

"First Families of Virginia. You know—old names, old money. Of course, the former First Lady will come. You know we're still close friends. And your friend Pauline Howard will invite her German movie star friend and she'll get some other sparklies to show up. We'll wine and dine these people to the hilt. We'll let the hoi poloi mingle with the hoity toity, and it will be a positive experience. This will be the highlight of your campaign. I'll have three or four members of our staff working just on that project. We'll get you in an at-home atmosphere with all your family around you and that will do it."

"Well, you know, Denny," Johnathan squirmed a bit. "We have a big home and all and I know it won't be a problem with Betty. But how many people are we talking about?"

"At least five hundred or more."

"But we can't accommodate that many people inside."

"Oh, I know that. No, well have a tent attached to the back of the house. That's where most of the party will take place. In fact, we'll just let the guests parade through the front door, on through the drawing room, and then out onto the terrace and into the tent. We'll put a canopy over the terrace and have heaters on hand inside the tent."

How the hell did this guy know the floor plan of my house already, Johnathan wondered. He momentarily thought about what his brother might think.

"Listen, Denny. It's damn near one o'clock. Do you want me to order some lunch or should we end it for the day or go out somewhere or what?"

"Oh gee, I didn't realize. No, we need to keep on going. I've got some other points to go over with you. Just have the gal bring us some sandwiches."

"Great," Johnathan said, heading toward the intercom. "Turkey, ham and cheese...what would you like?"

"I'd love a big fat corned beef—lots of mustard—and a Coke. A real Coke. None of that diet stuff for me."

The two men took a break for a quick lunch. Johnathan went out to his secretary's desk and checked his mail and the telephone messages. Naturally, Isabelle had phoned. He'd see her later.

Denny Harris watched through the open door of the office as Johnathan went through the pink telephone message slips. He watched Johnathan put one of the pink slips in his right pants pocket. This would be the perfect opener on the subject. There was no doubt in Denny's mind who that message was from. He'd seen it many times before. And he was no slouch himself. He could hump and bump with the best. But he also knew discretion was absolutely essential.

He began when Johnathan walked back into his office.

"So, Johnathan," Denny Harris said. "Did Isabelle Stoker call this morning?"

The color from Johnathan's face drained instantly.

"Sit down," Harris said, patting the sofa. "Let's go over a few things here. First of all, not to worry, your secret is safe with me. I've been in this business a long time. You're not the first, and you certainly won't be the last. I intend to help you keep it that way. We just must take a number of precautions. If she's that important to you, I understand completely. Really, I understand, and we can make some adjustments."

Johnathan shook his head slowly back and forth. He wasn't looking at Denny Harris now. He clasped his hands and held them down between his legs, staring at his feet, thinking: *Shit, this is it.*

Harris read his mind. "There is something you should know about politics and the Other Woman, Johnathan. Contrary to what you may think, I'm certain your opponent will never bring up the subject. Think about it. There's an unwritten law among men in politics: never attack the other guy for sleeping with someone other than his wife. Just think about the last few elections. Sure, the Kennedy boys had plenty of flings and certainly Gary Hart had a fiasco. But it wasn't their opponents who blew the whistle on them, it was the goddamn media. It was that guy from the *Miami Herald* who nailed Hart to the wall. So don't lose any sleep over this. It's not a disaster by any means."

The color came back into Johnathan's face and he looked straight at Denny Harris, eager to get on with it. "Really?" he said, his face now beaming like a little boy just handed a lollipop by the bank teller at the drive-through window.

"Yes, really," Harris assured him. "The first thing I'm going to do is get you a private credit card for the telephone. Anytime you have to call this woman, use it."

"And for God's sake don't call her from home without the card. You'd be amazed how easy it is to get a copy of your phone bill. That's one thing that you can count on during this election. All kinds of people will be scrutinizing your phone records."

"Okay, fine," Johnathan said.

"The other thing is, no more hotels or motels. I don't know what your arrangements are—and frankly it'd be better if I didn't know the details. But you'll have to meet at her house at odd hours—during the day, late afternoons, mornings, things like that. I don't want you to be paranoid, but be aware that someone could possibly be following you. That's how they got Hart. Staked out his goddamaned townhouse, the bastards. You should also know that it would be virtually impossible for someone to follow you all the time, okay?"

"Sure."

"I see that Miss Stoker is a decorating assistant. I've come up with a plan. A good plan, a way we can keep her around and she can help us too. We'll put her on our staff for this hunt breakfast at your house. I assume she's fairly intelligent and could help arrange some of the logistics for the reception. That way, if anyone asks questions, we can explain the phone calls by saying she's on staff. If anyone really wanted to dig in here, they probably couldn't do the job until after the election anyway, and by that time, you're in the Senate and we can deal with it if we have to."

"Absolutely," Johnathan said. "She'd be a logical choice anyway. She helped us decorate when we hosted a party to promote a project we did down at Payne"s Corner. My wife uses her boss all the time. She'd be a logical choice to help put on the kind of party you're talking about.""

"Great," Harris said. "This is what I want you to propose. Ask her to take a leave of absence from her job until after the election. Offer to pay her twice her current salary. Tell her she"ll work out of our Alexandria headquarters. That way you can be close to her, see her for lunch, drive her home from work or whatever. I've been through this routine before Johnathan, and I know it will work."

"I'll definitely see what I can do," Johnathan said.

Definitely.

Chapter 18

Fried & Baked

Johnathan spent a quiet Labor Day weekend on the farm with his family. The boys came home and days were spent riding in the morning, taking long walks in the woods in the afternoon, and eating together every night. Johnathan specifically asked Betty not to accept any social invitations. "It'll be the last weekend we can be together until after the election," he explained. "And I want to enjoy it."

Johnathan sat on the terrace alone on Saturday afternoon to go over his campaign schedule. He loved Virginia—the lush countryside, the mountains in the distance, the smell of the horses and the fresh cut hay, the wild flowers. So far, he'd led such a charmed life, he thought to himself, and soon it could get even better.

Yet, he was torn. All his life he'd worked toward capping his career in law with a run for office. Now it was a so close. He imagined what it would be like to walk down the aisle toward his seat on that first day on the job, his family watching from up above in the gallery. He visualized his office: red leather couch, photos on the walls, and a constant flow of visitors, including lobbyists, constituents, and...Isabelle.

The image of Isabelle coming to visit him there in his inner sanctum kept popping into his head. He could see her now. She was standing in the middle of the room, tall and straight with her feet together. She was wearing navy blue pumps and a navy blue dress and she had a white sweater over her shoulders.

Her shoulders...he could smell them. *Shalimar.* They were so very smooth... he loved to kiss them. Someone was kissing his hand. He came to and it wasn't the smell of Shalimar. It was Eau de Dawg.

"Oh, you silly things," he said to Brutus, the black Lab. "What do you want?" Phillip, the Jack Russell, deposited a tennis ball at his feet. He picked it up and tossed it out over the terrace and the terrier went racing after it. He thought of Isabelle again. He would call her next week. They'd have dinner at her place—no more restaurants for a while now—and he could explain to her how and why she had to leave her job for a while.

They would make it work. He would never give her up.

Never.

He thought about all his traveling between now and the November elections. He decided to go everywhere by car and hired a driver for the next sixty days. He clearly had no desire to get in a small airplane, no matter how much time it saved. He glanced up at the sky, thought about his brother Bob and, for a moment, felt tears welling in his eyes.

On Tuesday after Labor Day, Johnathan Dent's campaign headquarters on King Street in Alexandria officially opened. His secretary, Thelma Wickwire, took a leave of absence from the law firm and was in charge of running the office. She put together an entire staff consisting of an equal mix of paid employees and volunteers, including representation from every ethnic and racial minority available.

From the moment they all walked through the door, the office took on a life of its own, with telephones ringing, copy machines humming, staffers chatting with each other, and callers offering money and time to the campaign. Staff members began to personalize their modest surroundings with plants and family photos.

Johnathan was off to a luncheon in Manassas with the Northern Virginia Chapter of the Association of Dental Hygienists, hand-shaking at the Ballston Metro station during the evening rush hour, dinner with the Northern Virginia Builders Association at the Tyson's Corner Marriott.

On Wednesday three representatives from the Battlefield Coalition in Manassas visited Johnathan. They came to lobby their cause of saving the ground around the historic Manassas Battlefield site. There was talk that developers wanted to put up a mall and office-condominium complex. They wanted assurances from Johnathan that he opposed the project.

He was, of course, ever so diplomatic. "I understand your concerns," he told them over a late morning cup of coffee and donuts. "Our history in Virginia is very important, and I'll do everything I can to preserve that history." He made a note to ask Sam Blackwell about the proposed project, the principals, and what it would mean to oppose such development, both in terms of history and his own campaign coffers.

The group leaders thanked him and indicated that a "substantial" contribution would be in the works once they had a "hard and true" declaration to align with their cause.

By the time he drove back to the country, had dinner, and crawled into bed it was ten-thirty. He stared at the neon green time on the digital clock. Betty was beside him reading and drinking a "late glass of wine" as she put it.

"Damn," he said, aloud.

"What is it?"

"Oh, I just forgot something," he said, turning out the light on his side of the bed.

It was Wednesday, he realized, and he had forgotten to call Isabelle.

Thursday morning, Johnathan was at the Alexandria office by eight a.m. for a ten o'clock meeting with Denny Harris. Then a lunch meeting with an abortion rights group. Johnathan was riding the fence on that one as long as possible. Most women in the cosmopolitan Northern Virginia region were solidly pro-choice, the predominately Baptist Bible belt voters downstate were just as vociferous in their support of pro-life candidates. It was a touchy subject that could determine the outcome of the election. Denny Harris recommended waiting as long as possible to see where Johnathan stood in the polls before issuing his official position.

Between Harris and the women, he called Isabelle, being sure to use his new calling card.

"Hey," he said.

"Hey," she said.

"Forgive me, please?"

"You know I will."

Isabelle had stewed all day and night when he hadn't called to talk about their usual Wednesday date. This was exactly what she had feared all along, that she would be lost in the shuffle as Johnathan moved on to greater glory in the U.S. Senate. Still, she also knew about his hectic schedule, and as they spoke, she was reassured by the tone of his voice.

"How about the Roma Restaurant tonight?" he asked.

"Great. What time?"

"About eight-fifteenish," he said.

"I'll see you then."

As they sat in her living room later that night after dinner, listening to Mozart on the stereo, Johnathan was more in love with this woman than ever. She meant everything to him, and he was risking his political career for her. He loved to watch her talk. She described a project she was working on with Michael Aldridge. It was a welcome diversion from the talk of preservation, abortion, tax reform, and the national debt he'd heard from the moment he woke in the morning until the time he went to sleep sixteen hours later. As she spoke, her hands and arms moved as she talked about swatches of fabric, antique furniture, and sconces over the fireplace. And each sip from her glass of dark, red Chianti added to the enchanting glow on that glorious face he adored.

She shared her work with him. It pleased her that he seemed interested, even now in the middle of a hectic political campaign. When she finished, he told her about the meetings he'd had that day, then talked about his new offices, which led him easily into what was the most important topic of the evening.

"I want you to come to Alexandria this week and see my office," he said.

"Oh Johnathan, I don't think that'd be a good idea." *After all,* she thought, *we do need to be careful.*

"Isabelle," he said, looking into her eyes, "I want you to come and work in my office for the next few months."

She was stunned, but by the time he explained Denny Harris's plan, it made sense and there was no doubt that she would do whatever he wanted.

By Monday of the following week, she was at her new desk on the second floor of the townhouse offices of senatorial candidate Johnathan Dent. She was ecstatic. Michael Aldridge hadn't been too happy about her request for a leave, but she was such a valuable member of his staff that he didn't want to risk losing her services after the campaign. Yes, it was the busiest time of the year, but she explained, she'd always wanted to work in politics somehow, someway. It was one of the reasons she came to Washington in the first place. Now, a candidate who went to school with her best friend's father was running for office. She'd met him years ago, followed his fledgling political career in the papers, and was flabbergasted when he asked her to join his staff. She told Michael she simply could not refuse. Anyway, she reminded him, it would give her entree to a host of potential new and well-connected clients. That helped soften the blow considerably, as did her assurance that she would help him whenever possible. She planned to be back at work the day after the election.

Reluctantly, he agreed.

Johnathan's schedule was strenuous. The constant travel was exhausting, yet exhilarating. He'd been at it a week, and this afternoon, seven days after Labor Day, the first in a series of tough television commercials prepared by Denny Harris was scheduled to air. The first would appear at 5:08 p.m., just minutes into the early news. Johnathan was anxious to gauge the reaction.

He made a half-day trip to the tiny town of Purcellville, forty-five miles west of Washington, to speak to a group of contractors. There would be a box lunch of fried chicken, biscuits, and cole slaw. He would return to the office by two or three, work on a few projects, and be able to see the news in order to get a firsthand reaction in the office.

Perhaps Isabelle would be there, he hoped.

The chicken was cold and greasy. The contractors were lukewarm at the start. They didn't really know what to make of a man who had made his reputation as a corporate lawyer, far from the concrete and steel and bare-chested construction workers they dealt with on a daily basis. Johnathan spoke for about twelve minutes and talked about his work on several building projects, including Payne's Corner. He gave them what he thought they wanted, assurances that the building industry would prosper in the state if he was elected. He also knew he was walking a fine line between the builders and the preservationists.

He was careful. And by the time he rolled up his shirt sleeves and sat down to eat fried chicken, they seemed friendly. He assured them that he'd encourage the resurgence of America's staggering steel industry. When he departed, he felt certain he'd made some allies.

Following the lunch and speech, Johnathan was back in his car, cruising down Route 7 toward Alexandria. He wanted to catch up on his reading and started with the front page of the *Washington Post* as the driver maneuvered the car through traffic around the beltway. He never even finished the front page. He was tired. He put his head back for a nap, and when he opened his eyes, they were two blocks from the Old Town Alexandria office.

As the five o'clock news began, staffers and volunteers gathered around two televisions at each end of the office. They sat on desks, on the floor, and on the arms of chairs. There was a round of applause following the commercial, one that focused on his opponent's unconscious mother. Isabelle was sitting on the floor with her back to Johnathan. He watched her and she turned and looked directly at him and gently nodded her approval.

He watched her leave, gathering her notebooks and canvas bag to go home. *Home alone*, he thought. How he longed to be with her. But he was quickly distracted when Miss Wickwire called him to the phone.

The rest of the week Johnathan traveled to southwestern Virginia for rallies in Tazwell, Bluefield, Dickenson, Washington, Smyth, and Grayson. The strategy was to do the smaller cities further away first so he would wind up in the highly populated area around northern Virginia during the latter part of the campaign. Betty Dent was also scheduled to cross his tracks and take her ideas for education and arts to the far reaches of the state later on. Early in the campaign, she would visit schools in Northern Virginia in Manassas, Arlington, and Alexandria. She still had a deep aversion to speaking to large crowds, yet was infinitely more at ease in front of children. She talked about the importance of Head Start programs, fighting illiteracy, and the dangers of drugs and alcohol.

Little did the children and their parents and teachers know that Betty Dent kept a chilled bottle of wine in the back seat of the limousine that carried her from appearance to appearance.

At the Republicans' Crystal City headquarters, media consultant Dan Warfield spit fire for five days. He was mad as hell at the tone of the Dent commercials and was working around the clock on a counterattack.

Warfield, a former vice president of one of the largest banks in Norfolk, was chosen as James Russell's campaign manager. He was a wiz with numbers with extensive experience in banking in Virginia. He was a brilliant tax attorney in Annapolis, where he settled after law school, primarily to take advantage of the Chesapeake Bay. He was an avid sailor, and his practice provided more than enough funds to indulge in several racing boats. He was on the water every weekend in some regatta or another, and at one point had even helped crew an America's Cup boat. He was a native Virginian, and his move to Norfolk to work with an old friend in the banking business in the early 1970s allowed him to keep sailing. Warfield also had a reputation as a skilled fundraiser, and Russell knew he had to raise a lot of money to keep up with Johnathan Dent and his heiress wife.

Warfield was stewing in his office and plotting strategy. This was his first foray into the upper reaches of politics. He hired several knowledgeable assistants, including Clifford Oates, a respected media consultant, the Republicans' answer to Denny Harris. He liked to get down and dirty, too, and was toiling on his own series of television commercials. The taping was slated to take place the next morning, in a studio on Capitol Hill. They would attack Johnathan Dent's Middleburg lifestyle, show pictures of his huge house, Johnathan riding in the hunt in full regalia, sipping drinks at a steeplechase event with a Rolls Royce in the background. *"The lifestyles of the rich and famous,"* the voiceover read. The spot ended with the question, *"Johnathan Dent says he's a man of the people, but which people?"*

"It's going to be simple and to the point," Warfield informed the group collected in the high-rise office building overlooking the Potomac. "I don't want to say anything straight out against Dent. I want to imply it. I've got an assistant looking into what they said in their commercials about Jim. Hell, we might sue the bastard."

"Now, Mike," as he turned to one of the men in the office. "What about that private investigator we hired? I want him to take a real close look at everything—Dent's mortgage payments, his credit card bills, phone records. Hell's bells, I want to know what the sonofabitch eats for breakfast."

"He's working on it."

"Well, what the hell is the goddamn holdup?" He didn't wait for an answer. "These pricks are way ahead of us in that department. We've got to get on the stick. If these guys have to work twenty-four hours a day, make 'em do it. I want to see that report. Right now, they've got us by the balls and we're running out of time."

Johnathan and Betty were home on the farm in Middleburg after their first two weeks on the campaign trail. Johnathan had no appearances scheduled, though Denny Harris was staying at the house and several strategy sessions were planned. The candidate and his wife did put in an appearance at the Episcopal Church in Upperville, with several camera crews from stations in Washington showing up to tape his entrance and exit from across the street.

Betty tried to get out of going, feigning nausea, which was actually a mild hangover. She was now downing glassfuls of wine before each appearance. No sips for Betty, and it took eating two or three Tic Tacs before she got out of the car to kill the smell on her breath. She realized when to stop. She'd been sipping wine for so many years, she was able to handle it now. No one could tell when she was just a bit tipsy. Her walk was steady, her speech impeccable. Truth be told, she was a genuine asset on the campaign—both for her unlimited bank account and her ability to charm the schoolchildren and their parents and teachers wherever she went.

Johnathan pointed out that an appearance in church was vital. "Betty, there's just no argument here, please, try to understand." He put his arm around her as they sat on the edge of their bed. "The press is following us everywhere. We've got to go to church. It's a great photo op."

Nothing else was said. They were seated up in the fifth pew, the family pew, for the eleven o'clock services and afterward, as expected, there were a number of photographers across the street as they exited. The media pack knew not to go on church property.

The next week brought more of the same.

Johnathan traveled to Portsmouth for two days. A luncheon with the teacher's union for deep-dish chicken pot pie, a dinner with dock workers for chicken breasts and cream sauce. Then a rally and on to the Norfolk area for an interview with the editorial board of the *Virginia Pilot* newspaper.

"This interview is vital," Denny Harris warned. "You're in Russell's territory. I don't want to scare you, but tread lightly."

By a lucky twist of fate, one of the editors had also attended the University of Virginia and remembered Betty from when she worked at Eljo's doing the advertising.

"I was working at the *Daily Progress* at the time," he told Johnathan. "Your wife did beautiful ads. I was the salesman and she was a joy to work with."

They chatted about old times in Charlottesville. And when Johnathan left the interview, he knew from the looks on their faces and the warm handshakes it was advantage Dent despite tough questions about abortion, development, and transportation. The flattering story the next day merely confirmed his initial impression.

Midweek, Johnathan was back at campaign headquarters.

Just in time to see Isabelle, he thought. It was Wednesday. He walked casually into her office. She was on the phone and motioned him to come in. She was going over details with the florist for the shindig on the farm, now ten days away.

"There should be a total of twenty-two small centerpieces," she said. "Right...okay...and what else do you have written down?" There was a pause while she listened.

"Right."

Pause.

"And the front door?"

Pause.

"And the front gate?"

Pause.

"And you'll also do the balloons, right?"

Pause.

"Wonderful, I think that's..."

Pause.

"No later than seven that morning, correct. And you have the directions I sent, right?"

Pause.

"Good. I'll see you then."

She hung up the phone and leaned back in her chair. She was still writing herself a memo in the margin of a legal pad.

"What's up?" she asked looking up at Johnathan in the doorway.

"Not much."

"Well, now, you can't say that. I know better."

"Well, I've been south."

"I know," she said, casting her eyes downward. She wanted to tell him how much she missed him, but she knew they had to be careful in the office.

He read her thoughts.

"It's Wednesday, you know?"

"How could I forget?" she replied. And there was an awkward silence.

"Well?" he asked, assuming she knew what he was really asking *"Will I see you tonight?"*

"I'm making Chicken Tempura."

He smiled. "Please don't."

For a half-minute she thought he meant he couldn't see her. "What do you mean?" she asked.

"Do you have any idea how much chicken I've consumed in the past ten days?"

They laughed.

"How about a steak? A nice T-bone, a baked potato, and a salad?"

And you for dessert, he thought.

"No problem," she said, smiling at him.

"What's this I hear about steak?" a voice from around the corner asked. It was Cindy Clark, one of the volunteers.

"Oh, nothing," Johnathan answered, giving Isabelle a quizzical look, as if to ask, "Did she hear us?"

Isabelle shook her head "no", she knew that no one heard them. *And after all, the conversation was perfectly innocent, they were talking about chicken.*

"He was just telling me about all the chicken he's been eating on the campaign trail," Isabelle said to her as she stopped in the doorway. "I don't have the nerve to tell him I've ordered barbecue chicken for the feast on the farm."

They all laughed.

That evening, in the coziness of her Georgetown apartment, Isabelle cooked two T-bones to perfection. Medium rare. Johnathan was famished. They watched the news together and sipped a deep red Bordeaux, snuggling up on the couch, each thinking how perfectly they fit into the other's arms.

The news was the same, mounting tension in the Persian Gulf. Isabelle pretended she was listening. But it was a simple fact. She could not simply sit next to this man. It was impossible. She ached for him and she didn't see any point in waiting.

"To hell with the news," she declared.

He turned and looked at her.

She rubbed her palm on his chest and started to unbutton his blue oxford shirt. He finished the task. He stood and pulled his shirt tail out and took off his shirt. She leaned over and took a big swallow of the red wine.

"Go ahead," she urged him. "Keep going."

When he was naked she leaned over him on the couch. She kissed him and he tasted the heavy wine. She was decisive in her movements. She knew where to touch him...lightly kissing him as she moved down his body and took him in her mouth.

He held her head and she continued...

Betty Dent's campaign to bring "art to children" if her husband was elected Virginia's next senator was off to a good start. She "borrowed" two antique primitive whirligigs from her family's art collection on loan to the museum in Washington. These colorful toys, often put together with wire and scrap metal by country folk artists, brought delight to the schoolchildren when she showed them.

She visited two or three schools each day, demonstrating to a rapturous group that huddled around to see the toys. The press was most receptive when invited to tag along and cover her presentations and her picture appeared in several newspapers and magazines around the state. Bertha had the dinner entirely prepared for Mrs. Dent and her daughter each evening. She always fixed an extra plate for Mr. Dent. Some evenings he made it home for dinner, but often he was on the road and called to say he just couldn't make it.

This was one such night.

Betty tried to understand. She attempted to tell herself it was all for a good cause. But, she was isolated and kept full-time company with Robert Mondavi and his soothing white zinfandel.

Her friends called and left messages with Bertha. Most of them went something along the lines of *"We miss you, good luck, let us know if there's anything we can do."* She unquestionably missed her friends, her charity auctions and customary way of life. Not to mention her husband.

On this evening she was home by four. Bertha was fixing a salad. Betty joined her in the kitchen to chat and catch up on a few household details. When the phone rang, Betty answered.

"Hello," she said, rather happily, even though she was tired.

"Why I can't believe it. You're home." It was Franny Collins. Betty was elated to hear from her. They hadn't talked in ages.

"Yes, I've been gone since six this morning, can you believe it?" Betty asked.

"Oh, I believe it," her friend said. "Everywhere I look and listen you and Johnathan are all over the newspapers and TV. It must be brilliant!""Well... yes and no. It's such a grueling pace, it's hard to think about it. But never mind all that. Catch me up. What's the latest news in town? How's the horse business?"

There was a momentary pause.

"I hate to bore you, especially with all your exciting news," she said. "No, really. I want to know," Betty said, pouring another glass of wine. She settled into a soft chair, preparing for a gossipy chat with her best friend.

"Well..."

"Well, what?"

"Forgive me Betty, I'm so sorry," Franny was crying now.

"What is it? Is somebody sick? Franny, talk to me," she pleaded.

"It's Jake."

"What's wrong?" Betty asked, then instantly recalled that she already knew the worst. Of course she knew. *Oh my God*, she thought, *I hope Franny hasn't found out about Claudia.*

She hadn't.

"He has AIDS, Betty. The doctor told him he would have six months to a year, tops."

"Oh, Franny," she said, tears now gathering in her own eyes hearing her friend's sorrowful tone. "I'm so sorry."

Franny cleared her throat. And gathered her emotions.

"Well, I'm not. I'm not one bit sorry," she said, rather indignantly. "That bastard. After all this time...and our children. Oh God, Betty...that's what gets me. How the hell am I going to explain this to them?"

"Oh, Franny...you've just got to be strong," Betty said, trying to be encouraging. But she couldn't quite understand the hostility. *Did she know about Claudia? Was that it?*

"Betty, I'm just so ashamed. And now I've got to go get tested myself. Can you imagine that? Me, sleeping all these years with a man who likes to screw other men. Oh, Betty. I could just die."

If she only knew, thought Betty.

If she only knew.

Chapter 19

A Royal Swivet

Johnathan's next week of traveling consisted of a luncheon in Blacksburg, followed by dinner with another group in Salem. He spent the night and spoke at a breakfast rally in Radford and then met with reporters from the *Roanoke Times* for a question-and-answer interview session.

Denny set up live television interviews with two stations in the area, followed by a forty-five minute on-air radio call in program popular in that part of southwestern Virginia. Johnathan left the area by eight to spend the night at home. He asked his secretary to alert his family. He looked forward to the comforts of his own warm bed.

At just past midnight he walked in the kitchen. The light on the stove was on. There was a plate in the oven. He opened the oven door and lifted the tin foil. Green beans, scalloped potatoes and—what else—chicken. He felt as if he'd soon lay eggs or crow at the crack of dawn. He couldn't look at it. Instead, he wrapped the fowl in foil. He put it in the refrigerator, had some oatmeal cookies and a glass of milk, and went upstairs.

In the morning, Betty was asleep when he left the bedroom. He showered and dressed and softly went downstairs for breakfast with Maude…no eggs just fruit. Next to Isabelle, she was his favorite female in the world, even if her mother did spoil her terribly. She showed him a science fair project on hair growth. They ate English muffins and he offered to drop her off at school.

"Is the chauffeur going to drive us Daddy?"

"I think so, is that okay?"

"Oh boy, I hope everybody sees me. Are you going to come talk to my class one day Daddy like Mommy?"

"Of course I will honey."

The next series of campaign sojourns included a rally in Sussex in southern Virginia. A lukewarm reception was no surprise considering that the area was heavily conservative filled with deeply religious Virginia Baptists. When Denny discussed the appearance later, he thought some small gains had been made.

"We'll increase our advertising in that area," Denny noted, adding "these people will love our television commercial about preserving Virginia for the future."

"Good idea," Johnathan agreed.

The thirty-second television spot for Johnathan Dent played heavily on the visual senses. It was impeccably executed by Denny Harris's production staff.

It presented Johnathan walking alongside an old stone wall on his farm. He ambled up to a paddock fence and reached out to pat a sleek chestnut thoroughbred. He continued along the fence and met up with his wife and daughter and twin sons. Even Phillip, the Jack Russell terrier, was in the picture. The camera pulled out to a wide view of the countryside, with the verdant mountains in the background. The voice-over began *"Johnathan Dent wants the good life for everyone in Virginia. As Senator, he'll work to serve and preserve the future of Virginia. Vote for Johnathan Dent on Tuesday, November 6."*

"This looks like a goddamned Hallmark Hall of Fame production." Dan Warfield screamed as he watched on his VCR in his Crystal City office.

"What the hell kind of crap is this?" he asked anyone who'd listen. "This makes me want to puke."

"Calm down, Dan, it's not that bad," said one of his co-workers. "Things are not that bad."

"Not that bad? The election is less than four weeks away. These commercials are great. They've got a ten-point lead in the latest poll in the *Washington Post.* We've got to come up with something, and fast. Any ideas?"

"I think I'm on to something," Chris Oakley, one of Warfield's young lieutenants, said quietly.

"For Christ's sakes—what have you got?"

"It seems our worthy opponent, the honorable Johnathan Douglas Dent, is as queer as they come...if you'll excuse the pun."

"Go on," Warfield said, sitting back in his swivel chair behind his desk. "Tell me more."

"Well, we've been going over his phone records, and it seems he's made a number of calls to a particular number in Georgetown. The place belongs to Michael Aldridge, a decorator, who prefers men. He'll swish into your house and collect thousands for recovering your sofa in chintz and knocking in a few sconces over the fireplace. He's almost a parody of himself."

"Tell me more. That's not enough." But Dan Warfield was intrigued.

"You want more? Here's more," Oakley was saying now, standing up as all eyes in the room focused in his direction. "In addition to a number of phone calls to Mr. Aldridge, there are several calls to that AIDS clinic over in Adams Morgan All their records are supposed to be confidential, but with a bit of digging and a few hundred dollars, I had a guy check the records. Sure enough, they had someone from Middleburg go in for a blood test sometime between the period of the first phone call and the second phone call. And where do you think those phone calls came from?"

Oakley was clearly enjoying this. A sinister grin spread across his lips as he prepared his final punch line.

"The telephone calls were made from Johnathan Dent's home phone in Middleburg."

Dan Warfield took a deep breath. He was delighted with this latest twist, but wary at the same time. He understood this was potentially explosive information, but there was no room for error. They had to be unconditionally confident, and even then it was risky. Voters could turn on Johnathan if it were true, but some might also feel some sympathy for the Democratic candidate, particularly if they thought this was a dirty trick perpetrated by the opposition.

Still, it was worth further exploration. Immediately.

"Damn. That's good work, Oakley. This may be just what we need. Wouldn't that be something—handsome, debonair Johnathan Dent—a flaming faggot. What was the name of that decorator?"

"Michael Aldridge."

"You know that name is so familiar, I think an old client of mine, Eleanor Hartley, used him in her home in Annapolis. I remember meeting some girl who worked for him. I'm almost positive. I'll give her a call. Matter of fact, I'll call her right now."

He buzzed his secretary, told her to look in the Rolodex, and to call Mrs.

Richard Hartley at home. She did as instructed, but there was no answer. Dan Warfield made a note to call her later. Meanwhile he had a better idea.

He buzzed his secretary again. "Get me George Jasper at the *Washington Post*," he ordered,adding, "This is the kind of information I think he might want to hear about."

Back on the campaign trail, Johnathan visited the south central section of the state. He started out with a rally in Danville, and felt good about it when he left. Johnathan noticed the crowd seemed more attentive than usual, something he hadn't felt at all in this part of the state when he first begin traveling. He figured as if many people had turned out more out of curiosity than anything else. But today he sensed something different.

Maybe, just maybe the commercials were making a difference.

There was no time to sit around and ponder all this. There was a lunch of Chicken Kiev with retired state employees, and then, on to a dinner of Lemon Chicken with Almonds with the Virginians For Horseracing.

The next day he was in South Boston, for a breakfast of scrambled eggs, country bacon, and grits with the Citizens for No-Tolls, a group that wanted to abolish all toll roads in the state. It was a small gathering, but once again, Johnathan felt they were genuinely interested in his views.

Lunch was hamburgers (*Thank God for red meat,* thought Johnathan) with the Wholesale Beef Industry. And dinner in Martinsville was more chicken—Provencal—with a small group of supporters.

He spent the rest of the week visiting a string of small towns: Patrick Springs, Laurel Fork, Stuart, Galax, Willis, Poplar Camp, Rocky Mount, Chatham, Clover, and Altavista.

He spoke to Isabelle late at night from his hotel room, being careful each time to use the credit card Denny Harris had given him. He also called the farm and spoke with Betty once; the other time he called she was out. He looked forward to returning home. After a quiet weekend, he'd be ready to hit the road again. The big party at his farm was to take place the following week.

As he drove up the driveway late Friday night, he didn't even notice the beginnings of preparations for the big event. Workmen had already started to erect the tent behind his house.

The next morning he got up before six and went downstairs to let the dogs out. Then he noticed the metal stakes in the ground beyond the terrace.

"Damn...that's going to ruin the grass," he said out loud.

"Don't worry, Daddy," said a familiar voice behind him. "Mommy told me it's worth ruining the grass."

"Oh Maude," he said, leaning over to gather her in his arms. "What are you doing up so early?"

"I waited as late as I could last night," she told him. "Mommy said I could. But I fell asleep. I wanted to see you, I wanted you to come down to the barn with me while I ride my pony."

The dog scratched to come in.

"There's nothing I'd like better."

They had one of the best weekends Johnathan could remember in a long, long time. Betty was in a enjoyable mood and he knew why. He noticed she didn't go anywhere without a glass of wine in her hand. Maude was thrilled to have him home and Johnathan was just as thrilled to watch her ride. She had finally become involved with the pony, and she was also becoming more adorable with each passing day. The three of them had long talks and a nice dinner. On Sunday evening, Denny Harris called to give Johnathan some news.

"The *Washington Post* is publishing their next-to-last poll and I got word that you're leading by six points."

Johnathan didn't know how to react. He knew that any lead was good, but it had been ten points a month ago.

Was it something he said? Or was his opponent finally beginning to make up for lost time?

He asked Denny Harris what it all meant.

"Johnathan, it's great news, but it also means we've really got to keep it going in these last weeks."

There was less than three weeks to go. Johnathan's itinerary was to take him to the Richmond area for most of the next week. In many ways it would be a challenging time. Even more than two months after the crash, he was still mourning his brother's death. Spending any time in Bob's backyard brought it all bubbling to the surface. And then, in an odd twist of events, he was not only booked in the same hotel where he had stayed during the convention the previous summer, he was in exactly the same room.

The room where he had stayed with Isabelle.

As the driver headed south along I-95 past Dale City, Woodbridge, Fredericksburg, and Bowling Green, Johnathan thought about her. It was ten days since he had seen her, which meant that it was over ten days since he had any sex. It didn't seem to present itself at home much anymore. For one thing, Johnathan was tired. For another, Betty was either too busy or too hung over.

Oh well, he thought...*the train has left the station at home.* Maybe he could arrange to see Isabelle later this week. *Maybe she could come down to Richmond for the night.*

He hoped he'd have time to call her. Oh, how he yearned to wander around the Valentine Art Museum with her.

But there was no time now. They were approaching the city. And the first thing on Johnathan's agenda for the week was a meeting with the top editors and reporters of the Richmond *News Leader*. This was a large and influential paper read all around the state and yet another important interview, according to Denny, who had arranged the meeting.

Denny did not come along, preferring to spend the first half of the morning wrapping up a final series of commercials he was preparing for the last week of the campaign. But he'd been invited to join the group for a luncheon on the top floor in the executive dining room. He'd be flying into town in an hour or so.

Johnathan's car glided past the old buildings in the historic city. They exited onto Broad Street, then turned east to Grace Street and toward the offices of the newspaper. The car pulled up to the front steps. Johnathan left his papers and briefcase in the car; he didn't want to carry anything, particularly a rival newspaper. He'd been reading the *Washington Post* story on the latest polls, which appeared to be very much in his favor. But he didn't need to remind himself the victory winds can shift in a heartbeat.

"You know, this is going to be at least a three-hour proposition," he told the driver. "There's really no need for you to hang around." He put his hand on the door handle. "Let me see..." he thought for a moment. "Why don't you go ahead to the hotel. There's a block of rooms reserved for us...three or four or five—I can't remember what Denny said. Anyway, I know there's one for you and one for me. Go ahead and check us in, put the suitcases in the rooms, and I'll just get a taxi back with Denny. You don't have to plan to be around until at least three, okay?" He opened the heavy limosine door and stepped out. He was wearing his cashmere coat, suit and tie. His walk was purposeful. He looked every bit the part of a senator.

He poked his head back into the car for the driver's response.

"Sounds good to me."

A foul up in the room reservations forced the Dent party to combine some of their reservations. It was agreed that Johnathan and his driver would share the suite.

At the time, Johnathan thought nothing of it. After all, there were two bedrooms separated by a large seating area. Then on second thought, that meant he wouldn't be able to invite Isabelle.

On Wednesday morning, in his Crystal City offices, Dan Warfield received some attention-grabbing news.

"What do you mean, 'he's sharing the room with the driver'?" he asked one of his assistants. "Why didn't you tell me this sooner? Holy shit. The guy really is queer. The *driver*? Jesus H. Christ"

He put a second call into George Jasper at the *Washington Post.*

"I think we should have lunch George," he told the columnist, who listened to Warfield the first time but was skeptical about the information on Johnathan Dent. He'd known the man for years, lived in the same small town.

"It couldn't possibly be true," he told Warfield that day. "I'll need a hell of a lot more proof before I can go with that story. Christ, my editors would be all over me for sources. Get me the documents, get me the records, get me something and then maybe we can talk."

With the latest evidence of Dent's Richmond roommate, Dan Warfield believed it was time to talk to George Jasper again.

"I know you may feel uncomfortable about this," Warfield told the columnist. "Why don't we go somewhere quiet and talk? I think I have what you're looking for, and I'll bring you the records so you can see for yourself."

"Fine," George agreed. "I'll meet you at the Szechuan Palace over on H Street."

George Jasper didn't know what to think. All the information and possible evidence Dan Warfield presented so far seemed to indicate his friend Johnathan Dent could very well be gay.

His journalistic instincts were in disarray. First, he knew he could not allow his friendship with Johnathan to get in the way of a good story. His wife and the candidate's wife friendship had to be irrelevant. There could be serious repercussions to his career and their social standing in the community if his name was attached to a scandalous story about one of the town's most respected citizens.

He took copies of the phone bills from Dan Collins. He went back to his glass-enclosed office on the fifth floor of the 15th Street offices of the newspaper. He sat there staring at the numbers, then started to call the ones that were highlighted in yellow. Sure enough, one was the office of Michael Aldridge Designs, the other the AIDS Screening Clinic in Adams Morgan. He hung up both times and damn near broke into a cold sweat.

He was a reporter first, he told himself, *and a friend second.*

He knew he needed more than this rather flimsy evidence to get this story in his newspaper. What if one of the farm hands had snuck into the house to call the clinic? What if Betty Dent was having her living room redone by Aldridge himself?

Then he opened the large brown envelope Warfield handed him. He pulled out two photos of Johnathan and his driver coming out of a hotel room. But that still wasn't enough to ruin a man's life. He'd dearly love to break a big news story, but not like this. Not one that hit so close to home. He needed more and he needed to think.

He spoke to one of the national editors, on a "suppose basis." As in "suppose I told you I had this information about a certain candidate. Suppose I had some physical evidence that he might be gay. What would it take to get that kind of story in the paper?"

He didn't name any names, just posed the hypothetical questions, even though he already knew the answer. His editors confirmed what he already knew: Get more facts and documents, and ultimately, you'll also have to confront the guy with the story before it saw the light of day.

George Jasper wanted to discuss it with his wife, Claudia, that night.

When Johnathan called back to Middleburg to check in with Betty, he was told she'd be out of town until Thursday. She and Maude were down in the Roanoke area and were planning to stay for a few days to campaign and see the countryside.

It triggered a thought. Johnathan called Isabelle. He asked her to meet him in Middleburg and stay overnight at the house. No one else was home. He gave Bertha a couple of days off. It was a two-hour drive from Richmond. He could take the car after dinner on Wednesday night and come back by seven the next morning and no one would be the wiser.

That was it. He had fantasized about sleeping with her in his very own bedroom, and his wife was making it happen.

He called her. She agreed. They'd rendezvous at his house at tenish that night.

George Jasper was home for dinner early. He was anxious about what he had to tell her. He churned over it in his mind as he made the ninety-minute drive out Route 66 during rush hour to Middleburg. As he walked in the door, he had no inkling how to broach the subject. But he couldn't even ponder writing this kind of story without her advice, and perhaps even her consent.

She welcomed him gladly. Knowing he'd be there at a decent hour, she prepared a steak and baked potato and opened a bottle of red wine. They barely spoke as they made their way through the meal, when George ultimately began…

"I felt I had to tell you this, Claudia. I've gotten some very distressing news about Johnathan Dent that could put him out of the race."

Claudia listened as her husband presented his "evidence." She put down her fork and stopped eating and took a big gulp of wine. By all appearances she was composed, though she swore she could hear the pounding of her heart.

"The guy gave me a copy of the phone bills with calls to the clinic in Washington, for crying out loud," he told his wife. "There are dozens of calls from his office phone to his decorator in Washington, who everyone and their cousin knows is gay. I feel terrible, Claudia, but I've got to keep asking questions and digging on this one, even if it means knocking on Dent's door and confronting him. If it's true, it's one hell of a story."

She sat still. She dried the palms of her hands on the napkin in her lap. She did not cry, but wanted to very badly.

All she could say was, "Isn't there someone else who could check these things out a bit more?"

"No, there isn't. Why the hell would I want anyone else to have my story. This is whopping material .It could mean a bonus. Hell—it's potential Pulitzer material."

"Well, we certainly could use the money," she said, getting up and taking the plates away.

She cleaned up the kitchen, then went upstairs to her daughter's room for a while. She sat on the edge of the bed.

What a disaster. How could she drag Johnathan down when his wife had been so kind to her? Still, there was one nagging question. *Why would Johnathan Dent be calling Michael Aldridge from his office?* She knew Betty hired him a long time ago to decorate the living room, but that was five years back, at least. Her daughter was watching a Disney video and hardly acknowledged her mother's presence. She left the room and went back downstairs. She just had to talk to Betty, who was out of town with Maude.

She called Pauline Howard to get a number for Betty.

"All I know is they were going down to Roanoke for a couple of days," Pauline told her. "Why don't you try the Hotel Roanoke?"

"Good idea, thanks a lot."

Bingo. Yes, Mrs. Dent was a guest in the hotel, but no she wasn't in her room right now. No, she didn't care to leave a message, she would call back.

Claudia stewed. Her husband might wonder what she was doing downstairs this late. She went upstairs to talk with him. It was close to ten o'clock.

He was watching the early news.

"Oh, I was just looking for my book..."

He held up his hand to her. "Shhh, I want to see what these guys say about the election. I haven't seen your book."

``Well, I'll go look downstairs again."

Claudia roamed around downstairs for twenty minutes. She worked herself into what Southern friends called "a royal swivet." She dialed the Hotel Roanoke again. This time, thank God, Betty answered the phone.

"Betty," she whispered, "It's me."

"Oh, Claudia, how are you? Is something wrong? Why are you calling me so late?"

"No...well...no...not really."

"What is it?" Betty pleaded.

"No, everyone's fine, really..." She was stalling a few precious seconds. *How do I word this? What do I say?*

"I need to talk to you," Claudia blurted. Suddenly she realized, they couldn't talk on the phone. After everything George told her tonight, maybe Betty's phone was bugged.

"Go ahead, Claudia, talk...tell me, please. What is it?" she pleaded.

"No...no...um...when are you coming back?"

"Late tomorrow, why?"

"Well...we must meet before that, it's...important..."

"Can't it wait until I get back?"

"No, it can't. And as a matter of fact, it really can't. This is urgent Betty, really."

"Okay, okay...let me think. Maybe I could make it back by midafternoon?"

"Betty, I know what you're doing is very important. I know you're helping Johnathan with the election. But please believe me...this is more important. I can't say anything more than that, but it has to do with the election and I have to see you as soon as possible."

Claudia had made her point.

"Okay. I'll get up first thing tomorrow morning and be back before nine. Is that good?"

"Yes. Call me at home as soon as you arrive."

At the precise moment Claudia Jasper and Betty Dent were concluding their telephone conversation, Johnathan Dent turned into his long driveway. It was after ten. The house was dark and he hoped that Isabelle hadn't arrived before him. After a long day, he should have been exhausted from the endless hours of travel. But meeting Isabelle tonight energized him for what he expected to be an exhilarating night. He visualized it so many times. He'd take her on a tour of the house, and then he'd whisk her to his bed. He yearned to wake up early and walk with her around the farm—even if it'd be close to freezing, even if they'd be awake half the night making love. As he stepped out of his warm car into the darkness, the stillness was soothing. There were no dogs at home, someone must have taken Hobo to the Fursman Kennels. And Bertha forgot to leave the outside lights on. The garage door was locked and he went around to the front to use his keys. It had been so long that it took a few tries before he found the right key. The house was usually unlocked.

He opened the door and turned a light on outside. Isabelle would be coming up the drive soon. He took his coat off and went back to the kitchen. He thought about having a drink, but decided against it. His senses needed no priming this night. He would wait and watch television.

No, he thought, *I've had enough television.*

He clicked it off and turned on the stereo instead and found Frank Sinatra crooning.

Perfect.

He checked the thermostat...way too low. He turned up the heat and then had an idea. He would build a fire in the bedroom fireplace. He felt slightly nervous, much like the first night he'd taken her to bed. He knew he was taking a huge risk, but was confident everything would go on schedule. Once again, he ticked off a mental list: Betty was in Roanoke, Maude was with her, Bertha had two days off, the boys were at school.

He went upstairs.

The phone rang.

Damn, he thought. *What the hell do I do?*

It was one thing he hadn't even thought about. Maybe it was Isabelle, maybe something had happened...maybe she couldn't make it...maybe she was lost.

Three...four...five...he counted the rings.

What if it was someone else and he got caught answering the phone?

How the hell could he explain that? He was standing in the middle of his bedroom with newspapers in his hand to start the fire.

Six...seven...

He picked up the receiver.

Simultaneously the remote automatic listening device ordered by James Alexander Russell kicked in.

"Johnathan, it's me," Isabelle said, instinctively knowing that he would be reluctant to answer the phone.

He sat down on the edge of the bed and took a deep breath. Just hearing her voice sent him soaring.

"Where are you?" he asked. "Has something happened?"

"No, no...nothing," she explained. "I was here before ten and I came to your house and it was all dark. I'm in a phone booth in Middleburg. I'm on my way now, I just wanted to make sure you were there and that everything is okay."

"Come on over," he said.

And they hung up.

He quickly lit the fire, putting extra logs on the hearth. He stood up and surveyed the room. It was too bright. He turned all the lights out except one on the nightstand. His mind was racing. He still had a suit on, should he change? If so, what would he put on? A robe?

Heavens no, he thought, *how corny.*

He went downstairs to wait. His heart began thumping when he heard her car pull up.

They went in the kitchen and each had a Coke. They sat and talked; there was so much to catch up on. She took off her shoes and curled her legs up under herself on one end of the loveseat. She narrated her plans for the party next week. She waved her arms and stopped in mid-sentence and looked at him. He was half-smiling.

"Why are you smirking, you haven't heard a word I've said," she frowned, curling her lip ever so slightly. She looked at him with eyes that danced with delight.

"Oh," Johnathan said, "just because."

She smirked back. "*Because?*"

"Because, I love sitting here and talking, but I can't stand it any longer."

He took her hand, which she held up to him and they silently walked up the staircase. He closed the bedroom door and turned the old-fashioned brass lock. They peeled off their clothes and left them in a heap.

He slid under the covers and she stood for a moment before him. She threw back her head and her hair shook off her face and down on her bare shoulders. As she slipped under the soft sheets, they became interwoven in a desperate tangle.

They kissed forever. Just one big,longing kiss after another. Then he kissed her on the ear, then on her neck, and then he took a little bit more of her body in his mouth. He kissed her intensely on the mouth again. They hugged, stroked and snuggled.

It was one a.m. when they curled up tightly, turned out the light and drifted off to a deep sleep.

At four a.m., Isabelle began to stroke Johnathan on the inside of his thigh. She rubbed his chest and kissed him half awake, just enough—as she worked her way down his body to the object of her desire. Minutes later, they slept again.

It was a few minutes after six in the morning when Isabelle opened her eyes. She did not have to look around the room for a clock. It was right on the nightstand next to the tiny crystal lamp. She slipped out of bed, gathered her clothes and left the room.

She stood in the large upstairs hallway. She was naked. She looked around at the family portraits and the gilt mirrors for a moment. Oh, how she loved this man yet she realized how impossible their situation had become.

No one could ever leave this. This was his home, this was his life.

Isabelle felt she was in a royal swivet and crashing in an odd way. Then she caught herself. She immediately dressed and headed down the carpeted staircase, being careful not to make any noise. She stopped at the foot of the stairs and gazed around again. She had a feeling she might not ever be back.

CHAPTER 20

Seeing Stars

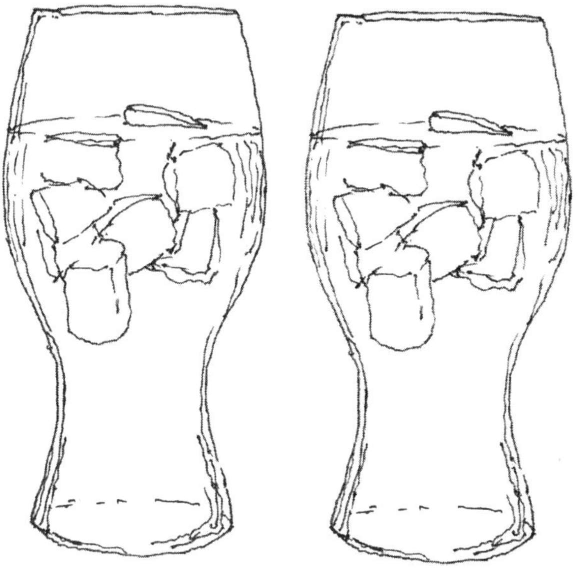

Johnathan heard a car start, then pull down the gravel drive.

He bolted out of bed. He saw the clock. It was after six. He had to be back in Richmond, but now, he heard Betty calling from the kitchen.

"Johnathan?"

He didn't answer. He was panicked. He was certain Isabelle had slipped out early. He looked at the bed. It was torn apart. He could still smell Shalimar. He went into the bathroom and wrapped a towel around himself.

"Johnathan?" She was in the doorway…

"Daddy?" It was Maude.

He was in his towel.

Betty looked at him.

She looked at the bed.

She looked at the fireplace.

She looked at him.

She knew.

He tried to tighten the towel.

She did not say one word.

Maude stood by her mother, sensing an awkward moment.

"I had to come home early," she explained, almost apologetically.

"I just wanted to get a good night's sleep," he explained.

"I see," she said.

"I...uh," he stammered.

"I know you have lots to do."

He took a half-step toward her as if to kiss her and his little girl. He knew he couldn't. He hadn't showered. His body reeked of sex.

Betty Dent was trembling with anger. She knew her husband had been with someone in their bed. She smelled the perfume, but she controlled herself. She would not confront him now, but she would never forget this moment. And yet, she still loved him. She didn't know why.

Not now, not after seeing this.

They had been together so long. They had so much to live for.

"Go ahead, take a shower," she said through clenched teeth. "I'll meet you in the kitchen.I'll make some coffee." She turned and left.

Betty Dent knew that a compulsion acted out in an instant could destroy her marriage. She would wait.

She would wait.

Johnathan had a quick cup of coffee and was gone. When he leaned over to kiss his wife good-bye he noticed the two empty coke glasses in the sink from the night before. They agreed to speak on the telephone later that night. Maude went upstairs to get ready for school.

Betty called her friend as soon as Johnathan was out the door.

Betty was in shock when she heard Claudia's tale of the phone bills and the theory that Johnathan was gay.

"You can't let them print that story in the paper," she ordered her friend. "It just cannot be true."

"I know that. I know that. I just had to tell you." Claudia was crying now. "I don't know what good I thought it would do telling you. I know I have to tell George the truth. It's going to be so awful. I guess I knew all along this would come out. God only knows how long it will be until I get sick. But I guess I just didn't think this would be how he would find out."

Betty tried to be compassionate. But on the heels of this morning's sordid scene in her very own bedroom, she knew that nothing could be further from the truth than some outlandish story about her husband being gay.

"You have to tell George and you have to tell him right away. Before that story gets out."

"I know it."

"Claudia, I'll do whatever I can to help you. And I don't like to remind you that I never told a single solitary soul—not one soul—about what happened with you and Jake Collins that night, let alone trudging down to that clinic. But we're talking about my husband's career here, and this just can't happen. Please."

"Consider it done."

Back on the campaign trail, Johnathan breathed a sigh of relief as he pulled out of the driveway that morning, heading for another day of speeches and appearances. As the day wore on, he had a difficult time concentrating on his work, stumbling over the words of his prepared text at a noon rally in Fairfax County. That afternoon, he forgot the name of the man who had just introduced him at the Arlington Rotary Club meeting. He was certain his wife knew he was having an affair, just from the look she gave him at their bedroom door that morning. He knew he had to be far more careful about Isabelle, particularly in the final days leading up to the election. He would call her later that night, right before he would call home. In the meantime he had a luncheon date.

At the offices of James Alexander Russell, Dan Warfield was starting to put the pieces of the Johnathan Dent puzzle together. His sources reported that a female visited the Dent estate in Middleburg the night before. They had his telephone conversation on tape. It was vague and her name was never mentioned, but the man who had followed Johnathan from Richmond had her license plate number and they were working on tracking that down.

Claudia Jasper decided to dress for the city and visit her husband at his downtown office at the *Washington Post.* She wanted to make her confession away from the house. She was confident her husband would not make a scene sitting in his glassed-in office in the middle of the newsroom.

She would confess all. She would tell him about Jake. She would tell him about her blood test, and about the call from Johnathan Dent's house to set it up. And finally, she would admit she had tested positive and had no idea how long it would be before she began suffering from the full blown dreaded disease. She understood if he wanted her to leave. She held out optimism that he'd forgive and allow her to remain in the house. All she wanted now was to able to spend the last days of her life with her daughter, Lisa.

Isabelle Benton Stoker was up to her ears in work for the Middleburg reception in honor of Johnathan Dent. She had a list a mile long of last-minute details. She was frantically trying to find extra men to park cars. She had averted a major disaster earlier in the morning when departing Middleburg. She felt it would be better to leave Johnathan and head for home. Her intuition was on target, particularly when she passed Betty Dent going down the road less than a half-mile from the entrance to their farm. Had she dawdled another minute or two, Betty could very well have caught them in her own bedroom. She questioned if Betty had spotted her as they drove past each other. She doubted it. She wished that Johnathan at least had the good sense to change the sheets. She was going to remind him before she left, but hadn't wanted to disturb her lover's deep sleep.

Betty Dent attempted to put the morning confrontation out of her mind. She called the maid and told her to clean the bedroom and change the sheets. She took Maude to school. She came home as if it was just another day in the life of a Middleburg wife and mother. Soon, she was sitting in the kitchen writing out a grocery list for that night's dinner.

Life went on. She was furious with Johnathan. She couldn't believe he'd sacrifice his lifelong ambition and family for a few minutes of extramarital pleasure. She realized her husband was tempted every day. He was the best-looking man she'd ever seen, and surely other women were equally attracted to him—especially now as he stood on the brink of election to the U.S. Senate. She had no idea who the other woman might be, but it didn't matter. She would do anything she could to keep her husband. He was the only love of her life, and she was not prepared to lose him. Not now.

The telephone rang, interrupting her train of thought.

"Betty? It's me Pauline."

"Oh, how are you?"

"Great and you?"

"Well. A bit tired, but hanging in there."

"Well...have you heard the news?"

"What news?" Betty asked, holding her breath. God only knows what could be on the streets of Middleburg before noon.

"About Jake Collins?"

"Jake?"

"Yes, darling. He has AIDS. And he's left Franny and moved in with Rusty Stewart."

Yes, life went on.

The Hunt Country reception to be held at the Dent's Middleburg farm was scheduled for Saturday afternoon. The tent was almost finished. Overseeing the entire project, Isabelle was obligated to drive out to the country and check on things. There were extra heating generators to be installed, along with wiring that had to be completed. She drew a detailed chart for the men to follow.

As she pulled up the estate driveway, thinking about her night upstairs in his bed, Isabelle's heart began to race. She thought about their night at the Lincoln Memorial. It was an evening forever etched on her memory when Johnathan came close to confessing his love for her. He'd held her hand tightly as they walked up the marble steps and said simply, *"Isabelle, you mean the world to me."* Then he had squeezed her hand.

He told her how much he admired John Kennedy and of his lifelong ambition to run for the Senate. *"I have just always known that my life would not be complete unless I gave it a try,"* he'd said, still holding her hand. He looked up, gazing at the reflecting pool toward the Washington Monument and concluded, *"Somehow, someway. I just have to try."*

As Isabelle pulled around behind the main house and looked out over the fields filled with horses, she understood how John Kennedy and Johnathan could love it so much out here in Middleburg. It was serene.

Johnathan's dog, Hobo, came to the car.

She did not go inside, partially out of fear that Mrs. Dent would be there and partially out of politeness so as not to disturb anyone. This entire party was enough of a disturbance.

The men were securing the poles and unfolding the massive white tent. She talked to the foreman, gave him her instructions, and walked around to the slate terrace in the back. The party would take place under the tent after guests had flowed through the receiving line in the main house. She was finished within an hour and returned to her Alexandria office before lunch.

On the morning of the reception, Isabelle dressed early and made her way to the country. She wore a white wool suit with brass buttons and a silk blouse. Her hair was pulled back in a French braid and she looked smashing. She decided to put on a little make up.

The guests were scheduled to arrive at eleven-thirty.

She made sure the flowers were properly arranged. She reminded the caterer one more time of the schedule for serving drinks, hors d'oeuvres, and lunch.

A jazz trio would play softly throughout, except for a brief period just before dessert, when the former First Lady would introduce Johnathan. He'd say a few words, thank all the proper people, and of course, she knew, introduce his wife and children to the crowd.

Things were moving along smoothly. It appeared that everyone was busy executing their tasks—the florist, the caterer, and the extra serving staff. The kitchen was filled with workers—one person was slicing lemons and limes for the drinks, another was arranging ham biscuits on a silver tray, and another was washing fresh shrimp to be passed before the lunch.

She wanted to go over a few details with Johnathan and his wife, the First Lady and Denny Harris. Those four people would stand in the receiving line in the foyer.

Denny Harris came into the kitchen.

"Oh, good, there you are," he said to her.

"I was just about to say the same thing," she said.

"We need to go over some things."

"Yes."

"Let's go in the living room, the rest of them should be down in a minute."

Though Isabelle had been in the house before, this was the first time she'd looked around at the furnishings and the paintings. It was stunning.

No, better than that, she thought. *It really was magnificent*, a look accentuated by the late-morning light gleaming across the old wide pine floorboards.

Still, she was uneasy. It was challenging being in the same room with Johnathan, regardless of the occasion. But to be in his own home, in his presence and the presence of his wife, was worse. Isabelle deliberated if Betty knew that she had spent the night. Then there was the party itself. Isabelle had spent weeks making sure no detail was overlooked. She chose to sit in the window seat, knowing that the light behind her would be most becoming when he finally did enter the room.

The living room was packed with treasures. There were dogs and horses everywhere—in paintings, on needlepoint pillows, as small statues, and as large bronzes. The only animal in the room that was not a dog or a horse was an antique copper rooster weather vane sitting atop a cherry wood highboy that Isabelle guessed dated from about 1750.

A Federal period pine mantel with a gilt mirror was flanked on each side by gas lamps that had been wired for electricity. A number of old family photographs graced the mantle. A Queen Anne tea table with even more family photographs filled a narrow space along the wall near the doorway. Several small trunks were placed strategically beside chairs as side tables. One of them, from the Federal period she guessed, appeared to have the original pale blue paint.

Something from her parents' collection, no doubt, Isabelle thought.

There were three miniature chests that Isabelle adored. They were placed on top of other chests or beside a small chair. One was tortoise and bone inlaid ebony wood and another she identified as Victorian and walnut. Overall it was a remarkable collection of antiques. Yet unlike some homes, every piece seemed totally in context, exuding a feeling of comfort and warmth. Isabelle had been in some houses where she'd been afraid to sit down. Michael had decorated some of them after the client had insisted on "priceless antiques."

She heard them coming down the staircase. She remained seated. Mr. and Mrs. Johnathan Dent entered the room. Isabelle hated to admit it, they looked like an ideal couple.

He wore a dark blue worsted suit, custom made in London, with double vents in the jacket. His Egyptian cotton shirt in a cream color had come from Turnbull & Asser in London, as did the silk tie, a darker cream than the shirt with diagonal stripes. It made his face look tan and Isabelle even thought it made him look somewhat rested, though she knew better.

Mrs. Dent was the embodiment of all that is proper and all that can be executed properly with the proper amount of money. Her designer mohair navy blue suit was adorned with satin braid on the pockets and large brass buttons. Simple yet elegant. A modest solid gold pin, no larger than a quarter, in the shape of a star also caught Isabelle's eye. Betty Dent had it pinned on the right side of her suit, over her heart.

She greeted Isabelle and Denny first.

He walked behind a few steps. And didn't speak.

They went over the schedule of events. First, greeting the guests in the receiving line. Isabelle would stand just inside the front door while two maids would check coats. She'd ask their names and pass it on to Denny, who would be the first in the receiving line. The former First Lady would be next followed by Betty Dent, and finally Johnathan. If Denny had any pertinent information about the guest, he'd pass it on as he introduced them. *"This is Mrs. Stephen Oliver,"* he would say, *"She's been most generous with her support in the campaign."* That gave Johnathan a cue to personally thank Mrs. Oliver for all her help.

Bertha came in and asked if anyone cared for a drink. Everyone declined except Mrs. Dent. She asked for a glass of Piedmont Chardonnay with lots of ice.

Finished with formalities, Denny excused himself to go to the men's room and Isabelle was left to make small talk. She stood up from her place on the window seat and joined the Dents in front of the fireplace, already hissing and crackling and adding just the right ambience to the room.

Johnathan broke the awkward silence. "We're so grateful for all your help Miss Stoker," he began.

"Oh, yes," Betty chimed in solicitously. "I just can't imagine how we could have done any of this without you. What a mountain of work this has been."

Isabelle smiled as sweetly as possible and replied, "and all for such a good cause, Mrs. Dent. It's been my pleasure."

Bertha brought the glass of wine on a silver tray and sat it down on the mahogany pie crust tiptop table next to the couch.

"Are you sure you wouldn't care for something, Miss Stoker," Johnathan asked. For some reason Isabelle was furious with him for calling her Miss Stoker. Certainly anyone could see through his formality.

"No, thank you," she said.

"Are you quite sure?" Mrs. Dent chimed in yet again.

"Quite," Isabelle said.

Isabelle looked quickly at Johnathan. She could tell he was nervous. She wasn't sure how much of it could be attributed to today's event, how much could be attributed to her presence, being so close and yet so far.

Betty took a long drink from her glass, nearly draining it, and sat back in the couch.

"That's such a good-looking outfit you have on," she said to Isabelle. "Very becoming color."

"Oh, thank you," she answered and immediately reciprocated. "And I can't help admiring that gold star you're wearing. It's so pretty."

"Isn't it simply divine?" she said, looking down at the pin. "Johnathan gave it to me just this morning. I simply adore it, don't you?"

Isabelle was sorry she'd ever mentioned it. It was the first time in her entire relationship with Johnathan she actually felt jealous. She didn't mind sitting here in his antique house filled with antique furniture and antique paintings. She was envious maybe, but certainly not jealous.

But when his "antique" wife told her that he had just given her a "simply divine" piece of jewelry, that was enough. That was too much.

"Yes, it is," Isabelle said, being careful not to look Johnathan in the eye. She rose to leave. "I think I'll visit the powder room before everyone gets here." She wanted to freshen her makeup. She also felt like crying.

Isabelle waited in the entry hall for the guests. She poked her head into the dining room, to the right of the front door. She was still upset, but realized that the show had to go on. She was curious enough to study the design and layout of the house. The original pine woodwork was hand grained. She noted that a number of early American painting techniques had been used throughout the house. On the far wall of the dining room was a painting of a horse, a bright and shining chestnut with a flaxen mane and tail. The name of the horse was painted in the lower left hand corner: "Tom-Tom." There was an old English Sheepdog, "Sudsy," lying in the grass beside the horse. She recognized the artist as a friend of the family, Rusty Stewart. A Chippendale settee in a traditional stripe sat in the front bay of the dining room. The walls had been glazed a dark, bright red. In the center of the table a rather tall Edward VII silver mounted cut crystal vase held three bird of paradise flowers. The chairs were mahogany Sheraton with leather panels. The three-part mahogany sideboard was flanked with antique knife boxes. Isabelle was unable to identify the period and right now it didn't matter. She heard the first guests pull into the driveway. She turned to the front door.

"Good morning," she said, extending her hand to point them in the right direction. "This way please, and may I have your name?" She checked the guest list and ushered them forward to the receiving line.

The procession grew in numbers and strength. Within ten minutes, a line stretched out the front door, fifteen people long. The car parkers were running back and forth as fast as they could and Isabelle was juggling it all very calmly. Mrs. Dent put her glass of wine on a side table behind her and periodically took a drink whenever there was a momentary break in the line. She asked to have it refilled three times. Johnathan, for the first time ever, urged her to "wait until later."

Everyone in line was a serious contributor to the campaign, either with their time, or more important, with their money. James Ayres, Col. James Ludley, Mr. and Mrs. William Nelson, Cynthia Jenkins, Bryce Lingo, Michele Buchanan, Elizabeth Calvert and on and on.

Then there was the glitteratti.

Jack Kent Cooke, owner of the Chrysler Building and the Washington Redskins, and his latest wife arrived, causing a small commotion when he bypassed the line outside and headed straight for the Dents, kissing Betty on both cheeks. He was bubbling over with greetings for everyone, ordering the maids to take his coat upstairs right away.

"Why of course, Mr. Cooke," they obliged, as if they worked for him.

A small group of invited reporters and photographers huddled nearby behind a velevet rope. Veteran chroniclers of such events, they included Jane Podesta of *People Magazine*; local television reporter Sophie Shephard; Janet Hitchen, who was shooting pictures for the *Middleburg Life* newspaper; and Rudy Maxa, a columnist from *Washingtonian* magazine.

There was at least a ten-second silence as the First Lady entered the front hall. She and fund raiser Nancy Dutton stood in line like everyone else until it was their turn to greet the candidate.

"So good to see you," Betty Dent said. "Have you been out fox*funting* today?" she asked the First Lady rather innocently. (So much for the white wine on ice.)

"Fox*hunting*," Johnathan chimed in, repeating "Have you been fox*hunting* today? We'll have to go cross-country sometime. I'm so glad you came."

"Thank you," she said, laughing to herself about Mrs. Dent's inquiry.

The guests were directed down the entry hall, past the living room, and out onto the sun porch. From there a wide, full canopy-type tent had been attached, as guests proceeded down five steps and out along to a larger tent that covered the entire slate terrace and beyond. As they stepped down into the canopy, waiters took their drink orders.

Servers circled with silver trays of hot ham biscuits and three tables in the tent were overflowing with cheeses, crudités and dip, and the fresh shrimp cocktail.

Out in front a long, bright red Mercedes-Benz limousine pulled up.

There had been a number of limousines that morning, but not a Mercedes, much less a red one. It was unusual. Most limos were Lincolns or Cadillacs. Those who followed such things would have known exactly whose car it was.

Pauline Howard emerged first. The parking attendant extended his right hand to her and she nodded and said "Thank you." He turned back to extend his hand again.

It was Helena Winkler, the actress. Her red hair positively sparkled in the bright sun. She was wearing a cashmere dress that clung to her tightly in her signature color red.

The Vincent Perons arrived along with Marshall Allison III, D. H. Bedford with his latest newfound love, Ann MacLeod, Phil Thomas, Helen Wiley, Leslie Brown. Willard Scott, the nationally known weatherman, and his wife were greeted warmly by the Dents, as was Margaret Stone—the cookie heiress, vineyard owner Sis Worrall and writer Jane McClary.

The Dents' longtime friends, Raymond and Smith Curtis, Spencer O'Brien from the bank, and Betty's old friend, Franny Collins, arrived. Thank God she was just behind her soon-to-be ex-husband, Jake Collins, who had arrived moments earlier with his newfound love, Rusty Stewart. Fortunately, they were not holding hands.

Holly Hawk, a close family friend, came with Claudia and George Jasper, who were beaming. The week before, they had three separate sessions with a marriage counselor over in Leesburg. They were sorting out their problems, and they seemed to have rekindled their love.

Democratic fundraiser Pamela Harriman arrived with her usual escort, Frederick L. Rodgers. Ambassador True Davis, Elmore Mason, and an attractive new brunette moved through the receiving line as well as steeplechase jockey Todd Sweet and his latest love, Jane A. Wagner, who most agreed had now "had" every jockey on the circuit. (And those who had experienced the pleasure of her company said that she had now been "rode hard and put up hot.")

Political supporters present for the Hunt Breakfast included Governor Sam Cooke, who arrived by helicopter, throwing the animals in the barnyard into a frenzy. One goat impaled himself on an old feed tub so badly that he later had to be put down. Retiring Senator Lee Blair was "more than happy to be part of this special occasion," he said later when asked to speak after lunch. Bruce Sundlun flew in for the event. He was busy on the campaign trail in his "home" state of Rhode Island, where he was running for governor. Most Middleburg people knew he preferred to spend most of his time on his Salamander Farm right down Zulla Road.

The mayor of Alexandria, James P. Moran, Jr., who was running for Congress, also took time off from his campaign to be on hand. "After all," he said, "In this business, one hand washes the other."

The Very Reverend Andrew Edward Mayhaw of the Episcopal Church in Upperville came and said grace before lunch was served.

The party was in full buzz, with everyone standing in clusters seeing and being seen, talking about the latest polls and about what a fine senator Johnathan would make. But they were also talking about Mrs. So-and-so's latest facelift and Jake Collins leaving his wife for Rusty Stewart.

This did not seem to affect Mr. Stewart's career in any way. Because at that very moment the former First Lady was asking him if he could paint her favorite hunter "in the next few months or so...whenever you have time."

"Oh, you know I'd be honored to do that," he told her, knowing full well he could also up his price by several thousand dollars.

A group of ten stargazers had gathered around Helena Winkler. She was basking in the attention and was into a monologue now. She was waving her arms in the air as she explained why her current husband, an obscure Yugoslavian count, was not with her this day.

"But my dears," she said, (she was always saying *"But my dears"*) "He's off in France stag hunting. Besides, I'm too busy working on my memoirs for him to be around. He'll have a grand time, but then so will I."

"Your memoirs?" asked one of the guests.

"Oh, yes, you know it keeps me busy," she threw back her head laughing, and added, "just like all my husbands."

"And what will be the title of your book?" another woman asked.

"Oh, my dears...I think I shall call it *Equal Parts*. Because, you know I have loved each one of them in equal parts."

Betty and Johnathan mingled around the tent. Johnathan was anxious to speak privately with Isabelle, but was having a hard time moving five feet in any direction. Everyone wanted to shake his hand and congratulate him on what seemed to be a highly successful campaign.

Sam Blackwell grabbed his arm. "Did you see the paper today?"

"No, what did it say?"

"We're way out front, Johnathan, it should be smooth sailing from here on in."

Johnathan's eyes searched the tent. She had her back to him, standing by one of the food tables.

"Oh, Sam, excuse me. I don't mean to be short, but I need to have a word with one of the volunteers." He shook his hand. "How about we have lunch or even dinner next week?" Johnathan had another thing in mind as well when he suggested dinner. He could arrange to see Isabelle, too. But he wanted to get over to her...

In the opposite corner of the tent, Betty Dent chatted with Rusty Stewart, Jake Collins, and the First Lady. She acted as if nothing was out of the ordinary. As if it was just an everyday occurrence that you left your wife for another man. She had been steadily drinking wine for an hour-and-a-half.

"So what are you working on these days, Rusty?" she asked giddily, only half-listening as he told her. She was watching Johnathan on the other side of the tent. She still loved him so much and she was certain he soon would be the next senator from Virginia. She was actually thinking about what she would wear on the day he was sworn in. She nodded to Rusty and watched Johnathan make his way over to Isabelle Stoker.

What a sweet girl, Betty thought.

But then...

She saw Johnathan step up behind her, put his hand on her shoulder, and whisper in her ear.

Betty saw the girl turn her head over her shoulder. She saw her face light up as she looked at Johnathan. She was sipping a Coke.

Betty Dent felt an instant hot flash. It had nothing to do with hormones. It had everything to do with anger as she remembered the two glasses in the sink with a bit of Coke in the bottom when she returned home early one morning. She turned around for a moment.

How could he, she asked herself over and over.

She took a deep breath and gathered herself up, like an actress with stage fright. She didn't yet know what to do. But she realized one thing and one thing only.

Isabelle Stoker and Johnathan Dent were in love.

Nine more days remained until the election.

Newspapers and television reporters were now referring to James Alexander Russell as a longshot. In a *Washington Post* story just one week before the election, Russell took one last stab at Johnathan Dent.

A Washington Post reporter wrote:

"There is a certain spring in James A. Russell's step these days, and he has the kind of anything-is-possible glow that longshot candidates get in the days before an election."

The writer claimed that Russell admitted he has had trouble raising money and could not begin to equal the *"seemingly bottomless money pit available to Johnathan Dent from his heiress wife."*

"Money is everything in a political campaign," Russell told the *Post*.

He also criticized Dent for his liberal views on abortion and development. *"He's in the pocket of the big developers in the area and everyone knows it,"* Russell said to the reporter. *"People are ready for my politics. We need higher taxes on the rich and Johnathan Dent is one of them."*

Johnathan sat back in the front seat of his car after reading the report. His first reaction was that of irritation. How the hell could this man have the nerve to drag his wife into the campaign? The fact was she had contributed very little money so far. Granted, they were running in the red, but Johnathan was assured that if he won, the party probably would be able to make up the difference in funding.

Then, he thought about it. This was a desperate man who took shots like this and surely the voters saw through such tactics. What Johnathan didn't know, and probably never would know, was just how desperate James Alexander Russell really was.

Betty Dent knew. She had singlehandedly seen to it that the potentially damaging word that Johnathan was gay never would see the light of day. She ran interference with her good friend George Jasper at the *Washington Post*.

She secretly set up a meeting with Johnathan's campaign advisor, Denny Harris.

"I just wanted you to know what this man has tried to ruin Johnathan," she told him one afternoon over tea. "And I want you to fight fire with fire and do whatever is necessary."

She then passed over an envelope with $100,000 in cash. She pushed it at him. "Use this however you think it will be best put to use," she instructed him. She emphasized Johnathan must never know about this.

All final campaign efforts were put into the Northern Virginia area. Johnathan choked down what he hoped would be his last chicken concotion for a long time: tarragon chicken, chicken smothered in gravy, sweet and sour chicken, ginger chicken, fried chicken, and baked chicken. He kissed babies. He shook hands. He spoke at rallies, luncheons, and dinners.

He managed one last visit with Isabelle before that first Tuesday in November. They snuck away to her Georgetown apartment. They didn't eat. They didn't drink. And, they didn't sleep. He was there for one hour and thirty-five minutes before he drove back to Middleburg.

"I told you I had a nice piece of jewelry for you," he whispered as he handed her the velvet box.

She smiled at him and leaned over and playfully teased him. "There is really only one piece of jewelry I'm interested in," she said.

Isabelle fell back against the door after bidding him good-bye. She was full of energy, as always after they made love. She walked into her living room and sat down on the sofa and admired in amazement the large heavy gold bracelet in the shape of a lover's knot he had given her.

Johnathan turned on the radio and listened to some country music as he drove west. He rolled down the window of his Mercedes for some cold air in order to stay awake on the long drive back to Middleburg.

From time to time he wondered what life would be like if he were with Isabelle full-time. How they would make love in every room of their house. He could almost see it. But then he had to stop and ask himself, "What house," because he knew he could never walk away from Betty with enough money to continue his current lifestyle. He was a victim of circumstance. He also wondered if he could be happy living a simple life with Isabelle.

She never asked him for anything. She was always there...just there... waiting quietly, ready to please him in every way.

He made the turn into his driveway. It was late. It was dark. Betty was always there, too, although lately she seemed distant. Still, they had a well-ordered and predictable life together: children, horses, dogs, good friends, and lots of parties. They even *looked* as if they belonged together.

His life was about to change if the voters gave him their stamp of approval. He hated to think about the election. He wanted to win, it meant everything to him...but he couldn't help question how much of his time it would take.

Too late for that now, he told himself. *There was no turning back.*

Safely home and parked behind the house, he turned the car off and sat for a minute. He could still smell Isabelle and her Shalimar. He opened the car door and stepped out into the country night. Clouds streaked the violent blue colored sky. It was cool, the kind of coolness you get on your face when you poke your head in the freezer looking for ice cream.

He sighed. Perhaps Johnathan Douglas Dent was destined to continue a life in equal parts.

Perhaps.

By Vivienne Rees
Washington Post Staff Writer

Democrats picked up strength by winning races for governor in Florida and Texas in midterm elections yesterday, while almost all congressional incumbents, including Senator Jesse Helms (R-NC) survived despite some surprisingly tight contests.

Overall, the elections appeared likely to produce little or no change in the Senate and small Democratic gains in the House, with a 97 percent reelection rate for congressional incumbents.

Key gubernatorial races in California and Michigan were too close to call early this morning, but with victories in Florida, Texas, and Rhode Island, Democrats had made significant gains.

Bruce G. Sundlun (D), 70, a wealthy Providence businessman upset three-term incumbent Edward D. DiPrete (R) in their third face-off, winning a race tipped in Sundlun's favor in a battle over ethics.

Sundlun, who owns a horse farm in Northern Virginia's countryside, is a former World War II bomber pilot and Harvard Law School graduate who headed a communications company that operated television and radio stations. He is chairman of Sundlun and Company, an investment banking firm.

Full-time resident of the Virginia hunt country, Johnathan Douglas Dent (D), was elected senator from Virginia. Dent, a partner in the law firm of Duke, Graves, and Coggin, had a well-financed campaign, including a posh Hunt Breakfast at his Middleburg estate in the last week before the election that was highly criticized by his opponent, James Russell Alexander.

With an extravagant financial allowance of over $2 million, Dent collected 70 percent of the votes. He captured all but two of the state's 97 counties.

Epilogue

For as long as Isabelle would live, Wednesdays would always feel different.

Wednesdays were for Johnathan.

She had no idea what would happen now. It had been ten days since they had spoken. He was busy with all the celebrations surrounding his victory. There were receptions and cocktail parties.

But now it was Wednesday and Isabelle would not see Johnathan today. She had no idea what the future would bring.

Would this be the end?

Would she see him next week after he got settled?

Or would he simply drift out of her life?

She pulled on a pair of grey wool slacks and a grey cashmere sweater, the most appropriate thing she could think to wear on a cold and grey November day. She put on the English crystal pin he'd given her years ago.

Isabelle decided to take the afternoon off. She wanted to wander around the Hirshhorn Museum, one of the first places she'd visited with Johnathan. Maybe she'd feel better there. They often roamed around the sculpture garden, gazed at the oversized bronze sculptures and then gone to her place for dinner and all that followed.

Isabelle took a cab to the museum. As she stepped out on to Jefferson Avenue, the U.S. Capitol loomed large on the eastern end of the mall. The Washington Monument towered on the opposite end.

There was an exhibition at the museum featuring major contemporary artists from all over the world. Some of it, Isabelle didn't understand. Oh, how she missed Johnathan, he would have explained it to her.

One artist had contributed a bizarre video. Another had glued green and brown glass bottles and bricks to the wall in the shape of a Mercedes Benz logo.

Isabelle lingered and walked slowly from room to room in the circular museum. She was trying to take it all in and understand what each artist had in mind.

One piece by Jeff Koons consisted of two real basketballs floating in an actual fish tank half-full of water. An entire room was devoted to racial discrimination, with wallpaper etched with the image of a black man hanging from a tree limb.

Very depressing, she thought, *this isn't helping at all.*

She edged her way slowly to the final gallery. It was filled with the work of Jenny Holzer, who combined writing and art. She wrote "Truisms"—brief one-liners about life. All the truisms were reproduced on five panels along one wall in the narrow room.

Isabelle took a seat on a cold, hard marble bench and began to read...

A single event can have infinitely many interpretations.

Solitude is enriching.

You must have one grand passion.